ADVANCE PRAISE FOR *WHITE PLAINS*

"In David Hicks's captivating debut, an English professor realizes he can no longer stand to live a life of quiet desperation. Comic and tender by turns, *White Plains* is a big-hearted novel about awakening—and reawakening—to love."

—LENI ZUMAS, AUTHOR OF *RED CLOCKS*

"For the single man, in this case dear Flynn in *White Plains*, it can be a rocky road to climb toward grace; and David Hicks shows us every glorious bump on the way I found myself groaning at each of Flynn's stumbles, but always hoping for him (especially as he assembles himself as a parent) in this glowing set of stories, a book that reads like late night messages sent from a friend. This is an honest look at a man moving from punishing bad faith toward something he finally hopes is good."

—RON CARLSON, AUTHOR OF *THE SIGNAL*

"What happens when a man risks everything in search of a real home and big love? David Hicks shares the answer in *White Plains*, a thrilling and thoughtful take on what it means to live life to the fullest."

—SOPHFRONIA SCOTT, AUTHOR OF *UNFORGIVABLE LOVE*

"David Hicks has written a novel with sentences that dance and sing on the page, as we follow Flynn Hawkins, our protagonist, in his quest for redemption from the debilitating effects of divorce, abandoned children, and consuming guilt. Introspection is key here (where so few tread), and there are no tricks in this writing, only honesty."

—ALLEN LEARST, AUTHOR OF *DANCING AT THE GOLD MONKEY*

"On first glance, David Hicks' witty and melancholy *White Plains* is a novel of the academic life, in the tradition of Lodge, Amis and McCarthy, and it deserves a place in that most excellent tradition. But White Plains exceeds this subgenre and rewards us with dynamic shifts in point of view that reveal an unsparing and original look at aging through a literary life and events that seem to have a mind of their own. Hicks writes spot on spots of time covering thirty years: St. Marks, Shea Stadium, Creede, Colorado. . . . momentary stays against confusion and concentric circles of diminishing expectations. With characteristic and devastating restraint, we're asked, "How many chances does a man get [does anyone get] to set his life straight." The answer: read this extraordinary novel."

—DAVID LAZAR, AUTHOR OF *I'LL BE YOUR MIRROR: ESSAYS AND APHORISMS*

"*White Plains* resonates with our desire to do right by those we love and offers a compelling tale of self-inflicted destruction and redemption."
—**BENJAMIN DANCER**, AUTHOR OF *PATRIARCH RUN*

"Flynn's half-lived life comes of age post-marriage, in the time of tender fatherhood. He's not just the flawed but adored professor living inside an English teacher's dream of a book. He's an American man growing up, finally, right when this country needs him the most."
—**REBECCA SNOW**, AUTHOR OF *GLASSMUSIC*

"In this intensely psychological story, David Hicks gives us a panoramic understanding of his protagonist, Flynn, as he investigates the human condition. How can we live close to the bone? With characterization reminiscent of Richard Powers and John Williams, *White Plains* is as intriguing as it is beautiful."
—**ERIKA KROUSE**, AUTHOR OF *CONTENDERS*

"*White Plains* is wise, sincere, intimate; Flynn's self-reflection refreshing, if flawed. A novel comprised of a patchwork of perspectives, each its own swelling wave, so full and beautifully realized, show us Flynn as father, as friend, as professor, as son, brother, lover. As human. A man sometimes silent but never resigned, never disengaged. This book is a blueprint for a life lived, seized. A book that guts, but holds you fast with exquisite sentences and offers, yet, a measure of hope."
—**ANGELA PALM**, AUTHOR OF *RIVERINE* AND *WORK WITH ME*

WHITE PLAINS

WHITE PLAINS

A NOVEL

DAVID HICKS

CONUN
DRUM
PRESS

CONUNDRUM PRESS: A Division of Samizdat Publishing Group.
PO Box 1353, Golden, Colorado 80402

print ISBN: 978-1-942280-39-2

epub ISBN: 978-1-942280-40-8

mobi ISBN: 978-1-942280-41-5

Library of Congress control number: 2017936789

CONUNDRUM PRESS BOOKS MAY BE PURCHASED WITH BULK DISCOUNTS FOR educational, business, or sales promotional use. For information, please visit Conundrum Press online at conundrum-press.com.

Conundrum Press is distributed by Independent Publishers Group: IPGBOOK.COM

PUBLICATION ACKNOWLEDGMENTS
Earlier versions of some chapters first appeared in the following magazines:

"Once Upon a Time at the Kiev," *Specs*, Fall 2011.

"Higher Laws," *Saranac Review*, Fall 2014.

"Diamond Dash," *Colorado Review*, Summer 2003.

"Us and Mom in a Fancy-Schmancy Restaurant, If You Can Believe That" in *Crack the Spine* 164, September 2015

"Sunday Morning at the Silverado" (originally titled "Sunday Morning at the Silver Spur"), *South Dakota Review*, Summer 2011.

"Spring Creek Pass," *Glimmer Train*, Spring 2006.

"All the Wrong Moves," *Saranac Review*, Fall 2012.

"In Love with Louise," *Trachodon*, Spring 2012.

This book is dedicated to my parents, Albina and Richard, for all their love.

And to Cynthia, always.

§

This is either a dream or it happened. I'll never know.

My father at my bedside, saying he has to go, he's sorry he won't be at my baseball game.

I don't know what I say back.

As he leaves my room, his shoulders are slumped. He doesn't look at me when he closes the door.

NEW YORK

IN A COMPLETELY DIFFERENT
PART OF THE COUNTRY

Professor James Augustus Faustino was a large man. His head was a stalwart dome mopped by black-and-gray hair, his enormous face swathed by a trimmed white beard. He draped his whale-shaped torso with a linen shirt he bought at the Big and Tall shop in Jamestown, along with a leather vest that used to be his father's. The last time he had weighed himself, over two years ago, he had topped off at 306.

Faustino was the chairman of the English Department and a beloved professor of American literature at Devlin College in Madisonville, New York. On this day—August 29, 1994—he was sipping coffee from a mug that said "Papa" while preparing to welcome the new recruits, the six graduate assistants entering Devlin's two-year Master's program on scholarship in exchange for teaching College Composition. He could hear them already, down the hall. They would begin teaching and taking graduate classes in a week. One of them, a kid named Hawkins, was only twenty-two and had no teaching experience at all.

Faustino was a "toss them in the water and see if they could swim" kind of guy. There would be no mollycoddling on his watch. After all, nobody had ever "mentored" *him*. At age twenty-nine, only three months after earning his PhD at NYU (studying under the famed Hemingway biographer Philip Young), he had launched right into his teaching career: four preps, publish-or-perish, and absolutely no mollycoddling. He had been hard at it for thirty years since.

He pressed his fingers to his temples while scanning his office for the "Grad Ass" folder. The previous evening he had attended the wedding of Mary Anne Tscherpel, one his colleagues, and while his wife Joanna had left early, complaining of lower-back pain (she caught a ride with the Slowicks, who didn't drink or dance), Faustino had been among the last to leave and was now paying the consequences.

He found the folder and flipped through the files. The usual pie-in-the-sky types: book lovers, strong recs from their English professors, and 3.9 GPAs—except for the Hawkins kid, who was accepted only because Slowick's good friend at SUNY/Binghamton had called the young man "one of our most promising graduates" despite his 3.1. Hawkins had asked if he could move to Madisonville as soon as he graduated (something about not wanting to spend the summer in White Plains, his hometown), so Faustino had contacted another recent admit, Mason Briggs, a Devlin alum who in the three years since his graduation had done time as a substitute teacher in the Cheektowaga School District and as a patient in the "blue room" of Buffalo Psychiatric Hospital after (allegedly) trying to kill his mother. Briggs, now "fully recovered" and already in town, had said yes, he sure could use a roommate, you bet, and arrangements were made for Hawkins to move in with him at 17 Younger Drive, a mile or so from campus—and as further evidence of his good will, Briggs had secured his new roommate a job at Honest John's in Jamestown, where he was employed as a waiter.

When the clock on his desk flipped to 9:00 a.m., Faustino heaved himself up, hefted a box filled with composition textbooks and other materials, and shuffled over to the GA Office. He spotted young Hawkins right away, an affable-looking kid with wavy brown hair who squinted when he smiled, but was taken aback by the sight of Briggs, who had gained at least forty pounds, further embedding his deep-set eyes and giving him a scruffy, half-crazed look. Faustino introduced himself, welcomed them all to the program, announced he was eschewing any "team-building" nonsense, and passed out textbooks along with the same sample syllabi he'd been distributing to GAs for over a decade. "Feel free to improvise," he told them as he took one of the student seats, worrying it might collapse underneath him. "And if you have any questions, don't ask me; ask Slowick," for he hadn't taught composition in seventeen years.

He gave them the run-down: the usual HR bullshit; the location of the infirmary, gym, dining hall, and Student Life office; how to open a library account; how to use the new personal computers they had recently installed (he pointed out the monstrous printer in the corner), how to open a new "electronic mail" account ("Don't ask me about *that* either"); where to get their IDs; where their classrooms were located; the new touchy-feely rules about dealing with students of the opposite sex; and the location of the Tutoring Center for the idiots that Devlin seemed to be admitting to college these days. At the end, he asked if anyone had any further questions, and the Hawkins kid raised his hand.

"I wonder if you could say a word or two about why you do this."

Faustino looked at the young man. "You mean *this*?" he said, pointing at his notes.

"No," Hawkins said. "Teaching English. Do you consider it, you know, a worthy vocation?"

Faustino tossed his folder onto the nearest desk. He really needed this kid to teach two sections of Comp, and if Hawkins or anyone else quit before even embarking on this enterprise because he didn't think the profession was "a worthy vocation," Faustino would be completely screwed. "Just to be clear," he said, "you're questioning what I do for a living."

The young man swiped away a stray hair. "Not questioning exactly," he said, and then shrugged. "Asking for guidance. I'm trying to figure myself out."

One of the other GAs hacked out an aggressive cough, and Briggs appeared to scoff—he had once told Faustino his lifelong dream was to be an English teacher. And one of the female students, Amita, was staring at the general vicinity of Hawkins' thighs.

Twenty-one months later, after missing the Commencement ceremony at which these six graduate assistants received their diplomas and realizing he would never see any of them again (except perhaps Briggs), Faustino would look out the front window of his house as Hawkins' beige, boxy, stuffed-to-the-gills 1984 Dodge Aspen (nicknamed "the Coffin") pulled away from the curb outside his house, would remember the young man's first question to him, and try to recall his response. No doubt it was something about the value of showing young people their own humanity and the humanity of others through stories, of exploring the dark and ambiguous aspects of human nature in a world that avoids such exploration at all costs, of such work being of the highest calling. He may have quoted Northrop Frye. Whatever he said, it was apparently good enough, for he would remember the kid nodding and saying, "Okay sir, count me in."

ON MONDAY MORNING, FAUSTINO WAS WRITING UP A NOTE TO HIS COLLEAGUES reminding them about the Add/Drop deadline, which his secretary would type into an electronic-mail memo for him and send to everyone, when the Hawkins kid, Flynn, stopped by.

"Well well," Faustino said, settling back into his chair with a creak, "look who just broke his cherry. How was your first class?"

Flynn wrinkled his nose. "My knees were actually knocking," he said. "Behind the podium. I thought that was just an expression." He told Faustino he had broken out in a sweat as soon as he walked into the room.

Faustino smiled, remembering his first time in front of the classroom, thirty years earlier. "You didn't perchance ask, 'Is it just me or is it hot in here,' did you?"

Flynn laughed. "How did you know?" He told Faustino that after class a female student had come up to him, asked him how old he was, and when he told her, she put a hand on her hip and said, "I've *dated* men older than you."

Faustino scratched his beard. No Devlin freshman would dare to speak like that to their professor, not even to a graduate assistant. It must have been a community-college transfer.

"I could feel myself blushing," Hawkins said. "Not very professorial. Has that kind of thing happened to you?"

Faustino glanced up to see if the young man was kidding, then tapped the desk with his pencil. "Oh," he said, "back in the day." He pointed the pencil at Flynn. "Word of advice," he said. "No dalliances. With students, I mean. We had an incident, a few years back. Didn't end well."

After Flynn straightened, clicked his heels together, and saluted—"Yes sir!"—Faustino smiled and pointed two fingers toward the door, a gesture he had perfected to signal students that he needed to get back to work.

It wasn't very kind of Flynn to call his roommate "Mason the Matricidal Maniac," but that's the nickname he came up with after a few months of living with him and then two weeks of sharing an office. When Briggs graded essays, he hunched over, fists to temples, and shouted invectives at the offending authors: "Who on *earth* uses a semicolon to introduce a series? You *moron!*" Once, when Flynn was returning from a class and heard Briggs spewing this kind of vitriol at what he assumed was a student, he ran down the hall to put a stop to the abuse, only to discover Briggs alone at his desk, the back of his neck red, fists clenched. "Idiot! When are apostrophes *ever* used to create plurals? Aargh!"

Whereas Briggs seemed of the mind that bad grammar signified the onset of the Apocalypse, Flynn took a more conciliatory approach. "They're just kids, Mase," he said one late-September evening at home. "Besides, Slowick says it's more important to teach them to express their ideas well, give them some confidence. Grammar comes later." Dr. Slowick taught the Practicum they were all taking to help with their first year of teaching.

Briggs rolled his eyes. "Fuck off, Mister Wonderful," he muttered—which is what the hostess at Honest John's had been calling Flynn.

The thin and slightly teetering house they rented for two hundred seventy-five dollars a month was across the street from an abandoned factory that had at one time employed nearly all the men of Madisonville. Now it was where kids went to smoke pot, and there were rumors of a meth lab. All that was left of the town itself was the Ace Hardware Store, the Kum N' Go gas station, a smattering of houses, and a few old shops, including Dave's Sporting Goods, which sold mostly ammunition and bait (Lake Chautauqua was a few miles away), Margie's Beauty Shoppe, and three run-down bars, one of which, Jack's Joint, was a favorite among Devlin students. For groceries, Flynn and Briggs drove to nearby Jamestown or Lakewood. Their house at 17 Younger Drive sat scrunched between its leaky-roofed twin rented by four Devlin seniors and a dilapidated faded-blue edifice occupied by a ragged young couple with a flinching four-year-old of indeterminable gender and a disgruntled German Shepherd named Baby chained up in the back yard. Baby's lean and tattooed master made a habit of screaming at his dog, and at his wife and son, with such ferocity that Flynn and Briggs were more than once tempted to phone the police. When they finally did, after hearing the child shrieking nonstop, the officer who picked up the phone chuckled at Flynn. "19 Younger? That's my brother Ray! I'll call him and tell him to settle down, don't you worry. Now who's this? You renting the white house next door? College kid?"

After Flynn hung up, Briggs slammed down the upstairs phone and stomped down the steps. "Inbred rednecks! That's who's running this shit town! Cauliflower-eared pedophiles!"

By then Flynn had learned that the Matricidal Maniac was not simply angry with low-life townies and ungrammatical freshmen—he was angry at the world, angry at how he had been treated at Buffalo Psychiatric ("I mean, electroshock? I told the doctors—and I use that term loosely—what is this, Victor Frankenstein's lab? What's next, *leeching*?"), angry at Flynn (mostly for being so damned *pleasant*), and angry at his mother, not for refusing to die after he had tackled her to the floor, wrapped his burly hands around her neck, and banged her head against the hardwood in a blind rage that had been building for two decades, but for exacerbating the audacity of her survival on a daily basis by calling to offer tender, tentative inquiries about his physical and mental health. He had told Flynn the whole story of the "acute psychiatric episode" while at Jack's Joint shooting pool on the first day they met, seeming surprised when Hawkins didn't bat an eye at the details. Typically, he said, people looked aghast, or found an excuse to leave his company, or pretended to be sympathetic but never called him again, or attempted a lame joke about wanting to kill their own mothers; but Flynn had simply sighed, then shook his head. "Tough deal, man."

"Idiot," Briggs had muttered as he blasted the six-ball with a sharp crack into the corner pocket.

As for Flynn's mother, once an attractive blonde with pronounced cheekbones, a keen sense of humor, and a sultry way of interacting with strangers (Flynn's earliest memory is of standing waist-high to her at the supermarket checkout as she complimented the "bronze, muscular arms" of the teenaged bagboy before asking him to carry her groceries to the car), she had, following the death of Flynn's father, taken the life insurance money as an excuse to quit her job as the principal's secretary at White Plains High School, acquire some cats, step up her smoking habit, and scale back her already limited culinary activity, gnawing on a piece of toast in the morning, skipping lunch entirely, and heating up a TV dinner for Flynn in the evening while crunching Charles Chips from the extra-large tin.

In contrast, the young scholars at 17 Younger Drive ate like Romans, most of their meals taking the form of piled-high plates from Honest John's buffet, pre- or post-shift. When they were not working at the restaurant, they spent their free time watching television (*The Simpsons*, *Northern Exposure*, and *The Martin Short Show* were among their favorites), grading, preparing for classes (which were, that first semester, Restoration Drama, American Modernist Poetry, and the Teaching Practicum), or discussing pedagogy. Of the two, Flynn was proving to be the more thoughtful and innovative instructor. He required his students to write op-ed columns and mail them to their hometown newspapers; he led them on walks through the poor neighborhoods near campus so they could interview residents to get their life stories; he facilitated "silent conversations" during which they discussed current events by way of writing to one another in small groups; he asked them to grade their own essays before he did. If he had a flaw, it was in the generosity of his grading; by November, Faustino was calling him "The Fresh Prince of B+." Even though he felt not a glimmer of the kind of certainty Faustino seemed to feel about the professoriate ("Teaching literature to young people," their fearless leader had pronounced that first day, breathing through his nose like Orson Wells, "is the most satisfying way to earn a paycheck that I can think of"), he did enjoy his new work environment. Not his actual, physical environment—for after a crisp and sunny week in early October, the sky above Madisonville had turned morose, and there seemed no relief in sight from the pervasive gloom—but the campus environment, so rife with young people on the verge of changing the world, including young women seemingly determined to defy the encroaching autumnal chill with their exposed and goosebumped flesh. He enjoyed as well the company of his fellow graduate assistants, who were kindhearted and quirky; he even had a friendly date with one of them, the nasal-voiced Pakistani named Amita, which ended with a healthy front-seat makeout immediately followed by the news that her boyfriend would soon be returning from his military tour in Somalia. At the same time, he sensed no potential for a genuine kinship with any of them (with the possible exception of Briggs, now that he was lightening up a bit, cooking late-night pots of chili and relishing Flynn's cinnamon-raisin French toast on Sundays), to say nothing of a legitimate romance—although he did enjoy, in late October, what most people would call a one-night stand, but what Flynn privately classified even in the very heat of the moment(s) as an enriching educational experience, with a thirty-nine-year-old single mom he met at Jack's Joint while shooting pool with Briggs. And regarding his students, while their youthful vigor made him smile, and while he freely engaged in rigorous nocturnal fantasies featuring a select few, he was well aware that he was in a position of authority and thus resolved never to abuse that position, and he was aware as well that emanating from most of them was not so much sexual fantasies about their young professor but a resistance to, even a resentment of, what he was offering them, a manifestation perhaps of their middle class bitterness over what they were beginning to glean was, at bottom, an insanely expensive and cleverly disguised form of imprisonment.

Still, he treated them with compassion (after all, hadn't he been in that very prison only months earlier, sitting in a similar classroom with the same gray sky out the window?), and taught them earnestly, seeking to improve his craft as well as theirs with each passing week. Rest assured, he made his share of rookie mistakes: he once walked into a crowded classroom and started writing on the board, preparing his lesson on Aristotelian rhetoric, only to have a Biology professor enter and inform him he was in the wrong room (after which Faustino called him "the Absent-Minded Trespasser"); and during a conference in the GA office with one of his students, a fetching blonde named Linda Gustafson, she started crying about failing her Chemistry test, and Flynn gave her a hug (inhaling the scent of her shampoo as she sobbed into his shoulder), only to see Slowick walk in, turn on his heels, and return to his office, afterwards telling him, "No hugging students. Ever. Not a good idea."

After which Faustino dubbed him "The Norse Whisperer."

But despite these and other transgressions, he had what by all accounts must be deemed a successful first semester. Certainly his freshmen found so endearing their young professor's lanky pacing, his cheerful forgiveness of their clumsy errors, his encouragement of their rebellious impulses ("Screw what your father thinks! You're all legal adults now!"), his self-deprecating jokes, and his insistence that they voice strongly their tentative ideas and "think with complexity," that by Thanksgiving Break, Flynn, of all the graduate assistants the least well-read and most ill-equipped for the profession of professor, had become one of the most popular professors at Devlin College.

Faustino noticed. One Monday in December, when the kid passed his doorway at the usual time, wearing his corduroy jacket and carrying the worn leather satchel he had probably purchased at a thrift store (which made him look like a teenager dressing up as a professor for Halloween), Faustino barked out his name, and Hawkins back-stepped in a clunky moonwalk, Michael Jackson style, until he stood in profile at the doorway.

"I'm going to Chicago for a conference," Faustino said. "Want to cover for me?"

Hawkins raised an eyebrow. "Cover? Your classes?"

Faustino held up a meaty finger, as if pointing to God. "Just one. The upper-level." He had already decided that at the end of his Intro to Lit class on Tuesday he would give his students the day off on Thursday; then in the midst of their euphoria and gratitude, he'd pass out course evaluations. Bada bing.

"The upper-level?"

Faustino nodded. "American Tragedy," he said. "We're doing *Death of a Salesman*."

"*Salesman*?" Hawkins said.

"Is there an echo in here?"

What he would never tell Hawkins is that when he taught *his* first upper-level class, he had broken out in a sweat as soon as he walked in the room and said, *Is it just me or is it hot in here?*

"I'll give you my notes," he said.

THAT THURSDAY, FLYNN WALKED INTO AMERICAN TRAGEDY (THE ENGLISH majors regarding him with a chilly skepticism), introduced himself, and immediately distributed the quiz Faustino had told him to administer. As the students bent to the task, Flynn scanned the quiz himself, stopping at question number six: *At the end of Act One, Biff finds a rubber hose. Exactly where in the basement does he find it?*

What a ridiculous question. He glanced up at the students and cleared his throat. "Excuse me, everyone. If you want to skip number six, be my guest. I'm changing it to a bonus question. Extra credit only." The students sighed with relief, except for two girls in the front, who seemed disappointed.

Once he collected the quizzes and opened the class discussion, he found himself in an oasis of liberal humanitarianism and nuanced analysis. For every question he asked, several hands flew up. The students argued over whether Willy Loman deserved their admiration or sympathy, and whether Biff's story mattered more than his father's. They asked intelligent questions, some of which Flynn couldn't answer. "If Miller really wanted us to sympathize with his 'tragic hero,'" one student said, making air quotes, "why is he such a despicable, egotistical wife-beater? What is it about this play that everyone thinks is so great?"

Willy Loman as a despicable wife-beater? A nineteen-year-old challenging the value of an American classic? This was nothing short of thrilling.

THE FOLLOWING MONDAY, JAMES FAUSTINO SAT IN HIS OFFICE WITH HIS DOOR wide open instead of the usual six-inch crack that, he hoped, deterred would-be whiners. When his young protégé walked past at the usual time, Faustino cleared his throat and held up the stack of quizzes he had found on his desk.

"Oh," the kid said.

After an uncomfortable plane ride that forced Faustino to realize it was no longer physically possible for him to sit in coach, he had arrived in Chicago, where it was snowing sideways, and caught a monster of a cold. To add insult to injury, only four people showed up for his panel on "Does the White Male Perspective Still Matter?" He had proposed it to the American Literature Conference solely so he could enjoy a reimbursable dinner with an old friend from his NYU days, but as it turned out, his friend injured his back while shoveling and was incapable of leaving the house. On top of all that, every time Faustino called home

Joanna had complained of odd pains in her lower back, and in spite of Faustino's insistence that she go to the doctor or the Emergency Room (he suspected a kidney stone), she chose to suffer in silence (except when speaking to him, of course) until he returned. When he did so, after another uncomfortable flight (the woman seated next to him made a point of sighing audibly and leaning away from the parts of him that spilled over the armrest, even more so when he hacked out a series of phlegmy coughs), he had a restless night's sleep and had arrived at his office to this stack of quizzes, on one of which was scribbled, "Professor Hawkins said we could skip #6 because it's such a lame question."

He took off his reading glasses. "Lame?"

"Well, no," Flynn said, reaching to see for himself. "I didn't say—"

Faustino pulled back the quizzes. "Let me tell you something, 'Professor' Hawkins. When I ask you to give my students a quiz I've been giving them for over twenty years, you give the quiz. As is. Capeesh?"

Flynn nodded. "Yes sir," he said.

Faustino put his reading glasses back on and lay his fist on the desk, poised for the "Dismissed" gesture.

"But . . ." Flynn said.

Faustino raised his eyebrows, which, he knew from looking in the mirror, had the effect of forming three creases in the acre of forehead above them.

". . . it *is* an unfair question," Flynn said.

Faustino sat back and threw his reading glasses onto his desk. Did he need this? He let out a series of violent coughs, his ribs sore, his lungs watery.

"I re-read the play before class," Hawkins said, "and even *I* couldn't tell you where exactly Biff found that rubber hose. You've read it, what, thirty times?"

Faustino let out a lip-fluttering exhale, like a tired mule. He could see where this was headed, but he had learned, in three decades as a professor, that it was better to let young people fully express their moronic opinions instead of interrupting to correct them.

"And that was the first time for most of them," Flynn said, turning around the Ernest Hemingway bobble-head doll on Faustino's desk "It's a little picky, is what I'm saying. With all due respect. It's not a learning tool, which is what quizzes should be. According to Dr. Slowick."

Faustino templed his hands and took a breath. *With all due respect*, he wanted to say, *you should shut the fuck up*. What was it with kids these days?

"It's *supposed* to be picky," he said. "It's *supposed* to be unfair."

Flynn frowned.

"It makes the kids who read closely feel good about themselves. And it makes the knuckleheads feel like they may have skimmed too quickly. Biff finds the hose behind the fuse box, the power center of the house. Willy, the human power center, is impotent. Biff has potential, but he's been rendered impotent as well, by his father's grandiose dreams for him—he can't ever live up. The way America can't ever live up to its potential. Get it?"

Flynn nodded. "Okay, but . . ."

"So I was curious to see how closely they read. I was guessing Dani and Nicolette, the two girls in front, would know the answer. And they did. They read more closely than you did, apparently. Anyway I don't even count the quiz. It's meant to be a 'conversation starter.' They take the quiz, I go over the questions, and each one starts a conversation. That particular conversation would have been about the symbol of the hose, the symbol of the fuse box."

"Oh," Flynn said.

"So you see," Faustino said, "it's not just a quiz, it's a 'learning tool'."

The kid nodded, his face turning red. Faustino sat back and reminded himself that this was a twenty-two-year-old he was talking to, one that was getting a little caught up with how good-looking and "cool" he was.

"Listen, son," he said, "these kids, they need to be challenged. Our job is not to be liked, or popular, or fair. It's to make them better thinkers. Better people."

Flynn nodded. "I'm sor—""

"Save it," Faustino said, flicking out his two fingers, and Flynn bowed his head and exited.

But as soon as the kid left, Faustino missed him.

By spring semester, word had apparently spread among the faculty that Flynn was a worthy substitute, so others also called on him when they attended conferences or fell ill. One afternoon in April, after teaching Keats's "Ode to a Nightingale" for Slowick's Brit Lit survey, the two star English majors, Dani and Nicolette, approached him with a proposal: they wanted to create a "literary garden" on campus.

"A what?" Flynn said. He pictured old books stuck on spikes inside a labyrinth.

Nicolette took out a map of the Devlin campus and drew a big arrow pointing at a blank patch outside Palmer Hall. "Here," she said. "There's a bunch of dead bushes there right now. We want to clear that area and plant flowers."

"Flowers that appear in literary works," Dani said.

"Like 'the coming musk-rose'," Nicolette said, widening her eyes at Dani, and they burst out laughing.

"So can you help us?" said Dani.

"Maybe bring it up to your 'elders'?" said Nicolette.

Flynn nodded. "I'll do what I can," he said, wondering what Faustino would think.

"Garden, schmarden," is what his professor said when Flynn relayed the students' idea. But then Faustino sat back in his desk chair, lifted his eyes to the ceiling, and spread his massive hands like a priest at the altar.

"God made a beauteous garden,
With lovely flowers strown,
But one straight, narrow pathway
That was not overgrown.
And to this beauteous garden
He brought mankind to live,
And said, 'To you, my children,
these lovely flowers I give."

Flynn stuck his finger in his mouth and pretended to vomit. "Ann Bradstreet?" he said. "Your grandmother? A Hallmark card you picked up for Mother's Day?"

Faustino shook his head. "Bobby Frost," he said. "Worst load of crap he ever wrote. I had to memorize it in grade school." He picked up his phone. "I'll call my buddy over at Buildings and Grounds."

Three days later, the dead bushes outside Palmer Hall had been cleared and a mound of dark, loamy soil had been dumped there, along with some shovels and spades. Dani and Nicolette were outside, along with some other English majors, and Briggs was there too. He and a few of the students were digging and planting while the rest stood around trying to come up with literary songs to sing, like "Wuthering Heights" by Kate Bush and "Richard Cory" by Paul Simon. When Briggs chimed in with the boisterous chorus of "Don Quixote" by Gordon Lightfoot, waving his spade in the air, Flynn straightened and stared at him.

When he went inside, he found that Faustino had covered Briggs's name plate with a handwritten sign: "Chauncey Gardener."

BY THE TIME THE STUDENTS CAME BACK FROM SUMMER VACATION, FAULKNER'S honeysuckle was waist-high and trellised, Marquez's geraniums were bright with color, Blake's lilies were tall and elegant, and Millay's strawberry bushes had fruited and multiplied. When Flynn approached the east entrance of Palmer Hall for his first day of his second year of graduate school, he found some English majors sitting on a stone table near the garden, eating bagels and drinking coffee, and two others on the ground, their bare legs stretched. And—he had to look twice—under the nearby pear tree, his feet bare and the sleeves of his linen shirt rolled up, was Dr. Faustino, absorbed in a book.

ON THE THIRD MONDAY OF OCTOBER, 1995, JAMES FAUSTINO, WHO KEPT THE same schedule every semester (office hours Mondays and Wednesdays, classes on Tuesdays and Thursdays, Fridays free for meetings), was composing a difficult evaluation of his junior colleague Mary Anne Tscherpel when Flynn rushed in. *"Ciao, professore!"*

Faustino put down his pen. *"Figlio mio,"* he said. "How was your class?"

"Good. So, registration begins tomorrow, right?"

Faustino nodded; he had been conferencing with his advisees all week and couldn't wait for registration to be over.

"And I'm graduating at the end of next semester," Flynn said. He seemed a little out of breath.

"Yes, provided you pass your classes and the MA exam," Faustino said, his voice sounding a bit more gruff than he had intended. "Is there a point, son?"

"The point," Flynn said, holding up the Spring 1996 course-selection booklet, "is that you're not teaching a graduate course. In my final semester here."

Faustino scratched his beard. He had last taught a graduate course, on American Modernist Poetry, during Flynn's first semester. "We all take turns," he said. "There's a rotation. In your two years here, you take each of us at least once. Twelve faculty members, three courses per semester, four semesters."

"Well, right," Flynn said, opening the booklet to the English page, "but here's Tscherpel teaching a class on people I never heard of, which is fine of course, but I already took her for Restoration Drama, my first semester."

Faustino nodded. "That's because Dr. Slowick will be on sabbatical in the spring."

Flynn lifted his head to the heavens, then dropped his chin to his chest. "Okay that's not the point," he said. "Here's the point. Let me just put it out there. You're this great Hemingway scholar, you studied with Phil Young, your nickname is Papa, you used to be a boxer, et cetera et cetera."

Faustino placed his right hand on the desk, in the dismissal position, and wondered if he should tell the kid the truth, which was that he had never boxed, but he had once joked to a student that he had almost qualified for the Olympics, and once that legend was born, he had done nothing to dispute it.

Flynn flung himself into the student chair—a move he had developed to counter what he called the Faustinian Finger Flip. "So in an ideal world," he said. "I mean, if I could have one wish . . . you know, before I leave here . . ." He clasped his hands together. "It would be to study Hemingway with you."

"Ah," Faustino said. "Well thank you. But, you know. That's life." He smiled thinly, but as he did so, he had an idea. Nonetheless, he flicked out his two fingers. "Off you go now, son."

The following Monday, as Faustino left the building on his way to a Core Curriculum meeting, he saw Flynn chatting with some undergrads on his way back from class. He called out and Flynn jogged over, holding his satchel to prevent it from flapping.

Faustino opened his bag and handed Hawkins a completed Independent Study form for Spring 1996. Next to "Course Title" he had written, "Hemingway."

"Sign this and bring it to the Registrar," he said. "You can drop Dr. Tscherpel's course. I've already spoken to her about it."

Faustino started to walk away, but Flynn put a hand on his arm. "You spoke to her about it?"

"Yes," Faustino said. *Again with the echoing!* "Oh, and I was thinking we'd have it at my house."

Flynn gaped open his mouth. "At your house?"

"Yes! My house." Faustino turned and walked away, thinking of replacing the course title with something like Echo and Faustissus, or Echo-Roman Wrestling, or Echo and the Funny Man. He continued on towards Bateman Hall where he would sit for two hours daydreaming about the Yankees' chances in the playoffs and worrying about Joanna, who, after months without much pain (except for a consistent backache), had doubled over in pain that morning and had finally agreed to make an appointment with her gynecologist.

THREE MONTHS LATER, ON THE THIRD THURSDAY EVENING OF JANUARY 1996, at 5:45 p.m., Flynn set off on the fourteen-block walk from 17 Younger Drive to 105 St. Anne Street. It was damp and cold, and as he tramped through the hardened snow the sky deepened to black. He was greeted at the door by Faustino's wife, a corpulent woman with gray-blonde hair and moist blue eyes. "Jim hasn't done this for years!" she said as she led Flynn to an armchair, scurried into the kitchen, came out with a tray of finger sandwiches and a glass of soda, and set them on the coffee table. "Did you eat dinner, sweetheart?"

Flynn stared at her. She was so . . . *maternal*. He scanned the living room for photos of children, but remembered that at the English Department Christmas party, Slowick had told him, his voice confidential, that the Faustinos had never been able to conceive. It was, Slowick said, the unspoken tragedy of their lives.

When Faustino came lumbering down the stairs, Mrs. Faustino seemed to vanish, and Flynn and his professor sat opposite each other in the living room. Faustino began by chatting about Hemingway's life, focusing on the author's boyhood, and they proceeded to discuss a few of the Nick Adams stories Flynn had been assigned, including "Indian Camp," which ends with a man killing himself during his wife's violent childbirth and Nick's father, a doctor, saying, "He couldn't stand things, I guess." They talked for two hours straight. When Mrs. Faustino quietly re-entered the room, replacing the sandwich tray with a plate of cookies and a mug of tea, Flynn met her eyes (such kindness!) and smiled a thank-you.

"Shouldn't the young man be allowed to take a break?" she asked Faustino. "What if he needs to go to the bathroom, for heaven's sake?" When Faustino gave her what seemed the marital equivalent of the finger flip, she scowled and held out the tray. "I'm giving you the finger right now," she said, "even though you can't see it." Then she winked at Flynn and laughed. "I've never done that before!"

As Faustino dropped the book to his lap and raised his eyes to the ceiling, Flynn picked up a raspberry-thumbprint cookie and popped it in his mouth. "You have as many as you want, dear," she said as she left the room. "There's plenty more." Then Flynn had to stare at his *Collected Stories of Ernest Hemingway* so his professor wouldn't see his eyes well up. Nobody—not his mother, not any of his aunts (nasal-voiced, reedy Bronx women who overcooked their meals and communicated via sarcasm and clichés)—had ever spoken to him as this woman had.

When he looked up, Faustino was staring at the kitchen door. "She's a piece of work," he muttered. Then he scratched his beard and looked down at his book.

For the next month, Mrs. Faustino had dinner waiting when Flynn arrived: eggplant parmigiana with a side of braciole and salad; penne pasta with pesto and chunks of mozzarella and sausage; flank steak with mushrooms and macaroni-and-cheese; a roasted chicken with carrots and potatoes. But on the first Thursday of March, she was nowhere in sight. "My beloved is indisposed," Faustino said as he opened the front door. He pointed upstairs. "She said to help yourself to whatever you'd like in the fridge. Can I warm up some lasagna for you?"

"No thanks," Flynn said, even though he was hungry. The idea of his esteemed professor preparing food for him seemed inappropriate. He glanced upstairs, hoping Mrs. Faustino would appear after all, but everything was quiet.

They sat down to discuss "Fathers and Sons," which Faustino called "Quite possibly the best short story ever written," to which Flynn replied, "Quite possibly an overstatement?" and instead of emitting a deep chuckle, Faustino frowned.

"Quite possibly *not*," he said.

"Better than 'Rip Van Winkle'?" Flynn offered.

Faustino snorted. "I'm talking stories, this guy gives me a fairy tale."

"'Young Goodman Brown'?"

The professor shook his head. "Too heavy-handed."

"'Life in the Iron Mills?' 'Bartleby, the Scrivener'?" In the preceding semester he had taken a course in 19th Century American Literature and had loved all the symbolism.

Another snort from his professor. "What are you, a socialist?"

"How about 'The Dead'?" Flynn had also enjoyed a course on the Irish Renaissance—such bleak portrayals of the human condition balanced by a perpetual impulse towards humor. The Irish treated a joke as a serious thing and serious things as a joke, according to a character in one of the plays he'd read, and Flynn had felt himself missing the grit and sarcasm of New Yorkers. He was still in New York State, but here in Madisonville, six hours away, it was a completely different part of the country.

Faustino shook his head. "Best ending ever," he said, "but too much dilly-dallying beforehand."

Flynn smiled, thinking of what his other professor would say to that. "How about 'The Shawl?'"

"Ooo," Faustino said. "Good one. Top Ten."

Flynn snapped his fingers. "'Beast in the Jungle'."

Faustino pursed his lips. "Christ," he said. "You might have me there."

After they discussed "Fathers and Sons," also based on Hemingway's relationship with his father, Faustino asked Flynn to read the final dialogue out loud. Flynn did so, his voice softening as he imagined himself as the boy in the passenger seat watching his father drive with a cigarette between his lips. When Flynn came to the part where Nick brags about his late father's sharpshooting skills and his son says, "I bet he wasn't better than you," Faustino suddenly closed his eyes and folded his meaty hands over his belly.

"'Oh, yes he was,'" Faustino said, quoting the story's next lines. "'He shot very quickly and beautifully. I'd rather see him shoot than any man I ever knew. He was always disappointed in the way I shot.'" He kept his eyes closed, then suddenly wiped them with his fists.

He cleared his throat and grabbed a napkin. "Gets me every time," he said.

Flynn sat still, not knowing what to say. He hadn't been nearly as moved by the story when he had read it the night before. "Should I continue?" he asked.

Faustino removed the napkin from his face, which was now ruddy, and shook his head.

"I'm sorry," Flynn said, remembering what Dr. Slowick had told him. "Is it because you always wanted . . ."

Faustino cut him off with his hand. "My father passed away," he said. "Christmas Eve.. He was eighty-nine. But still."

Flynn shifted in his armchair. "Shit," he said. "I'm sorry."

On the mantle behind his professor was a black-and-white photograph of a couple. The man had broad shoulders, mutton chops, and a whale-shaped torso. "Is that him?" Flynn asked, pointing to it.

Faustino nodded, then blew his nose.

"Handsome man," Flynn said, even though the man wasn't especially handsome. He bounced his palms on the arms of the seat. He wanted to say something like *Well, at least you had your old man around as long as you did,* but he supposed the pain must be the same—or maybe worse, because with more years there would be more memories, more time to screw up the relationship and regret what you never said to him.

"And yes," Faustino said, picking up his book and thumbing the pages. "Yes I always wanted a son. Okay? Now then. Next story."

FROM MID-MARCH TO THE END OF THE MONTH, THE WEATHER THAWED, THEN chilled, then turned outright offensive before thawing again. Then it snowed for four straight days. On Sunday, March 31, 1996, Flynn stared out the kitchen window, which overlooked the yard where Baby sulked in his doghouse, his fur matted. The doghouse was surrounded by stacks of rotting firewood, piles of bricks, three car tires, sheets of roof shingles, various auto parts, waterlogged boxes of old tiles, and cinder blocks. Flynn watched as the snowflakes splattered the doghouse roof and the trees dropped clumps onto the ground still patched by November's sooty snow. The branch of a crabapple tree bent perilously over the stretch of mud where Baby, in nice weather, would run back and forth, hooked to his chain.

One flake after another, without much accumulation or grace. Flynn watched the snow galumphing down from the gray heavens, attempting to reinterpret it as beautiful, as a pastoral cascade, but there was nothing attractive about it.

At that moment, James Faustino was in the waiting room of WCA Hospital, five miles from Flynn's house. The pap smear at the gynecologist's office had revealed nothing, but Joanna's back pain had persisted, so now she was undergoing an MRI. If they found "anything weird," they would do a biopsy right away. Faustino fingered the book he had brought with him (*Winesburg, Ohio*), but instead found himself staring out the window at the pathetic snowfall, a cantankerous and insistent blight determined to obstruct for an infuriating length of time the onset of spring, the inevitable return of his wife's health and vigor.

There had been a time, in his forties, when Faustino had fantasized about his wife's death. He would have been freed to explore his options in a way he never had in his youth. He was still a large man then, but more "big" and "broad-shouldered" than obese. He had been finding Joanna's matronly personality—her fussing over their cats, her cooing over their friends' and family members' children—a constant irritant. Her lilting, caressing voice, the very voice he had found charming during their courtship, had struck him as phony; he mocked it privately at first, then out loud on occasion, and finally, once, in public. The night he did so, they drove home afterwards in silence, and once they stepped inside their house, Joanna turned and smacked Faustino across the face. She tried to say something, her face scrunched and red, but it never came out. Instead she turned, went upstairs, and locked the door to their bedroom. Lying on the couch that night, Faustino realized how mean he had been, and vowed to treat her from that day forward with the respect she certainly merited. The fifteen years since had been a steadily enhanced period of kindness and camaraderie, along with a burgeoning patience, fastidiousness, and prudence he at once disdained and appreciated. He was a better person now than when they were first married, and he had learned to treat his wife with gratitude and compassion. That was enough. And the love he received in return, the tenderness, in such abundance, was beyond what he either deserved or expected.

Now, he at sixty, she at sixty-one, he was in no mood to imagine what his life might be like without her.

Back at 17 Younger Drive, Flynn Hawkins put his hand on the cold window, feeling a slight draft through the rotting frame. He had not gone home for spring break, as he had planned. He had spent the week reading on the couch, drinking tea, and recovering from the flu. And he had received a letter from NYU, accepting him into their PhD program, with a full scholarship and teaching assistantship. So things were going well. All things considered, it had been good to spend the last two years, excepting his sister's wedding and a few holiday visits, away from White Plains. He had done okay on his own. Rent would be much higher in Manhattan, but he could take out another student loan and try to sublet a rent-controlled place in the Village. Then, when he became a professor, he would make a real salary and start paying off his loans. It was all going to work out. In the back of his mind, he knew he should think more about it—he should decide whether or not this was what he actually wanted to do with his life—but he told himself he was on track, and it would be a good life.

ELEVEN DAYS LATER, WHEN FLYNN ARRIVED AT THE FAUSTINOS' HOUSE, IT was quiet inside, and the living room smelled stuffy. He hadn't been there in three weeks—first due to spring break, then because Faustino had canceled (without explanation) the following week. Mrs. Faustino was nowhere in sight.

Faustino went into the kitchen, microwaved a Pyrex container full of baked ziti, and brought out two plates. Flynn thanked him, then ate quietly as his professor took a seat at the table, opened his copy of *A Farewell to Arms*, and took a bite of his food. Faustino always wrote his favorite line of a book on its title page, and typically he read it to Flynn as a way of starting their conversation, but this time he stared at the page while eating. Flynn tried to read the line upside-down.

"'The world breaks everyone,'" Faustino finally read, "'and afterward many are strong at the broken places.'"

Flynn sat back. He had liked that line when he read it, but now it felt different. "Don't some people stay broken?" he asked. "Or pretend they're stronger but never get there? Like a bone that mends the wrong way? Or something?"

Faustino huffed while chewing his food—"Or something?" he muttered—then took a gulp of Bud Lite. "And what, may I ask, do you know about being broken? You're what, twenty-three?" He lowered his head and chewed like a rhinoceros.

"Twenty-four," Flynn said.

Faustino reached for the grated cheese. "Let's have this talk again when you're fifty," he said.

THE FOLLOWING WEEK, FAUSTINO CAME HOME FROM THE HOSPITAL JUST IN time to open a bag of pretzels and order a pizza. The doorbell rang as he hung up the phone. He took a deep breath, then opened the door for Flynn. As he went into the kitchen to get a couple of beers, he noticed the kid looking around, then up the staircase. "I hope you like pepperoni," he called out. When he came back, Flynn was still standing by the table, and for a moment Faustino considered telling him about what he had just seen: his wife, blanching first at what the oncologist had told them, then again at the "chemo plan" that would begin immediately. Faustino had held her hand, feeling her grip fade at first, then tighten fiercely, just as it had during their wedding, at the little church where she had served as acolyte and lector. She hadn't let go of his hand for the entire service, not even when they kneeled, her nails occasionally digging into his palm. When he had bent to kiss his bride, she had squeezed even harder and hissed into his ear, "Now don't you ever, *ever* leave me."

Faustino handed Flynn a beer, told him the pizza was on its way, then settled the mass of his body into his armchair and picked up his copy of *For Whom the Bell Tolls.* "Let's get right to it," he said. "No small talk." And he opened the book as a monsignor would open the Bible.

THAT SATURDAY WAS MILD AND SUNNY, AND THE TREES ON YOUNGER DRIVE were finally beginning to bud. Flynn and Briggs were sitting on the front stoop, drinking the iced tea Briggs had made, when the students next door—a different group than the year before—came outside carrying garbage cans. They waved to Briggs and Flynn and told them they were having a kegger that night. "You guys want to join us?"

Flynn started to say "No thanks," but then Briggs said, "Sure, we'll call our friends!"

The students arrived that evening by car and by foot, from all directions, as if magnetically drawn to the gleaming aluminum keg. The other grad assistants came to Flynn's house, and Flynn anxiously scanned the growing crowd from his front stoop, hoping he wouldn't see any of his students. But then he did: three freshmen from his fall composition class, who, when they spotted Flynn, slunk away into the back yard.

The party lasted well into the evening, during which Flynn and the other graduate students sang along to the music the seniors were playing on their boom box, took swigs of schnapps that Amita had brought, and complained about Professor Tscherpel. By ten o'clock the crowd had spilled over onto Flynn's front yard. Some tee-shirted male students were gathered around the keg, taking turns sitting in a beach chair and having beer funneled down their throats, their chanting growing louder each time, and Flynn saw one of his freshmen in the scraggly bushes making out with an upperclassman. The smell of marijuana wafted over from next door, and at one point Flynn noticed Dani and Nicolette, the English majors, but as soon as he lifted his hand in a wave, Nicolette stumbled and fell to the ground, her legs splayed, her panties revealed in the glow of the porchlight.

Then the students decided to abandon the boom box and blast music from the stereo inside their house, sticking the speakers out the windows:

AC/DC's "Thunderstruck." Briggs ran over to tell them that wasn't such a good idea, that their angry neighbor had already yelled out from his window to shut the fuck up and their elderly neighbors would probably call the cops on them, and this left Flynn and Amita alone on the stoop. "Come on," she said, taking his hand and pulling him into the house. She kissed him at the base of the inside stairway, her lips tasting minty. Then she led him up to his bedroom.

"What about G.I. Joe?" Flynn asked, but it came out slurry. He told himself that was enough drinking for the night; in high school and college he had overdone it at times, and he needed to learn when to hit the brakes.

"Never mind him," Amita said, as she unbuckled his belt. For a moment, Flynn worried he was too drunk to be aroused (he pictured Faustino replacing his nameplate with "Jake Barnes, English Department") but then he turned his head away, belched, and everything was all right after that.

Afterwards, Amita curled into him on his bed, her black hair soft on his shoulder, her arm a rich-brown boundary separating his pale heart from his pale loins. Flynn felt a small wave of shame—he hadn't washed his sheets in months—but then closed his eyes, trying to enjoy the smell of Amita's perfume, feeling her breath on his neck (acrid and minty from the Schnapps) and remembering the passage from "Fathers and Sons" in which Hemingway describes Nick's isolated, faraway feeling after sex. That's when he heard a boisterous roar in his back yard, and when he sat up he saw licks of flame out the back window. He jumped up, dressed quickly, and ran outside to find that the students had started a minor bonfire, using twigs and branches, with Briggs and the other grad students (three of whom were in their underwear) looking on, drunk and amused—but apparently they had run out of branches, so several of them were off looting the neighbors' yards for wood.

That's when they all heard Baby growling viciously, and Flynn looked over in time to see the dog hurling himself repeatedly against the length of his chain until he tore it from its holdings and sprinted after the student who had climbed over the fence to get at the firewood. The kid screamed and leaped back over just before Baby got to him, but the dog's owner then appeared at the back door wielding a rifle and yelling at Flynn to get "these goddamn faggots" off his property before he "put some lead in their pansy-asses."

Flynn immediately called out that the party was over, ran over to the garden hose, opened the valve, and began to douse the fire with water, much to everyone's chagrin. He was still doing that, making sure it was out, when he saw the partygoers suddenly running in every direction.

He dropped the hose and walked out to the front yard, where there were two police cars at the curb, their flashing lights sweeping into the windows of the houses across the street. Two officers got out of the lead car and went next door, and the two in the rear car came right up to Flynn and asked if he resided at this property. "I do," Flynn said, checking to make sure his fly was zipped. He looked around, but Briggs was nowhere in sight. Then one of the officers held out handcuffs.

"What?" Flynn said. "What'd I do?" He started trembling.

"Disturbing the peace, for starters," the officer said as he dropped the cuffs, took Flynn by the arm, and led him to the squad car. "And stealing firewood. Firewood's very important to people around here."

"Plus serving alcohol to minors," the other officer said, his voice sounding familiar to Flynn. "We got a whole bunch of stuff on you college boys."

"I'm not a college boy," Flynn said as he got into the back seat. "I'm a professor." And the two officers burst out laughing.

At the police station, which was oddly bright and welcoming, he and the students waited a long time in the lobby before they were all finger-printed, charged, issued a summons to appear in court, and told they were free to go. Flynn thought about calling Briggs for a ride, but then he remembered how much his roommate had drunk that night. One of the seniors put a quarter in the payphone and told Flynn he could ride back with them, but when the car pulled up outside the station, Flynn recognized the driver as one of the tee-shirted guys who had been funneling beer, so he shook his head. He knew the way home, he said, and in any case he needed to sober up.

He walked along Route 394, trying to keep a steady course. He wondered if he had just been officially arrested, if this was the kind of thing that would hurt him in the future. But if he had been, they would have taken a mug shot—that was something they did—and he would probably be in a cell, "awaiting bail." Besides, what evidence did they have that he had done anything wrong? Stealing firewood—how stupid was that? He hadn't stolen any firewood. And what kind of lame-ass cops in what kind of lame-ass small fucking town arrested people for stealing firewood? Briggs was right—what a stupid fucked up depressing place this was! (Briggs was right about everything, actually! He would tell him this when he got home.) And serving alcohol to minors? Well, he'd like to see them make *that* stick. First of all, it wasn't his beer, he hadn't paid for it, it wasn't on his property, actually it wasn't even his property, it was his landlord's property, and yes, people were drinking it, but he certainly never served it, not technically speaking anyway, to anyone he knew for a fact was a minor. But that probably didn't matter. He hadn't asked for anyone's ID—nobody had—and ignorance was one-tenth of the law, or something like that. The freshmen! He had known damn well they were minors and he hadn't said anything. Fuck. He was screwed. He was guilty in the indirect way that someone who drives without knowing his taillight is out is guilty . . .

He was trying to remember the other charges against him when a station wagon pulled over to the curb, ahead of him. Flynn saw the reverse lights come on and thought about fleeing, but then he recognized the license plate: "PAPA."

"They called you?" Flynn yelled into the open passenger window.

Faustino leaned back. "Who?" he said. "I saw you walking. It's getting cold. You're three miles from home." He gestured. "Get in, son."

Flynn opened the door and flopped into the seat, keeping his eyes on the dashboard.

"What's going on? I was at the hospital," Faustino said, pointing behind him.

"I'm so sorry," Flynn said, then felt his throat close up and tried not to cry. "Is your wife okay?" He had heard from Slowick that she had cancer. Then, "I think I've been arrested." As they approached downtown Madisonville, Flynn told him, trying to keep his voice steady, what had just occurred.

"Well, did you do it?" Faustino asked, after Flynn was finished.

"I did not," Flynn said. He was trying to pronounce his words carefully so Faustino wouldn't know he was drunk, but he felt sure he had already incriminated himself. His breath probably smelled like Amita's. "Of course not. Never."

"Well, you stood by as minors were served beer, correct?'

"Well yes, but—"

"Then you're guilty," Faustino said. "*And* you're drunk. And students were there? *Your* students?" He shook his head, staring at the road. "Jesus."

They rode in silence past campus, Faustino quietly scratching his beard. Finally he clenched both fists around the steering wheel. "You can't imagine what I would think of you," he said in his gravelly voice, "if you allowed my 18-year-old child to drink beer on your property, and he died in a car accident on his way home." He made a left turn onto Younger Drive.

"Well, you don't ha—" Flynn said, then stopped himself.

When they pulled up to Flynn's house, Faustino kept the car idling, staring at the litter of red cups on the lawns. Flynn smelled the dampened ash and realized he had left the hose on this whole time. He put his hand on the door handle. "I am so sorry," he said. "I am."

Faustino lifted two fingers from the steering wheel and pointed toward the house.

On Monday morning, James Faustino hung up his office phone and kept his hand on the receiver. He had considered canceling his next class meeting with Flynn, had considered aborting the course altogether. He had even considered kicking Flynn out of the program. But after speaking with Slowick and (just now) to the dean, he knew he should exercise restraint and show some compassion.

By the time Flynn came by his office that afternoon, Faustino had spoken to his friend Allen in the Madisonville Police Department, the one who had been on duty the night of the party.

"You're off the hook," Faustino told Flynn. "Your neighbor dropped the charges."

Flynn sat back in the student chair, swiped his wet hair (it was raining outside) from his forehead, and looked at the floor.

"It was trumped-up anyway," Faustino said, "according to Allen. Some kid stealing firewood, no idea which kid it was . . ." Faustino sat up straight and folded his hands on his desk. "But serving minors," he said, pointing both index fingers, "that's serious." He paused to see if Flynn recognized the gravity of the situation. "You're lucky Allen isn't up for a witch hunt. 'No harm done, but make sure the kids never do that again', you know, with graduation parties coming up and all that."

Flynn shifted in his seat, his head still bowed. "I *did* do it," he muttered. "I *am* guilty. There *were* freshmen there."

The kid looked like he was going to cry.

"I should turn myself in," Flynn said. "Make a full confession."

Faustino blew out a sigh. "Oh, I don't know," he said. "After all, thank God, nothing happened." Flynn had his hands over his eyes now. "After the party," Faustino said. "According to Allen, I mean. No accidents, no crimes." He rested his hands, palms down, on the table. "I suppose I myself was guilty of my own"—he breathed deeply through his nose, his belly extending—"youthful indiscretions. When I was your age."

He considered reaching over and patting the kid on the arm. "Easy, son."

THAT THURSDAY, FAUSTINO CAME HOME FROM THE HOSPITAL A FEW MINUTES after six and found Flynn waiting on the porch, looking no longer sullen, but something else: repentant, perhaps, or determined to redeem himself; but it came across as defiant. They went inside, Faustino offered him some chips ("I'm afraid this is all I have"), but Flynn said no and held up his book, ready to get to work. Faustino shook his head and went over to his armchair, thinking, *If this is what it's like to have a son, I'm glad that ship has sailed.* He picked up his copy of *The Old Man and the Sea*, licked his index finger, and turned to the opening chapter, his mind suddenly elsewhere—on what had just happened in Room 312 at WCA.

"What's your line?" Flynn asked, and Faustino lifted his head. The kid was pointing at his book, opened to the title page. Faustino held it up so that it faced the kid. *Man can be destroyed but not defeated.*

Flynn widened his eyes and showed Faustino the title page of his own book, where he had scribbled the same line.

Faustino offered a weak smile. "That one true sentence," he said. "He finally got it, in 1952."

But Flynn looked down at the book, shook his head, and mumbled something.

"What," Faustino said.

"Nothing," Flynn said.

Faustino sighed. "Come on, son. What is it."

The young man looked down at his book. "Well, I loved this book."

Faustino thrummed his fingers on the lamp table next to him. "But?"

"But," Hawkins said. "This line—it's a great line. But after I wrote it down, I realized . . . it might be a lie."

Faustino cringed. A *lie?*

Had he been like this, at that age? He remembered having strong opinions, but at the same time he had been acutely aware that he was an inexperienced person reading lines written by men of experience—and a certain amount of deference came with that. And now that he was older, he indeed found that great works spoke to him with more truth and relevance than when he was young. This kid, he was just inventing ways to be contrarian and skeptical, taking issue with some of the most beautiful lines in the English language simply to feel intelligent, to bolster his frail ego.

"I mean, a man *can* be both destroyed *and* defeated," Flynn said. "I've seen it with my own two eyes."

WHEN FLYNN ARRIVED AT FAUSTINO'S OFFICE THE FOLLOWING MONDAY, HE found the professor's door shut and a note in his mailbox: *"Could you cover my classes this week and maybe next? Syllabi and notes attached. Also let's skip Islands and Feast. No more class meetings, in other words. Just work on your essay, which I'm sure will be stellar. — Papa."*

Flynn stood by his mailbox and looked over the syllabi. For Modern Drama, *Long Day's Journey into Night* was scheduled for the final two weeks; Flynn would stay up all night if necessary to read the play and study Faustino's notes. But he wondered: was Mrs. Faustino in dire straits? He put a note in his professor's box: "Don't worry, I've got you covered."

Four days later, after trying his best to teach the longest and most depressing but most magnificent play he had ever read, Flynn received an email from Faustino: HOPE CLASSES ARE GOING OKAY. WATCH OUT FOR JACOBY BY THE WINDOW, HE'S A BULLSHITTER AND HE HAS SOMEONE'S NOTES FROM LAST YEAR. VISIT IF YOU CAN. JOANNA WOULD LOVE TO SEE YOU. CALL FIRST.

But Flynn knew he wouldn't.

TWO WEEKS LATER, HE HAD FINISHED FAUSTINO'S CLASSES, ADMINISTERED the final exams, and encouraged the students to send their professor cards and notes. After the American Drama final, Dani and Nicolette stopped at the front of the room looking worried. "I'm sure she'll pull through," he said. He pictured Mrs. Faustino's eyes, her smile, her faded yellow cardigan. She was hearty; she would be fine. "She'll beat this thing," he said.

A half-hour later, Flynn was sitting alone in the Graduate Assistants office, staring at the M.A. in English Examination grades posted on the wall. He had passed with a B. He had officially earned a Master's degree. Briggs had earned an A. Flynn probably could have pulled off an A too if he hadn't spent so much time preparing for Faustino's classes.

He heard a gentle cough in the hallway, then Dr. Slowick came in and sat down in the chair opposite Flynn. The professor ran his hand over his bald head and straightened his glasses. Flynn was afraid to speak. What would compel Slowick to come into school during his sabbatical?

"It has fallen to me . . ." Slowick started to say, but then his face flushed and he got up and left the room.

JAMES FAUSTINO LAY FACE DOWN IN HIS MARITAL BED, CLUTCHING THE SIDES of the mattress as if he had been flying through the air, hanging on for dear life, before landing with a profound thud in this room. His face was buried in his wife's pillow, his hair spread like an old mop over the white collar of his pressed shirt and the jacket of his black suit. He had never allowed any part of himself to touch her pillow—his body odor would stain the cloth, or a long strand of his gray hair would mar its smooth surface—but a half-hour earlier he had plunged his face into it, choking out sobs and not bothering to wipe his nose.

He heaved himself over and stared at the ceiling, at the cheap plastic squares he had always promised his wife he'd replace, at the water stain above the closet door. This was nothing he could bear. This was not the outcome he had planned on. *He* was the one: Type A, gargantuan, poor eating habits . . .

"Jo—" he choked out, but on his mind was not his wife's name but a phrase from *A Farewell to Arms*, one he had quoted to her in the hospital three days earlier as if it were his own line, after she had told him (her hand stroking his beard, touching the lids of his eyes), "If this gets me, honey, I want you to move on. I want you to live and love again."

"I don't live at all when I'm not with you," he said back, and then imagined young Hawkins finding his statement ridiculously romantic. *Well to hell with him*. He loosened the tie that was strangling him.

He lifted his head at the sound of a creaky car door slamming shut, then footsteps on his front stoop. Flynn. It was Flynn, coming to pay his condolences, or to apologize for not visiting when Joanna was in the hospital. Faustino went up on his elbows—yes, it might help him to see the youngster—but then realized what he must look like. He could never answer the door in this condition.

FLYNN HAWKINS STOOD ON HIS PROFESSOR'S PORCH, HIS HAND BELOW THE doorbell, his finger poised. A light rain was falling. The bells of Devlin campus were chiming. The 1996 Spring Commencement had begun.

Two hours earlier, he had been lying in bed with a headache, listening to Briggs getting ready. Flynn and the other graduate assistants had gone out the night before to celebrate, and toward the end Amita had offered to come home with him, but Flynn had slipped out when her back was turned and walked all the way home. Amita was smart and kind and beautiful, sure, but how was he supposed to compete with a soldier?

Briggs knocked on Flynn's bedroom door, but Flynn said nothing. The door was locked. He lay on his back, the covers under his chin.

It was Saturday, June 1. Their lease was up, but their landlord had given them the weekend to move out, since there was nobody else renting the place until September. Briggs had already packed his things and would be heading to Buffalo after graduation and the wake for Mrs. Faustino, which would take place at the Williams and Gardner Funeral Home at two o'clock. Flynn had planned on leaving the following morning. He would drive to White Plains and stay with his mother while looking for a cheap place to live in lower Manhattan. Neither his mother (who rarely drove farther than Macy's or the DMV and was certainly not going to risk the six-hour trek to Madisonville, "wherever on God's green earth *that* is") nor his sister (who was six months pregnant) would be coming to his graduation ceremony.

Briggs clapped up the stairs with his dress shoes and rapped on his door again. "Hawkins!" A pause, then a jiggling of the door handle. "Flynn, we gotta go, for fuck's sake! What's going on, is Amita in there?" He banged on the door. "Amita! Flynnie! Wake up!"

Flynn held his breath until Briggs gave up and tramped down the stairs.

Once he heard the front door slam and Briggs's car pull away, Flynn got up and rubbed his face. He would pack up and leave. Now, not tomorrow. He would get on Route 17 and head east. He'd skip graduation. Most of his professors would be there, along with his fellow graduate assistants and their families, including Briggs's infamous mother and Amita's macho soldier-boy, probably in full military garb. But no one for him.

And he would miss the wake. But Faustino wouldn't want him there anyway. The man would surely prefer to be left alone. Can you imagine? That beautiful woman. The love of his life. It wouldn't even register if Flynn was there. Besides, he knew how Flynn felt about him. Flynn didn't need to line up at some ritualistic service, paying respects and whatnot, to show his professor how much he cared. He didn't need to see Mrs. Faustino in the coffin, her lips sewn up into a clownish smile, her middle collapsed from the removal of her organs, her overbrushed hair arranged strangely with chemicals. He didn't need to touch her skin to know how cold and taut it would feel. He didn't need anyone grabbing him around his waist again, pulling him away from the coffin.

He washed himself, packed his car, cleaned his bedroom, put his house key on the kitchen table, and left 17 Younger Drive for good. As he pulled away, he saw the flinching child on his neighbors' porch and realized it was a boy.

But as he headed through town on 394, a soft rain began to fall, and just before driving past the Devlin campus, he impulsively turned right onto St. Anne Street.

When Faustino had talked about Ernest Hemingway's death, he had put down his book (*The Old Man and the Sea*), set his huge paws on the armchair, and described the famous writer going up to the roof of his Idaho home and blowing his brains out, just as his father had done. "He couldn't stand things, I guess," Faustino had said, putting on a downcast face.

But Flynn had read a more recent biography than the one written by Faustino's mentor, and it painted a more complicated picture of the author's final years: plane crashes that left him with cracked discs, a broken skull, a ruptured kidney and liver; second-degree burns sustained in a fire; treatment for arteriosclerosis and hypertension; paranoia (justified, as it turns out) about being tracked by the FBI; heavy drinking; electroconvulsive therapy at the Mayo Clinic; a deep and abiding depression; and very likely hemochromatosis, a genetic disease he had inherited from his father. It wasn't simply that he couldn't stand things. The man had been destroyed. And then he had been defeated.

Flynn flicked two fingers away from the doorbell, pulled up his collar, ducked his head, ran through what was fast becoming a downpour, and got back into his car. He U-turned on St. Anne Street (sensing his professor watching from the front window) and drove back toward 394, where he would head east on the slick road, past the Devlin campus, past the police station, past the hospital, and past the Williams and Gardner Funeral Home, before following the ramp onto Route 17 East.

But somewhere between Jamestown and Elmira, unable to see clearly, Flynn would pull over onto the shoulder of the highway. He would grip the steering wheel with both hands. He would drop his head, listening to the rain thunder onto the hood and roof of his dead father's car. He would sit there, in the heavy rain, for quite some time.

ONCE UPON A TIME AT THE KIEV

ONCE UPON A TIME AT THE KIEV, ON THE CORNER OF EAST 7TH AND 2ND, a bowl of soup with two slices of challah bread and a glass of water was $2.99, and the waitresses left him alone. One day potato pickle, another day matzoh, another day pea. He could never remember which soup was which day, but it was all on a schedule by the front door.

That day, beef barley. There were only two other regulars in the place: the mopey Hasidic guy and the magenta-haired *artiste*. He couldn't bear to look at the front pages, so he flipped over the *Post* and *News* and read the sport sections, then the *Times*'s Arts & Leisure. Outside, floating flakes of ash, sheets and sheets of paper on the street.

Flynn never ate at the Kiev with anyone besides his friend Peter, except once when Rachel visited. She had taken in the chain-smoking Ukrainian waitress, the toothless homeless guy gnawing on a knish, the girl with eleven eyebrow rings. "You *eat* here?" she said.

After the soup and buttered challah, he went back across the street to his apartment, covering his nose and mouth. Inside, he lay on the couch, surrounded by Wyeth prints: weathered women, all of them Helga. New England wind, wailing and grating.

He kept the windows shut.

HE HAD THE WORLD AT HIS FINGERTIPS, ALTHOUGH HE DIDN'T KNOW IT. He was twenty-eight years old. He was getting his PhD in English Literature at NYU, full scholarship plus a stipend. He worked at the St. Mark's Bookstore. He was living in the greatest city in the world. He was tall, wavy-haired, and charming, and he was meeting smart, attractive women, and sometimes he had sex with them. Rachel was someone he had dated once in college, lost touch with, and recently reconnected with. She lived in Binghamton, almost four hours away, so they saw each other every other month. It wasn't exactly a relationship, but it was fine. She was feisty, bighearted, and cute, and she thought Flynn was the bee's knees.

That Friday, the bookstore opened back up for business, even though lower Manhattan was a ghost town, even though the stench was everywhere. They had only one customer: a girl with jet-black hair, enormous eyes, and a red leather jacket. She gave Flynn a sad smile as she headed towards Fiction.

To pass the time, he bet Peter he could find a grammatical error in any book within two minutes. And he did, in one Nonfiction book after another, until Peter grabbed one by William Safire.

The black-haired girl came to the counter. "At a time like this," she said, "you're arguing about grammar?" She handed Peter *La Muerte de Artemio Cruz*. Peter nodded in Flynn's direction.

"Flynn might look like an L.L. Bean model," he said, "but in real life he's a dangling modifier."

When the girl smiled at this, her cheekbones jutted out.

"At a time like this," Flynn said, leaning his elbow on the counter and pointing to her book, "you're reading *realismo mágico?*" She put her hands on her hips and sized him up. "What we need now," Flynn said, sounding like a former roommate of his, "is not escapism; what we need now is good grammar and rhetoric. Precise language. Carefully selected nouns, well-placed adjectives, active and appropriate verbs. The fate of the free world hinges on what we say next."

Peter gave the woman her change. "This" she told Flynn, jabbing the book out like a weapon, "is not 'escapism.' This is reality." She twisted her lips. "You need to change the way you think, *guero*." But she said *guero* the way someone would say *guapo*. Then she left, her boot heels thudding on the hardwood.

On Monday, Flynn visited his mother in White Plains. She was in the kitchen smoking a cigarette and watching the President on TV.

. . . hide and burrow in.

"Are you a professor yet?" she asked. It was the same question, every time he went there. He had finished his course work, had recently passed the grueling three-day written exam, and was about to take the oral exam, but he was dreading the dissertation. Once he completed it, he'd have to look for a teaching job, and he wasn't sure that talking about books was what he wanted to do for a living. He was thinking he might want to do something bigger, something good for the world, something that would help it to heal.

He was thinking he might want to change the way he thinks.

From next door, he heard his sister shouting or laughing at her kids—it sounded the same—and something thumped against the wall. His mother shook her head while taking a drag. "Every day is a wrestling match," she said. She looked nothing like the mother of his youth.

The enemy knows no borders.

"A professor," she said. "Now that would have made your father proud."

Flynn's father had died when he was a junior in high school from a heart attack brought on by cirrhosis of the liver. Apparently no one had known his liver was rotting. Nobody had even known he'd been drinking—or not that much, anyway. Coors Light while watching Jets games, martinis at restaurants and weddings, but nothing that seemed imminently fatal—at least not to Flynn. And he had steadfastly refused to go to the doctor.

"How could you not know?" Flynn asked, after his mother told him about the cancerous condition of Fungus, her cat, whose actual name was Fergus.

His mother sucked in her cheeks. The ash of her cigarette crisped.

When I was a kid . . .

She exhaled a locomotive breath. "These things don't conveniently announce themselves," she said.

Flynn sat in silence.

. . . dead or alive.

FLYNN WROTE POETRY. HE FANCIED HIMSELF A POET. TUESDAY MORNING AT Lil's Diner he handed Peter his latest, titled "Coffee Spoons." The diner wasn't called Lil's—for a long time it was the West Fourth Street Diner, and then it changed to the Violet Café—but Lil had been there forever (*Morning, sweetheart*) and she always knew what Flynn wanted. She had charcoal fingers, skeletal wrists, Japanese palms. Sometimes while sipping his coffee Flynn drew a sketch on his pad, or wrote a poem, and showed it to her.

Amid the clatter of dishes and silverware Lil came to Flynn's place at the counter and asked if she could read what he had written. When she finished, she put down the coffee pot and tapped the back of Flynn's hand. Her long fingernails scraped his knuckles. "This is nice," she said, as Peter reached for it. "But if you ask me, poetry should be more . . . direct. Not so many metaphors and such."

Flynn started to laugh, but then he saw Peter nodding in agreement.

"Where were you last week, sweetheart?" Lil asked. She shook her head, her voice clouding. "Saw a white man covered in ash, looked just like you. Like the livin' dead."

Two eggs over easy, wheat toast, home fries: $2.99, $3.33 with tax.

"You were open?" Flynn asked, but then the cook slapped the bell and she left to pick up an order.

Peter handed Flynn's poem back to him. "You're hiding behind allegory," he said. "And Prufrock? Enough already. This is no time for Prufrock."

FLYNN USED TO MAKE CHILI. AN ART FORM, HE CALLED IT. *MULTEITY IN UNITY*— that's what Briggs, his former roommate, used to call it. All those ingredients at a low boil, congealing so slowly you didn't even notice. When ground beef went on sale at D'Agostino's—really on sale, like ninety-nine cents a pound—he'd buy a family-sized pack, fry it up with onions and garlic, and dump it into a spaghetti pot with kidney beans, peppers, tomatoes, the works—the way Briggs used to do it. All those things cost money, but in the long run it was a good investment. Because he cooked that chili all night long, sometimes waking up to stir it, then had it for lunch and dinner all week.

Tuesday night in the meat section, holding the 89%-lean package and gazing longingly at the rib-eyes, Flynn pictured the second airplane, heard the endless keening of sirens, felt the quake of his apartment floor. He saw the faces plastered on the arch at Washington Square, flapping on the fences at Union Square:

Nicknamed "TJ"
JESSICA, TURQUOISE DRESS
Gray suit pink tie

And two days later:
Chain tattoo on left arm
BLACK PUMPS WITH HOLES ON BOTTOM
Perry Ellis glasses

And after four days:
Gold tooth
SEASHELL EARRINGS
Wedding ring inscribed "B♥K"

And on the bottom:
If found, call Janna: 212-538-9971
ANYTHING AT ALL, CALL US: (914) 677-0082
Call please please please 7182483872.

He put the beef into his basket and headed towards check-out, but in the middle of Aisle 4 he doubled over, he dropped the basket, he fell to his knees.

THE NEXT MORNING HE LAY IN BED, THINKING ABOUT THE BLACK-HAIRED GIRL. Eyes so big she had taken in all of him at once. Eyes like a Klaus von Döngen painting. Eyes like white serving trays carrying giant black pearls. And hair the black of her leather jacket. Lips, blood-red, that wanted to swallow him. Skin like coffee with an exact measure of cream. But her eyes, her eyes were bottomless wells of sorrow. He could lower himself in and drown.

"I'M LONELY," HIS MOTHER SAID TO HIS ANSWERING MACHINE. ON HIS DRESSER was a picture of her, one his father used to have on his desk. In it she wore a V-necked sweater, her hair so blonde it shimmered even in black-and-white.

"Don't hate me," she said. "I did my best with you." A muffled croak, then a few hacking coughs. In the background, a Tums commercial. "I think I'm dying," she said. "I think we're all dying."

He painted, too. One of his paintings was of a field of sunflowers blooming under an oyster sky near Silver Lake. In it, a Ryder truck idled on a hill between Saint Anthony's Church and the deli where he used to ride his bike to get bread for his mother. Most of the flowers yearned toward the sun, but one was turned away, arching its blossom—the brightest yellow, the blackest core. He called it "Defiance."

Back then, Christine's on 1st Avenue had an all-you-can-eat special: kielbasa, pierogies, red cabbage—anything and everything for $9.95. The fat Polish waitresses wore miniskirts. On Wednesday night, after finishing his third plate, Flynn sat back, patted his belly, and told Peter a story.

One evening, when Flynn was a sophomore in high school, his mother had baked a chicken and fried some potatoes, but gave Flynn boiled broccoli instead of fries. She brought the plates into the living room so they could all watch Channel 4 News with Chuck Scarborough and the new co-anchor Flynn's father called "the Token".

"You need to avoid oily foods," his mother said, pointing to his chin, which hosted a colony of scabs that, before he shaved them with his father's razor and dabbed them with his father's Brut, had been a tiny colony of pimples.

"Oil!" his father said, still concentrating on the *Post* crossword puzzle and ignoring both the news and the plate of food in front of him. He found the word he had skipped. "Three-letter word for slick." He lifted the paper close to his face, scratched the word in with a pencil, and looked over at Flynn. "You got a lot of three-letter problems, champ," he said. "Oil. Zit." He pointed at Flynn's chin, and Flynn quickly covered it with his hand. "And cat!" he barked, plucking Fungus off the footstool and tossing him onto the floor. He laughed and slapped Flynn's knee. "I'm just giving you the business," he said. He rustled the newspaper and leaned over. "You mustn't take life so seriously."

Flynn pushed away his dish and stood up. He wanted to ask his father something. He wanted to ask him when he had decided that selling cabinet parts all week and sitting on the couch all weekend would be his life.

"What is it," his father said, leaning back in his armchair. "You need more money? Don't bother asking, you just piss it away." He pointed. "You have to learn to be *frugal!*" As Flynn turned away, his father lurched up and tried to grab his arm. "Come on," he called out as Flynn vaulted up the stairs. "Don't be so morose!" He lumbered over to the landing, rustling his newspaper. "*Sad!*" he yelled up. "There's another one!"

Flynn acted out the story to Peter as other diners glanced over. But he left out what happened in his bedroom afterwards. What happened in his bedroom afterwards was that he stood before the full-length mirror and stared at his eyes, dark and angry. At the scabs on his chin. Then he tiptoed to the bathroom, spread some of his mother's cover stick on the scabs, then spent the next ten minutes trying to wash it off.

"You do your father so well," Peter said, "it's as if you were born for the role."

Thursday morning, a week after his soup at the Kiev, Rachel called to propose moving in with him, even though her parents were going to hate her for it. She was willing to do it, for him. For the relationship. "It's been hard for all of us," she said, "even upstate. We can't keep putzing around like this, Hawk. Life's too short. Like shit or get off the pot, right?"

"Right," Flynn said. If there was one thing he really needed to do, it was to shit or get off the pot. And that's what he loved about Rachel: she never stayed on the pot. She got things done. She made decisions. She took charge. She spoke with authority. She lit up the room with her smile, and Flynn never had to guess what she was thinking. He could certainly stand to be a little more like Rachel.

He looked around his tiny apartment. He didn't have a picture of her anywhere. There was one in his desk drawer, one he had taken of her at Jones beach: she had spontaneously joined a soccer game with a bunch of kids, and she was kicking the ball while laughing, three children at her heels, the ocean in the background.

Flynn heard her say that her parents might not be too upset, so long as marriage was in the long-term plan. He thought, *I didn't even realize we were a couple.*

"Hey, are you there?" she said.

"No, it'll be great," he said. He pictured her bright green eyes, her tousled red hair. *Energy* is what she had. The woman had *energy*. That, and she loved him. She adored him. He was the man of her dreams. He had never been the man of anyone's dreams—at least not that he knew of.

Outside his window, a flake of ash hovered in the air.

"Whew," she said, pronouncing her exhale. "Okay, I'll tell them. Mom will be furious."

"Oh well," Flynn said.

"Easy for you to say," she said. "You're not the one taking a risk here."

"Are you kidding?" Flynn said. "Everything's a risk."

On lunch break with Peter, on their way towards Washington Square Park, they saw the black-haired girl. She was walking toward the NYU classroom building, her red skirt flouncing about her strong legs.

"Rosa Flores," Peter said. "Now there's an allegory you can hide behind." He dropped into his personal-ad voice: "Early twenties. Grad student in Comparative Lit. Likes Garcia Lorca, Chilean wine, and long walks under *la luce de la luna.*"

"It's as if I'm destined for her," Flynn said.

"Destined," Peter said. "Active verb, or passive adjective?"

"I'm picking up Rachel on Saturday," Flynn said. "She's moving in with me."

"From Penn Station?" Peter asked.

"From Binghamton," Flynn said. "Oh, can I borrow your car?"

Across the street, Rosa saw them, stopped, and waved. Peter pointed with his cigarette. "Trust your instincts," he said.

What Flynn's instincts told him was to dash madly across the street, embrace Rosa Flores, and twirl her around so that her skirt lifted and her enormous eyes opened wide with delight.

When he did nothing of the kind, she shrugged, turned, and entered the building.

Hours later, she walked into the bookstore, strode past New Arrivals, found Flynn in Self-Help, and stood with her arms crossed. Flynn was squatting by the Deepak Chopra shelf. When he looked up, she raised an eyebrow.

FRIDAY NIGHT IN SOHO. ROSA WORE A DRESS THAT WAS ALL WHITE. WHITE like a high-school prom queen. White like a sixteen-year-old at a town-hall wedding. It had *lace*. But she wore it with no bra, no stockings, nothing. The curves of her flesh were shameless and alluring. Flynn wore a gray linen jacket with black chinos and a gray shirt, and he reminded himself not to slouch.

In line at the ticket booth for the tiny Off-off theatre, Rosa took his arm and said that in her opinion, a little *realismo mágico* would be most beneficial to him. She said he had sad eyes that made her want to take care of him, and when she said *take care of* it sounded like *fuck*.

The play was a campy gay version of *Long Day's Journey into Night*, a play Flynn had once taught. In the second scene, when the drunken father sang a song called "I Coulda Been a Contendah," Rosa put her hand on his leg, threw back her head, and laughed.

At Veselka's afterwards, where he had the Ukrainian stew with a side of mashed potatoes and beet salad for only $8.95, he couldn't stop smiling. At what? Hard to say. Possibility? Potential? Finding such a readily available solution to his ambivalence? His surprising capacity for whimsy in the midst of such a stench?

When he finished, Rosa suggested taking a cab to her apartment in Queens, and he felt his neck heat up. The fare would cost more than dinner. But what the hell, right? You only live once.

Inside the taxi, Rosa slid away from him, lifted her leg over his, and pressed her calf into his groin. As the taxi burrowed into the Midtown Tunnel, she was illumined in pulses: a sliding hem and bend of knee; lips, full and open; shadowy tresses fanning the window. In the dusked throbs between punctuated light, only the white dress, the white gleam of teeth, the white turban on the cabdriver's head.

On Borden Avenue Flynn kissed her, keeping his eyes open as the street lamps tolled, but her eyes swallowed his, he could see only one at a time, so he leaned back and tugged down the top of her dress. In half-notes of lamplight her breasts arched up toward him. In quarter-notes of asphalt bumps her bared thigh throbbed against him. He saw, or thought he saw, his father's eyes in the rearview mirror.

Vernon Boulevard: $12.90.

Hunters Point: $14.35.

THE FOLLOWING MONDAY, HE WALKED WITH PETER OVER TO PANE E CIOC-colato for a bowl of spaghetti: $6.95 with a big basket of bread. A sepulchral waitress, her eyelids drooping from the weight of her mascara, took their orders with a look of blank resignation. Restaurants had been empty for two weeks. The whole world loved New York, but nobody was willing to say so in person.

"So she's all moved in?" Peter said.

"Already got a job," Flynn said, curling spaghetti around his fork, then sliding it into his mouth. "Teaching a Pilates class even as we speak."

Peter put down his fork. "I'm going to pretend you didn't just say 'Pilates'."

"When I was loading her stuff into the car, her mother sat by the window like Mrs. Bates. When I kissed her cheek, it felt like ice."

"You kissed her mother?"

Flynn poured some beer into his glass and took a careful sip. He checked his watch. He took another forkful of pasta, only as much as his mouth could manage. He wiped his lips with the corner of his napkin. Students at a nearby table burst into laughter.

"We got into a big fight," he said. "On Saturday, our first night together."

"Over what?"

He shrugged. He couldn't remember.

When Peter asked about his date with Rosa, he focused on evenly distributing the butter on his bread.

He had taken the subway home from Queens, rehearsing the call to Rachel he knew he wasn't going to make. She was taking a big risk. It would be terrible to cancel everything, the day of. She would be furious. By the time he got back to his apartment, the sun was coming up, and he had to shower quickly, get Peter's car, and head north. During the drive to Binghamton he kept himself awake by fantasizing about Rosa, but by the time he exited I-81, he had calculated the cost of being with a woman like her and concluded that he couldn't afford it.

As he bit into the slice of bread, his eyes clouding, Peter bent his head and said something to his bowl of spaghetti, like the downbeat of a prayer.

SUNDAY MORNING IN THE FICTION SECTION: THE SQUARED-SHOULDERED BACK of her. Black hair caressing the back of her black leather jacket. Reading, but shifting her weight. As Flynn approached, she held up the book, a Borges paperback. "Such a sad man," she said to the air in front of her.

"Dead now," Flynn said.

She turned to face him. "Fiction is truth," she said. "I need you to understand that."

Flynn nodded, considering it.

"Nonfiction?" she said. "Pack of lies."

She put her hand on Flynn's arm. "You said you'd call. I thought it was good." Her enormous eyes welled and opened in wonder, as if revealing to Flynn the vastness of all he was denying himself. "I thought it was magical."

"I'm sorry," Flynn said. "My mother." It's the first thing he thought to say. "I had to go to White Plains."

"Your mother what?"

"Sick," he said, looking at the floor. "Terribly sick. She may be dying."

He kept his head down as Rosa Flores walked out of the store, the book still in her hand, the alarm going off.

ON WEDNESDAY MORNING, FLYNN AND RACHEL WALKED PAST LIL'S DINER on their way to the new café on Waverly, where a fresh-baked bagel with cream cheese and a bottomless cup of coffee cost $2.49. When the waitress refilled Flynn's cup, she put her hand on his back and brushed her breast against his shoulder. Rachel's eyes turned to ice.

ON THURSDAY, HE RECEIVED THE FORTY-EIGHTH REJECTION OF HIS POEM, "A Terrible Beauty is Born." The editor had scribbled, *While beautifully written, this is a terrible poem.*

"Missed you again last weekend," his mother said on the phone. "Your sister's worried about you." Flynn knew this already, because his sister had left eleven messages on his voicemail. When he promised to come not this weekend but the following, she said, "*Next* weekend? I could be dead by then."

So he took the train to White Plains, walked into the house, and kicked Fungus out of his way. A migraine had seized the back of his neck. The house smelled like an old man's t-shirt. He could hear the faint strains of the *Barney* theme song from the other side of the wall.

Flynn's mother wore her gray bathrobe. She didn't get up from her gray seat at the gray kitchen table.

"So Rachel moved in," Flynn told her by way of news. *And I rejected a Puerto Rican girl you would have hated*, he almost added. *Also, you'll be pleased to hear I have abandoned poetry altogether.*

She leaned over to flick ash into the saucer, stopped midway, and attempted to hook a stray hair behind her ear. "The gray ones grow straight out," she said, holding the strand between her fingers. "They're dead, so there's no curl. And they keep growing after you're dead," she added, as if to herself. Flynn calculated her age: fifty-nine. "You've got a few yourself now," she said, pointing to his temple. "Startin' to look like your old man."

On the floor were gray strands of hair, flecks of cigarette ash, and the gray fur of Fungus. From behind the wall Flynn could hear his sister yelling at her husband Mitch, and Mitch responding with a roar.

His mother sighed. "They're always at it, those two."

"I'm going to ask her to marry me," Flynn said, surprising himself.

She looked up, her painted eyebrows arched. "The Protestant?" she said. "Looks like a matchstick?" She leaned back, her wrist drooped over the arm of the chair, her cigarette dangling, the cylinder of ash about to cascade to the floor. Flynn had forgotten that his mother had met Rachel at his college graduation.

"Come on, Ma," he said.

In the baby picture hanging on the wall behind her, Flynn's face seemed no longer cute or innocent, but doughy, pliant. He imagined removing the photo from its frame and taping it to the Union Square fence:

Missing.
Zits on chin
Early-onset OCD
Below-average penis

~~*If found, call Peter.*~~
~~*If found, call my mother.*~~
~~*If found, call my sister.*~~

His mother waved her cigarette like a wand, arching disdain. "Best you could do," she said, and for a moment, Flynn considered tackling her to the floor, clutching her by the throat, and banging her head against the linoleum until she cried out for mercy. But she probably wouldn't have cried out. She probably would have stared at Flynn as if she had known all along he would do this. She probably would have smiled, happy she finally got to him. She probably would have seen it as proof that he cared.

A wisp of smoke wafted across the table. Flynn inhaled it into his lungs.

THE NEXT MORNING, BEFORE WORK, FLYNN WALKED OVER TO LIL'S. THE acrid smell on the streets seemed to be dissipating; he was surprised to realize he would miss it when it was gone. Peter was at the counter, reading the Op-Ed page of the *Times*, wiping egg yolk from his plate with his rye toast, extra butter. He didn't look up as Flynn sat down.

"Good morning sir," is how Lil greeted Flynn. She waited, holding her pad, until finally he ordered. "Whole wheat or white?" she asked.

"You know," Flynn said.

"White," Lil said, tearing off the order and slapping it on the shelf by the kitchen. She picked up a pot of coffee but then turned, wagging her long finger. "What's wrong with you? You found some other breakfast place?"

The other customers looked up with accusatory stares.

"Wheat," Flynn said. "It's always been wheat."

She set down the pot, laid her hands flat on the counter, and sighed, her face softening. She looked at Flynn as if he were in a hospital bed. "Listen, sweetheart," she said. "You're smart, creative . . ." She clicked her long nails on the Formica. "Why aren't you *doing* something?"

When Flynn didn't answer, she stood taller and straightened her shoulders. "That day?" she said. "The cook, he went home. Right away. But me and the girls, know what we did?" She knocked on the counter. "We stayed right here and we gave those poor people some coffee."

"Coffee?" Flynn pictured it: thousands of people coated in ash, pouring cream and sugar in their Styrofoam cups.

"That's right," she said, lifting her chin. "Coffee. We had them masks on." She put a hand over her mouth, her long fingernails stretching to her ear, and motioned with the other toward Flynn, as if handing a cup to a ghost. Then she put her hands on her hips. "And what did *you* do, Mister Artist? Mister Poet?"

He watched television.

He had just come out of the shower when he felt an odd movement, as if the air had changed. In the sky over the building across the street, he saw only a piercing blue. But then: a line of smoke, the color of pencil lead, being pulled up to the heavens.

People gathered on the street—his neighbors, apparently. An elderly woman came out on the roof of the building across from his, looked southwest and cried out, "My god!"

Flynn leaned out the window. He had a towel around his waist. "Hey!" he called out and she turned to him, her eyes wide. In that moment he felt closer to her than he'd ever felt to anyone.

He ducked inside and turned on the television.

Later, sheets of paper billowed by, chunks of ash. A page stuck to his window screen—an invoice, unpaid and overdue. He shut the window, tied a rag over his mouth, and dropped to the floor.

He should have gone to White Plains.

He should have headed to the towers to see if his cousin Jessica, who worked there, had made it out.

He should have called Rachel.

He should have gone to Peter's, to see if he was okay.

He should have dashed across the street, run up the stairs to the roof, and hugged the old woman.

Instead, he stayed in his apartment. He stayed there for two days, trying to keep out the smell, until he ran out of food. And that's when he went to the Kiev for beef barley soup.

FRIDAY NIGHT. HE LAY IN BED WITH RACHEL, FLAT ON THEIR BACKS, SIDE-BY-side. He had banged his head into the headboard when she told him to *Fuck off*, when she screamed *You need help!* and refused to speak for a half-hour as he tried to get her to take fifty percent responsibility for the argument. Mice scratched at the box of old newspapers in the broom closet. Asthmatic air drifted in through the window. A spider web in the corner of the ceiling shimmered red from the fluorescent bar sign across the street. Music and voices burst out as somebody opened the door to the bar, then muffled again as it closed. Two women clacked their shoes as they walked past. It was the fourth argument they'd had that week. He was starting to lose his voice.

He wondered what would happen if he called Rosa Flores.

Rachel sighed. "Maybe we should call it quits," she said. Her words floated to the ceiling and hovered above them.

Flynn closed his eyes and felt the scrape of Lil's fingernails on his knuckles.

You're gone, is what Peter had said over his bowl of spaghetti at the Pane e Cioccolato. *Goodbye.*

"No," Flynn said. "Let's work at it. We'll be okay."

The little finger of Rachel's right hand, and that of his left, were almost touching.

THE LONELY COOL BEFORE DAWN

I MET FLYNN HAWKINS IN 1997, IN A CHAUCER CLASS AT NYU. I WAS GETTING my third master's, he was getting his PhD. We were in the NYU Classroom Building: nothing on the walls, windows sealed shut . . . a nondescript room to say the least. But Professor Reynard spoke Middle English so beautifully, so perfectly . . . we were all entranced. Although Flynn, typical Americanist, democratic to the core, didn't show him much deference. At the end of our final class of the semester, we all paused at Reynard's desk to hand in our final essays, and when it was Flynn's turn, he shook our professor's hand and said, *"Sire clerk, wiltou drynketh with us a pitaunce of ale?"* Which stopped the rest of us in our tracks. We waited to see if Reynard would correct Flynn's grammar, but he just grinned.

"This gooth aright!" our esteemed professor exclaimed. "Unbokeled is the male!" And we all let out a cheer.

Reynard took us to his favorite pub, called the Burp Castle, which was just down the road from Flynn's apartment on East 7th. It's a shabby little place with murals of monks on the wall, and the bartender "shushes" everyone when the conversation level gets too loud, so we've referred to it as the Shush Bar ever since. Flynn felt right at home there; being shushed was his natural condition, he said. Reynard didn't stay very long, he had a pint of stout and then had to get home to his wife, and the rest of our classmates left soon after that, but Flynn and I stayed for hours, talking nonstop. We discovered we had a lot in common. We had both lost our fathers when we were in high school; we were both raised by religious mothers, but now rejected our religions completely; and we both considered working at a bookstore to be our dream job, however quaint an occupation "the noisy set . . . the martyrs call the world" would consider it.

At one point, he put his hand on my shoulder in a gesture I can only describe as fraternal. "Pete Silverman," he said. "I've been looking for a friend like you my whole fucking life." Then he bent his head, belched quietly, and stumbled to the bathroom.

I was working at St. Mark's at the time, and by the end of the week I had convinced the owner to hire Flynn part-time. Flynn took to the job right away: great with customers, totally in love with books . . . it really was his dream job. He said he'd much rather work there and at Dojo, where he waited tables on weekends, than be a college professor.

At the end of his first week I asked him if he wanted to come to a party my friend Jack was having at his apartment on Astor, he said sure . . . and we all wound up getting drunk on Jack's Bombay gin. Flynn is one of those guys who can be pretty shy, but at a party, he comes out of his shell. He says hello as if he's absolutely delighted to meet you, looks as if it just made his day that you shook his hand, and acts as if he can't wait to hear all about your most intimate secrets, skip the small talk. We drank so much that night and had such a good time that we wound up putting on bathrobes we found in Jack's bedroom closet. We discovered a golf bag in there too, so we improvised a game of putt-putt in their tiny living room. At first we set down empty wine glasses and were trying to putt the ball into them, but then one of the glasses broke, so we used coffee mugs instead. Then we set up obstacles, and before you know it Flynn had taken out the nine-iron and executed a perfect chip off the carpet. The ball sailed right through the open window and as it fell five stories we all cringed, thinking we'd hear the sound of a windshield smashing or someone screaming out in pain . . . but instead we heard the sharp tap, tap, tap of the ball bouncing across Broadway. Everyone roared their approval and high-fived Flynn, and he fell to the floor laughing and apologizing at the same time. That's when Jack's wife came home, saw Flynn on the floor in her bathrobe, and kicked us all out, so we piled into cabs and went to Puglia's in Little Italy. I don't remember much about that part of the night except that Flynn flirted with the waitress and told her he was part Italian, which was an outright lie, and when she told him to come back when he was a *full* Italian we all toasted her for her wit and Flynn for his audacity. After that he led us to the Café Palermo (boldly declaring it was better than Ferrara's), slapped down a twenty and said "Cannolis for everyone!" and my god they were the best damned cannoli I ever had. I remember both of us mocking each other because we got some of the cannoli cream in our beards, and on our way out Flynn hugged us all and said he was so happy to have made such good friends, at that moment he was happier than he had ever been in his life, and as if to punctuate his little speech he walked up to a girl on the sidewalk and kissed her on the cheek, and she shoved him away but laughed as she did so, and then her friend said "Wait, I'll take some of that action" and gave Flynn a big smooch on the lips and mussed up his hair, and this is the kind of thing that used to happen in the city late at night but no one ever talks about it.

Our friendship grew. We met for breakfast at the West Fourth Diner (or Lil's, as we called it, after our favorite waitress), worked together at the bookstore, took our lunch breaks together (at Dojo, the Kiev, Eddie's, the BBQ, or Pane e Cioccolato), and often had a few beers together at night. We never, not once, ran out of things to say to each other. We were brothers. I don't use that word lightly. We went to Knicks and Rangers games, saw a bunch of concerts at the Bottom Line, and our favorite thing was to go to readings at the 92nd Street Y. We saw Alice Walker there, Mark Doty, Kazuo Ishiguro, Sam Shepard, Richard Ford, and a cool tribute to Herman Melville by a bunch of novelists on the 150th anniversary of *Moby-Dick*. Good stuff.

Then, 9/11. Then, Rachel. Flynn changed from this fun-loving guy to the poster child for Codependency. It was all so surprising to me. I'm still a little blown away by it, and hurt too, I suppose. I went from seeing him every day to hardly ever—and if I did, he was usually with Rachel, and she and I inevitably got into some friendly bantering that turned into an argument. I couldn't tell if she was flirting with me (Flynn later said she had a little crush on me) or establishing her dominance, but it was as if arguing was the way she communicated with people. She had strong opinions about everything. If she ever did one of those personality tests, she would be 100% "J."

So when he told me they were engaged, I wanted to say "Gah! Don't do it!" but instead I reminded him of what he had told me the previous year. I had been in a relationship with a woman, Debra was her name, an ardent feminist, and I had committed the heinous crime of attending Jack's bachelor party (she called us "a bunch of Neanderthals" but all we did was go to a Mets game and out to a bar afterwards) . . . and the relationship had turned sour after that. Flynn had gently pointed out to me that I seemed to be trying to make up for all the men who had done Debra wrong in the past and was staying in the relationship out of a perverse sense of obligation. He understood my behavior, he said, because he had always felt guilty over what he "had done to" Rachel in college. Apparently they had gone out on a date, and to Flynn it was just a friendly date, but to Rachel it was like the prince had come into her house with the glass slipper and it fit . . . followed by nothing: no phone call, no second date, just friendly hellos whenever he saw her on campus. Years later, when they met up again at some softball game, she gave him shit about it and he spent the entire evening trying to make it up to her, and then promised to "make every effort to cultivate a real relationship" afterwards, despite their geographical distance. I shouldn't make the same mistake he had made, he said. But now here he was, still trying to make it up to her, this time by proposing. So I reminded him—"Remember when you told me never to stay in a relationship out of obligation?"—and asked him if that was the case, if that was why he was marrying Rachel. But he just said, "No, it's not like that anymore, I really do love her now."

After that . . . there was nothing to say. I sat there as he explained why he was going ahead with it, and I guess in retrospect I regret my silence, I regret not calling him out on his lie, I regret not telling him straight out that he was making a big mistake. They got married a few months later, they moved to White Plains . . . and I didn't see him anymore.

Then, they had a baby of course, and when Nathan was a few months old, Flynn came down into the city with the little guy and we met at the Alice in Wonderland statue. Flynn was pushing one of those collapsible baby carriages, and his hair was cut short, and he had shaved his beard, so it all felt very different. But we had a decent day. We went to the Frick, but Nathan started crying (no doubt at the offensively trite Fragonards), so we left the museum and walked around the neighborhood to settle him down, had lunch at a diner on Lexington. We did that kind of thing a few more times ("Sundays with Uncle Peter," Flynn called them), including one visit a few days after my mother died, when Flynn embraced me as soon as he saw me, and when I tried to pull away he kept me close, saying how sorry he was for me, until I felt the unspoken permission to let down my guard—you know how that goes, when you're with someone who knows you better than you know yourself—and I found myself sobbing into his coat. "I'm an orphan now," I kept saying. I knew I was being melodramatic, but it really got to me, losing my mom. He doesn't have too great a relationship with his own mother, but he kept his hand on my shoulder as we walked and he told me about his father's death, and how he remembered little things about him all the time . . . like the whistle, the one his father used when he wanted to let Flynn know he was in the stands during baseball games, and then Flynn did the whistle, two short chirps, right there at the park, and then he started to cry too. See, this is why I love the guy.

On another visit, we met in Harlem, had lunch at Amy Ruth's, then walked the length of the park toward midtown. He told me things were good . . . but to me, he seemed suspiciously upbeat. You know when people say things are great but they nod their head a lot, as if they're trying to talk themselves into it? He had bags under his eyes and he had an even-more-terrible haircut. Still, he was . . . buoyant. This is who he was. I suppose it can be frustrating at times, because you never know what you're getting when you see him. Are you getting the real Flynn or Flynn the talk-show host? He's like one of those guys who commits suicide and afterwards all his neighbors say, "But he always seemed so cheerful!"

When it comes right down to it, I've decided, almost every relationship involves two people with intense insecurities masked by whatever behavior it takes to keep those insecurities from being exposed, while at the same time revealing their equally desperate need to have them exposed, even embraced. It's a recipe for disaster. And yet it gets repeated every day, all over the world.

We went on like this, seeing each other only once in a while, with the occasional phone call, until one day, he called me out of the blue and said he needed a "Big Pete Silverman Talk," so he came down without Nathan and we met at McSorley's, in our old neighborhood. He looked terrible. Very thin. His eyes were red.

"I think I have to leave her," he said.

"Ah," I said, nodding. Good for him, I thought. And yes, I'll admit, I also thought *Finally! I'll get my best buddy back*. "Then leave," I said.

He shook his head. "Not that easy," he said.

I took a sip of my beer. "If you need a place to stay . . ." I said. But we both knew I had a studio with a twin bed. "I have a friend who has an air mattress."

All around us was bustle and noise. McSorley's is the opposite of the Shush Bar. Everyone's shouting to be heard over everyone else, and the waiters carry eight mugs at a time, shouldering their way through the crowd, not worrying if there's a little spillage along the way. The sawdust on the floor catches everything.

"Simple," Flynn said, "but not easy."

His eyes were watery and fearful, and he kept looking around, as if now that he had declared his marital misery he would be executed by firing squad.

I don't know much about what happened after that day. I only know I didn't get my friend back. In fact, it was even harder to get a hold of him from that point on. Once when I called he picked up the phone but I couldn't hear him; all I heard were the sobs of a dying man. After he hung up, I called back, but he never answered. Whatever it was, I never spoke to him or saw him again.

It's been over two years.

THE BEST TIME OF MY LIFE, THE VERY BEST TIME I'VE EVER HAD IN MY LIFE, was with Flynn. We were at the Cedar Tavern, watching the Super Bowl: St. Louis versus Tennessee. He was rooting for the Rams (me, I didn't care much who won, but I cheered for the Rams for his sake), and it was a great game. Afterwards, we stayed in our booth for hours . . . and we wound up closing the place. We were friends already, but that night, that's the night that solidified it. That's the night I told him what happened. How my father died. He was in a bath house, on 28th Street, you know the kind, when it caught fire, and he died of smoke inhalation. I didn't know this at the time. At the time, I was told he had died of an aneurysm, a word I didn't understand. That's what my mother told everyone . . . everyone who called, everyone at the wake, everyone at the funeral. Then, when one of my father's friends asked why it was a closed coffin, she burst into tears. My uncle was the one who told me the truth, after my mother died. I had no idea my father had this double life. He was a sweet man, very nice to my mother. But think about it: that must have been very hard for her.

Now, I live near that building. I walk past it every day.

Flynn listened to the whole story and he didn't say anything bad about my father; he just shook his head, said "What an awful way to die," patted me on the arm and said something about how hard it must have been to have to deal with his sudden death, and all the lies and cover-ups, when I was only sixteen. That was the same age he was when his own father died. He told me he had found out at a baseball game, just after he had made a terrible play in the outfield, and because of that he always associated his father's death with a feeling of failure and humiliation, not loss or grief.

"That's me too," I said.

By the time we left it was late, maybe one in the morning, and it was cold outside, and we were pretty drunk. We were walking with our arms around each other like buddies, half-holding each other up, when we heard a car drive by blasting the opening harmonica notes of "Thunder Road." We started singing the song together, we knew every word, and we kept singing it, louder and louder, as we walked down University, and at the end of the song we went under the arch, and while he pretended to wail the sax solo I pointed at him, shouted out "The Big Man!" and then we both ran through the park, jumping on benches the homeless guys weren't sleeping on, and we started drunk-parkouring with our heavy coats on, leaping up on railings, knocking over garbage cans, swinging from tree branches, sprinting down and up the little amphitheater, our breath clouding the cold air. Flynn fell hard on his shoulder when he tried to side-jump one of the statues, so after that we left the park and jogged down 8th Street, past the NYU classroom building, then turned down

Mercer and jogged past where he used to have his cubicle when he was a grad assistant, then past the Bottom Line, past Lil's diner, across West 4th toward the Tisch building, then back up towards Tower Records, and on Broadway Flynn jumped up on the hood of a cab while it was at a red light and the driver opened the door and starting flipping out on us but we were too drunk to care.

Now, Tower Records is closed. The Cedar Tavern is closed. 269 Mercer isn't even a valid address. The Kiev, closed. Lil's diner became the Violet Café, and now it might as well be closed because it's a fucking Starbuck's. The Polish place, Christine's, where we used to get cheap dinners, that's closed. Eddie's closed a loooong time ago. The BBQ relocated. The Bottom Line, fucking closed. All the places we loved: closed.

I love this city. There's no place like it. But nobody's here anymore.

HIGHER LAWS

PROFESSOR FLYNN HAWKINS CAME HOME FROM WORK, TOSSED THE MAIL ONTO the kitchen counter, poured dog food into Mollie the Collie's bowl, opened the package of chicken breasts he had set out that morning to defrost, and set the oven to 375 degrees. He began to wash the chicken under hot water, but then felt a wave of dizziness, so he dropped the breasts into the sink, grabbed hold of the rim, and lowered his head.

Chicken was one of the few foods his wife Rachel liked, but only if it was baked, so they ate it that way once a week, with Ore-Ida frozen potatoes and canned corn or raw carrots, along with "salad," which for Rachel meant iceberg lettuce with ranch dressing. Of late her tastes were even more restricted, as she was five months pregnant. When she had come home from her gynecologist's office and broken the news, Flynn's first thought was, *How?* They hadn't had sex in what seemed like a year. But then he remembered: Thanksgiving night. Flynn had cooked the turkey, moist and delicious, but Rachel's mother had refused to eat it, saying it was undercooked, wondering aloud if they were all going to die of salmonella, then manufacturing a coughing fit the moment Flynn's mother lit a cigarette. But then Nathan and his cousin Marianna sang a song for everyone, Mitch, who was a cop in the Bronx, told some funny stories about the idiotic crooks he had recently arrested, Annie brought out her famous rhubarb-and-cherry pie, and after everyone left or went to bed, he and Rachel pulled out the couch, Rachel said, "Thank God that's over" and they had sex, quick and muffled so her parents, sleeping in their bedroom, wouldn't hear.

His second thought: *I'm done for.*

When the wave passed, he put the chicken into a Pyrex pan, sprinkled on some rosemary, tossed in a quarter-stick of margarine, and slid the pan into the oven. When he straightened, he saw his reflection in the back window, dark and gaunt, as if a criminal were standing outside his house, looking in at him.

He sorted the mail on the kitchen table, leaving the American Express statement unopened so Rachel wouldn't accuse him of spying on her. It was usually between four and nine hundred dollars, with a long list of purchases—mostly clothes for Nathan, she'd say, but there would be other charges: Liz Claiborne, Ann Taylor, Filene's. He took out the stack of bills from the antique desk, added the new ones, and reordered them according to urgency: mortgage first, then gas and electric, car loans, credit cards, school loans, insurance, AT&T, and payments for the sailboat Rachel had bought without his knowledge and kept on a lake near Binghamton, where her parents lived. Flynn would write some checks for the first of the month and delay others so they'd have enough for groceries, gas, and birthday presents for Nathan, who would turn four in a couple of weeks. Five years earlier, when Rachel had moved into Flynn's apartment in the East Village, he had worked three jobs (clerking at the St. Mark's bookstore, teaching part-time at Cooper Union, and waiting tables at Dojo) while researching and writing his dissertation (on Hawthorne's ambiguity as a response to self-assertion in 19th Century canonical works), and Rachel taught Pilates at three different places while getting her master's degree in Physical Therapy. Now, they made more than twice as much as they did back then, but it seemed twice as difficult to balance the books. And soon there'd be more hospital bills. Another mouth to feed.

A girl's, apparently. They had seen an image of her, milky and alien, during Rachel's last ultrasound, and the doctor had said, "I don't see any dots between the legs." On the way home, Flynn had suggested the name Emily, as in Dickinson—or Emilye, as in "The Knight's Tale." He wanted his daughter to be strong, creative, and smart. But Rachel had announced the baby's name would be Jane.

"Okay, like Jane Eyre," Flynn had said. "Plain Jane. Or Yeats's Crazy

Jane. Or Springsteen: Crazy Janey and the Mission Man.'"

"No, as in that's my mother's name."

Mollie the Collie finished eating, and Flynn interrupted his mail-sorting to let her outside. Rachel had brought home the dog a few years back, over his objections: Nathan was too young, he had said, only eight months old, and the dog might see the baby as competition. When Mollie then nipped Nathan on the cheek, nearly taking off half his face and leaving a red welt, Flynn turned to Rachel with his screaming son in his arms and said "Now see what you've done!"

There was one piece of mail for him, from Gayle Cullen of Penn State's Worthington-Scranton campus. His paper, on Emerson's influence on the works of Hawthorne, had been accepted for the Hawthorne Society's annual conference, which was being held in Concord, Massachusetts on May 21st. Enclosed were registration materials and a tentative schedule.

Concord. Flynn closed his eyes, picturing it. The Old Manse. The cemetery. The pond.

As it happened, he was teaching *Walden* in his Early American Litera-ture class, which satisfied the core Humanities requirement at Fairfield University, but the book was gaining no purchase with his students. Earlier that day, as he read from the second chapter, he felt his left eye twitching and found himself thinking about his morning drive, when he had steeled his way down the Merritt Parkway, smearing back tears. It was the trees that had triggered them, the stooped trees lining the road: a blur of bowed branches, glazed with ice, from a rain storm the night before accompanied by a plunge in temperature. The trees, and all the houses behind them, the thousands and thousands of homes crammed into what was once a thickly wooded paradise. *I'm thirty-three years old*, he had thought. *Why am I crying in the car?*

"As long as possible live free and uncommitted," he read. "It makes but little difference whether you are committed to a farm or the county jail.'"

A hand shot up—Mark Pietrovic, the crystal-eyed baseball star and closet singer-songwriter, majoring in Business. "I don't know, Hawk," Mark said, shaking his head. "Maybe back in Nineteen-Whatever you could go out on a piece of land somewhere and live without any commit-ment, but it's 2006, man. Those days are long gone."

"*Eighteen*-whatever," Flynn said. He liked Mark, but worried the kid would end up taking over his father's car parts business instead of doing what he loved. "Forty-six," he said. "Published 1854."

Quentin Scirocco, known as "Q," nodded in agreement with Mark. "Too late for me," he said. "Un-free, committed up the wazoo. I graduate in three weeks and then I'll have to get a job to pay off my loans." He looked around the room. "We're not here by choice," he said, making a rapper's gesture. "It's *indentured servitude*, y'all."

Flynn winced, eyeing Wanda and then Chuck, the two English majors in the class, but Wanda was re-reading the passage, her brow furrowed, and Chuck was texting someone under his desk. The rest of the students seemed mildly disgusted that they had to read such ancient drivel.

Flynn heaved a sigh, clasped his hands, and asked them to take out some paper and pick a sentence, any sentence, from *Walden* and write a reaction, any reaction, to it. Some students groaned, most playfully, but they all began searching through their books for something to write about.

Flynn looked out the window, at the oaks and maples veneered with ice just as they had begun to bud, at the tulips by the tennis courts, now crushed. He thought of Ron Kruger, his colleague in History, who had recently gone through a divorce and acquired a new girlfriend. Everyone had noticed the change—he practically bounded now when he walked, and had lost weight—but Flynn was waiting for the inevitable collapse. Kruger had not waited, had not figured out what his issues and patterns were, before launching into the next relationship. And as everyone knew, rebounds never worked.

Flynn himself was seeing both a neurologist and a psychologist, although he hadn't told anyone about the psychologist. He had sought out both six months earlier after nearly wrapping his car around an exit sign on a drive to West Point where he had given a lecture on Edgar Allan Poe. The dizziness that had been visiting him in brief, abrupt waves for months had turned into a full frontal assault, and he could barely keep the car on the road. When it happened again on his way back, he pulled over on the Bear Mountain Bridge and braced for a vehicle to slam into him. After four drivers careened past, one blasting the horn, Flynn put on his hazards, got out, and stepped up onto the steel rim of the bridge.

As he stared down at the Hudson River, gauging the distance between his feet and the metallic water, he knew he should think of Nathan, what it would be like for his son to grow up without a father; but all he could focus on was the barge loaded with garbage heading toward him, and then a lone sailboat, soundlessly gliding the other way, toward the city. On the west bank of the river, near the town where Toni Morrison lived, the land was green and fertile. On the east bank, not far from White Plains, there was garbage and dead shrubbery where there had once been trees and high grass. The banks on that side seemed to erode into the river, deteriorating even as Flynn stood, wondering what the impact would be like.

The following semester he adopted a five-day schedule, even though the goal of most of his colleagues was to dwindle their work week down to as few days as possible. (Kruger, for example, had secured a two-day schedule, with a course release for research, and was fast gaining the reputation of an easy grader.) A five-day schedule made Flynn feel like a normal person and a good employee, not a slacker like Kruger. He commuted in the morning like everyone else, complaining mildly about the traffic to the department secretary as he deposited his umbrella in the umbrella stand. When he wasn't teaching, he could be found at his desk, surrounded by his plants and books, which included a rare first edition of Browning's *Men and Women*, a first American edition of Dostoyevsky's *Notes from Underground*, and five years' worth of *American Literature* and *American Literary Quarterly*, among other essential journals. On his walls hung a poster of a waterfall (with the inscription "In Wildness is the Salvation of the World"); a facsimile daguerreotype of Ralph Waldo Emerson; a print of a William Blake etching depicting the somewhat violent creation of the world, and his plaque for Outstanding Faculty Member, 2004-2005. On his desk was a framed picture of his son playing in a sandbox (Nathan holding the back end of a truck, his forehead furrowed) and a large crystal from MacNair Richards, a student who had graduated two years earlier and traveled extensively—waiting tables in Prague, teaching English in Japan, and working as a ski instructor in the Colorado mountains. He had found the crystal after the Commencement ceremony on his desk, with a note: *From Alaska, where I spent last summer. Thanks for everything, the beautiful and kind Flynn Hawkins.* Flynn had picked up the crystal, felt the weight of it, and put it back where MacNair had set it. It had stayed there ever since.

Flynn, who wore mostly tweed, corduroy, or herringbone jackets with button-collared shirts and Eddie Bauer chinos, was what some might consider handsome, with a high forehead, wavy brown hair, a well-trimmed moustache, and a face that reminded people of someone else: a cousin, an old high-school friend, or an actor (Matthew Perry, or a skinny John Travolta). He had never had an affair with a student—in fact he was the chair of the Ad-Hoc Committee on Sexual Harassment and a member of the Women's Studies Advisory Board—but occasionally he caught a female student's eye, complimented her hair or an attractive item of clothing, then looked away, as if he'd meant nothing untoward or lascivious by the remark.

Now that he thought about it, he had never had a nine-to-five schedule before. When he was first hired at Fairfield, Nathan was a newborn and Flynn was finishing his dissertation, so his department chair had kindly given him an evenings-and-weekends teaching schedule so he could spend his weekdays at home (feeding and changing Nathan, taking him to the park and supermarket, driving him around with a Motown CD on until he fell asleep, sneaking in revisions of his last three chapters) until four p.m., when he would get ready to go to work—glancing out the window as he changed Nathan's diaper, looking up at the clock after squeezing a drop of antibiotics into his son's clamped mouth, scribbling a note to Rachel about what was in the fridge to warm up for dinner. If she was late, he'd imagine her barreling down the Bronx River Parkway in her red Pathfinder and getting into a terrible accident; he'd imagine being sad at her funeral. He'd imagine quitting his job, selling the house, and moving with Nathan to someplace quiet, a place where they could live simply and front all the essentials of life.

That's when his migraines had intensified. They were accompanied not only by a sickening discomfort and nausea, but also by pain so penetrating that he longed to decapitate himself. His neurologist told him they were caused by a combination of stress, irregular sleep, dehydration, bad eating habits, and caffeine, and he needed to completely change his lifestyle;

but who could do such a thing? His students needed him. Rachel needed him. His son needed him. After his evening class he would come home, bathe Nathan, read him a story, and put him to bed, then do the dishes, straighten up the family room, join Rachel in the bedroom to watch a TV show and hear about her day, then grab the baby monitor and go up to the attic, where he would grade papers or work on his dissertation until he fell asleep with his head on his desk, only to wake up at the first squawking cry to warm up Nathan's bottle.

In the fall, when their daughter was born, he would give up his five-day schedule and return to teaching evenings and weekends, return to caring for an infant. Only for another couple of years, until she too was ready for preschool. He could handle it. So many people had gone through so much worse, raising children with no steady income and nothing like tenure, which Flynn was sure to get when he applied next year. Who was he to complain? He had a good job, a beautiful son, and a wife with bright green eyes, a fit body, and a boisterous personality everyone was drawn to. He just needed to drink more water, regulate his caffeine intake, and he'd be fine.

Quentin's hand was up. "Any passage at all, right?"

Flynn nodded, pretending to notice another student's hand—Audrey's—too late. "Q" cleared his throat and read the passage about how Thoreau went to the woods to live deliberately, to "live deep and suck out all the marrow of life.'"

"Okay," Q said, "so this is telling us we should all live close to the bone, right? *Austere.* But I'm also thinking it means we need to party hard, you know? *Carpe diem.*" He made the rapper's gesture again.

Flynn shook his head. Q was a sweet kid, but he hadn't read a single line of a single book the entire semester. "He *is* talking about seizing the day," Flynn said. "But not in that way." He folded his arms and glanced outside again, where a Physical Plant worker was bent over the crushed tulips. "You can too," he said. "Even in college. Even in Connecticut. I mean, you don't have to wait until you graduate to live every day deliberately, to make the most of your short life." He looked out beyond the vast and well-manicured campus lawn toward the once-sleepy seaside hamlet of Fairfield, now cluttered with mansions and quaint shopping plazas in the second-most crowded state in the Union, and beyond that the decaying docks jutting out into Long Island Sound, murky, seaweed-strewn, and polluted. An image came to him, of MacNair Richards swimming in a river somewhere in the mountains of Colorado, then stepping out of the water and up onto the rocky shore, the clear water streaming from her auburn hair, rushing over her breasts and down her muscular thighs.

"Mine's on the same page," Audrey said, still with her hand up. Flynn nodded, bracing himself.

"'Our life is frittered away by detail'," she read. "'An honest man has hardly need to count more than his ten fingers, or in extreme cases he may add his ten toes, and lump the rest. Simplicity, simplicity, simplicity!'"

Audrey slapped her palm on the book. "I mean, shut up, Henry! If you want to live like this, that's *your* problem! I *need* my iPad. I *need* my iPhone. I *need* my car to get to school. I *like* wearing nice clothes." She looked around, but the other students were ignoring her.

Wanda's hand went up next. "Mine's on eighty-five," she said. She waited for everyone to get to that page before reading Thoreau's boast that only once during his two-year stay in the woods had he felt lonely; but then a gentle rain had made him aware of a "sustaining congeniality" in the atmosphere that "made the fancied advantages of human society insignificant," and he never felt lonely again.

Wanda looked up. "I wrote that this feels sad. *The fancied advantages of human society?*" She tilted her head like a puppy. "What I was wondering is, did Thoreau have any friends?" She leaned forward and opened her palms. "Did he ever fall in love?"

Flynn pictured Thoreau, "long-nosed, queer-mouthed, and ugly as sin," as Hawthorne called him, walking into town every day, eating a piece of his aunt's apple pie, picking up a newspaper, ice-skating on the Concord River, chatting with the locals at the general store—all the things he left out of his book. He shrugged at Wanda. *Some of this is pure bullshit*, he wanted to say. "He *needed* to be on his own," he said instead. "He needed to figure things out." He looked at the slumped students in the back row. "So do all of *you*," he said, his voice rising a bit. "Instead of just, you know, jumping into a career at age twenty-two and getting married at twenty-four like it's some kind of government mandate. You should get your act together first, right?" He scanned the room: his students looked mildly alarmed.

He softened his voice. "The truth is," he said to Wanda, "we don't know if Thoreau ever had sex, or if he was ever in love." Wanda frowned, and Flynn wondered who he had meant by *we*. We the members of the Thoreau Society? We the biographers who pore over the journals and letters of 19th Century writers and philosophers who wrote in an age when people didn't talk about sex, didn't confess to erotic urges, would set down with minute care the measurements of a pond but who wouldn't come within twenty hectares of disclosing the true measure of their longings?

He took a breath. Wanda—bright-eyed, smart, kindhearted—was the kind of girl Flynn hoped his unborn daughter would grow up to be. "Truth is, he wasn't good at sustaining intimate relationships," he said. "Neither was Emerson, for that matter."

Chuck looked up from his phone. "Emerson?" he said. "I thought Emerson had it all, the way you talked about him: wife, kids, good friends, upstanding member of the community." Chuck grinned. "Like you!"

Flynn grimaced. "Don't be deceived by appearances," he said. He thought of Emerson's fondness for intelligent single women like Caroline Sturgis, Elizabeth Peabody, and Margaret Fuller, at the anger those women may have felt about the mixed messages they received from the Great Original Thinker. Emerson played with words, cast kindling smiles, but when push came to shove he waxed eloquent on the nobility of friendship, caressed these women with his liquid voice, then hid behind his words.

"Emerson's wife wasn't very happy," he said, still waiting for the next volunteer. "His true love had died tragically, and he married Lidian out of convenience." He tapped his copy of *Walden*, thinking of two strong, dark-eyed women he had known during grad school. He must have lacked then whatever it was that was required—courage, self-confidence, forthrightness—to be himself, whatever that meant, with either one. To fully assert himself. To *claim* love rather than hope for it. One of them, a girl named Rosa, had certainly deserved better.

"You never marry your true love," he muttered.

His students were now staring at him.

Flynn opened his book to one of the pages he had marked with a paper clip. "Let's jump to the end for a minute," he said. "Page 209, bottom paragraph."

As his students flipped wearily to the page, Audrey sat back and folded her arms.

"'If one advances confidently in the direction of his dreams," Flynn read, "and endeavors to live the life which he has imagined, he will meet with a success unexpected in common hours. . . . In proportion as he simplifies his life, the laws of the universe will appear less complex. . . . If you have built castles in the air, your work need not be lost; that is where they should be. Now put the foundations under them.'"

Flynn shut his book. "You have to give him that, at least," he said. "If you live according to your ideals and not what someone else says your goals should be, you'll feel good about yourself and other things will fall into place, even though there will be suffering, or consequences—people, like your family, will be mad at you . . ." He took off his glasses and ran his hand through his hair. "I mean, I know a lot of you have your lives all mapped out, but . . . listen, you need to know this: *nothing* ever goes according to plan. We get married to the wrong people, we find whatever jobs we can to make money, then figure out ways to enjoy our lives apart from that, like on weekends or vacations . . . and meanwhile we're not happy on a daily basis, we don't live the way we want to—I mean, look at you guys, you've all been medicated out of your depressions instead of confronting what you're really sad about, and you're still not happy, you're numb, you're just trying to—to *steal* it, happiness, instead of *earning* it, and then, you know, you stare at your cell phones while the world goes to shit, you major in Business because you want to make money even though you *know* that's not what makes you happy, I mean there are *studies* . . ." He was starting to sweat, thinking frantically. "And then we end up dying, all disappointed, wishing we hadn't . . ." He tapped the book in his hand. "So, you know, why don't you figure out not what you want to *do*, but *who* you want to *be*, and conform your lives, your decisions, to *that*? Why do we do it the other way around, conforming to our stupid, mundane lives?" Flynn waved at the blackboard, thinking he had put some key expressions on it, but that was in a previous class and he was waving at nothing.

"There are bills to be paid." A voice from the back: Troy Dougherty, who had yet to hand in either of the two essays required for the class.

"But what are those bills *for*?" Flynn said. "I mean, look at you, Troy, you drive a red Miata, so you had to get that job at the department store catching shoplifters so you can pay for your car loan and insurance, so you didn't read *Walden* because hey, you don't have the time, so you don't ever think about how you're living your life, right?"

"Right," Troy said. "I'm doing fine. I like my job; it's good for my career. I probably make more money than you do."

"*An unexamined life is not worth living*," Flynn said.

"Socrates," Wanda said.

"Was Socrates an American?" Troy asked.

Wanda rolled her eyes, and Flynn sighed. He despised Troy. Loathed the very sight of him. He wanted to flunk him for the course, but knew he would end up giving him a D, if only so that he would never have to see him on campus again.

"Did Socrates have credit card debt?" Troy asked.

"Listen," Flynn said, addressing everyone, "don't you want to just, I don't know, go to Europe for a year, bum around, have some fun, instead of starting your *careers* already? I mean, you're so young!" Flynn thought of the unused Eurail pass he had bought before 9/11, before Rachel had moved in with him. As soon as he got his PhD he had planned to go to Europe for a few months before returning to New York and looking for a teaching job. Even though it was only five years ago, he felt far removed from the person he was in those days—the new millennium launched, his glittering potential as yet unrealized. One night he had gone out with his friend Peter, and they had stumbled home through Washington Square Park at two in the morning, singing loudly. Where was that person now?

"Something I'm not handling well," Flynn told Rachel that evening. She was in bed with Nathan, watching television, with Mollie the Collie lying at their feet, even though Flynn had repeatedly requested that the dog be prohibited from their bed. "It's not like when we were in college," he said. "I mean, I admit, SUNY Binghamton was no hotbed

of intellectualism, but I can recall *thinking*, engaging in spirited conversations, you know, about *ideas*."

"Hotbed?" Rachel said. "Use real words, Hawk."

Rachel delivered statements loudly and with precision, as if perpetually engaged in public discourse or the star of her own reality TV show.
When they were first married, she had worn her red hair long and thick,
but she had recently cut it short, shorter than his, and added streaks of
fuscia. A wisp of it hovered over her left eye. "Anyways you drank a lot
in college, as I recall."

"No, in my *classes*, I meant."

A rerun of *Seinfeld* came on, and she turned up the volume. "Oh my
god I love this one!" She grabbed the phone and jabbed a speed-dial
button; she and her sister would watch it together.

Flynn stood at the doorway, thinking that the show's off-color humor
might be inappropriate for Nathan. When they had first moved to White
Plains, he had steadfastly refused to put a television in the bedroom. It
would be like admitting defeat, he said; that's when you know a couple
has stopped having sex. But once he finally relented, he was grateful. It
gave him some time to himself. After that, the televisions kept appearing—a total of four now, one in each bedroom, the big one in the family
room, and a little one mounted in the kitchen. If he objected to any of
her "impulse purchases," Rachel would laugh at him. "I love you, Hawk,"
she'd say, "but you really need to lighten up."

Flynn went back to the kitchen and saw the stack of bills he had left on
the table. He knew, from an article he'd read, that people who shopped
a lot were unhappy, trying to fill a void. He wondered if he was the one
who had made Rachel unhappy. What sad life had he assigned to her,
proposing marriage out of a sense of obligation, telling her he loved her
when he didn't even know what love was?

In therapy, he had retraced his marriage back to the beginning, back
to their first meeting, trying to locate a time when he had been madly in
love, when his heart had been full with her. If he could remember such
a time—if they both could—then, in theory, they could reclaim, and
reconstruct, that original love. But he couldn't. They had met in college,
but she was ruddy-cheeked and naïve then, and something about her

green eyes—she seemed to make them sparkle at will—had both attracted him and warned him off. Five years after graduating, however, when he had returned for his college reunion, she had shown up at his alumni baseball game thirty pounds slimmer, with a cute haircut and a white top that showed off her freckles. When they had gone to her apartment afterwards she had suddenly run to the bathroom and vomited, then stayed in bed all night while Flynn took care of her. He would later find out she had an eating disorder, and she had starved herself for weeks before the reunion, knowing he'd be there. He talked about all of this to his therapist, and when she asked him to describe some fun moments they'd had together, he told her about the time they drove to Virginia Beach and pulled over to have sex in the car; the time they played golf with her father, sneaking kisses behind her father's back; the glow on her face as she came down the aisle at their wedding; the time she sang the Barbra Streisand song "My Man" to him, her eyes full of love. But he also remembered his agitation over her aggressive driving on that trip to Virginia; his consternation over her repeated cheating during the golf game; the unease he felt during their wedding, sensing the whole thing was a façade; his discomfort when she sang to him so theatrically.

Rachel laughed at something her sister said on the phone, with Nathan still lounging in the crook of her arm and the dog fast asleep at her feet. She was not the kind of person who needed therapy. She was perfectly happy with the way things were. She knew who she was. And she adored her husband, her son, her house, and her job. *He* was the one with the problem. He was the one hamstrung by guilt and strife, all stemming from his Catholic discomfort with flamboyance, bombast, or anything that smacked of narcissism. What on earth was wrong with him?

A SUNNY DAY. FAIRFIELD WAS GREEN AND RESPLENDENT. FLYNN HAD TAKEN his students outside, and they were sitting in a semicircle as he read to them, no longer caring what they thought.

"'No man ever followed his genius until it misled him. Though the result were bodily weakness, yet perhaps no one can say that the consequences were to be regretted, for these were a life in conformity to higher principles. . . . If the day and the night are such that you greet them with joy, and life emits a fragrance like flowers and sweet-scented herbs, is more elastic, more starry, more immortal, —that is your success.'"

Flynn took off his glasses. Most of the students were looking up at him expectantly; Audrey was watching two shirtless men tossing a baseball.

"That's from 'Higher Laws,'" Flynn said. "Page seventy-nine." He knew he should say something else to spur their participation, but he was afraid they would ruin it for him.

Finally, Mark Pietrovic nodded, looking down at the book in his lap. "Awesome," he said.

Chuck, who was student teaching that semester, went back on his elbows and blew out a sigh. "I've had a bad week," he said, and Q patted him on the shoulder. "That . . . was medicinal." He sat up and pointed to the book. "What he's saying here, Hawk, is we should get our shit together so we don't go up or down with everyone else, and we'll just feel this . . . *peace*. Simple things will make us happy."

"Yeah, like the other day," Q said, "I was at a concert and my friends were getting all coked up, but I told them no thanks and they got all up in my face about it. But I felt good about myself, you know? *Resolute*."

Cocaine? Flynn thought.

Wanda raised her hand. "This is telling you to be the person you know you really are, to do what you *know* is right, even if your father and your boyfriend tell you you're a loser and your whole family thinks you're worthless." She smiled sadly, her eyes watering.

Then Troy spoke up from his spot under the tree: "This is telling *you*, Hawk, that you gotta take the bull by the balls!"

After class, Chuck and Wanda followed Flynn to his office, chatting with him about what they were going to do after graduation. Chuck was going to stay on at the school where he was student teaching, and Wanda, who had been admitted to grad school, said she was now thinking of taking a "gap year," maybe traveling for a while. As Flynn took his place at his desk, they stopped talking, and Chuck closed the door.

Wanda sat down, leaned forward, and clasped her hands in a gesture that smacked of such heartfelt sympathy that Flynn wanted to laugh at her. "So . . . we want to know if you're all right," she said.

"Yeah, we heard you had cancer," Chuck said.

Wanda opened her hands. "If there's anything we can do . . ."

Flynn tilted back his chair. "Cancer?"

"You don't look so good, man," Chuck said.

Flynn shook his head. This had never happened before. Students talked to *him* about how stressed *they* were; they told him about their breakups, their homesickness, their relationship problems; but they never asked about him; they never wondered how he was doing.

"I'm not cancer," he said.

Wanda's brown eyes were full of concern. "Well then what are you?" she said.

When Flynn arrived home, he went straight to the bathroom mirror, peered at the dark semi-circles under his eyes, and weighed himself. The last time he had done so, a year and a half ago, he had weighed 208. Now: 157.

He walked through the kitchen, the dog following him, and fell onto the couch. He wedged a pillow under his neck and closed his eyes, trying to lighten the weight of his head, trying to lessen the effect of his encroaching migraine. During his drive home he had been hit with another dizzy spell, and when he turned onto his street he had rammed into a stone pylon at the entrance to his neighbor's driveway.

He rubbed his neck and worried about his insurance rates.

For years, he had been living minute by minute, focusing on the next chore, the next thing he had to do. But what had happened? He hadn't even noticed the deterioration.

He closed his eyes, trying to will away the pain. If he could take just five minutes. If he could completely rest his head for five minutes.

But Rachel and Nathan would be home soon.

He got up and took some hamburger meat out of the refrigerator, along with the half-empty bag of Ore-Ida French fries and a head of iceberg lettuce. As he turned on the oven and made patties, he ticked off the warning signs: the dried blood in his mouth every morning; his erratic driving; six to eight Advils a day. And all the pathetic weeping—in the car to and from work, upstairs late at night, on the floor of the family room after everyone was asleep.

You're a sad dad, Nathan had said a few days ago, after Flynn had read him a Dr. Seuss book. *It's too bad that Daddy's so sad.*

And now, the frightening loss of weight. He hadn't realized what a habit it had become, hitching up his pants all the time. After putting the burgers on the frying pan and the French fries in the oven, he went to his bedroom closet, gathered all his belts, and went down to the basement with Mollie the Collie, who was wondering about her own dinner. Flynn put the belts on his workbench and began boring new holes in them. He was working on the last one when he heard the garage door open and close, followed by the kitchen door slamming, Rachel's footsteps above him, and then her voice screeching his name. He stayed quiet, gripping the augur.

Upstairs, the kitchen was filled with smoke. Rachel was running water onto the burnt burgers and the frying pan, trying to open the window at the same time. Flynn rushed over and shut off the oven—but the fries were burnt as well.

"What the hell, Hawk!"

Nathan plugged his nose and looked wide-eyed at them as they ran around opening windows and doors. "Disaster!" he shouted. "This is a disaster!" Flynn plucked him up, carried him into his room, and opened the window there, too.

Once things calmed down, he got on the phone and ordered a pizza.

Afterwards, with Nathan in his room watching a Thomas the Tank Engine video and Flynn standing on a chair, installing one of the smoke detectors they had bought when they had first moved into the house, Rachel asked where on earth Mollie the Collie was, and when he told her, she went downstairs to get her. When she came back up, she stood below Flynn with her hands on her hips, pooching out her belly. "Hawk, what happened to the car?"

Flynn lowered his screwdriver. "I'm so sorry, Rache. I got dizzy—"

"Do you have any idea how much that's gonna cost? Did you hit someone? Are we going to be sued?"

Flynn shook his head, came down from the chair, and tugged out the waist of his pants. "Look, Rache, I weigh—"

"Are you having an affair?"

Rachel's eyes reddened, and Flynn saw, and felt, what it must be like to be married to a man who didn't love you. Who didn't even like himself. Who had no idea who he was.

THAT NIGHT, FLYNN STAYED IN THE ATTIC UNTIL WELL AFTER MIDNIGHT, revising the draft of his conference paper and preparing for the final week of the semester. He was surprised to feel so lonely, so removed from everyone, in his own home.

Soon he would be renovating this room, to make it Nathan's, and the baby would take over Nathan's room downstairs. Flynn would keep the bookcase up here, but take out his books and replace them with Nathan's. He stared at the spines: *Hypocrisy and Ambiguity in Nathaniel Hawthorne's Work* (an outgrowth of his dissertation); *Living Through Others* (a multicultural composition reader, co-edited with a colleague at Fairfield); and *Leading Half-Lives: Nineteenth-Century American Women Writers* (an anthology he had co-edited with Gayle Cullen). They would be enough to ensure him tenure, but not a single one of his books—or articles, for that matter—had been read by anyone he knew.

Why do you stay here and live this mean moiling life, when a glorious existence is possible for you? Those same stars twinkle over other fields than these.

Kruger had been talking about ditching it all and going back to his music (he had once been a jazz pianist), even if it meant a much-reduced income. A year ago another of Flynn's colleagues had quit right after earning tenure, and he now owned his own Harley-Davidson shop in Wyoming.

But how to come out of this condition and actually migrate thither?

He looked out the attic window, at the starless sky. In his Early American Lit class he would be covering the last chapter of *Walden*. They would discuss the one-hundred-year-old bug, the one that came out of the larvae inside an old oak table, warmed to its hatching by a lamp. *Who does not feel his faith in a resurrection and immortality strengthened by hearing of this? Who knows what beautiful and winged life, whose egg has been buried for ages under many concentric layers of woodenness in the dead dry life of society . . . may unexpectedly come forth from amidst society's most trivial and handselled furniture, to enjoy its perfect summer life at last!*

He would write on one side of the board, *The mass of men lead lives of quiet desperation.* He would talk about his father, about the old notebook he had found in the attic filing cabinet, where his father described his dream of quitting his job selling kitchen parts and becoming a baseball coach once Flynn went off to college. It was dated a month before his death.

On the other side of the board, he would write, *Awaken.*

He would write, *Simplify.*

He would write, *Renew.*

He slumped into his desk chair. What would it be like to enjoy his perfect summer at last?

How long had it been?

Since September 10th, 2001.

He reached out for the economy-sized jar of Advil he kept on his desk, and downed four without any water.

Could a man be saved by words?

*

THE FIRST SURPRISE WAS ALL THE PEOPLE: FIFTY OR SIXTY, ON AN UNSEASON-ably warm May afternoon.

The second was how unremarkable the pond looked. How democratic.

The third was the facsimile of the shed. A tiny edifice. More than one guest and you would feel claustrophobic.

And finally, the pile of stones. It was customary for visitors to toss them onto the original site of the cabin, and Flynn had imagined it as the size of a highway department supply. Instead it was a modest mound.

The shore is composed of a belt of smooth rounded white stones . . . and is so steep that in many places a single leap will carry you into water over your head . . . .

He squinted into the sun and found a spot near those very stones. He tried to tune out the music and conversations, tried to imagine what the pond looked like without the coolers, the canvas folding chairs, the people. An orange Frisbee glided by, a dog dashing after it. Kids splashed around in the cold water. Nearby, a husband and wife carried on a hiss-ing argument, while about a dozen overdressed academics strolled the perimeter, their conference lanyards hanging like albatrosses from their necks. Along the shore, wooden scaffolding braced the soil, to stave off erosion. Flynn wondered how strong the braces were. He wondered how much longer they would hold.

Could a pond be saved by faith?

He settled back, opened his bag, and took out the sandwich he had bought in town: roast beef with melted Muenster on a toasted hard roll. He took a bite and closed his eyes, chewing. Then he pulled out the batch of final essays he needed to grade. On top was Mark Pietrovic's.

At first I thought Thoreau was a flake. Then I realized who else we called flakes: Christ, Galileo, Q Scirocco. As Emerson said, "To be great is to be misunderstood" . . . .

Thoreau believed we should advance confidently in the direction of our dreams. It's hard to argue with that. So why am I a Business major? Because my father told me to be. Why do I want to get married and have two kids? Because everyone else does. Is everyone else happy? I don't know anyone who is—not even my professors. So why do I want to be like everyone else? What's my dream?

Then, at the end: *This paper has no thesis.*

Flynn took out his pen and stared at the essay, but his heart was pounding. He put away the pile of papers, stretched out on the ground, and put his bag behind his head, suddenly exhausted.

But how to come out of this condition and actually migrate thither?

Words arrived from far off and hung in the air, just out of reach.

Transience.

Starry.

Winged.

When he awakened, the sun was setting, and people were packing up. He had slept deeply. His head was lighter, and his forehead felt sunburned. He knew he should go back to the conference hotel for the keynote address, but he decided to stay a while longer, until the pond had cleared out. Then he would see it for what it really was: more trees than when Thoreau was there, the landscape lush and green, the water still bejeweled, still deep.

Still alive. Still a kind of temple. Still sacred.

By the time the last person left, it was twilight. Flynn stripped and stood on the shore. He looked down at his body, at his ribs, his skinny legs. He needed to put some flesh on his bones.

He stepped into the pond. Although the temperature had reached at least eighty degrees that afternoon, the water was still cold. It was even colder with the next step, as the bottom dropped out from under his feet. He resisted the impulse to climb back up to shore. Instead he treaded water, shivering but invigorated. *To be awake is to be alive.* For the first time in years, he felt aroused. He looked up at the appearing stars, stirring from his long slumber:

Heaving exuviae.

Carpe diem.

Resurrection.

He cast out toward the middle, knowing it was unwise. *Hypothermia. Paralysis. Rigor mortis.* He shivered violently, noting the water's depth, its darkness. But he kept on, with smooth, careful breast strokes, the icy water bathing his body. He imagined the cells of his skin hydrating and awakening. His head had cleared; he felt a curious lightness in his brain.

Resolute.

He plunged down into the wet sky, the cool liquid stars.

OH MY MAN I LOVE HIM SO

IF YOU KNEW US IN COLLEGE YOU WOULDN'T HAVE SEEN THIS COMING. HE was a nice guy then. Quite the charmer! He was on the baseball team, but he wasn't a jerk like some of the other guys. The first time I saw him he was injured, he had a broken leg, he was sitting on the ground while his teammates practiced, and he was cheering them on, telling them to hustle and stuff like that. He had shorts on. Say what you will about Hawk, he has nice legs. Plus a flat stomach—back then. This was a long time ago. He was a sweet guy, or at least I thought so. That's what we all thought! Not Mister Mope as I call him now. He drank a little too much maybe, but he did great in school, he got mostly A's as I recall, except in Math. Statistics—that was the only class we took together, and we both got C's I think. He hung out with the potheads too but he didn't smoke much, or at least that's according to him. Anyways the first time I saw him, out there on the baseball field, he waved hi, I waved hi back, and I felt my heart go pitty-pat. It was that thing you hear about, you know? I just knew it, I knew he was the one. His smile. The way he smiles, his eyes almost close up, it's so adorable. I told Mickey, she was my best friend back then (these days she goes by her real name, Michaela), "I'm going to marry that man."

Me, I didn't drink or smoke pot or anything. Still don't. Well right now I'm having a little wine, but that's because I'm upset, understandably I'd say. Justifiably. Plus I'm an adult, but we're talking about back then, back in college. So you know, from the beginning—I guess this is what I want to say—from the beginning, contrary to what you might think from the separation agreement, or what I like to call the "pack of lies," I was the responsible one.

At first we were friends. I'd see him around campus, the school wasn't very big. He called me "Mad Dog" because apparently there was some notorious Irish terrorist with the same last name as mine and that was this terrorist guy's nickname. Him I called "Hawk," because that's what the guys on the team called him. Anyway, it was cute. I'd say "Hey there, Hawk!" and he'd say, "Mad Dog!"

Why him, you probably want to know. I've been asking myself that a lot. I had a boyfriend before him from back home, Sam was his name. Tall and preppy. But you know, you can't make sense of these things. You either feel that flutter in your stomach or you don't, right? And I certainly felt it with Hawk.

There was this time. He was in the cafeteria, loading up his tray of course, he was and still is quite a big eater, and Mickey and I were at the end of line, and the girls in front of me were talking about him, you know, kind of checking him out—he was a junior and we were freshmen—so I called out "Hey Hawk, save some food for the rest of us!" and everyone laughed, and he kind of leaned back, gave us a big smile and said, "Mike and the Mad Dog!"—which was apparently the name of some sports show in New York City. When we walked past his table, he handed me a little plate from his tray with a piece of coconut-chocolate cake on it and said, "Here you go, there was only one piece left." I blushed like you wouldn't believe, thanked him, and went to my table. And I know this is such a little thing, I'm sure it seems silly, but that, the fact that he had noticed that I liked that kind of cake, well that meant a lot to me, that's all.

Not long afterwards he asked me out, and he was very sweet. He called me Rachel instead of Mad Dog or "Rayche" or "Ray-mac," which is what everyone else called me. He said, "May I have the honor of taking you to a movie on Friday?" Well sure, mister smooth-talker! We saw *Sleepless in Seattle*, which is still my favorite movie of all time (I absolutely adore Tom Hanks!). We wound up back in his room, which I won't get into right now, but let's just say he was a gentleman and didn't pressure me to do what I wasn't ready to do. But after that night, nothing. No phone call even. I was pretty naïve back then. I thought we were a couple! But we never, like, agreed to that I guess, so to him it was just a casual date. I'll never understand men. Mickey said well he's from the city and remember, you're an upstate girl. And she was right. I grew up in a very sheltered environment, the youngest of six, so I was the baby, and boy did I get spoiled, as my brothers will tell you. I was cute as a button, I was. Quite the little tomboy. Bright red hair and red cheeks too. By the time I went to college I hadn't done anything: no sex, no drugs, and not much rock and roll even, and I was commuting from home, which was just fifteen minutes away, so nothing much changed. Then when I was a junior, after Hawk graduated (we're the same age, but I got left back a year when I was in elementary school and he skipped a year), I moved into Mickey's apartment and then I went through some stuff we're not going to get into here. All part of growing up, in retrospect.

Anyhoo, it wasn't until years later I saw my chance. Hawk was part of a group of guys called the Marathon Men, him and all of his buddies from Newing Hall. In their senior year they played softball for three straight days on Memorial Day weekend, dawn to dusk. They played a different team every hour, like the third floor Mountainview girls at one o'clock, the Athletics coaches at two o'clock, a group of professors at three—and they charged every team an entry fee that went to that charity that helps the kids with cancer, I forget the name. It was all Hawk's idea. I think he missed being on the school team, because he quit after the year he had the broken leg, and this was his way to relive his glory or something. But it was a nice thing. They played softball all day and they drank all night . . . well what am I talking about? They drank right on the field, there was a keg at third base! Then at the end, on the last day, one of the kids who had cancer came to the field and accepted the check and I think there was a TV camera there. And so after Hawk and his buddies graduated the younger guys kept up the tradition, and five years later the younger guys invited the original Marathon Men to play them, like an Old-Timers Day, and the youngsters probably thought the older guys were out of shape but what actually happened was that the old-timers kicked the young bucks' butts! Anyways I heard about this reunion game and I was already losing weight from my Pilates classes and I knew this was something Hawk would show up for, so I kicked it into high gear and by the time that weekend came I had lost a total of twenty pounds and I had a tan and I was looking pretty good if I do say so myself! When Hawk saw me he didn't recognize me at first and then he did and he said "Wow, Mad Dog, you're a knockout," which is the kind of expression my dad would use. Part of his charm I guess. By the end of the night he was back at my apartment. Hey a girl's gotta do what a girl's gotta do! But I was so nervous and I hadn't been eating much so what actually happened was before we could go all the way I got sick to my stomach and he took care of me all night. What a sweetie he was.

WAS.

Anyways I was hooked at that point. I took some pictures that weekend and I had them developed immediately. One was of him out in centerfield, his hands on his knees, looking towards home plate. His hair was kind of long, his forearms were tan . . . yep, I used to stare at that picture. This is going to sound silly but I used to kiss it before I went to bed. You know that Barbra Streisand song, "My Man"? I used to sing that in my room at night, I imagined singing it to him when we were married. I imagined dancing with him at our wedding, with my parents watching. What would they think of their little tomboy daughter then!

At the time, three years after graduation, I was back living with them in Binghamton, and he was in New York, living in the Village, so we did the long-distance thing for a couple of years, and I never told him about this but I actually started dating Sam again, just once in a while, nothing serious, but then 9/11 happened and Hawk and I decided to move in together. I had a huge fight with my mom over it. He always joked about it, but he had no idea how much that devastated me, how hard it was for me to be so bold to her. She's a tough cookie, that one. So I moved into his apartment in the east Village, which is by the way a disgusting neighborhood. (Two words: rats and cockroaches!) But I kept pestering him about it, so we were only there a few months and then we moved up to White Plains, near where he grew up, and he took the train down to the city when he needed to and I found work at this great place called Body Fit where I helped middle-aged men with arthritic knees and taught a couple of Pilates classes as well.

Oh I forgot to mention how we got engaged! Best day of my life! Or was, anyway. He took me to a beach. There's one not too far from White Plains, though you'd never guess because it's so crowded there, absolutely stuffed with people, but if you drive a little bit you end up in a town called Rye and there you are at the Long Island Sound. The beach is right next to Playland, that's where Hawk worked when he was in high school, and that's also where they filmed my second-favorite movie "Big." (Tom Hanks again!) So we were still living in the city at the time, and we took the train up to White Plains, I met his mom (no comment on that, she's a bitter old coot) and his sister (she's quite the pistol, we're friends to this day), and he borrowed his mom's car and we drove there. On the way we stopped at his father's grave, and he told me a little story about how when he was little he loved to ride his banana-seated bike with the high handlebars, and one day the chain came off, and he didn't think his father could fix it, but he did, and when Flynn went to hug him his father pushed him away and said, "You're a big boy now, no more hugging." Now what do you think of that? That probably explains a lot. For me it's the opposite, my dad's a big mush but my mom, good luck getting a hug out of her.

I was *so* nervous the whole time we were at the beach. It was cold out, this was in the winter, so absolutely nobody was there. In fact I was worried he was going to break up with me! But instead what did he do? First we played the penny game, which is when we both toss a penny in the air and if they both landed on heads we kissed and if they both landed on tails the game was over, but if it was split then the one with heads got to ask a question and the one with tails had to answer truthfully. To be honest, it usually ended with a fight, he's really stubborn and he always thinks he's right, his mother spoiled him rotten if you ask me, but a little fight once in a while never scared me, no sir. But he was sweet that day, that whole day was sweet, so when he got heads and I got tails he dropped to one knee, reached into his pocket and held out the cutest little diamond ring you've ever seen, and I just started bawling. Dreams *do* come true— that's what I always tell my Jane, my daughter, my mini-me, she's such a dreamer, that one. So we put together a wedding, he took out a loan for it because he was still a graduate student, and it was a wonderful wedding if you ask me, at Saint Mary's, my little church where I used to be in the choir. I have a huge family and they were all there. Father Bart said I was the most beautiful bride he ever saw, and that's certainly how I felt.

After we were married, everything changed. Not obviously, mind you. It was subtle. He would make fun of my upstate accent, of the way I dress—everything was sarcasm with that man. Constantly making fun of me or making jokes that weren't really jokes if you know what I mean. One time we were out with his professor friends, the most boring people on earth, and his buddy Kruger was saying something about a TV show and Hawk said, "Well Rachel watches eleven hours of TV a day so I'll let her answer that question." Yep, that's when I stormed out, and he came outside and apologized left and right but Jeez, that hurt, you know? Then afterwards all he talked about was how I made such a scene in front of his friends and he was totally joking, why did I get so upset?

I would like to say this to him and to all New Yorkers: sarcasm is mean.

Long story short: I'm the one who supported him all through his PhD, or the last part anyway, and his horrible defense, all that stupid stuff. So phony. So intellectual, these people talking about things that have no basis in reality. Plus I gave that man two beautiful children! And what does he do? Our little girl wasn't even two years old when he up and left us. Just left! God, it makes my ears burn just thinking about it.

Still, I'm holding out hope. I know he's having an affair. I can see it in his eyes, I can smell it on his clothes. Once he gets that out of his system, he'll come back. If not for me, then for the kids. He is, I'll say this, he is a great dad. I can't see him living without them. But in the meantime, I'm hedging my bets, as they say. I've been on a few dates with Gary, my sweet garage mechanic over at Quality Auto Care, and let me tell you, it feels GREAT to be treated like a lady again. A little flutter in the stomach. Not a big one, but it's enough for now. Just in case this doesn't work out.

DIAMOND DASH

DURING THE LONG WAIT IN LINE WITH THOUSANDS OF CHILDREN AND THEIR parents and guardians, a line that wrapped all the way around Shea Stadium and then some, I had twice resolved to leave, had twice determined that whatever this promotional gimmick was it couldn't be worth it, standing for over an hour like this in the heat and humidity after sitting through yet another three-hour Mets loss, and I was also aware that in order to establish a trusting co-parenting relationship with my soon-to-be-ex wife I needed to bring our son back *on time* after such special outings; but Nathan, who was six, kept insisting it *would* be worth it, whatever "Diamond Dash" was, so we hung in there, shuffling forward, Nathan holding the back of my tee shirt from behind me, occasionally burying his face into the small of my back as he matched his steps with mine.

NATHAN WAS FIVE, JANEY NOT EVEN TWO, WHEN I HAD LEFT MY MARRIAGE, following the Most Miserable Christmas of 2007 when my son and I shared a stomach virus and took turns vomiting. I waited until after the holidays because I didn't want everyone to have such a lousy memory attached to that time of year. A few days after New Year's, after putting the kids to bed, I spent an hour in the basement, sitting on the concrete floor with my head in my hands. I couldn't bear to hurt Rachel, couldn't fathom what this would do to the kids—I guess you could say that being a father was *who I was*—but I had lost over fifty pounds, I was crying every night, I had ferocious migraines, and I had been utterly unable to revive or manufacture any feelings of love for my wife. I had resolved to hang in there until Janey turned eighteen—*Only sixteen more years, man, you can do it*—but when I found myself standing on the side of the

Bear Mountain Bridge, staring at the Hudson River rushing under me, I knew I wouldn't survive that long.

Finally I got up off the basement floor, trudged upstairs, and told Rachel I was sorry, I was terribly sorry, but I couldn't go on, I could no longer live this charade, I didn't love her anymore, I felt ashamed and awful but I didn't know what else to do. She heaved the coffee table at me: *Get out of my house!* So I spent the night at my sister's. I was lying in the guest-room bed, miserable and guilt-ridden, when my mother, who lived next door to Annie, came into the room without knocking and told me how disappointed my father would be, may he rest in peace.

The next day, after Rachel called to tell me Nathan was confused and crying and I'd better be the one to explain it all to him, I picked up my son and drove him to the neighborhood pizzeria. Nathan hung his head as he came out of the house, kept his head down as he got into my car, and lowered it even further as we got out at the pizzeria and I guided him to a booth. In the corner was a kid around Nathan's age playing a video game, firing a toy gun at men who popped up out of nowhere. In a split second the kid had to decide if it was a hero or villain, to hold fire or shoot.

Our pizza slices sat on paper plates before us.

"I'm not leaving you and Janey," I told him. "I'm leaving Mom. Your mother."

I checked my impulse to call the whole thing off, to tell him it had all been a terrible misunderstanding, I would be moving back in immediately. My wife was a fun-loving, attractive woman and I was an idiot for leaving her. So many people, millions and millions, including my parents, had learned to shelve that silly dream of happiness and true love and settle for a working, fraternal partnership with their spouses. Why couldn't I?

I sought out Nathan's eyes, hidden under the Mets cap I had given him for Christmas, but when he raised his head I looked away.

"You are, you *are* leaving me," he said. He lowered his head again as his face clenched, his breath grating and catching in his throat. I reached out to keep his forehead from touching the pizza sauce. "I woke up and you were gone," he said through his chokes. "Mom said you just left, you left us."

I considered explaining everything to him: how his mother and I had been too young to marry, how it had been a mistake from the beginning, how we hadn't yet learned to love ourselves, how we had fought all the time before he was born and afterwards repressed it all so that it came out in bitter parries and brutal asides delivered with sarcastic smiles. I considered telling him how important it was for him to love himself or at least know himself before committing to someone else. I considered advising him to be deeply in love, crazy in love, before he married. I considered apologizing for ruining his life; all the articles I'd been reading concluded that children of divorced households were far more likely than "normal" kids to become addicted to drugs, commit violent crimes, and grow into coldhearted atheists who hated their fathers.

Nathan lifted his head. "Why don't you just come back?"

He thought the solution so simple, so obvious, that for a moment his eyes brimmed with certainty. But when they met mine they again collapsed, and his tears dropped onto the oil of his pizza, his shoulders convulsing. *Nothing will ever be as hard as this*, I wanted to tell him, but I knew that would be a lie, that in fact he was in for a lifetime of hardship and hurt and patricidal fantasies, and who could even predict whether or not whatever city he lived in would be obliterated by terrorists or completely underwater by the time he was my age. Instead I watched as he slipped away from me across the table, the space between us opening like a canyon, and I understood that nothing for him would be easy for a long time, and nothing I could say would help. All those months I had considered leaving, all the inner debates and bargaining, I had known it would destroy him, and that alone had kept me from acting on it. But I had never put a face to the destruction. Here it was, in front of me, and I had at the ready no offerings of solace, help, or hope.

As we neared the centerfield gate he took my hand, and when we finally entered the ballpark and heard the stadium usher say *Stay on the warning track, this way please*, I saw immediately how the Diamond Dash worked. The long line of kids and adults followed the warning track to the right-field corner, then turned along the foul line towards first base where the children made a sharp right and took off, dashing around the bases as parents and guardians continued to stroll towards home, shouting encouragement, until they met their little ones at the plate and ushered them out of the ball park. A dash around the diamond.

Nathan broke into a slow, almost stationary trot, as if he had to go to the bathroom.

ONE SATURDAY IN JUNE, FIVE MONTHS AFTER I LEFT MY WIFE, MY SON AND I had sat together on the baseball field at Silver Lake Park. "Are they the same swans we saw last time?" he asked, pointing.

I looked over and nodded, thinking of Yeats's swans, especially the fifty-ninth one, then noticed, at the far end of the lake, an SUV that looked like Rachel's, fire-engine red. It rolled slowly on the shoulder before stopping under a tree. "They're beautiful," I said. "But territorial." Nathan threw the baseball up in the air and caught it in his new glove, waiting for me to define *territorial*. His little fist clenched around the ball. I told him the swans decided a pond was theirs, and then dominated it. "They kill ducklings at night," I said. "They drown them." I started to demonstrate, as if forcing his little head under water, then stopped.

Nathan shuddered. "Why don't the ducks just stick together and fight back?"

I watched the swans glide in unison, dipping their long necks toward each other—such grace, such enmity. "I guess they're afraid to," I said.

"Do you still not love Mom?" Nathan asked.

"I'm sorry," I said, glancing across the lake at the car.

"Do you love someone else now?" He was still watching the swans.

I hesitated. There was a new Student Life director at my university, with recklessly curly hair. After meeting her in the fall, I had thought about her every day. In mid-December we had met for lunch, I told her of my situation, and we spoke of the possibility of dating once I left my marriage. She was smart, energetic, and had a great, throaty laugh. "It would be exciting to date the famous Professor Hawkins," she said. "The students adore you." When I drove her back to campus I held her arm as she started to leave, pulled her to me, and gave her a long, desperate kiss. But a few weeks later, when I did leave my marriage, she refused to answer my calls or emails. And when I went to her office to find out what had happened, she shook her head sadly and closed the door on me. For a while I kept up hope—maybe she simply didn't trust that I had left my wife for good—but the next time I saw her on campus she had a glittering diamond on her finger.

Then, in early February, I had tried to contact someone I had met in graduate school, a woman with enormous black eyes that had haunted me off and on for the past seven years. But while I learned from a web search that she had graduated NYU with her masters in Comparative Literature, she seemed to have disappeared afterwards—or more likely got married and changed her name.

"No," I told Nathan.

He was shifting his weight, standing on the dusty path between first and second base, pounding the glove with his little fist. I was squatting on the infield grass, a few feet away.

"Mom still loves *you*," he said, "even though you left." He kicked the bat with his foot. "So now you must love her again if you don't love anyone else. You have to love *someone*."

I tore up some grass, fisted it in my hand. *Your mom doesn't really love me; she loves the* idea *of me.* "I love *you*," I said. "And Crazy Janey, of course." When I had picked up Nathan I had seen my baby daughter in the back yard, in the turtle sandbox. ("Leave her," Rachel had said. "Nathan's the one who needs you. She's fine.") Janey, I thought, would never remember anything from the two years I had spent with her in the house. No memories of her father rocking her in the blue chair, feeding her pureed apricots with her Ariel spoon, singing "Good night, it's all right, Jane" before bed. Would it be easier for her, then, than it would be for Nathan? Or would she be even angrier at me when she came of age?

Nathan shook off his glove, picked up his new bat, and tried to toss the ball in the air and hit it, but again and again he swung and missed. After the fifth try, he flung the bat away. "I *hate* this!" he said, his face reddening. "It's too *heavy*."

I could see that the bat, which I had also given him for Christmas, *was* too heavy, and that his shoulders were in discord with the rest of his body, but that soon, in a few years perhaps, he would be strong enough to rip line drives with a smooth, level stroke. But who would teach him how to swing, how to shift his weight from back leg to front, how to follow the ball with his eyes right into the catcher's mitt?

Nathan crumpled to the ground and began flinging pebbles in my direction, though not far enough to reach me.

"I was lying on the floor every night," I said quietly, "crying. After I read to you and rubbed your back. After you fell asleep. After Mom and Janey fell asleep." I began to curl my face into my armpit, mimicking how I must have appeared on the family-room floor, but then stopped. No child wants to picture his father like that.

Nathan straightened his shoulders. "If you come back I'll be good all the time and you won't be sad anymore. And if you do get sad you can come in bed with me like you used to and I'll rub *your* back now."

I shook my head, looking at the torn grass in my hand. I could, I thought. I could go back. I had been making it work, hadn't I? *Fake it 'til you make it*, my mother had once told me, when I confessed to her I was unhappy in my marriage. *How do you think your father and I made it as far as we did? Before the son of a bitch up and died on me.*

"Mom says you're going to hell," Nathan said.

A cyclist rode past us then, down a dirt path that led into the woods. Nathan and I had ventured that way many times, but I still didn't know where the path ended. Once he found a butterfly on the ground there, its wing bent, and thought that by picking it up and holding it, he could save it. I had to tell him that if you hold something too tightly, you could kill it.

"This is not your fault," I told Nathan, "and it's not your mother's fault." I stood up and brushed off my shorts. "This is my fault."

ON THE RIGHT-FIELD WALL OF SHEA STADIUM WERE THE JERSEY NUMBERS and names of the most famous Mets: Casey Stengel, Gil Hodges, Tom Seaver. Men of strength, confidence, humor, and grace. When I bent to scoop up some gravely clay from the track, Nathan yanked on my shirt so we wouldn't lose our place. I started to tell him about the stadium, which would soon be torn down—I had been to over a hundred games here—but he furrowed his brow. "Why did that man call it a warning track?" he asked, but I was thinking of my father, of a time he had taken me here, and I heard Nathan's question in some arid distance, as if he had asked it in his thin voice through a tin can on a string from his room in our former house in White Plains and it had somehow carried all the way to the other tin can here in Queens.

WHEN HE WAS FOUR, NATHAN AND I SAT ON THE LIVING-ROOM COUCH AS I prepared for the class I was teaching that night. He was reading a pop-up ABC book featuring a variety of animals and insects, and Rachel was in the family room blasting an old Pat Benatar CD while vacuuming the carpet. We had just found out she was pregnant again, and I was feeling like a prisoner whose sentence had arbitrarily been extended.

Nathan was inventing a narrative to go with the pictures, occasionally identifying a letter. "B," he called out over the noise, "Butterfly. Butterflies are pretty. They fly with their pretty wings and drink from the pretty flowers." He flipped the page.

I put my finger to my lips as I went back over the page I was trying to read. I was completely unprepared for class; I hadn't even re-read the novel I was teaching, to say nothing of how I was going to fill three hours of class time talking about it. "Go in your room if you want to read out loud," I said.

The music pounded. The vacuum whined. Maybe I would put the students into small groups, give them themes to discuss.

"C. Crocodile. Butterflies like to visit their friend Mister Crocodile." Another turn of another page.

"Nathan, please. Daddy's trying to work." I held the book closer to my face.

Love is a battlefield.

"D," he said next. "Doggie. Daddy Doggie." He was still looking at the crocodile; he hadn't turned the page. "Daddy Doggie is cranky today." He raised his voice to be heard over the music, craning his neck so his lips came close to my ear. "HE CAN'T EVEN SEE THE PRETTY COL—"

I snapped my book shut and clamped my hand over Nathan's mouth, forcing his head against the back of the couch. His eyes widened. He couldn't breathe.

"*Will you be quiet,*" I hissed.

"It's so the outfielders know the wall is coming," I said. I told him they feel the track under their feet and that's how they know they might crash into the fence. I was ready to add that I myself had been an outfielder, and that whenever I raced back for a long fly ball I'd feel the crunch *one two* and brace for the fence, and that once, at a field where there was no warning track, I had sprinted back and collided into the fence, hurting my shoulder and missing the ball—*And so sometimes, you see, there is no warning*—but Nathan was looking up now and wondering about something else, like how the stadium lights had come on even though the game was over and the sky wasn't dark yet, so I didn't tell him any of those things.

As we reached the right-field corner and turned toward home, I strayed from the track to step on the outfield grass, to feel it under my feet. When I was Nathan's age, my father had taken me to Fan Appreciation Day, and while I don't remember anything about either game of the doubleheader, I do remember that between games, clutching the wooden stake of the poster I had made, I had walked across this same outfield with hundreds of other fans. I had first been ushered to the end of a long line outside the stadium that led to the same centerfield gates Nathan and I had just walked through, and we had split into two parades, one streaming towards first base, the other towards third. For days I had dreamed of feeling the grass beneath my feet, of seeing my heroes leaning over the dugout rail, appreciating my poster. But once on the field, I found myself frantically searching for my father. He had walked me to the outfield gates, but now where would he be? Still back behind the outfield wall? Up there in our seats, in a section I couldn't possibly locate? Out in the parking lot, smoking a cigarette? As I approached the infield I gripped my poster with both hands, searching the stadium for his maroon windbreaker. By the time I reached third base, I had dropped the poster and was running towards the exit behind home plate, and when I found my father there—standing at a reasonable distance from the rest of the parents, a snuffed-out cigarette at his feet—I clasped my arms around him, breathing in his musky smell.

"What the hell?" he said.

A few months after I left my sister's house, Nathan and I had sat on my bed in my tiny apartment in West Harrison on the second floor of a cottage, formerly the horse groomer's quarters, in the back yard of a small estate. A divorced woman in her sixties lived by herself in the main house. As soon as the weather had begun to warm I saw her outside every day, wearing a floppy hat, digging in the big garden beds out back, humming to herself. She was lean and fit, with gray-blonde hair. In mid-May she had given me some fresh lettuce, and a week later she left a bag of seed packets by my door with a note: I could start my own garden if I wanted to, in the little plot alongside the cottage.

The kids and I spent the day outside, planting together. Before picking them up I had aerated the soil and added some compost, and once they were with me, I scooped out holes with a spade as Nathan dropped in seeds, all the while keeping an eye on Janey to make sure she didn't eat the dirt. Now inside and freshly bathed, Janey sat on the floor in her happy-face pajamas watching a Winnie the Pooh video while Nathan showed me some drawings he had made in his first-grade class. In one of them, stick figures in red crayon stood side-by-side on orange construction paper. There was a mommy, with a thick smile and a tuft of red hair; a daddy, tall and skinny, with brown hair and a moustache; a chubby baby in a bright blue stroller; and a slight little boy. But between the boy and the daddy was a strange man with a thick and hideous grin. The tallest member of this crayon portrait, he was clearly not a member of the family. And although the stranger was smiling, his head was on fire. An orange blaze raged up from inside his skull, the top of which had apparently been blown off.

"Who's that?" I said.

Nathan looked puzzled. "That's a man with his head on fire," he said.

I looked at the other drawings: a cow with green stripes, a boy with hands so fat they blotted out the scenery. I thought, maybe sometimes a man with his head on fire is just a man with his head on fire. But then I remembered: on our way out of the pizzeria, he had kicked the soda machine as hard as he could.

"Are you angry?" I asked. "That I left? That would be totally normal, you know." *My god, of course he's angry. He'll be angry with me until the day he dies.*

"No," Nathan said, fingering the button on his shirt. "Just sad some-times, but I see you almost every day and Joey Vinnola says you're better than his dad because his dad is always—"

I gathered his angular body to me. "It's okay if you are," I said. I was thinking of what my therapist would say about Nathan's drawing. *That one's going to have issues when he grows up.*

"Okay, but I'm not," Nathan said. "You're the best dad ever."

I held him at arm's length: his mushroom-cut hair, his spindly body, his wet mouth opened in an O, and the baby teeth inside making way for the grown-up teeth. *You have no idea how amazing you are*, I wanted to say. *You're already a better person than I am.*

"I got it," Nathan said, his eyes widening "I'll just live here with you!" He rapidly patted my knee. "Jane can live with Mom and we could play catch in the back where all the grass is and you could read to me every night and we could watch *Thomas the Tank Engine . . .*"

I touched my finger to his lips, but he slapped away my hand. "Don't you want me to live here? Why don't you tell Mom you want me to live with you?"

I caught my breath. In a preliminary talk with a lawyer, I had proposed that very compromise: *If I have "no chance whatsoever" at full custody, could I at least have custody of one of them?* The lawyer had shaken his head. "They never split up the children," he said.

I took both of Nathan's hands and pulled him into me, breathing in the smell of his hair. If I pried open the top of his head, would an orange fire leap out and devour us both?

"Natty," I choked out. "You're the best boy. The very best boy. In the whole wide world."

Two months after Nathan was born, I carried him to the couch with me at three in the morning, after the clangy radiator in his room had awakened him from a deep sleep. I shuffled into the kitchen, holding him in one arm while getting his bottle ready. With his cracked squawking in my ear, I plucked the bottle from the pot of hot water, squeezed a drop of Rachel's breast milk onto my wrist, arranged my son in the crook of my arm, placed the nipple in his mouth, and made my way over to the couch. "Natty is the best boy," I sang to him, "the very best boy in the whole wide world." I found an old movie on television as he slurped the milk. When he fell asleep in the middle of it, waking up in time to belch into my face, spit up onto my shoulder, and drop into sleep again on my chest, his heart beating rapidly against mine, a wave of tenderness came over me, a rush of something I had never felt before, and with that the certainty that he and I had just sealed something, something permanent, something more natural and unbreakable than a wedding vow.

NEAR FIRST BASE WAS A SIGN: *PARENTS AND GUARDIANS, PROCEED TO HOME plate*. When we reached the base, Nathan, no need for directions, broke from me towards second, and as he ran in line with the other kids, I surveyed the adults, wondering which were parents and which were guardians, which were heroes and which were villains. Then I turned and noticed my dashing son.

At first he ran with his fists closed, legs windmilling, knees and elbows jutting out as he followed the children in front of him. The rest of the parents and guardians strolled to home plate, looking right and cheering encouragement, while I stood arrested at first base. For just before reaching second, as Nathan leaned forward and dashed past a taller boy in front of him, a strange thing happened: his body began to collect itself, began to come together in flight.

His chin rose, his shoulders relaxed, and his fists opened as he took the inside corner of the second-base bag with the side of his right foot (*Where did he learn that?*), passed two more dashers, then accelerated confidently past an entire line of jogging and laughing kids—tall kids and short, bad kids and good, kids of all colors, kids with stepdads or stepmoms, kids with single moms or single dads, kids with no parents at all, kids with parents who hated each other, kids with parents who loved each other. As he rounded third, the Mets third-base coach smacked him on the ass and he ran even faster, sprinting past four more children as he streaked towards home, and just then he lifted his arms, the gallant victor in the throes of his own grace, and smiled a smile of triumph, of freedom, of an escape from suffering. And when he alighted in the air above home plate, hovering like a butterfly and landing so lightly it would hardly count as a run, he didn't seem to notice that his father wasn't where he was supposed to be, that he was in fact still lingering at first base as parents and guardians streamed past him, a man who seemed to have popped up out of nowhere, neither hero nor villain, grinding some warning-track dirt in his fist and standing at a reasonable distance off to the side.

§

I COULD SEE THEY WEREN'T EATING WELL—PILLSBURY CINNAMON ROLLS OR Eggo waffles in the morning, mac-and-cheese or Pizza Hut at night—so whenever I "babysat" them at my former house, now their mother's house, I tried to give them nutritious lunches and snacks. Janey, who wouldn't knowingly eat vegetables if her life depended on it, could be tricked into eating them in soup as long as tortellini was involved. Nathan would eat soup too if I told him there was a dinosaur at the bottom of the bowl. He'd slurp and slurp, gazing into the murky broth, and halfway through I'd point to something outside or tell him there was a caterpillar on the floor, and as soon as he looked away, I'd take a tiny plastic dinosaur out my shirt pocket and drop it into the bowl. He was stunned and delighted each time he discovered it, no matter how many times I had done it before.

Sometimes I put chopped-up fruit in bowls and set them on the floor, so they could eat from the bowls like puppies. That's how I got them to drink milk, too. I made smoothies and secretly mixed in broccoli or kale. Nathan would gladly eat veggies if hot dogs came with them, so I'd get the kosher all-beef kind, slice them up like miniature hockey pucks, and mix them in with beans and corn or carrots. Once, he abruptly stopped eating, his eyes wide. I smacked his back, then tried to give him a mini-Heimlich, but what finally worked was picking him up, flipping him upside down, holding him by the ankles and pounding his back until the pink chunk of meat popped out.

Two weeks later, while eating spaghetti mixed with fried spinach, Janey stopped chewing, eyes wide, mouth open, and I saw a strand of pasta sticking up from her throat, so I reached in and pulled it out like a magician yanking a ribbon from his assistant's ear. Janey coughed and cried, and then laughed as I held up the noodle and scolded it for almost killing her.

Sometimes, while eating, I remind them of these incidents. I tell them to take their time, to chew their food. "Remember when you almost choked to death?" As if I want them to know: given the opportunity, I could still be their hero.

US AND MOM IN A FANCY-SCHMANCY RESTAURANT, IF YOU CAN BELIEVE THAT

As soon as Famous Author came on the scene, we knew there was going to be trouble. We met her when Flynnie asked us to pick her up at Laguardia, but then we didn't see her again until months later, and that was at the fancy-schmancy restaurant. The total amount of time we spent together, like an hour when you add it all up, she never *once* asked us a single question. It was all "I this" and "I that," every sentence out of her mouth started with I. "I, I, I." No exaggeration.

We all had a pow-wow about it, after our warm and fuzzy family dinner. Talk about a mismatch! They're like complete opposites. Flynnie's more like "you, you, you." He wants to make everyone happy. The rest of us, we can be a little gruff. That's putting it mildly. But Flynnie, he was always the sweet one. Like when he was a kid, whenever one of us was sick, he would come into our room, kiss our forehead, get us a ginger ale, that kind of thing. When it snowed, he would go across the street and shovel Mrs. Leimus's driveway. When Pop wanted a beer, Flynnie would jump up and get it for him. Pop used to call him his golden boy. (Me, he called Anna Banana. Not quite the same.) And after he grew up and got married, he was all about his kids. When Nathan was born, he quit his softball league, stopped going to the rec center, quit hanging out with his friends—they all bitched to me about it, like *Where the hell's yuh brothuh, what is he pussy-whipped or somethin?*—but I was like what do you want me to do, he's with his kid, shut your face! And my friend, the one that works at Fairfield, she says he's like that with his students, too, he always makes time for them, he goes to their whatchamacallits, their music recitals, he stops by their baseball games, she said he won Professor of the Year once but he never said anything about it, at least not to us. When we were kids Pop used to always tell us about the martyr types, like that girl who died in Africa, down there helping the poor or something like that, maybe it was the Peace Corps, it was on the news and Pop was all over it, he said that we, meaning me and Flynnie, we should grow up to be just like that girl (there were, like, *tears* in his eyes) and I was like, "What, you mean *dead*?" but Flynn must have taken all that stuff seriously because he did end up like that girl and now look what's happened, it's like a whatchacallit, a backlash or something.

At his wake, at Pop's wake, Flynnie was the one who held us all. He wrapped us up in his gangly arms and made us cry with him like in a football huddle. (Mom did that thing where she squeezes her eyes shut like she's trying to force her tears back into their sockets.) He was, let me think, sixteen. I was in college, that was my sophomore year, so yep, he was sixteen. But, even then, even so young, he was the one we could count on for that kind of stuff. Not the practical stuff, and definitely not the financial stuff, but you know, the emotional stuff. And the family stuff too. Like no matter how busy he was, he always came over to Mom's for Sunday dinner. With the kids, of course, and Rachel came too back then, but toward the end, like in the last year of their marriage, he came without her a lot, I mean with just the kids. Always in a good mood, too, no matter how bad things were. He'd give my Mari a hundred kisses, put his ear to my big belly to see if there was any action (this was when Robbie was in there), ask Mitch how many criminals he's caught lately, and tell Mom dinner smelled good even though, let's be honest, he knew damn well there was a slim-to-none chance it was *actually* good. She's the absolute worst cook. She could burn boiling water. Last week she was over our house and we had just got one of those electric teapots and she decided she wanted some tea so she filled it with water, put it on the oven, turned on the gas, and burned the shit out of it. Melted plastic everywhere. The smell was terrible. But I digress.

The only time he wasn't like that, like sweet and nice, was, you know, right after 9/11. Things got a little weird there for a while. Missed a lot of Sunday dinners. I mean he was living in the city at the time, which had to totally suck, not to mention the smell, and our cousin Jessica she died in Tower 2, she was on the 93rd floor, he said he kept imagining her jumping, he was sure she was one of those people that fell down the side of the building, remember that? Like the towers were crying or something. But after he married Rachel and they moved up here and Nathan was born, he got back to normal. That's what saved him, Nathan's birth. I'm convinced of this. Saved his life. He cheered up one hundred percent after that. Absolutely loved being a dad, from Day One. He worked at it, too, unlike my Mitch; he got up in the middle of the night to feed Nathan and he cooked all their meals and did all the grocery shopping and laundry and diaper-changing. Rachel said once it's a good thing he didn't have boobs or she would have nothing to do! (She's a pisser, that one.) Last summer he was Nathan's tee-ball coach, cutest thing you've ever seen. And with little Janey, my god, sweet as can be, he sings to her and kisses her toes and makes her giggle all the time, that girl is such a pumpkin. A few weeks ago I was in the car with the three of them, we were going to Mari's school play, she was a cow in *Charlotte's Web*—a cow! Like that's not typecasting or nothing! Like, um, let's see, who can we get to play the cow, oh hey what about the overweight retarded kid? Only Mari was so happy about it she never knew it was an insult so she was the best freakin' cow you've ever seen. And so here's the point, while me and Flynnie were talking he put his hand back and the kids grabbed onto it and he drove like that, his arm bent back while talking to me, like that's how they always drive now, even when he needs to hit the blinker or turn down the radio, he keeps his right hand back there. Not exactly safe, but you know.

Oh, and can I tell you what they do at night sometimes? Nathan, he's the one who told me. They all go over to the park, and they stand out there, the three of them, holding hands and looking up at the sky, and Flynnie tells them stories about the constellations. And when he says "Okay kids, time to go home," Nathan says something like, "Wait, what about those, are those the seven sisters?" and Flynn stays out there, telling them stories, until they get so sleepy he has to carry them home. See, it's like he became an even better father after he left Rachel. And her too; all of a sudden she's like supermom. I know, right?

In other words, my point is, they were doing just fine before Famous Author showed up. Flynnie was starting to adjust, Rachel was starting to calm down after a year of being separated and she was letting him see the kids once in a while, though to be honest that was only when she went out with Mr. Blue-Eyed Garage Mechanic and needed a babysitter, and the kids, they seemed to be adapting to their new lifestyle. But my God, in the beginning? In the beginning it was terrible. He cried *so much* about them, that first month he stayed with us. He'd be in our guest room, door shut, but still, we could hear it. He ate with us sometimes, and he came out the room of course whenever we asked him to watch the kids. He's like the ideal babysitter. He's one of the few people who really "gets" Mari. We all have to tiptoe around her sometimes, she requires a lot of extra care and I'm not gonna lie, it's stressful. I mean I'm raising her more or less by myself. Mitch is gone a lot because we need the overtime, oh I forgot to say he's a cop in the Bronx, and she's destroyed a few babysitters, my Mari has, just completely annihilated them, but Flynnie's great with her, she just adores her Uncle Flynn. She was so worried about him when he was in there, in his room I mean, crying into his pillow. Is Uncle Flynn okay? Shouldn't we go in there? No honey, we'd say, he just misses his kids, and she'd say, Well why doesn't he just go back home? And we never knew what to say to that, because let's face it, he should have. He should have just gone back home.

P.S. He was like this when he was a kid. Big crybaby. Don't get me wrong, he was normal and all, always running around playing sports and riding his bike and reading his books, my God he was always reading books, but Jesus Christ what a cry-baby, forget about it. Even now, even as a grown-up—what is he, thirty-six, thirty-seven? Thirty-six—he was mostly crying about his kids at first, but then he was also moping about some woman, some woman at his college who had promised to go out with him back when he was thinking of leaving Rachel but dropped him like a hot potato as soon as he was actually available. But, Mitch and I talked about this, and let's be honest, that makes sense, what she did, I mean Flynn was quite the mess. What woman in her right mind would jump into a relationship with someone who's crying every day? Not a healthy woman. Not a woman who has her shit together. So that must be why she said uh sorry, no thanks, changed my mind.

To be perfectly honest it was hard to have him in the house. To be perfectly honest. You get used to your home being a certain way, and you already got a mentally handicapped kid, and you throw a depressed adult male into the mix, and it doesn't matter if said depressed adult male is your baby brother, it throws everything out of whack. That's all I have to say about that.

Anyway it got better once he moved into that little whatchamacallit, the carriage house, over in West Harrison. The first week, I went over with Mari to bring him some books he left at our house, and you could tell, he looked much better. He actually smiled and gave me a hug, or he tried to. I'm not very good with hugs. Mari, though, she's like my surrogate hugger. She can kill a man, the way she hugs. I have to keep her away from my little Robbie or she'll give him internal combustion. She gets a little enthusiastic, is what I'm saying. She *really* likes having a little brother.

That's how we used to be, me and Flynnie. When we were kids, we slept in the same room, we played in the little pool together, we took baths together when he was a baby. I know for a fact I saved him from drowning a few times even though Pop once said if he left us alone *I* would have drowned *him*! (Apparently I had issues about being the princess of the house and then having to share the spotlight after he was born, blah blah blah.) But I took care of my baby bro, I would never let anything happen to him. But then, according to Flynnie, I turned mean, back when he started to get stronger, back when he shot up and got as tall as me and then went through puberty and started stinking up the house. But I don't see it as me being mean. All I was trying to do was keep him on the straight and narrow. Pop was gone a lot, Mom wasn't exactly the most attentive parent, and then they were both *really* gone when Pop died, I mean like gone gone, and somebody had to see to it that Flynnie went to church, that he did his homework, that he came home right after baseball practice instead of hanging out with the troublemakers. He acts like this is the reason why he had a bad marriage and why he always went out with bitchy women, but that's obviously his therapist talking. His therapist thinks he gets into relationships with quote-unquote emotionally unavailable women who remind him of quote-unquote the women in his family because he's trying to quote-unquote resolve his issues. The only problem with this theory is that I am not a quote-un-quote emotionally unavailable woman. My emotions are very available, I can tell you that! Yes I can be bossy, this will not be news to anyone, but I am not, like, coldhearted or mean or anything like that. What I *am* is well organized. What I *am* is a realist. What I *am* is the person in our family who does what needs to be done. Not cold. *Practical.* As for Mom, she can be a little stiff, I grant you that, but you should have seen her back before Pop died, she used to sing, play old records, dance with us around the living room, la di da. Not all that affectionate, that's a given, not "emotionally available" perhaps, she had a tough childhood, not for nothing she and Pop had their problems in the sack, but that stays right here, okay? Still we all have our issues, and I wouldn't go so far as to call her cold. *Guarded*, that's it. Guarded. Appropriately, no *necessarily*, guarded. Anyway, I'll just come out and say it, it hurt, it still hurts, to be portrayed in this manner. I've been his rock, his true defender, all his life. When he got his permit and he went out with his friends and came home drunk at four a.m. with a dent in the car, Mom freaked out, absolutely freaked out, but I was the one who told her to back off, he was just a stupid teenager, make him pay for the repair and that's it, and all of this while he was sound asleep upstairs. That was just after Pop died. He was pulling all kinds of crap back then. One time he came home and shit the couch while he was passed out drunk. I know, right? Disgusting. And when he was nervous about marrying Rachel, saying he wasn't sure if he loved her, I'm the one who told him, this was right outside the church for God's sake, I'm the one who told him to man up, get in there, and do the right thing. And this year when he needed to hire a lawyer but didn't have any money because he kept giving Rachel his entire paycheck even though they were freakin' separated (see what I'm talking about?) I'm the one who loaned him a thousand dollars. A thousand dollars! And then he meets this Famous Author and he takes my hard-earned money, okay Mitch's hard-earned money, and he flies way the hell out to Colorado with it! Comes back looking different, like he just saw the Purple-Mountain-Majesty-Above-the-Fruited-Plains with his own two eyes.

Agh. See? This whole thing is giving me *agita*.

Anyway, Famous Author, whose name shall henceforth never be uttered in our household, *that* one is cold. We heard about her for months but we'd never met her, because Flynn is apparently now embarrassed by us, his own flesh and blood. Then, we finally met her. Here's what happened. I'll tell you. Flynn called us from his house, well it was pretty much Rachel's house then since they were separated, in a total panic. He was watching the kids, and Rachel said she'd be back home by seven but when he said "Okay good because I have to be at the airport by eight," she apparently got a little gleam in her eye and by now it was eight thirty and Famous Author was sitting alone at the World's Shittiest Airport and who knows when Rachel would be back so could I please please go to the airport, pick her up and bring her back to our house and by that time Rachel would surely be home? And when I said "Geez, just bring the kids over here! Or I'll come over there!" he said the kids were sound asleep and he had sworn to Rachel that nobody else would be present whenever he babysat and that included family and he also swore to her that he wouldn't take them *anywhere* without her knowing and he didn't want to piss her off and she would absolutely freak if she knew he had a girlfriend visiting and then he'd never get to see the kids and she was not answering her phone so I said "Oh for Christ's sake all right" and I asked Mom to come over and watch the kids and told Mitch to grab the blue cop light and we blasted down to the airport to pick her up, I mean we flew down the Van Wyck so fast I swear Mitch hit warp speed. Took us seventeen minutes, new world record. When we got there we spotted her right away, (A) because we googled her picture and (B) there was a crowd of people like always but she, she was the only one standing there all annoyed with her hand on her hip like her chauffeur was late.

We didn't get much out of her on the way back. Sullen. Like Mari when she misses her nap. *And* I don't recall her ever saying thank you for the police escort. When we got to our house, Flynn was waiting in the driveway with the car running, looking embarrassed beyond belief.

When I told him he should bring his new girlfriend inside so she could meet Mom, he said "Some other time, Annie," and drove off. Now how do you think Mom felt about that? I mean, we saw her looking out the window and all. It broke her heart, that's how it made her feel. She couldn't even talk about it. She just handed me Robbie's binky, told me they were both sound asleep, and went back into her house. That's right, we live next door to Mom. Flynnie always teases me that it's symbolic or whatnot but it's not, because, again, I have to say this: *practical*. Have you seen what real estate is going for around here? So we just built onto Mom's and *wal-la*! Affordable property in Westchester County, *and* an instant babysitter, on-call 24/7.

Anyway, Flynnie stopped showing up for Sunday dinners after that, or he'd show up but he wouldn't say much, or he'd show up without the kids because Rachel, after she got wind of the new girlfriend (okay, because I told her), she went into Defcon V and started telling the kids their father was an adulterer who would go to hell for his sins and they couldn't see him anymore. So when he came over he'd just sit in Pop's old armchair and stare out the window like something was out there, something besides the train tracks I mean. Then he missed one of his weekends with the kids because Famous Author was visiting again and then the next weekend he flew out to Colorado, and I had to say something then, I had to say listen, little bro, I love you, you know that, but these are weekends you should be spending with your kids, right? And what's the deal with missing three days of work? And—I had to say this—I wouldn't have loaned you that money, I said, if I knew you were going to donate it to United Airlines instead of your lawyer. And he was like "Annie, don't do something nice for me and then impose conditions on it, okay? I'll give it back. You want it back now?" But we both knew he didn't have it. Please.

"Listen, Flynnie," I said, "I read her book." (I'm talking about the paperback, not the one that's out now in hardcover. Who spends $24.95 on a book?) "This girl," I said, "forget about it, she's messed up. What do you get out of living like that, out in the freakin' wilderness? I'll tell you what you get. You get dead."

I had just seen that movie, *Into the Wild*. Great film, stupid kid.

"Or you grow hair on your tits," I said, which is my way of saying the girl might be a little too, you know, testosteroney.

"Please, Annie," he said, and he put his hand on my arm, right here. "I'm in love with her," he said. Which of course melted my heart. *And* scared the shit out of me.

"No you're not," I said. "You're in love with *that*," and I pointed out the window, at the "out there." You know, the "out there" that everyone's in love with. The "out there" that everyone thinks is going to solve their problems until they realize that they can go way out there, as out there as they want, but they're still going to be walking around with whatever's *in here*. "This is what counts," I said. I was pointing at my chest—which let me tell you, is pretty impressive. I use it to make all kinds of points.

"I'm thinking the two are connected," he said.

Whatever.

No matter what you might think right now, let me tell you something. My brother has a good head on his shoulders. Not for nothing he got a PhD when nobody else in our family graduated college. (I went for two years but then I married Mitch and got my PhD in Pregnancy—two friggin' miscarriages and one stillborn before Mari was born.) But when it comes to women, he's always been a dork. He never had a date in high school, but in college, as soon as his zits went away, he got so cute so fast that he had a lot of girlfriends all at once, not that he knew what to do with them. Mostly he dated these artsy forlorn types and then all of a sudden Rachel who's the opposite of artsy forlorn. And now Famous Author, same as Rachel, very outspoken and opinionated, I can't stand people like that.

Anyway, when we met her for the second time, that's when it was at the fancy-schmancy restaurant and that's when the shit hit the fan, so to speak. Flynn wanted to bring her over for dinner and finally meet Mom—she had already met Nathan and Janey in secret once, out at the park, and according to Flynnie it "went very well" but according to Nathan "she bought us puppets." (Hello? You cannot *buy* the affection of children. They are *too smart for that*.) And Janey just made a face, what a mug she has on her, she looked like she might start crying, and as for Rachel when that happened, it was the first time she had let him see the kids in a long time, when that happened it pissed her so off she said he would need a court order to see them again—but anyway as I was saying we were all set to host this momentous get-together, we were all set to cook up a big dinner and eat in the back yard, my Mitch had actually *cleaned the grill the way you're supposed to* instead of just scraping the crusted meat off with the dirty metal brush, but then Flynn called to insist we meet at a nice restaurant instead, Famous Author's treat, even though he knew damn well that us and Mom in a fancy-schmancy restaurant is not a good combination. But what was really going on was that Famous Author must have said no dice on going to a place where she didn't have any power, meaning Mom's house or my house, looked up "best places to meet your nasty future in-laws in White Plains without causing a scene" on yelp.com or some place like that, and came up with this restaurant with a French name, "La Reserve." Regardless. We wanted to be nice to Flynn, we all have to treat the baby of the family with kid gloves (it was always like this, poor Flynnie, such a sensitive boy, he doesn't have any friends, he needs a little extra love, that's all), so we said okay okay and went downtown and met them at "La Reserve," which was, let me tell you, there's no other word for it, *swank*. Which is probably the reason why we never heard of it before. The Hawkins clan doesn't exactly traffic in *swank*.

Flynn was all smiles. Mister Sunshine Blowing Up Our Asses. Mister Head-Over-Heels. Mister I've Seen the Rocky Mountains and They've Calmed Me the Fuck Down. He can light up a room, that boy. He's tall, he's got the thick wavy hair (seems to be growing it out these days, no comment, *cough* hippie *cough*), and those long eyelashes I was always jealous of. (Once in middle school I actually trimmed them when he was sleeping, but we're not going to get into that.) But me and Mitch and Mom, we saw right through it. We knew the deal. And there, right next to him, with a new haircut (like a forty-year-old trying to look like a twenty-five-year-old) and this flowing Asian sarong-type thing (to cover up her belly, which looked like mine when I was four months pregnant, no make that five), and a pair of those hipster glasses celebrities wear when they can see just fine without them, there was Famous Author. "So," I said after shaking her hand for the second time, which is, by the way, like a man's, "our place not good enough for you?" But Flynnie, he kept chatting about how Famous Author was kind enough to take a break from her book tour to visit with us and blow us to a big meal, then he kind of leaned in, grabbed my arm and said, "She didn't want to go straight into the lion's den, surely you can appreciate that, so just roll with it, okay sis?"

I nodded—Mom *can* be a handful, this is true (as he well knew, I once went an entire year without talking to her), and I do love my baby bro, I do—so I gave Famous Author my nice smile, how do you-fuckin'-do, good to see you again. And I'll give you this, she has a *presence*, that one. I mean, people notice her. She looks like a fucking lioness. Real pretty, plus a cute nose, nice smile, smoking hot boots. When I asked her where she got them, she lit up and talked about some little shop in Tibet and she gave the exact location even though we both knew I would never be caught dead in Tibet (and yes I do know where that is so shut your face), and then she went on to tell us, with Mitch looking bored out of his mind and Mom squirming in her seat like she was going to shit her pant suit over the cost of the drinks, where she had gotten *everything* she was wearing—the Asian sarong thing was from Laos, one ring was from a Hopi jeweler in Telluride, another was from a quote-unquote artisan in Morocco, her brooch was from an ironsmith in Selma, Alaska, her socks were from a wool factory on the Aran Islands (okay, now that, I have no idea where that is)—and that's when my stupid husband butted in: "You ever travel to someplace normal, like France?" and that set her off.

"I think that what we, or the Western world rather, calls 'normal' is typically a place that's been overrun by tourism and where everyone speaks English and there's a McDonald's and Starbucks downtown and they've lost their true character" blah blah blah "so that's why I choose not to *frequent* such places."

"Except for book signings, of course," Flynn told us, like I care. "Her last book was translated into German and Italian, so she had to travel there to give readings. Sweet, huh?" He put his hand on her back, but like he was afraid of hurting her. My Mitch would never do that. What my Mitch does is he grabs my shoulder and pulls me into him like he owns me. I love that shit. Total turn-on.

"So you're like one of those anti-American artists?" Mitch said, and I thought *You hit that nail on the head, hubby* and of course that set her off again, this time on a liberal tirade against capitalism and how we are destroying the planet and spreading our quote-unquote consumerist values to other countries "much to the detriment of their native cultures" and she used words no normal person uses like *jingoistic* and, uh, wait-let-me-think *ethnocentric* and in the middle of all this the waitress came by, smelled trouble, and gave us the "I'll come back after the tsunami's over to collect the dead" look and at the end of it Mitch said "What's *wrong* with consumerist culture? Isn't that how you got rich, by us capitalists buying your little books?" and even I had to cringe at that one, 'cause he said "little books" like he would say, I don't know, "ditties." My dear husband does bring a lot to the table, mainly Overtime Cash, but one thing my dear husband does not bring to the table is couth.

"Well, not us capitalists specifically," Mom said, because no one in the family had ever bought any of Famous Author's books. (Okay true confessions, mine I "borrowed" from a friend.)

Famous Author gave Flynnie a look, and Flynnie cleared his throat and glared at Mitch, who had that face on him, like he had just grilled a perp in the examination room and gotten all the information he needed without even buying the guy a Subway sandwich. No further questions, we got everything we need, lock this scumbag up. "Are you done?" Flynn said, and Mitch put his hands up, like it wasn't his fault, he didn't do nothin'. "Because we have something to tell you guys," Flynn said. And that's when he said it, and man did that shut my Mitch up. And Mom, she sat there with her mouth open and her eyes welling up. Me, I looked at Famous Author but she was doing her best Mona Lisa impression. I knew I promised my baby bro I was going to be nice, but that did it for me.

"You have any idea what you're doing?" I said. I may or may not have poked Famous Author in her chest. "You're separating this man from his children. From his family."

"*I'm* not doing anything," she said.

Then Flynn dropped Bomb Number Two. "We're pregnant," he said. "I mean, you know, she's—." And she looked at him like *we agreed you weren't going to say anything about that*. Mom let out a groan like she'd been stabbed in the gut and her innards were coming out. Me and Mitch, we were too stunned to speak. I don't know if you can tell but I am not one who is typically at a loss for words, but there I was, I couldn't speak. I literally had no words. Then Mitch sat back and blew out his cheeks, like *game over*. Like the perp they just booked had killed himself in his cell. That actually happened once.

"*How!*" I blurted out, but then I felt like an idiot. "Never mind," I said.

The waitress came by again—by the way, she was wearing a tux, and she was super hot, and yes, I saw that, in spite of the situation, my Mitch managed to give her the once-over, twice—but she pulled another U-ee and went right back to the bar.

"You shouldn't be flying in your condition," I said to Famous Author. I don't know why I said that. But she just waved her hand, like it's no big deal to fly when you're pregnant. "How many months?" I asked, thinking, like I said, about five, but she held up two fingers. What? If she looked like this now, what kind of whale was she gonna resemble when she was ready to burst? Humped-back?

"Don't do this, Flynnie," I said to my baby brother. But I could see that my baby brother wasn't my baby brother anymore.

"His name is Flynn," Famous Author told me, and that's when I almost jumped her. I swear to God, I almost jumped her and gouged her eyes out with my fingernails. I didn't even feel Mitch's grip on my arm until afterwards. It left a mark.

"I *am* doing it," "Flynn" said, looking me right in the eye, like *I'm not afraid of you anymore*, but I could tell he was. "At the end of the semester," he said. He looked around. "And I really would love some *support from my family*." But when nobody said nothing, he looked at Famous Author and held his hands out like this. "I'm sorry," he said to her. Then he looked at us. "We're leaving," he said. And they got up to leave. And the waitress came by again.

"Are they leaving?" she said as they were leaving.

"They're leaving," Mitch said. Mom put her head down and folded her hands like she was praying. Then Mitch told the waitress we were leaving too, we wouldn't be needing the table after all, thank you very much he said while checking her out again, and we all got up, kind of like zombies, and we left.

The *agita*!

Out in the parking lot, Mitch took the keys from me—I was too shaken up to drive, you know?—and he drove us down Mamaroneck Avenue to Walter's for some hot dogs.

"We've lost our golden boy," Mom said, dramatic as usual. She was in the passenger seat, of course. I was in the back.

I patted her on the shoulder. "It'll be okay," I said. "He'll come to his senses. I'll talk to him." But I knew she was right. We all knew.

What a dumb-ass, right? He always was a dumb-ass. Stupid little shit. He was like this as a kid. A dreamer. He used to just sit and read for hours. "Our Little Professor," Pop used to call him. But you know the problem with books? They're not real life, that's the problem. They're not real life.

December 24, 2009

Dear Nathan,

I am writing to you because I have been unable to see you or talk to you on the phone, even though I have tried many times. ~~Your mother is angry with me. I want you to understand that she is~~ You are such a good boy and I am so proud of you. You have been very ~~patient~~ good during this hard time. I am sure you miss me and I hope you know I miss you and Janey too, so much that my heart hurts~~, and I have been crying at night abou.~~

The reason why I have been trying ~~so desperately~~ to see you and talk to you is that I want to tell you I have to go away ~~for a while~~. I am sure you and your sister will be very sad about this, and I feel terrible about it, but I have to do this. ~~I made a mistake and I have to make things right.~~ I will still try to see you and I will still try to call you but so far that has not been working ~~because your mom is still very mad at me.~~ ~~Eventually~~ Soon I hope ~~she will no longer~~ everything will be more normal and we will be able to talk on the phone and there is also a way we can talk on the computer and see each other's faces like on TV. ~~It may be helpful if you tell your mom you miss me and want to talk to me.~~

I hope you get this letter. I am giving it to Vanessa's mom, and I am giving her your Christmas presents too, so she can give them to you next time she sees you. ~~I was supposed to be with you toni Here I am on your porch and~~

~~I was hoping to spend~~
~~We were supposed to go to Grandma's~~

I love you and Janey so much. I will always be your dad and I will always love you. You are both so beautiful.

Love forever,
Dad

COLORADO

WRESTLING APOLLO

IT WAS BECOMING INCREASINGLY CLEAR TO FLYNN THAT HE WAS LOST. DEEPLY, perhaps irretrievably, lost. In the desert. And on horseback, no less.

He was doing his best not to panic, but the sun was descending towards the horizon and he and Casey, his new girlfriend, were somewhere near the Utah/Colorado border. When they first started riding, Flynn had been awed by the landscape, the pale rusts and yellows, a sky bluer than he'd ever thought possible. *Nathan would love it here*, he thought; it looked like the landscape from one of his son's dinosaur books. But now it seemed dauntingly barren, like the surface of Mars. He thought of a novel that ended with the main character handcuffed to the man he had just killed, with no water left in the canteen, surrounded by a vast desert like this one.

Casey had led them into this predicament—or at least that was his view of things. His tendency was to allow himself to be manipulated into bad situations, feel sorry for himself, and blame others for it. When they had pulled up to the Desert Spring Ranch and saw the note—"Back soon, feel free to go for a ride"—Casey had immediately gone to the stables, pulled down two saddles, and told Flynn (who reminded her they didn't even know these people, and by the way he had never been on a horse in his life) that things were different out here, more hospitable and less formal, and as for riding, there was really nothing to it; with his long legs and athleticism, he'd be a natural. So now that they had gone out too far and lost their way, Flynn fully expected her to be the one to get them back. She was, after all, a former wilderness guide, whereas he had no idea where they were; it was all he could do just to stay on the damn horse. It pitched into and out of gaits, and had twice tried to buck him off, but Flynn had held onto the saddlehorn for dear life, yelling out

"Whoa!" to no effect whatsoever.

Casey, on the other hand, sat in the saddle as if it were an extension of her sacrum. "You okay?" she asked. They had just given up looking for the animal trail they'd more or less followed on their way out (the patches of snow, the long stretches of smooth rock, and the change in lighting had made it impossible to find as they backtracked), and Casey had suggested they head back "in the general direction" of the guest ranch; but it was hard to determine what that general direction might be.

"Doing fine," Flynn said, as he leaned over to pat the horse's sweaty neck. He knew Casey had counted on a brisk ride so as to make it back before dark, but the unexpected extent of his incompetence, and the "orneriness" of his horse, had slowed their progress.

"Except for the whole being lost thing," he added. He was wearing his Mets cap, a pair of old jeans, a fleece Casey had bought him at a little shop in New Mexico, and new hiking boots that kept getting caught in the stirrups. Casey wore ostrich-skin boots, an old suede coat, and a dirty cowboy hat, all the same color as the sandstone around her, the same color as her hair as well, the ends of which hid part of her mouth when she smiled. She was a bestselling author, known for her depictions of Western women, Western men, and Western landscapes. Flynn was—or until two weeks ago used to be—a professor of Literature at Fairfield University in Connecticut. They had met on campus when she had given a reading from her new essay collection, *Like Walking on a Glacier*. She had stood straight and strong at the podium, her hands fluttering the air like she was shooing away butterflies. During the signing afterwards, Flynn, who had been separated from his wife for a year and a half, waited until the last book was autographed before approaching her, and the ensuing conversation, followed by a pleasant stroll around campus, had led to a tryst at her hotel. A month later he flew out to visit her at her ranch in Sanctuary, Colorado, where he gazed at the Continental Divide and felt his chest expand. The trip back to New York saw a return of his migraines, renewed legal negotiations, and futile waits in parking lots on the days he was scheduled to have the kids. So when Casey told him she was pregnant, Flynn—after first asking how on earth that could have happened, given their precautions—knew what he needed to do. At the end of the fall semester, on the cusp of being awarded tenure, he quit his job, packed up his Accord, and drove across the country to set things right. When he arrived in Sanctuary, he got out of his car, took in the big blue sky, the grove of aspens, and the horses out grazing in the hundred acres of high grass that abutted the base of the Divide. Casey came out of her log cabin with uplifted chin, a big smile, and outstretched arms, and told him that by way of welcoming him to his new life, she had planned out a week-long tour of the Wild West: it would begin in Santa Fe and end in eastern Utah, at this place called the Desert Spring Ranch.

Which was somewhere "back that way," Casey said, as they slowed their horses to get their bearings. They were approaching the edge of the mesa, at least a thousand feet up, so Flynn held back as Casey walked her horse right to the cliff. "There's the Green," she said, pointing to a snake-shaped impression in the land far below. Casey's skin was cast in an orange glow, and she sat in the saddle with her belly pooched, a Buddhist cowgirl. She pointed to some distant peaks. "Between us and those mountains," she said, "maybe thirty or forty miles, not a single house or road. No tents, no campsites, not even a line camp."

Flynn nodded, even though he had no idea what a line camp was, or how it was that any human could see for forty miles. He was tired of asking questions that made him feel like an idiot. He needed to fit in here; he needed this to work. He had left New York to an eruption of disgust and confusion—from his colleagues, his students, his family, and of course, his wife. He was being impulsive and irresponsible, everyone said. He was abandoning his children, and it was useless for him to explain that his wife had already alienated him from them, hiding them at her sister's or taking them out of school early when it was his day to be with them, shutting off the ringer to the landline so he couldn't even call to say goodnight. It's not as if Colorado offered any form of redemption—it had all metastasized quite beyond that—but he had cut so many ties, had offended so many people, and had heard all who were dear to him say that Casey was totally wrong for him, that at the very least he needed to prove, if only to himself, that moving here hadn't been a huge mistake.

When Casey turned and moved her horse into a trot, Flynn gave his horse a polite kick, but nothing happened. "Kick him like you mean it," Casey called back, so he heeled the horse again, harder, and then again, worried he would injure the animal, until finally it snorted and lurched into its new gait.

As Flynn bounced along behind Casey, the last red slice of sun disappeared beneath the horizon and the mountain peaks slowly dropped to black, while the sky silhouetting them remained a clear and radiant blue. This had become Flynn's favorite time of day, but now he dreaded it, since it signaled the onset of a long night: fifteen hours of darkness and high-altitude cold. It had warmed up to around seventy that afternoon, but Flynn knew it was capable of dropping to below zero overnight.

The bottom half of Orion had appeared, the rest of it hidden by clouds. But with no moon, and their headlamps stashed in Casey's Forerunner back at the ranch, they soon wouldn't be able to see. They looked for any sign of lamplight, sniffed the air for smoke. The yips and howls of coyotes cascaded from all directions.

Casey stopped her horse, dismounted, and nodded her heard towards Orion. "That's south," she said, then pointed to her right. "So we need to head this way." She patted her horse's flank. "These guys gotta be hungry. If we let them go they'll probably head home, and we can follow them on foot."

This made no sense to Flynn. Horses were like homing pigeons? And even so, wouldn't they gallop faster than he and Casey could run? How would the owners of the ranch feel, having a couple of tourists lose their valuable horses?

"If I thought there was any chance you could stay on your horse," Casey said, "I'd say we loosen the reins, kick 'em hard, and we'd race right home." She shrugged. "But I don't want to risk that. That's how people die."

Flynn wanted to say he could do it. He could tighten his thighs, lean forward, and stay on his horse as it galloped home. But they both knew otherwise.

Casey held the reins as Flynn dismounted, then handed him the reins of both horses as she removed their headstalls and pulled out an old blanket that was tucked under her saddle. "Okay, let's head home now," she said, and slapped her horse on the flank. Flynn, taking her cue, let go of the reins and smacked his horse as well, hard, the way a man was supposed to smack a horse. "What are you doing?" Casey cried out as his horse stepped away, skittishly at first, and then both horses burst into a single-minded gallop in the general direction of where the sun had set. Casey and Flynn hurried after them, but the horses went too fast and were quickly out of sight, the tromping of their hooves fading back into the vast and chilling silence.

Flynn and Casey slowed, gasping for breath, then gave up. Before coming to the West, Flynn had never known how the altitude could grip your chest, tighten your head, seize your lungs. Casey had her hands on her hips, her chest heaving. *Now what?* he wanted to say. All week, she had been completely in charge: she had brought all the gear, taught Flynn how to set up a tent, shown him how to make a fire, supplied and cooked their meals, demonstrated what to do if they saw a bear or mountain lion, shown him how to put a saddle on a horse, and taught him how to ride the horse. But now? He had arrived in Colorado only a week ago, and already he felt more like a burden than a boyfriend.

Casey, still panting, asked why he had done that; she meant for them to hold their horses by the reins as they walked alongside them.

"Fuck, I'm sorry," Flynn said.

She shook her head as she opened her water bottle, told Flynn to take a sip, and drank a little herself. Flynn understood they were rationing now, something people did in movies when they were hopelessly lost. "We'll be fine," she said. "Let me think."

He looked up to the sky, hoping for some moonlight, even a sliver, but they had seen the last of it while camping the night before, the slimmest of crescents. And since half the sky was overcast, they weren't getting much starlight, either.

They kept walking in the direction the horses had gone, stepping around sage brush. As they walked up and down inclines of rock, Flynn kept apologizing for his boneheaded move. Then he felt Casey's hand on his—at first a touch, then a clasp. "Don't worry," she said. "We have our coats. We have a blanket"—she held it up—"we have each other. Each other's bodies. And it sure is gorgeous out here, isn't it?"

Which probably meant they were going to die. Flynn pictured it: the discovery of his skeleton in the clutches of another, his flesh picked off first by coyotes, then by turkey vultures. His children would hear about it and shake their heads: *What was Daddy doing in the middle of the desert with a strange woman?*

They walked in silence, Flynn's eyes adjusting, until it was so dark he couldn't see anymore, no matter how wide he made his eyes, how intently he peered. It was completely different, the desert, than he had imagined. In the daylight there was more color, more life, with yellow and rust-colored rock instead of sand, vegetation somehow growing from the dry, rocky surface. But at nightfall, bitter cold—and starker, more austere.

They heard the coyotes again, madly yipping, and Casey stopped walking. "I was hoping we'd see house lights by now," she said. "If we're too far off, we could bypass the ranch entirely." Flynn stopped with her, even though he felt they should keep walking—even in the dark, if only to keep their blood circulating, or in case the caretakers of the ranch came looking for them. Hey, why hadn't they hollered out for help?

He inhaled and belted out a yell—then another, as loud as he could muster. *Help! Hooooh!* He stood waiting, holding his breath, as he felt Casey staring at him.

When nothing—no sound at all—came back, he turned his attention to Casey's plan, which was, apparently, to sleep in the desert. They had done so every night of their trip (in the Four Corners area, in Bryce Canyon after traveling through Monument Valley)—only now they wouldn't be in an insulated sleeping bag inside a tent but out in the elements, exposed and vulnerable. He had never been in any situation, ever, even close to this—in so vast a land, so steeped in it as to be undetectable, a six-foot pole of flesh and bone in the chilling blackness of nowhere. He tried to work up an appropriate amount of terror, but there was also something else going on. *Dear god, she's right: what a big amazing land this is.* Here he was, thirty-six years old, and he'd never known.

Casey was pulling at brush, breaking off branches or tugging them out by their roots, and Flynn understood they would somehow be using these for warmth, so he got down on his knees, groping in the dark and yanking out brush with her, until they had formed a large mound. Then they came together, smelling of sweat and sage and juniper. He could see starlight reflected in her enlarged pupils, like a miniature cosmos he could get lost in.

She told him to take off his coat, then began to unbutton his shirt.

"What are you doing?" he asked.

While camping, they had slept naked together in the sleeping bag, since according to Casey that was the best way to stay warm. And it had worked. But sleeping naked out in the open air? That was another story, especially with coyotes around. Casey explained that they needed to take off their clothes to let the aridity dry the sweat from them. "You don't want to sleep in sweaty clothes," she said. "That would be bad." She draped his shirt over a juniper bush. "Plus," she said, "you're wearing all cotton. Not good."

While their clothes were drying, she said, they should make love on the blanket, so the heat from their bodies would keep them warm.

Flynn began to protest, but what did he know? A New Yorker was going to tell a Western wilderness guide how to survive a frigid night in the desert?

He made sure his wallet, with photographs of his children inside, was deep in his coat pocket before taking it off; then he pulled off his pants. Once he was naked, but for his socks, he shivered at first, but he breathed deeply and told himself it was all in his mind. Someone had once told him he needed to change the way he thought, and here was his opportunity. This was a new life he was starting, and there was, clearly, a different way of being out here.

Casey laid out her clothes on nearby bushes and led him to the blanket. They clutched at each other right away, their noses and lips cold, their breath warm. As they embraced, Flynn closed his eyes, conscious of his breathing, and after a while, his trembling ceased. Casey had a large frame, her weight about equal to his: he was long and thin, while she had strong legs, full breasts, and a Buddha belly. With her mouth on his neck, her breasts pressing into his ribs, and her hands rubbing his skin, he quickly warmed. As he was breathing her in, and as she swung her leg over his hips, Flynn imagined he felt the heat from their pulsing baby, the tiny homunculus giving him life.

Afterwards Flynn, still in the wool socks Casey had bought him, went off to urinate, as Casey pulled on her clothing, now dry. She had been easy with him on their rocky bed, tender even—"We can't sweat during this," she'd said—and the whole thing was forcing Flynn to reconsider her. She was forthright and headstrong, that was true; and that drew him to her. But there was also something fragile about her, something that yearned for whatever it was he had to offer, whatever it was she saw in him that he didn't see in himself. He was surprised he had anything a woman like her would want, but whatever it was, he would surely give it to her.

He put on his clothes, which had indeed dried out. There was no longer even a hint of warmth in the air. Casey called out, telling him she had separated the brush into two piles, was lying down between them, and he should hurry. He found her by crawling forward and clasping her socked foot. She told him they needed to stuff their shirts with sage and juniper twigs, cover their torsos with their coats, lay the horse blanket over their legs and feet, and sleep with their hats on. After they did that, they piled the rest of the brush on top of their bodies, entombing themselves. They were poked and scratched, but as they held each other, their breath warm, Flynn breathed in the scent of horse sweat and pine, knowing he wouldn't be cold for much longer.

"You're good at this," he said.

He felt Casey nod.

When he woke up, the hairs of his nostrils were frozen, but the rest of him was warm. He was alive. And something tiny was crawling across his belly.

He wiggled his fingers and toes: no frostbite.

A few years earlier, he had immersed himself in Walden Pond at twilight, swimming naked in the frigid water, feeling lightheaded and delirious before he came back up from its depths, blinked his eyes, and realized he was losing sensation in his legs. After he swam hard to the shore, he jumped around, massaged his toes, rubbed himself down with his shirt, pants, and some napkins from his lunch bag, then put his wet clothes on and half-walked, half-ran the mile or so back to his hotel, where he took a hot shower.

There are so many different ways to die, he thought now.

Casey was breathing soundly in his arms.

And so many different ways to live.

The landscape was tinted with something, a glint of light, and at first he thought the moon had come out, but then he remembered there was no moon. It must be the sun, he guessed, still an hour or so from its rising, giving off a glow from where it had already risen over the plains of Nebraska and was poised to climb the eastern slope of the Rockies. He pictured the million or so citizens of Denver, awakening to the bright day.

He felt cold and hungry, and there was that insect on his belly, or maybe it was a lizard; but he lay still, listening and breathing, trying to remember what day it was.

Monday. Nathan and Janey would be going back to school—the end of their Christmas break.

He looked up at the now-clear, fathomless night sky. There were millions of stars, an unspeakable spectacle, and Flynn realized *they* were the source of the dim light, not the sun. It was probably only one or two a.m. He imagined his children sleeping in their beds—Nathan in the attic, which used to be Flynn's office, and Janey in Nathan's old room. Nathan would be on his side, curled up into himself, his face elf-like and fair; Janey would be on her stomach, her cheek flattened on the mattress, her pillows tumbled on the floor.

The house would be quiet. But soon, before the sun was up in White Plains, Rachel would awaken them and get them ready for school.

When Flynn awoke again, day was breaking; there was a distinct glow from the east. His mouth tasted bitter and pasty, as if he had swallowed something, leaf or bug. He swept aside some of the brush, rolled over, and spit. Casey stirred and reached for him.

"We did it," she said.

They held each other for a while, then stretched off their sleep and kicked themselves out of their nest. They stood, stripped, and shook out their clothing. The cold was piercing, but the sky was still clear and the sun would soon warm them. And they were alive.

Flynn's stomach rumbled. "I'm hungry," he called out. "Let's shoot a rabbit and make a fire."

IN THE SHARP LIGHT OF DAWN, EVERYTHING WAS CLEARER. IF THEY FOLLOWED the edge of the mesa, Casey said, eventually they would have to meet up with the road they came in on. So they walked. Flynn carried the rolled-up blanket with the headstalls wrapped inside. His legs were stiff at first, from the hard ground and from riding, but he soon found himself moving more and more freely. As the sun continued its ascent, they talked as if they were on an excursion, the kind of pleasure hike they'd been taking every day. Flynn brought up his need to get a job when they got back to Sanctuary, apologizing for being so broke, and Casey told him about a nice couple that owned the only hotel in town; he could wait tables for them if he wanted. "We'll be okay," she said, and Flynn understood that this meant she had enough money for both of them. He told her more about his financial difficulties and missteps, keeping it general, as well as how Rachel had been preventing him from seeing the kids ever since he had filed for divorce, and about his lawyer's refusal to do any more work on Flynn's behalf until his back fees were paid. When he finished, Casey kept walking for a while, watching her feet. Then she said, "You need to stop engaging with all of them. You're just giving them more power."

"All of them?"

Casey nodded. "All of them."

They walked along the ridge of the mesa. The sun began to warm the back of Flynn's neck. He had been thinking that what he needed to do was not to disengage but to redouble his efforts, be more forthright and aggressive, especially about seeing his kids. He'd been passive his whole life. And to disengage now might mean losing them forever. He clutched the rolled-up blanket, watching Casey's confident walk from his position a half-step behind her.

Just then, she lifted her nose. "Smoke," she said.

As they approached the ranch, a lean black dog sprinted out toward them and jumped onto Flynn, paws on shoulders, nose to nose, its teeth wet and gleaming. Doberman. He drooled on Flynn's shoulder while humping his hip, then growled and nipped at Flynn's wrist when he tried to push him away. "Jesus!"

"Zeus!" a man barked out. He came charging up to the dog and smacked it across the nose. The dog yelped and trotted off a few paces. "If he does anything like that again," the man said to Flynn, "that's what you gotta do. Show him who's boss." He was a thin, slouched man, a little younger than Flynn, with tamped-down hair the color of cedar. He clutched a paintbrush in one hand and held out the other for a shake. "I'm Daniel," he said. "You must be Flynn and Casey." He looked back and forth between the two of them. "We weren't sure which was the guy and which was the gal."

"Well I'm the guy," Flynn said while looking at Casey, who loved dogs more than she loved people. As a girl she had a black Lab that slept in her bed, protecting her from her abusive father, and she always joked that she preferred sleeping with dogs to sleeping with men. "This is Casey," he said as he spotted the two horses out in the pasture, chewing grass, as if nothing had ever happened.

Casey lifted her chin as a kind of greeting. Daniel looked around. "Where's your gear?"

Flynn pointed to Casey's Forerunner, and Daniel gave a low whistle. "You slept out in that cold?" he said. "We figured you brought your tent with you, forgot to tie up the horses, and they ran off on ya."

Casey tilted her head toward Flynn. "He doesn't ride," she said. "And we were out pretty far." She shrugged a shoulder. "We were fine."

No, we were not fine, Flynn wanted to say. *We were lost.*

After they got their duffle bags from the Forerunner, they walked past the sign that Daniel had been painting when they arrived—*Welcome to the Desert Spring Ranc*, it said. Inside, they were greeted by a young woman with a baby slung in one arm and a box of kitchen matches in her free hand. She looked as if she had just lost something critical.

"When the horses came back without you . . ." She smiled nervously at Daniel, then at the cowering but unrepentant Doberman by his side. "We're so glad you're okay." Her voice reminded Flynn of a gurgling creek. She took out a Pyrex dish of enchiladas from the refrigerator and set them on the counter, then turned on the gas to the oven. "I'm Delia," she said. "I'll show you . . ." She struck a match, opened the oven door, and stooped to light the pilot, and as she did, the baby's face dipped close to the puff of blue flame.

While the enchiladas baked, Delia gave them a quick tour of the house, stopping in the small middle room between the kitchen in front and a living room, which doubled as guest quarters, in back. There were just three things in the middle room: a yellow loveseat, an end table cut in the shape of a heart (with a photograph of Daniel, a pregnant Delia, and a red-haired man), and, in the corner, a fat, mop-haired, bloody-eyed, malodorous white dog. The dog growled as they entered, growled when Flynn stood too close to Delia, growled when Zeus came into the room, and growled when the baby reached down from Delia's arms in an attempt to pet it. A wet, gravelly growl.

After they wolfed down their enchiladas and drank some instant coffee, Flynn and Casey went into the guest room to take a nap. The room had a large fireplace, a back door leading outside to a wood-heated hot tub, a folded-out sofa that would serve as their bed, a small television, and a DVD player. Flynn couldn't fathom how everything in the house ran on propane. Delia ushered them in and said she'd leave them alone until dinner was ready. "After all, this is your honeymoon, right?" She winked, smiled at her baby, and then winced as she hustled into the kitchen.

Casey and Flynn sat on the bed and took off their boots. "I told them that so we'd get the discount," Casey whispered. She shrugged and gave him her cute look. "But hey, you never know, right?" Flynn smiled, not knowing at first what she meant. They had yet to broach the topic of marriage. They had known each other for only five months, and Flynn had figured they were on the same page, taking it slow, given his still-legally-married status—until she had announced she was pregnant. Now, he wasn't sure what was expected of him. According to his lawyer, his divorce was "still weeks, if not months" from being resolved, "especially given the payment issue."

Casey stood, pulled off her shirt, and shook out her hair. "I am not having this baby out of wedlock, Flynn. That's not how I do things."

Flynn leaned toward her sympathetically and put his hand on her abdomen, but felt nothing—no heat. "I'm working on it," he said, while calculating how much he had in his checking account, how many more months before she gave birth, what an engagement ring would cost, and how much he owed his lawyer.

Casey bent her head as she tugged off her jeans. "If you really wanted to be divorced," she said, "then you'd be divorced by now."

As she headed off to take a shower, Flynn stared at her back, then stood up and unpacked his duffel bag. All his clothes smelled like dust and sweaty socks. In the inside pocket of the bag were a few things he'd been taking out whenever he'd had moments to himself: a picture of Nathan and Janey in their Halloween costumes (his son a cowboy, his daughter Pocahontas), a "prescription" Nathan had written him while pretending he was a doctor (*"Go owtsid and play mor"*), and the stem from a pumpkin he had carved for Janey back in October.

He had taken her to Roosevelt State Park, where the trees were spectacular, stopping first at a local farm to buy a small pumpkin. He held his daughter's hand and walked through the woods, then swung her onto his shoulders, as she told him in her three-year-old babble about all the events he had missed: their new cat Blackie, the man from the gas station who came to the house with flowers, the time the lights went out and they all read stories with flashlights. Flynn, who had spent the half-hour drive regretting that Nathan, who had the flu, couldn't come along, found himself entranced with his daughter's voice and enjoying her company. When they got back to the car, he took out the pumpkin, handed Janey a pen, and she drew a weird, crooked face on it. That's when Flynn realized he forgot to bring a knife, so he took the longest key from his keychain—the one to his office at Fairfield—and hacked at the pumpkin with it, trying to follow her design, and when he was done, having sweat through his shirt and bloodied his fingers, Janey beamed, declared it a "cuckoo crazy" pumpkin, and said she'd put it on the front porch when she got home.

Now, Flynn clutched the pumpkin stem, picturing his daughter's eyes. Was it possible to fall head over heels in love with his child, with both his children, to love them more than he had ever loved any woman? Was it possible to miss them with the kind of longing, the kind of desperation, he had only before read about in books?

He would never, ever stop engaging with them.

FLYNN AND CASEY WOKE UP TO A SHARP KNOCK ON THE DOOR. A MAN WALKED in—the redhead from the photograph. "Well, if it isn't our two Survivor contestants," he said, tipping his cowboy hat to Casey. "Rough night out there? It likely dropped below zero just before dawn." He stood iron-straight in tight Wranglers, cowboy boots, and a pressed denim shirt.

"It was fine," Flynn said. He sat up and wiped his mouth, embarrassed to be caught sleeping during the day.

The man strode over to the television, heels thumping on the old wood-plank floor. He held up a DVD. "Went to Junction yesterday," he said. "Stopped at the Walmart and picked up *Star Wars*, the original. Three ninety nine! We're fixin' to watch it after dinner." He picked up the television as if it were a rodeo calf. "Seen it probbly a dozen times," he said with a crooked smile. "Care to join us?"

Flynn nodded, then shook his head.

"And you are . . .?" Casey said. She sat up, her flannel shirt unbuttoned.

"Oh, Delia didn't mention me?" He half-turned and spit into the ash can by the fireplace. "I'm Butch," he said. He tipped his hat again to Casey, and walked out.

"You certainly are," Casey said to the closed door. She turned to Flynn. "So he's the brother?" she said.

Flynn dug through his duffel bag and found a cleanish shirt. "Could be the husband."

"No," Casey said. "Daniel's the husband. I can tell by the way Delia acts around him." She got up and pulled on her jeans.

"Something's off about *her*," Flynn said, finding the pair of cordu-roys he had worn in New Mexico. His jeans smelled too strongly of horse sweat.

"Oh, *her* I get," Casey said, buttoning her flannel shirt. "I've *been* her."

"I mean physically," Flynn said as he slid on the corduroys. "And she doesn't finish . . ."

"It's all connected," Casey said.

Delia herself came in then with a rap on the door, still holding the baby. "I'm sorry," she said. "I didn't want to disturb your nap earlier, but . . ." She pointed to the trunk at the foot of their bed. "Etta needs . . ." She held the baby with her arms straight out so Etta was facing them. "Isn't she . . . ?"

Flynn nodded. "Adorable?" he said. In truth, the baby looked like a bridge troll. But when Janey was a baby she had looked like that, chubby and complacent, with scattered hair, and she was turning out to be a beauty. As Delia bent over to open the trunk, which was stuffed with baby toys, Etta reached down for a rubber teething pretzel, her head swinging near the corner of the bed frame.

"So you like it?" Delia asked them, smiling with her lips pressed together. "We're so happy here, we're so . . ." She nodded, a lock of her hair floating over her nose.

Flynn nodded with her. "Content?" he said. "It is a great place."

Delia's eyes darted to the ceiling, to the door, and back to Flynn and Casey. "It's *sacred* is what it is, it's . . ." She set down the baby, and Etta tottered out into the middle room.

"At one time, maybe," Casey said. She had a strong, nasal voice that sometimes surprised people. "A long way back."

Delia nodded. "Lots of history," she said. "Butch and Sundance, Billy the Kid . . ." She pointed to the shelves behind the television stand. "There's books about it," she said. "Built more'n a hundred years ago. Used to be where horse thieves and cattle rustlers hid out. Part of the True West," she said, then sighed. "I'm just a little . . ."

From outside the door, the white dog, whose name was Apollo, snarled, a sound more sinister than the growling they'd already heard. Delia rushed out, and Flynn got up in time to see her scoop up her daughter, who had been pulling the old dog's hair. Apollo's bloody eyes were trained on Etta's throat.

"Dinner!" Delia called back over her shoulder.

BEFORE DRIVING OUT TO THE DESERT SPRING RANCH, CASEY AND FLYNN HAD stayed at a motel in Moab with wi-fi, the only internet access they'd had for the week. While Casey had taken a bath, Flynn had pulled out his laptop and found 294 new emails in his Inbox: friends at work, wondering why he had quit in the middle of the school year; a student, Audrey, sending him a link to the front-page article she had written for the Fairfield Mirror ("The Hawk Flies the Coop"); another student, Wanda, writing from Europe, saying she hoped it was "true love, and not escapism" that had triggered the abrupt move she had just heard about; his son's third-grade teacher, filling him in on Nathan's troubling behavior at school; his lawyer, insisting he be present for a court hearing in White Plains on January 12th; his friend Peter, begging him to call; and Rachel, detailing the many ways in which he was a terrible father and reprehensible human being.

And one from his sister. In it, she outlined how poorly Flynn was behaving: nobody should quit a good job in this economy; nobody should move so far from his family, especially with a mother as frail as theirs was; no father should ever leave his children; no sensible person should move to the Rocky Mountains, where there were no real job opportunities (that according to Mitch, her husband). Then, at the end: *It's not so much what you're doing that's wrong, Flynnie. It's how you're doing it.*

It might as well have been their father, writing from the grave.

AFTER DINNER (PRE-COOKED PULLED PORK, CREAMED CORN FROM A CAN, AND scalloped potatoes), Butch wiped his mouth and dropped his napkin onto his plate. "Delia darlin', that was delicious." Flynn looked at Casey as if she were wrong about which man was the husband, but Casey only looked amused. "What do you think, cowboy?" Butch asked Flynn. "Don't get too many meals like this where you're from, do ya?"

Flynn shook his head, looking at the empty box of scalloped-potato mix. "Sure don't," he said.

Delia released Etta from her high chair as Butch got up to collect the dirty dishes. As he began to wash them, Casey and Daniel started a conversation about dogs—Casey on the attributes of Labradors, Daniel on the Dobermans his friend was breeding—and as Daniel started telling a story about the death of his boyhood pooch, Butch dropped a dish into the sink with a clatter. As Daniel spoke more quickly—"As you can imagine," he said, lowering his voice and nodding towards Butch, "my little brother was devastated"—Butch pressed his hands to his temples, and Casey shot an alarmed glance at Flynn.

"That was one well-trained dog," Daniel said, shaking his head. "Our old man sure knew what he was doing. Like I was telling your husband here, you can turn even the meanest dog into a docile one if you know how to handle 'em." He glanced up at Butch, who had turned to face the table, still pressing into his temples. "I've almost broken Zeus," Daniel said, pointing to the black dog at his feet, "just like I did Apollo."

Delia jumped up to close a cabinet door Etta had opened, and on her way back, she squeezed Daniel's shoulder, and when Daniel patted her bottom Butch seemed to press even harder, a vein in his forehead bulging. He wheezed with his teeth closed as if clamped in a self-made, ever-tightening vice. "Always with the touching!" he hissed.

Daniel scratched Zeus's head and continued as if Butch hadn't spoken. "Yep, he was ornery, that one," he said, nodding toward the white dog in the middle room. "Then one day we had it out." He started to pound his fist on the table, but it landed softly, like a regret. "D'ja ever see *The Quiet Man?*" he asked Flynn, and Flynn nodded; it had been a favorite of his father's. "It was like that," Daniel said. "Me and Apollo, rasslin' on the floor. A regular barroom brawl." He mimed the fight, pretending to wrestle the powerful beast. He rolled up his sleeve to show Casey the scar on his arm where Apollo had bitten him, and Casey stared at him. "After that, as you can see, no more problems."

They all looked through the doorway to the middle room where Apollo hulked in the corner, wheezing like a lion that had gone too long between kills.

AFTER DESSERT—ICE CREAM SANDWICHES AND INSTANT COFFEE—DANIEL told Casey and Flynn how they had come to be caretakers of the place. Delia's uncle, the owner, had grown too old for the upkeep and was moving to Grand Junction, and they had just gotten married and needed a place to live; so they agreed to take up residency in exchange for managing the property. They had asked Butch to move in too, at least for the first few months, because he knew so much about horses and was handy with home repairs; had Flynn and Casey noticed the new roof?

"We've got big plans," Daniel said, and Delia smiled, taking his hand.

Butch was back in his seat, having calmed down during dessert. "Know what we're gonna do here, cowboy?" he said to Flynn. "We're gonna tap that spring out there, bottle the water, and sell it." He put a hand in the air, mimicking the label: "Desert Spring Water," he said.

Flynn frowned. "Don't you need, like, a bottling plant, permits and loans, that kind of thing? That seems like a big undertaking."

"Permits and loans," Butch said, folding his arms. "You're from New York, right?" he said, pronouncing "New York" as he would "Hades." "You have *no idea* how things are done out here." He took in Flynn's maroon shirt and long hair. "Look at you," he said. "You'd never make it out here."

"Easy, brother," Daniel said.

Flynn started to tuck his hair behind his ears, then stopped. "I don't know," he said, with a quick glance at Casey. "Maybe. I like it here. Well not *here*, exactly," he said. "But, you know." He pointed vaguely outside. "Here."

Butch's eyes darted around the room. "What's wrong with *here exactly*, cowboy?"

Daniel cleared his throat, got up, and gently took Etta from his wife's arms. "Movie time!" he said.

And that's when Flynn saw what was off about Delia, just as she handed her daughter to her husband. Her shoulders were turned perpetually inward. As if, when she was born, doctors had squeezed them into her chest and left them that way. As if they had forced everything in her that yearned outward back where it belonged.

IN THEIR GUEST ROOM, FLYNN STARTED A FIRE WHILE CASEY SCURRIED UNDER the covers, fully clothed. "You OK?" he asked her, after the flames flared up and caught the wood. He went over to the bed and leaned down for a kiss, but Casey kept her mouth closed. Her shirt smelled of old sweat.

"Do you get what's going on here?" she said, sitting up. "Did you see that guy having a seizure at the sink? How Daniel treats that poor dog? How *scared* that woman is?"

Flynn sat on the bed. *I'm not the one who picked this fucked-up place and took the honeymoon discount,* he almost said. "They're young," he said with a sigh, sounding to himself as if he were in his late fifties instead of his late thirties. "They're finding their way."

Casey craned her neck and shook out her hair with both hands. "This place is cursed," she said. "Bad things have happened here. I can feel it."

"Oh come on," Flynn said, with a bit of a laugh. He sensed the truth of what she was saying, but surely she could see she was being a little hysterical. What had happened to that calm, kindhearted woman he had slept with in the desert?

She pointed toward the door, her hair disheveled, like a witch. "He's *evil,*" she said, and Flynn sat quietly, unsure if she was referring to Butch, Daniel, or Apollo. He rubbed his thigh muscles, hardened and cramped. Casey kept untangling the ends of her hair.

"Case, I'm worried about the kids."

Her eyes softened. She had probably heard him sobbing in the middle of the night. She blew out a breath and put her head back on the pillow. "I think you have to get used to it," she said. "Rachel's going to marry her new boyfriend, and your kids, they're going to grow up with a different father. There's nothing you can do about that; it's just the way it is." She took Flynn's hand. "Especially Janey," she said. "Janey won't even remember you as her dad." She took his other hand and shook his arms a bit until he met her eyes.

"Hey sweetie," she said. "You need to do right by *us* now."

THE FLOOR OF THE WOOD-FIRED HOT TUB WAS SCALDING, TOO HOT FOR FLYNN to put his feet down, and the air was too cold to expose his wet torso—so he squatted on the bench, half-in, half-out, as Casey sat calmly, submerged to her shoulders, looking up at the night sky. Flynn cracked his neck and straightened his back, trying to relax, and when he did, he realized that his shoulders, too, were curled inwards.

Casey gave him a soft smile. "Maybe none of this is actually happening," she said. "Maybe we're characters in a Sam Shepard play."

Flynn pulled an icicle from the rim of the tub and pretended to stab her in the neck with it. She hunched her shoulders, gave him a quizzical look, then gently took the icicle from him and made it disappear in the hot water. Flynn looked out into the vast darkness, knowing the desert was out there, forty miles from here to the mountains, with nothing in between—not a house, not a road, not even . . .

He looked at Casey. "What's a line camp?"

Casey shifted her position and told Flynn it was a place, like a lean-to or shack, where cowboys stayed while herding cattle. Flynn imagined a scene from one of the Westerns his father used to watch: a bunch of cowboys sitting around a campfire, eating beans from a can.

"On their way to where?" he asked.

She shrugged. "To wherever they're going," she said.

She gathered her hair in a bun, her long neck illuminated by the starlight, and rested the back of her head on the rim of the tub, looking up. Flynn looked up with her. The sky was again spectacularly clear. They could see all seven stars of the Pleiades, and Casey pointed out Cassiopeia, the Gemini twins, four planets—Mercury, Mars, Venus, and Jupiter—and Cygnus swooping down the wide and milky Milky Way.

Casey pointed. "See that space there, between the first and second stars of the Dipper handle? They used to think there was nothing there. Then, you know the Hubble, the one in space? They pointed it there, right there, and they found galaxies, entire *galaxies* where there weren't any. Where they *thought* there weren't any."

Flynn took a deep breath. He was still thinking of what she had said inside, before announcing she needed to warm up and marching out to the hot tub, expecting him to follow. She could be right. Nathan, he was sure, would never call another man father for as long as he lived. But as for Janey, he had no idea. All their moments together at home—rocking her to sleep while singing "Janey Don't You Lose Heart"; putting her feet on his, holding her hands, and stepping around like a giant; waking up at two, four, and six a.m. to feed her and sing to her; asking "Janey, Janey, where are you?" when she played peek-a-boo—would be lost to her memory. She would grow up with her mother, brother, and stepfather, while receiving occasional visits from her biological dad, a tall man who carved pumpkins with keys and who lived far away with a strange woman and another child he probably preferred to her.

The baby. Flynn jolted upright and put his hand on the curve of Casey's belly, round and smooth under the water. "Whoa!" he said.

But Casey removed his hand and slid slightly away. "I'm not going to be like that," she said, and gave him a reassuring smile.

But Flynn was imagining the fetus boiling in her womb. "Come on," he said, grabbing her arm. "My god, this is stupid, it's wrong."

Casey's look turned cold. "I'll live the way I want," she said. "No baby is going to change that."

Are you kidding? Flynn thought. He lifted himself from the water and pulled her arm, about to insist on getting her out of the tub (*This baby's half-mine, god damn it!*) but that's when they heard a scream, loud and fierce, from inside the house. They both tensed, and when the second scream came, followed by the sound of the men shouting, they heaved themselves out of the tub and dashed barefooted through the snow to the back door, steam billowing from their skin.

Inside, Flynn, who had wrapped a towel around his waist, stumbled into the middle room behind Casey, who was stark naked, and saw that Apollo had Etta's shoulder in his jaw and was bearing down with a guttural snarl. Delia was the one screaming, clutching at her daughter's free arm as Butch, now in sweatpants and an untucked shirt, held an iron poker over his head and was about to slam it down on the dog when Casey yelled out "No!" Then Daniel grabbed the dog's snout and pried open his jaw, freeing Etta.

Casey pulled Delia, with Etta now in her arms, into the kitchen, and just then Butch stepped forward and slammed the poker down onto the dog's head with a sickening sound, triggering a child-like whimper and collapse from the beast. That's when the Doberman, Zeus, dashed in and leaped onto Butch, biting him in the hand until Butch threw him off, striking out with the poker until the dog yelped and whined with his head bent as he scurried back into the kitchen.

Butch dropped the poker and gripped the spot where Zeus had bitten him, which was crimson but not bleeding. "Delia darlin'! My hand!"

But Flynn could see Delia in the kitchen, her eyes wide and frightened as she set Etta on the counter and took off her daughter's pajama top as the child gulped in an endless, shocked breath, her skin chalky, blood bubbling up and now streaming down her arm. Casey, who was at the sink, told Daniel to hold Etta's shoulder under the water as she scrubbed the wound with soap, the child screaming now. Casey ordered Delia to get her a towel, and when Delia couldn't stop convulsively crying, Casey frantically looked through drawers, then ran to the bathroom to find one herself.

Flynn, still dripping wet, had picked up the poker, feeling its weight in his hand. Apollo was motionless on the floor, looking more like a giant stuffed animal than the beast who had attacked a child.

Butch was still gripping his hand where Zeus had bitten it. "My hand, Delia! It's broke!" He turned to Flynn, his face reddening, as Casey came running out of the bathroom with a clean towel, her breasts swaying. "Tell your wife to put on some damn clothes!"

Flynn lifted the poker, his muscles clenched. "She's not my wife," he said as he raised the poker higher, and Butch flinched, holding out his hands. Then Daniel screamed out that he couldn't find his keys and Casey rushed back into the middle room.

"Butch! Take them to the hospital, *now!*"

Butch straightened, sneered at Flynn, and hustled off to his bedroom.

Casey stared at Flynn, at the poker in his hand, at the dog lying listlessly in the corner. Butch came out of the bedroom with his keys in his hand, wild-eyed and red-faced. "Where . . ."

"Moab!" Casey yelled.

"I know where it is!" Daniel said.

"Go!" Casey yelled, and everyone trampled out. They heard the kitchen door open, then a yelp from Zeus, then the sound of the truck pulling away, kicking up gravel.

Flynn stood in the middle room, still holding the poker, still staring at the dog. For some strange reason, it reminded him of his mother—her mop of hair, the look of futility in her face. Why hadn't anyone seen this coming?

In their room, Casey had put her long underwear on and was stuffing clothes into her bag. She didn't look up when Flynn came in.

"We are *so* out of here," she said. She jabbed her finger toward the middle room, her body trembling, her hair tangled and wet. "What was *that* about?" she said, looking at the poker in his hand. "Who *are* you?"

Flynn stood over her, the poker cold and hard in his grip. He realized that she thought he was the one who had killed Apollo.

Casey pulled on her jeans and flannel shirt, zipped her bag, and stood, clutching its strap. "Are you going to pack," Casey snapped at him, "or do I have to do that for you too?" She hefted the bag onto her shoulder and stomped through the middle room and through the kitchen door.

Flynn followed, still in his towel, still carrying the poker. Everyone was right: this had been a huge mistake.

As he passed through the middle room he thought he saw a slight panting movement in the dog's ribs.

Outside, the cold air knifed into his skin, the gravel stabbed the bottoms of his feet, and he felt dizzy, short of breath, from the altitude. The stars were still a celestial spectacle. From the dark stables came a snort from one of the horses, and a frenzy of yips and yowls pierced the air, as if the coyotes were within striking distance now. From some dark corner Zeus emitted a low, menacing growl.

When Casey got to the Forerunner she turned to face him and he paused by the welcome sign. As if he had a choice. As if, were Casey to drive off without him, he wouldn't be lost in the desert. As if he would know exactly where to go, and what to do when he got there.

A GIRL'S GOTTA DO WHAT
A GIRL'S GOTTA DO

WELL, NOW HE'S GONE INSANE. OFF. HIS. ROCKER. SO I HAD TO PETITION for full custody, *and* to keep receiving the same child support, I don't care if he's unemployed, because what they don't know is that woman he's with is a bestselling author who makes a ton of money.

Soooo much has changed. Who knew my life would turn into this?

So this is what I want to say. Here it is. Before I go on and on, I'm just going to say this. This man, he's the love of my life. If you haven't had this feeling then you can't understand, and you shouldn't stand in judgment of me just because I'm about to file these petitions. If you don't know what it's like to have the love of your life look you in the eyes and say "I don't love you anymore and I'm not sure I ever did" then you *cannot* understand me. You. Can. Not.

Okay, now I'm going to cry.

We never had a chance. Not even when we were first married, living in that shithole. We didn't even have time for a honeymoon, we had to work. I mean, we did have a long weekend on Nantucket, that was nice, and we called it a honeymoon, but in retrospect it wasn't much of one. We rode bikes, we got completely roasted (I have fair skin, lots of freckles), we ate ice cream. Then three days of lying in bed sunburned and trying to kiss without hurting our faces. I still have this cute little ceramic lighthouse he bought me there. I love lighthouses!

Then Nathan was born, and everything changed. Not that it was Nathan's fault. God, no. We all know whose fault it was. Is.

It's been a year and a half since he up and left, but I don't think this feeling is ever going to go away.

I'll tell you this much: that man has some anger issues. He thinks I'm angry. He thinks I'm hysterical. Ha! I'd rather be the way I am than the way he is. The way I am, at least you know what you're getting. The way he is, watch out. You never see it coming.

Now you tell me which is more dangerous.

And now what's he done? Moving way the heck out to Colorado! My goodness.

What kind of father leaves his kids?

He's off in the mountains right now. God help me, I don't know where exactly but I don't want to know. It might as well be Siberia for all I care.

Just before he moved out, very sudden, he called to tell me what he was planning to do, and I slammed down the phone. I couldn't believe it. First the separation, then I was served with divorce papers (worst feeling in the world, by the way, I don't wish that on anybody), and now this. I didn't let him tell the kids; it would have been too painful for them. He tried for days, but I was like, no dice, mister. They would have been completely confused. You might as well say Daddy's going to Mars! This was in mid-December and he was supposed to see them on Christmas Eve, but I drove them up to Binghamton. I'll be damned if I was going to let him ruin their Christmas! Then he wrote them this pathetic letter and tried to get our neighbor to give it to them but she knew what to do. After that, after he left for Colorado, I took over operations. Sold the house in White Plains and bought a house in Binghamton, where they'd be safer, where I'd have my family to help me out. They're never going to see him again, no sir. Nobody's going to steal my kids from me, like that guy on TV. Did you hear about that? This guy, he took his kids to Florida, then he kept going and nobody knows where they are! That's why I had to petition for full custody. Somebody has to think of the children, am I right?

No offense but we're playing by my rules now.

SUNDAY MORNING AT
THE SILVERADO

CASEY'S HOME—AND MY NEW HOME, AT LEAST FOR THE TIME BEING—WAS A stone's throw from the Rio Grande, on the outskirts of Sanctuary, Colorado, an old silver-mining town. The town proper was only six blocks long and three blocks wide, so it was hard to believe that during the boom in the late 19th century as many as 10,000 people moved there, hastily erecting houses and shacks, at first all over town, then on the mountain slopes, then jammed into every available spot between dwellings, then even *over* the river (with floors made of slats stretched from bank to bank) when there was no more room left. Bat Masterson, Soapy Smith, "the dirty little coward who killed Jesse James"—at one time or another, they all made Sanctuary their home, living lawless lives at 9,000 feet. After the bust, everyone split, but two or three hundred stalwart souls kept it from becoming a ghost town, and that's still the case today.

The main street of Sanctuary was lined with establishments owned by folks who lived either right above them or close by: the True Value of Sanctuary hardware store, the Mane Event horsehair jewelry shop, the Big Bucking Deal saddlery, the Fat Brown Trout sporting goods store, the Eureka! silver gift shop (open only when its owner, Maybelle, was sober enough to stand), the Stumble Inn Motel and Bar, Sanctuary National Bank, no fewer than four art galleries, and the Silverado, my favorite place to get coffee.

It was early April the last time I went there, and it was cold that day, as in high-altitude cold, as in so cold my face hurt. Casey and I had more or less worked out our differences after the disastrous ending to our "Welcome to the Wild West" camping trip; or more accurately I had decided to keep my feelings to myself, just as I had in my marriage, and that had made for a more harmonious relationship. What was going on in the bedroom was a different story. In the three months since the camping trip we hadn't once made love, and when I pointed that out to her—more specifically, how we had rigorous and frequent sex when we had been visiting each other, but ever since I had moved out to Colorado we had done so only once, and that was for purely pragmatic reasons (to keep ourselves warm in the frigid desert)—she quietly explained that her therapist had advised her to abstain for a while, given that they were navigating the minefield of her father's abusive behavior when she was a child, and I immediately chastised myself for expressing my adolescent needs and decided to be a good supportive partner from then on and keep such lustful yearnings to myself.

In any case I had more or less settled into life on her gorgeous property, nestled in a curve of the Continental Divide, and since she had flown to England a week earlier to promote her latest book, I was on my own for a while, taking care of the horses and dogs while earning a little money waiting tables at the Sanctuary Hotel. My monthly income had dropped precipitously since leaving my teaching job back east, so I had recently petitioned the Broome County Child Support office in Binghamton (where Rachel had moved, to be closer to her family) to lower my support payments accordingly. This was bound to provoke anew the Wrath of Rachel, but what else could she do? She had already filed a petition to gain full custody soon after I had moved, and had spirited the children away "to an undisclosed location" when I had flown back for one of my scheduled visits.

And this far away, in such a secluded place, it hardly seemed to matter. Her anger, I mean. Her vitriol. Her vengeance.

The only vacant stool was the one closest to the door. Rosie, behind the counter as always, was wearing a John Deere hat and a white thermal shirt with an orange supermarket sticker on her left breast that said "Fresh." (Her second job was at the Mac's Groceries and Grub down the block, where residents shopped only out of desperation.) I hadn't seen her in weeks—everyone tends to hole up over the winter, according to Casey—and even though she gave me a nod and a howdy as she reached under the counter for a clean coffee mug, she seemed to avoid looking me in the eye.

When I moved to Sanctuary, Rosie had been the first to welcome me, shaking my hand as if she were the mayor. She had come by the ranch to check on her horse, which she paid Casey to keep in her stable. At first, she seemed surprised to see me there all alone (Casey had driven down to Santa Fe for a reading), but then she walked me out to the stables and showed me how to soothe Cielo, Casey's frisky Arabian, and how to administer a dietary supplement to her own horse, who was twenty-one years old. Rosie was lean and pretty, with starchy hair and tight jeans, and she looked right through me with her ice-blue eyes. The following weekend, when Casey was home, she and three other people (Maximilian Knox, an artist whose idea of fun was body-painting thong bikinis on livestock; Rosie's best friend Belinda, who brought her husband's skis for me to use, along with a six-pack of beer for the "after party"; and Eric Fretz, the only realtor in town) came by to cross-country ski across the hundred acres of Casey's property and then upslope to the top of the Divide. The landscape was an undulating blanket of white, and it didn't take me long to get the hang of skiing like that. Casey "broke trail" while Rosie lagged behind with me. She pointed out a bald eagle flying above us and showed me where to poke into the snow in order to find a glow of spectacular blue. We wound up on a ridge at 12,000 feet overlooking the valley, and when we looped back and skied downhill, I fell a few times, but Rosie again held back, offering encouragement, until I learned how to relax, bend my knees, and keep my balance. On my last downhill, the pine trees rushing past, I even tipped my head back and closed my eyes for a moment, feeling the sun on my neck and the crisp air on my face. "Atta boy!" Rosie shouted afterwards, and clapped me on the back.

Casey had kept an eye on me the whole time, in a somewhat proprietary way. In general, she seemed happy with how things had been going between us. She'd been wary but kind, and we had settled into what passed for domesticity in the midst of the uncertainty and disruption in my life along with the comings and goings of hers. As for me, I still had my doubts, especially after the recent stunt she had pulled in Alamosa;

but at the same time, I had fallen completely and utterly in love with Colorado. And maybe with Rosie. She had a big voice and a heart to match. She also had a boyfriend, and for that matter everyone knew I was Casey's latest, and in a town this small, there was just no getting around any of that.

Anyway, that day, the day of my last visit to the Silverado, I was in good spirits. My divorce had just been finalized (I had worked out a payment plan with my lawyer), and I hadn't even bothered to fly back to New York for the event. My lawyer was royally pissed about that (all I heard from him afterwards was a text: "Well, it's over"), and so apparently was the judge, but I didn't have enough money to go, and even if I did, I'd have used it to see my kids, not to feed Rachel's perpetual need for drama. (I heard she wore a pant suit with shoulder pads, and carried an attaché case into court.) Being in Sanctuary had shown me just how bad all that had been for me. I had changed so much since I'd moved. I had no desire to revert to the old Flynn, and that's what would have happened if I had flown back for the trial—or at least that's what Casey thought. Plus, I was starting to feel at home in Colorado. Even if it didn't work out with Casey, I thought, maybe I could still live there—if not in Sanctuary, then somewhere else, somewhere closer to an airport perhaps. It had been months since I'd seen the kids, and I'd been pining for them (privately of course). I tried calling them every day, at different times, but to no avail—Rachel, who had caller ID, kept the volume off on her house phone, and she never answered her cell when she knew it was me.

After breakfast at the Silverado, I was planning on stopping at the Fat Brown Trout to get the kids some fun Western gear (a sheriff's badge and pop-gun for Nathan, some red plastic cowboy boots for Janey), then mail it off at the P.O. and hope for the best. (According to an email from Rachel, the kids "never received" the Valentine's cards I sent them, nor the dozen or so post cards and letters—"They must have all gotten lost in the mail!"—nor did they get the "very touching" letter I had left with our neighbor after trying to see them for my scheduled Christmas Eve visitation and finding the house empty.) When I got back to Casey's, I'd give the horses some hot oatmeal to get them through the frigid day, then go inside, make a fire, and read over the court transcripts my lawyer had mailed me a few days earlier. My first official visit as a divorced dad—this much I knew—would be Memorial Day weekend, so I simply had to find a way to make that happen, and to enforce it if they were gone again once I arrived. But with all my debts and my maxed-out credit cards, it was hard for me to fathom how I'd come up with the four hundred dollars I would need for the flight, plus the hundred forty for two nights at the Binghamton Super 8.

The Silverado was packed. It was a Sunday, as I recall. There were three Texans wearing orange hunter caps (their truck at the curb, a dead elk in the bed), some rancher types bellyaching about the soaring price of alfalfa, and Samantha Leeds, the pretty bank teller, sitting next to the girl who worked at the Conoco. Trey Cross, who had been Casey's boyfriend before I came into the picture (apparently she'd kicked him out of her house the day before I arrived), was sitting at the opposite end of the counter, near the cook stove, where Belinda had six things going at once—eggs, bacon, sausage, and potatoes on one side, flapjacks on the other, and cinnamon rolls warming in the oven. The whole counter area was about the size of a living room, with about a dozen stools in a semicircle so that no matter where you sat, you couldn't help but look at Rosie.

After she poured me some coffee (all the while talking with Samantha about the lost snowshoers who had descended the mountains the day before and shown up on Main Street with frostbitten toes and fingers), the hunters got up, paid their tab, and headed out, and I was about to move to their seats to get closer to the heat, but just then a gaggle of artists burst through the door, on break from a weekend workshop being run by Maximilian Knox. You could spot them a mile away, either from the paint in their hair or their fancy glasses, even though the lone male, a longhaired New Englander, had bought himself some cowboy boots at the saddlery in an obvious effort to fit in. It was clearly their first time at the Silverado, so they settled on the hunters' stools and immediately started reading the signs on the walls:

Never kick a cow chip on a hot day.
Always drink upstream from the herd.
Don't squat with your spurs on.

The one seated next to me, with long black hair and a loose-fitting shirt, picked up a menu and asked Rosie how big the breakfast burritos were, and Rosie informed her that as a matter of fact nobody'd ever taken a tape-measure to it or set one on a scale, but let's just say she'd never seen a lone female eat the entire thing. "When I started working here," she said, "I liked them so much I started to look like one." She patted her belly when she said that, and ordinarily there would have been a lot more laughing—Rosie's voice projected as if she was on stage—but that's when we all noticed the pooch in her abdomen.

Manure happens.

She took my order, and the artists' drink orders, and when she turned to slap mine on Belinda's counter, we all saw another orange sticker on the back pocket of her jeans: "Boneless."

While I waited for my *huevos rancheros* (something else I was enjoying about Colorado: Mexican food) and Rosie chatted up the artists, I checked out the county newspaper's police blotter: a motorist who had sustained head wounds from a buck crashing through his windshield, a three a.m. investigation of "an incessantly barking dog," a reported domestic dispute that turned out to be old Todd Mattson yelling at the liberals on the TV, and a drunk man found "near frozen" near the river. Then, at the bottom: Dale Cross, hospitalized with a heart attack.

Trey's dad. One of those guys with a beer belly and no ass, the type you never see without a cowboy hat. I checked the date of the paper—last week—and looked over at Trey, but he didn't look like a guy whose old man had just kicked the bucket, and I hadn't heard anybody offering condolences.

"How's the old man doing?" I called out to Trey, but he either didn't hear me or was pretending not to. You might think he would see me as a rival, but no, he'd been friendly to me right from the get-go; we'd even had a few beers together at the Stumble Inn. But maybe that was only because he didn't think I'd last through the winter.

When Rosie delivered my breakfast, she took the opportunity to refill my coffee cup and slide over the ketchup. "For drowning your taters," she said, and this time I got a good look, and yes, she was indeed "with foal," as they said in these parts. I shook my head. She and her boyfriend hadn't been together very long; they certainly didn't know each other well enough to have a baby together. But who was I to talk?

"Now Trey over there," Rosie said to the artists as she pulled out her order pad, "he doesn't tolerate ketchup on his taters; he just unscrews the salt shaker and coats them with hoar frost"—to which Trey responded by lifting the shaker in salute and sprinkling on a little extra. He was rail-thin, with a rust-colored Fu Manchu, weather-worn already even though he was only around my age—a recovering alcoholic who had never really recovered. Rumor was he'd been married once, but his wife had walked out on him after he refused to talk to her for three straight months. Scary, right? Three months! And yet there was something I admired about someone who could be so . . . resolute.

There are two ways to argue with a woman, and neither one works.

"To each his own," Rosie said.

Since she seemed disinclined to speak to me directly, I raised my hand to get her attention and asked, with a friendly smile, about any "new developments" in her life since I'd last seen her. And even though I'd asked quietly, she broadcasted the answer.

"You mean this?" she said, pointing at her belly. "Honey this is the way we trap our husbands around here!" Which gave everyone a good laugh.

"Remember," she said when the black-haired artist ended up ordering the burrito on a dare from her friends, "no female, ever. But this gentle-man," she said, jerking her pencil at me, "he'll finish it for ya if you need him to, once he minds his own beeswax and settles into his *huevos*. I haven't once picked up his plate but it was wiped clean."

I smiled gamely and forked my eggs as the black-haired artist gave me a friendly look. I could tell she saw me as a local. I was wearing my corduroy coat (flaked with straw and hay, and smelling of horses), dirty jeans, and the old pair of Sorel boots I had picked up from a neighbor of Casey's whose husband had recently passed. Meanwhile Rosie took the other artists' orders, told the Connecticut Yankee with Cowboy Boots "Honey there's no such thing as decaf 'round these parts!" (but then winked and put on a fresh pot for him), advised Belinda to make the next burrito "a big'un," then slapped both hands on the counter in front of the newbies. "It's been a rough stretch, *artistas*," she said. She tipped her head towards me. "While the professor and his famous girlfriend were off on yet another tour of the Wild West, we were suffering back here on the home front. Nearly lost Trey's old man last week, and then"—she held up three fingers—"three customers in five days." Across the counter, the locals nodded with grim faces. "Two of our high-schoolers killed themselves," she said. "One day they're in here after drinking all night, next thing you know they're dead."

The artists clammed up at that, as did everyone else. I hadn't heard; Casey and I had camped at the Great Sand Dunes, then Mesa Verde, followed by a three-day sneak-on, sneak-off rafting trip on the Dolores River—one of the most blissful things I'd ever done. Rosie told the artists it was the high-school salutatorian and his girlfriend, one-third of the graduating class. Some sort of weird joint suicide. "The third was Big Toby Weiler," she said. "The diabetic." She pointed at my stool. "Dropped dead right where the professor is sitting, in the middle of a big-as-your-face cinnamon roll." She sighed and snapped her gum. "Everything goes," she said, then turned to Trey and rapped on the counter. "Not your pa, though, thank goodness."

"Good man," I said, raising my cup to Trey and catching his eye, but to be honest, I didn't know his father at all. I'd only seen him a few times, mostly in the hardware store, complaining about Obama and taxes and lazy teachers. But no matter: Trey was still acting as if he had just lost his hearing.

Indeed the whole place had grown quiet. Maybe we were all thinking the same thing: that it could all go, that *we* could all go, at any moment. I suppose you could say it was an honor then, a privilege really, to be alive, and I should feel fortunate to have such a strong, beautiful woman as my companion in this strong, beautiful part of the country. But that's not what I was feeling. What I was feeling was forlorn without my children—everywhere I went, I wished they could be there with me, could witness along with me the bald eagles, the majestic elk, the mountain peaks blanketed with fresh snow—and I wouldn't even be in these parts were it not for Casey's tearful phone call in December, which now felt like a manipulative ruse. I'd been living in something of a daze, traveling to beautiful places without a dime in my pocket, waiting tables for visiting

Oklahomans who left pocket change for tips, taking care of someone else's horses and dogs while pretending it was *my* 100-acre ranch I was gazing out on every morning. It had been all right for a while, but now that my divorce was final and there was no more baby on the way, I needed to set about restructuring my life. I mean, this was it, right? This was the only life I had. I needed to live it. I needed to show the world who was boss, live wherever I chose to live, make some honest money doing something I loved, and above all see my kids when I was supposed to see them. But how to meet my life and live it with such a gaping hole in my heart? With such a gaping hole in my checking account?

Don't let your yearnings get ahead of your earnings.

Eventually, everyone started talking again, and Rosie delivered the artists' breakfasts, refilled Trey's coffee, called out a *See ya* when someone left, and asked the artists how they liked Belinda's home cooking. The black-haired one had her mouth too full to answer, so Rosie turned to get Mr. Cowboy Boots his just-brewed pot of decaf. When she came back, I caught her eye and nodded towards her belly.

"So does this mean you guys are going to get married?" I asked.

I'd seen her boyfriend. He worked at the Fat Brown Trout and was a ski instructor at Wolf Creek—a soft-spoken Libertarian, always going on about how Ron Paul would save the country.

But this time, everyone heard me. The artists stopped gabbing. Samantha from the bank looked at me from across the counter. Trey scowled as he took a sip of coffee. But they clearly misunderstood my intentions. I wasn't some judgmental fundamentalist; I was fishing to see what my options were.

Rosie came over and picked up my dirty plate. "I'll get married when I'm good and ready to, Professor," she said. "Unlike some people." She dropped my plate in the bin and lowered her voice. "So what happened to *your* baby?" she asked.

And there we were.

In between the Tour of the Wild West and our most recent camping trip, Casey had gone to the Planned Parenthood in Alamosa for an abortion. She didn't tell me about it beforehand—she said she was going to load up on groceries and would be back in time to make dinner. But when she got back, groceries in tow, she confessed. She said she hadn't let me in on it because she knew I would try to dissuade her, but she also knew damn well it's what I secretly wanted her to do. When it came right down to it, she said, she "may have forgotten" to take her birth control pill when she had visited me in November out of some perverse subconscious need to compete with my ex-wife ("It's the one thing she has that I don't have"), and after thinking about it, she had come to the conclusion that maybe that wasn't a very good reason to have a child.

I looked her up and down. Had she even been pregnant? Yes, she had a protruding belly, but she always had; I actually found it attractive. If she *was* telling the truth, I knew I was supposed to be indignant. I knew I was supposed to say it was my baby too, she ought to have included me in the decision, and so on. But she was right; no matter what the truth was, I did feel relieved. So when she said she was going to tell her friends she had miscarried, and that I needed to corroborate her story, I said sure. If anyone asked, I said, I would tell them she had miscarried. And I did.

And one of the people I had told was Rosie.

It's better to keep your mouth shut and look stupid than to open it and prove it.

She dropped her order pad onto the counter and glared out the frosted window. I sat there for a while, trying to find the right thing to say. I sat there until Trey slid aside his plate, set down some cash, and walked out without looking at me. I sat there as Belinda (who, I remembered at that moment, volunteered at the Planned Parenthood in Alamosa once a week), rinsed off her spatula and took a bathroom break. I sat there as Rosie's boyfriend came in, bumped my shoulder as he leaned across the counter to grab a fresh cinnamon roll, and left without paying.

I sat there until Rosie set down my bill and refilled my cup.

"Listen," I said. "It wasn't my—"

She put up her hand and closed her eyes, and that's when I remembered that she had sent over a bouquet of flowers after I'd told her the news, and that she had driven out to Casey's ranch while I was at work, to give Casey a hug and keep her company for a while. She had sat in the living room, sipping coffee and telling Casey how sorry she was, telling her not to worry, a miscarriage could be a blessing because there might have been something wrong with the baby, and she and I would have plenty of chances to get pregnant again.

"Finish your coffee, Professor," she said quietly, her pooched belly now more like a badge of honor than a mark of shame. "And go on home to your famous girlfriend."

I put a little cream in my coffee and took a few sips, but if there's nothing to eat alongside it, coffee just doesn't taste that good. So I put a ten-dollar bill on top of the check, added a few singles, zipped up my coat, slid off the dead man's stool, stepped out into the bitter cold, and headed across the street to the Fat Brown Trout, where Rosie's boyfriend rang up my purchases while chewing on his cinnamon roll. When I went next door to the Post Office to mail the kids their gifts, I found a heavy envelope in my P.O. box: the transcripts of my divorce hearing. I opened it right then and there and skimmed through it, stopping at page 11: *Since the defendant has not seen fit to present himself at this hearing and therefore cannot defend his right to joint custody, the court rules in favor of Mrs. Hawkins—Ms. McGlinchey—on this matter.*

I stared at the sentence, reading it over and over.

Rachel had won full custody of the kids.

ME, THE FOX

WELL, WE DIDN'T MOVE TO BINGHAMTON EXACTLY. WHERE WE MOVED TO and where we still live is near the border of Binghamton and a super small town called Nanticoke, ten minutes from Grammy and Poppy. Everyone thinks, including my dad and my brother, that it's the most boring place in the world, but it's really pretty and peaceful and I would just like to say that I like it. We live off Route 21, but we're the only house on the right for a long way so it's easy to find.

I didn't always like it. Well, I always liked it, meaning where it is and the woods and everything, but it was hard at first for me, especially in school. If I could have just stayed home every day, watching TV or outside in the back yard, it would have been fine. We had a huge yard with a forest behind it (which my dad says is "really just a few trees") and farmland all around. We moved there from White Plains so for Mom it was back to her home but for me and Nate it was like a new world. Our own world. Nate had his side of the "forest" and I had mine, and he cleared a passageway in the middle so we could visit each other's forts. Excuse me, my mistake: so *he* could visit *my* fort. I couldn't visit *his* because he said his "moat" was filled with snakes and creatures that would eat me and I kind of believed him because I was really young at the time. His fort had an archery target and all kinds of stuff like Nerf guns and X-men, but mine had the best tree with low branches for climbing, and it was prettier too, I had a blue blanket hanging over a big branch and when I wanted privacy nobody could see me. I honestly never cared what Nate came up with for us to do every day, as long as he included me. He was my only friend.

Then one day, our cousin David came over, and just like that, I wasn't Nate's best friend anymore. I wasn't even someone he liked. When David came I ran out to the back to play with them, but before I even got there Nate yelled out, "Get out! Go to your own fort!" and David said, "Yeah, go away!" When I said I just wanted to see if they wanted to play "Slay the Dragon," which was totally Nate's favorite game, he said, "No! God, you're so annoying," and David laughed his mean laugh. So I went over to my fort and climbed up to my favorite branch. I knew if I went inside and told Mom about it then Nate would be furious with me, so I just stayed in my fort with the blanket pulled down and cried. Then I went inside, snuck into my room, shut the door, and sulked some more. But eventually I got over it (I probably played with my American Girl doll and told her all my troubles), and when I went back outside, I knew better than to go bother them, so I went back to my fort. But when I got there, I saw that my favorite climbing branch had been chopped down. I couldn't believe it! I looked over toward my brother's fort and I heard them both laughing.

"A pokemon destroyed your tree!" Nate said.

"Yeah, we saw it!" David said. "It was Mewtwo!"

I was only five years old at the time and extremely gullible, but I was smart enough to know exactly what had happened. *Betrayal*.

So then I had zero friends.

Of course, Nate had a whole bunch. He was really outgoing and played soccer, so, you know, boom: instant friendships. Me, I was shy. Whenever I told my mom I had no friends, she would pick me up and say, "Well you're *my* friend. You're my *best* friend!" She'd carry me to the mirror and wave to my reflection, saying, "Hi there, friend!" and I'd wave back and say the same thing. My mom has an irresistible smile, and she could always cheer me up. However, having your mom as your best friend isn't exactly something to brag about; so I had to do something. In a pathetic attempt to have a social life, I invited everybody in my kindergarten class to my sixth birthday party. My dad was there for it—it was weird, he came the day before, slept on the couch, and drove me to school that morning, and I don't know what he did all day long, but he was there when school was over and then my mom was home too, but Nate was at soccer practice, so there we were, the three of us, and the table was set with balloons and paper plates for eight people. And we waited.

The party was supposed to be at 4:00, but when 4:00 came, nobody was there. My dad kissed me and told me I was the prettiest and most wonderful six-year-old who ever lived, but then he kind of stood in the corner, trying to be polite I guess, and my mom kept fussing over the cake and cleaning the counter and saying, "Don't worry, even if it's just us, it's going to be a great party!" but with each passing minute I felt more and more like I was choking.

Finally at 4:15 the doorbell rang. We all rushed to the door, but they let me open it. It was Alivia Case. She lived down the road. She handed me a present, whispered "Happy Birthday," looked around the room, and quietly sat down. And so we had a party. They sang the birthday song to me and we all had some cake. Alivia and I barely said a word.

So then, after that, for a while anyway, I had a friend. For the rest of the school year we said *hi* to each other at the beginning of school, and sometimes we said *bye* at the end. But then we were placed in two different classes for first grade, so once again I found myself friendless. Plus the kids in my new class called me "Bug Eyes" because my eyes were apparently too big for my face.

Lunch was the worst. I sat alone every day. For the whole year. For the next three years in fact. I took my lunch and went to an empty table in the way back. Once, there were no empty tables, so I took my lunch to the bathroom and ate it in there.

It wasn't until fourth grade that I finally got the courage to sit with some other kids who were considered weird. They seemed happy to have me at their table. They told me about a game they played during recess: they chose an animal they liked, and as soon as they stepped outside they would become that animal. I decided I would be a fox. I liked foxes. Foxes were cool. So as soon as I stepped outside, I was a fox, sniffing the air with my long nose. We did this every day, and I started looking forward to lunch and recess for a change.

Then, one day, I stepped outside, fully prepared to transform into my fox self, when a girl grabbed my hand and told me I would be playing with her that day. I nodded and smiled. She was super pretty. She pulled me over to her friends. There were three boys and another girl with her. "This is Cal, TG, Tyler, Lexi, and I'm Rachel," she said. "We're the Boyz

Club!" I had no idea what I had done to deserve being included in such an amazing, exclusive organization, but I didn't care. From that day on, I started looking forward to school instead of dreading it, and all because my new cool friends who didn't sit at the "weird" table would be waiting for me at lunchtime.

Me and Rachel are still friends, and one day I asked her why she had approached me that day and she said, "Because you were different." I'm certainly not used to being different. Or I guess what I'm saying is I'm not used to being *considered* different. I do *feel* different. I feel different all the time. Everyone else I know, they have this life, with their parents at home, and friends from their neighborhood, and if their parents are divorced they see their dads all the time. I'm the only one I know who has to get used to being so alone all the time. All the time. Every day of my life. My whole life I have spent missing someone. I miss my dad all the time. When I get to be with him, though, I miss my mom. Now that Nate doesn't play with me anymore, I miss him, I miss the way we used to be. I miss my grandma too, and Auntie Anna Banana and Uncle Mitch and my cousins Marianna and Robbie, we used to see them all the time but now we never see them.

I'm used to it now, but still, if I'm honest about it, it's been a hard way to grow up.

SPRING CREEK PASS

It was only November, but to Flynn it had already been winter for far too long. Sanctuary was at nine thousand feet above sea level, located in what had been, in another epoch, the mouth of an enormous volcano. And while it had been a spectacular summer, filled with hikes above tree line, bald-eagle sightings, a raft trip down the Rio Grande, and camping in the Tetons, by mid-August the nights had grown cold, and by now he was beginning to dread the early dusk. Casey's property, which she had bought when her first book, *Destroyed But Not Defeated,* became a best-seller, sat four miles outside the town proper, bordered by the river at one end and the base of the Divide at the other. There was no insulation from the cold.

Flynn awoke just before the alarm, at 3:58 a.m., easing himself out of bed without waking Casey or Sage, the 110-pound Newfoundland that slept between them. Before going to bed the snow had started to fall, so he had ground his coffee, put out his clothes, and set the alarm a half-hour earlier than usual.

He opened the fireplace door and placed a chunk of pine wood, one he had chopped that summer, on the glowing ashes. After shuffling into the kitchen, he turned on the porch light and peered out at the thermometer: minus fourteen. And three more hours of darkness to go.

Wearing his flannel boxers and an old baseball shirt, Flynn slipped on his Sorels and stepped out to his car through a foot of fresh snow. The moon lit up the mountainside to the north; he could see the junipers a hundred acres away. One of the horses, Cielo, whinnied from the stable. In the spring, Casey had told Flynn that he could ride the skittish Arabian whenever he wanted; that way he could learn, she said. (She herself rode Rex, the bigger, more reliable quarter horse she had recently bought for four thousand dollars.) So he had, all summer. Cielo would skitter away from sticks on the ground, thinking they were snakes, and Flynn had trouble handling her at first, but he had learned to relax into the saddle, direct her without using the reins, and treat her with compassion and confidence. Over the past weekend, Flynn had taken her up the mountain, stopping on a ridge to feel the cold air in his lungs and look at the view. From up there, Casey's log cabin was just one of many dotting the landscape, and Sanctuary was just one of many pretty places to live in this part of the country.

He started up his old Sidekick, given to him by his new friend Len, a Spanish professor at Mesa State College. In April, after receiving the terms of his new divorce agreement, he realized he needed more money, so he had driven to the four colleges within a four-hour radius of Sanctuary, walked into the deans' offices with curriculum vitae in hand, and landed two job offers. He took the one at Mesa because of the nearby airport, which would make it easier to see his kids. Over the summer he had thrice driven four or five hours (to Denver, Colorado Springs, and Albuquerque) in order to fly back east, and while he wouldn't say it wasn't worth it (he spent a grand total of eleven hours with Nathan and Janey over those three trips, due to his ex-wife's maneuverings) it had been enough of a hassle to make him wonder if living on Casey's ranch would work for him long-term.

He put the heater on full blast, directed it onto the frozen, snow-covered windshield, turned on the rear defrost, got out of the car, and checked to make sure the wheel hubs of the Sidekick were on "Lock" for four-wheel drive. He took a deep breath, relaxed his body so he would stop shivering, and looked up to the eastern sky. The Leonids were due in a couple of days, and Casey had told him to watch for them just before dawn. He saw an isolated streak directly above him, then another to the south—but none where the meteor shower was supposed to be.

On a moonless night back in February, not long after he had moved to Colorado, several of the planets had been aligned, and Flynn had seen them with his naked eye, just before driving to the hotel to work the breakfast shift. He had walked into the restaurant gushing to the cook: he had seen the luminous Saturn and a rusty Mars; he had spotted a blue dot that was either Uranus or Pluto.

Now, the stars and planets seemed to have exploded into disarray.

After adding more wood to the revived fire, taking a shower, and dressing in the living room while the coffee brewed, Flynn put on his dry hiking boots, filled up his travel mug, put a banana in his coat pocket, grabbed his duffel bag, gym bag, and backpack, and headed back out, closing the door gently behind him.

The night before he had made this trip for the first time, back in August, Flynn had sat at the kitchen table with Casey, tracing the route on the Colorado page of her Rand McNally. It looked plain and boring, traversing what seemed to be barren land. He'd take the state road north to Gunnison, turn west onto highway 50, and follow that all the way to Grand Junction. "It's pretty," Casey had told him. "Keep your eyes open." She pointed to a crooked gray line, diagonally connecting 149 with 50 before 149 bent east towards Gunnison. "And take this cut-off right here."

The next morning, during the long drive, he had been stunned by the emptiness of the land, the depth of its silence. He had arrived at his new job open-mouthed and unaware of time.

By now, his third month on the job, he had fallen into a routine. He left every Tuesday morning at 4:30, stopped a few hours later at Jane's Kitchen in Montrose for some sourdough French toast (if he had time) or at the McDonald's drive-through in Delta for two Egg McMuffins (if he was running late), arrived on campus around 8:30, taught Basic Writing and two sections of Intro to Lit, and spent the night at the home of Len and his girlfriend Sydney, who taught English. On Wednesday morning, he hiked Black Canyon, then spent the afternoon meeting with students in his office (which had blank walls and only a few books); in the evening he taught a three-hour adult class on Greek Mythology. On Thursday, he taught his three classes again, gassed up, and made the long drive back.

Flynn eased onto Rio Grande Lane, feeling the fresh snow under his tires. Within a mile he saw some familiar bulges on the road: a herd of elk, belly-down on the snow. He slowed almost to a halt as they roused themselves and loped away. Flynn was grateful for the moon; it was like an enormous headlight in the sky, and it made driving in the middle of the night like driving on a dim afternoon. But in two weeks, he'd be without its aid both coming and going—during the coldest, darkest time of the year.

The road followed the river against the current, toward its headwaters. In the opposite direction it flowed through South Fork, bent west to Alamosa, then ran down and deep through New Mexico and along the Texas border before finally emptying into the Gulf. But here it was, so narrow you could leap across it in spots, and already frozen over, with fresh snow blanketing the icy surface. Back on March 20th, Casey and Flynn had stood on a bridge and dropped heavy rocks onto it, smashing the icy surface to expose the clear water gurgling underneath. After four hundred inches of snowfall, and no sign of spring's imminent arrival, Casey had decided it was time to force the issue.

Flynn eased onto route 149, a narrow road that would be empty of vehicles until it joined up with highway 50 an hour and a half away. He settled into his seat. There was nothing to do but drive and think. There was no radio reception; no place to stop and get gas or coffee; no cell-phone reception. On the passenger seat were a few CDs if he needed them—the Stay-Awake CD, the Keep-Awake CD, and the Wake the Hell Up! CD—with songs like the Ramones' "I Want to Be Sedated," Tom Petty's "You Wreck Me," and "Angels of the Silences" by the Counting Crows. But on most trips he left them there on the seat, next to the pens and notepads he used to plan for his classes or to jot down ideas he had about his unsettled life. A week earlier, he had scribbled, "Ask BC Fam Court if OK to call cops next time R hides kids"; "Use C's lavender soap to catch packrat in horse stbl" (which, after cheese, peanut butter, and tootsie rolls, was finally what worked); "Possible to sneak pay-as-go cell phone to Nathan?"; "For new custody hrng fwd email and phone rcrds—evidence of my atmpts to see them" and "Cut hole for stovepipe NW corner of shed," which he had been fixing up to use an office, but which Casey now wanted as a writing studio. Folded up under the passenger seat were the *Grand Junction Sentinel* classifieds (with one-bedroom apartments circled), print-outs of Craigslist rentals, the latest issue of the *Chronicle of Higher Education* (with circled job postings of schools near Binghamton), and the printout of an email from a former student, MacNair Richards, who had been living near Vail but had moved to Oregon with her partner.

Past the headwaters, the road curved out of the valley and began its

2,000-foot climb to the first of three mountain passes, Spring Creek. Flynn's headlights lit up the sign for the Oleo Ranch ("A Poor Man's Spread"), otherwise there were only pine trees and aspens. He could make out the glowering peak of Mount Baldy to the right, and knew that San Luis Peak, a fourteener, was behind it, and that another, Redcloud, lurked to his left. Flynn was riding up and onto the Continental Divide. On one side, Clear Creek flowed west, eventually ending up in the Pacific, but right across the road Spring Creek flowed east, on its way to the Atlantic. So much seemed to hang in the balance, and yet whatever the direction, whatever the obstacles, the water eventually found its way home.

He was driving through fresh snow, breaking trail, remembering a summer day when he and Casey stood at the top of Clear Creek falls, closing their eyes as the sun blazed down from a bright blue sky and the faint backspray of cold, clear water wet their faces. He remembered feeling free and happy and light.

He passed the sign for Spring Creek Pass, 10,898 feet; he was a few miles from Slumgullion Mountain, and this stretch of road was the last to be plowed during storms. Sometimes, after a big one, the plow from Lake City would spend all day going over Slumgullion and back, and wouldn't get to Spring Creek Pass until the next day. Flynn heard the howling outside, and felt the car shudder. It was always windy here, and snowdrifts tended to pile up, quick and deep, across the road.

When his headlights caught the eyes of an elk, Flynn slowed the car, his tires grinding on the dry hard snow. The massive bull, seven points on each antler, stood still, its moonshadow cast on the snow behind it. A few weeks earlier, on this stretch of road, a cow elk had bounded up from a dropoff and skidded on the icy surface with her hooves splayed, slamming her head into the corner of Flynn's car. The Sidekick wasn't damaged, and neither was the elk—she scrambled up, shook her head, and trotted away—but Flynn had taken it as a warning.

When he had first moved here, seeing a bull elk like that, all alone in the pitch of night, would bring tears to his eye. But today, he was all business. He shifted into first, then second, past the high-standing road-side reflectors that guided the plows when there was too much snow to see where the road was. It would deepen up Slumgullion, but Flynn's

Sidekick, with its high wheel base, would probably be okay. On the other side, however, the descent was angled and steep, a succession of switchbacks that at every turn would bring him to the edge of a cliff with no guardrails. Flynn called this stretch Slumgullion Slalom. There were five phases of his trip—Elk Alarm, Slumgullion Slalom, Deer Dodge, Rabbit Roulette, Cerro Suicide—and each one spelled trouble.

On the way up, Flynn lost the moonlight to a storm cloud, and the landscape was reduced to the snow in front of his headlights. There was nothing but the hum of his car and the sound of his wheels over the snow. But suddenly, on a curve that ducked under a projecting cliff face, the car lost traction when he stupidly stepped on the brakes, the back end sliding to the right and almost off the cliff before stopping. Flynn had been careless, forgetting that it was always slick on that curve, as it faced north and never saw the sun. He sat still in the driver's seat, afraid to shift his weight. His headlights lit only a trail of cat prints, bobcat or lynx, on the otherwise smooth surface of white.

He dropped into four-wheel low, easing the clutch up and the gas pedal down; but the back end slid a bit more, closer to the edge, a drop of about two thousand feet.

He got out of the car.

Snow was falling, large flakes that alighted on the road, on the bouldered slope of the mountain, on his thick, curly hair. Flynn knew that this is how people died around here, their cars dropping soundlessly into the abyss, and that he was sleepy and needed to think clearly. He looked down; his feet were deep in the snow, and he'd left his Sorels in the mud room. He lifted his face to the falling sky, calculated the time, added two hours, and pictured his children waking up for school.

He needed to focus.

He stepped over toward the cliff and peered at the back of his car. His rear right tire was inches from the edge.

Flynn put on his gloves, grabbed his canvas jacket from inside the car, and wedged it under the tire. It was bald, like all his tires, the snow caking onto it instead of being gripped by the tread and then released. For the last few weeks he had meant to replace them, but he didn't have enough cash. It was an issue: Casey, a best-selling writer, routinely received checks in the mail for thousands of dollars, while he was drowning in debt. When he had moved here she had set him up with a job at the hotel, but had discouraged him from looking for anything full-time. "It's full-time just taking care of this place," she had said, pointing out the log cabin, the shed, the horse stables, and the hundred acres of pasture. She'd buy the groceries and continue to pay the mortgage, she said, as long as he paid his own phone bill, chipped in for gas and electric, and managed the animals and property. When he brought up his child-support obligations, she frowned. "Why are you still paying that when Rachel isn't even letting you see them?" But he couldn't withhold money out of spite; he didn't want his children to go without, no matter how badly their mother was behaving, and he didn't want to give her the opportunity to depict him as a deadbeat dad. So that's when he decided to apply for a teaching job. It still wasn't enough—his instructorship at Mesa State earned him barely enough for child-support and credit-card payments while he was trying to save for a Christmas flight to New York, and he was also sending a hundred bucks a month to his sister to pay back a loan—but it helped. Meanwhile, he practiced austerity. In Grand Junction he took his meals with Sydney and Len, trying not to eat too much, or bought dollar-menu items at Wendy's or Taco Bell. He routinely stole money from Casey's change jar, and once he ate someone's turkey sandwich from the faculty refrigerator after it had been there for over a week.

Before he got back into the car he cleaned off his wiper blades, taking off his gloves so he could dig out the ice with his fingers. Then he sat there, the engine humming, his hand on the clutch, knowing that if he pushed the gas too hard and the back tire skidded out, he was a dead man.

He pressed down his foot as gently as he could, felt the tire ease up and over the jacket, and rolled the car out to the middle of the road. When he was past the icy section he stopped, retrieved his coat, and threw it on the passenger-side floor.

Okay.

He edged forward, letting the deep snow create its own traction. The flakes came at him directly, as if he were stuck inside a white kaleidoscope, slapping the windshield and forcing him to continually refocus his sight. As he crested the summit at 11,361 feet, the snow was falling straight down again. He sat back and heaved a breath.

On his way down the north side of the mountain, he followed the switchbacks like a drunken skier, veering left and right, as the flakes continued to lighten. Flynn dropped down to second and took it slow. He could see that there was less and less snow on the road, until eventually it was just a dusting. By the time he entered Lake City, the roads were almost bare.

At 5:26 a.m. the town was asleep, except for a pick-up truck pulling out onto the road behind Flynn and a snowplow warming up in a driveway. Lake City was only a little bigger than Sanctuary. It had been formed centuries earlier when a part of Slumgullion had broken off and descended into the valley, blocking up a creek and forming a sparkling lake that attracted settlers. But it was a tough place to live: the cliffs surrounding the town were so high, the valley so narrow, that in the winter it began to darken in early afternoon.

It took Flynn about a minute to enter and exit Lake City, with the window cracked so the cold air would keep him awake. He passed the café where, in July, he and Casey had stopped for breakfast before continuing on to Silverton, traversing what must surely be one of the most perilous mountain passes in America, spiraling around and up the mountain on a rock-jutted dirt road with no guardrails and barely enough room for one vehicle, every turn bringing them to the brink of an exhilarating death. Flynn's legs were wobbly when he got out of the car in Silverton, so they went for a walk in the tiny town, and Casey bought him a Hopi key chain made of silver and engraved with a bear, her power animal. He reached for it now, running his thumb over the sharp edges as he passed the Texaco station, which wouldn't open for another hour, and then a row of homes, converted miner's shacks mostly, some, judging from the faint smell of smoke, with fires still going inside.

Outside town, Flynn followed the bends of 149 alongside the Gunnison River. This was the beginning of Deer Dodge. They were everywhere. At first he saw only their eyes, but after a while the moon came out again and he could see a bevy of them lurking in the trees. Flynn swept his eyes left and right while keeping his foot on the gas, taking careful sips from his travel mug as he drove on.

When he lost the moon again, Flynn slowed, then saw the headlights in his rearview mirror gaining on him. As Flynn considered letting the vehicle pass so it could act as a buffer between the deer and his car, a second vehicle appeared, coming the other way—a bread delivery van, headed for the Texaco station—and at that moment a fawn darted out from the right. There was nothing Flynn could do. He hit the little deer's head as the delivery van churned past.

Flynn pulled over. The driver behind him stopped as well. Together they got out of their vehicles and looked at the fawn. Tiny stubs protruded from his head, the promise of antlers. He was stone dead. Snowflakes fell on his open eyes. There wasn't a sound in the air, not even the faint shudder of a last breath.

"You all right?" the man said. Silhouetted by his truck's headlights, he was tall and broad-chested, with blond backlit curls, and sharp eyes that glinted red from the Sidekick's tail lights. Flynn nodded, his hands in his pockets. It was cold, at least twenty below, and still dark. He'd have to make do with one headlight the rest of the way.

Back in his car, Flynn kept his eyes on the rearview mirror at first, waiting to see if the man wanted to go ahead of him, but when the truck didn't move, Flynn pulled back out onto the road. The truck pulled out too, but then stopped and went in reverse. It took Flynn a while to figure out that the man was picking up his dinner.

After Deer Dodge came Rabbit Roulette, on the cut-off from 149 to highway 50, the gray line Casey had shown him on the map. Soon Flynn wouldn't be able to take this short cut, a dirt path that was never plowed; he'd have to continue on 149 as it bent in the wrong direction to its intersection with 50. But for now, the cut-off would be passable.

He turned left onto the old road, which was barren at this end and dotted by a few trailers at the other, where some Natives lived. It was fairly smooth at first, with some washboarded stretches that rattled Flynn's teeth, but at the far end some sharp rocks jutted up from the road, and depending on what time it was, he either took it slow there or blasted through so that he could get to Grand Junction in time. Today, he had left the house early, but because of his mishap on Slumgullion and the dead fawn, he was now running late; he would have to go fast and hope for the best.

The road ran along the rim of a mesa, a stretch so lonely and uninhabitable it filled him with guilt and sadness for the Natives. But it was its own kind of beautiful. Here jackrabbits darted freely, scurrying off the road and back onto it. The only way to ensure he wouldn't kill any was to keep his speed under thirty miles per hour, which made the cut-off worthless; he might as well stay on 149 all the way to highway 50, as both those roads were paved. So he drove quickly enough to justify the shortcut, but slowly enough to give the rabbits a fair shot.

Three miles in, he stopped the car, got out, dumped the remains of his coffee, stretched, and relieved himself. To the west, the moon was on its descent. To the east, no Leonids; the sky there was blank due to cloud cover. In the distance he heard the faint yips of coyotes, then silence. The only sounds were of his urine hitting the dirt and his own tight shallow breaths. At Casey's ranch, this time of night, the silence was so thin you could hear electricity humming through the wires. Here, not even that.

He closed his eyes and pictured Nathan in his second-grade classroom, feet tapping the floor, eyes at once sleepy and restless; Janey, sitting in her pre-school semi-circle for story time, her eyes wide in anticipation of the next turn of page, the next amazing event in Peter Rabbit's adventurous life.

Rabbit Roulette began soon after he resumed his drive: a snowshoe hare scurried onto the road, brown with white flanks. Flynn swerved as it scattered first away from the car, then suddenly back in its path; he was finding it difficult to follow, absent his right headlight. They moved along like this, in spurts and swerves, Flynn and the hare, until Flynn finally slowed to a near stop and let the animal find its way off the road. In a month or so it would be completely white and harder to spot in the snowy landscape.

The second hare darted out in front of the car, then sped ahead of the front tire in a zigzag. Flynn followed it for a few seconds before it scampered off. The third jumped straight out into his path, and somehow avoided the tires; Flynn felt mildly disappointed when it made it to the other side.

The landscape was changing its hue: behind him a yellow glow, before him a dark blue. To the northwest, a meteor streaked long and silent, disappearing before it met the horizon. Flynn was staring at the spot, hoping to see another, when a flash of brown came from the snow-covered brush and he felt a thump under his tire.

He stopped the car and got out. All the times he had made this drive, he had always won the rabbit roulette—or rather, he had let the rabbits win. But this one lay half-flattened, its long back paws crushed, its front paws twitching. Flynn sighed and looked behind him, at the starless sky over Slumgullion. That storm cloud would hover over the summit until daylight, dropping several more feet of snow before dissipating—a self-made, self-contained storm. By the time Flynn made his trip back, the snow would have melted—the sun was strong at high altitude—but soon there would be a storm every week, and he would have to keep hoping it wouldn't come on a Tuesday or Thursday. It would be better for him to just stay in Grand Junction, where it was warm. He had friends there now, like Len and Sydney. He had his job. Great hiking trails. And the airport was there.

Flynn planted the heel of his steel-toed boot onto the rabbit's twitching ear and shifted the weight of his foot forward.

EVERY TIME FLYNN DROVE PAST THE BLUE MESA RESERVOIR, THE WATER looked different. The Gunnison had been stopped up by a dam and was now ringed by parched brown mesas, its hue changing with the altering light. At this hour it was a broad patch of darkness, shimmering silver at the surface, the mesas corniced by the first hints of dawn. During his first summer in Colorado, Flynn and Casey had stopped here on their way back from a drive to Crested Butte; they had sat by the water's edge, eating chunks of Asiago cheese stuffed into lumps of freshly baked bread and washing it down with mineral water.

That was a good day.

A solitary truck was parked by the shore, and as Flynn drove past he noticed a man stepping out onto the new ice, pulling a small wagon behind him. The ice couldn't possibly be thick enough; it had only recently started to form, and the middle of the reservoir was yet unfrozen. But the man looked peaceful and confident. He must know what he's doing, Flynn thought. He must have an intimate relationship with the lake. He must enjoy his own company.

Flynn headed directly west toward Cerro Mesa. The route ahead was a long, uphill straightaway that stretched for miles, plateaued at the top of a mesa, and then plummeted down in a series of twists and turns that flattened out through Cimarron and snaked back up to Cerro's Summit. Flynn wasn't looking forward to this stretch. Unlike Slumgullion, Cerro brought with it some company: tractor-trailers, for which highway 50 provided the only east-west route through the middle of Colorado before turning into the Loneliest Road in America. When the road iced up, there was nowhere to pull over; on one side was mountain, on the other, empty air. If at any point Flynn hit the brakes he would spin off the cliff, so his only choice was to think clearly, drop gear, and forge ahead.

It had rained on Cerro, frozen up overnight, and now it was snowing lightly—so the road was a thick glaze of ice under a dusting of white. Flynn took it slow, adjusting to the presence of traffic and to the low sunlight reflecting in his rearview mirror. As he rounded a curve, an eighteen-wheeler rumbled past him going the other way, its chained tires grinding into the iced surface. After that, the road straightened out, ran steep downhill, and then doubled back toward the bottom, a hairpin curve that demanded fifteen miles per hour and a stiff clutch. Flynn dropped down to second, then to first, and on the bottom turn Flynn felt his car drag. He muttered a curse, slowed down, and looked for a place to pull over.

When he got out, he saw that his left rear tire was flat—probably from a sharp rock on the cut-off. He put on his gloves.

For the first two months of his job, his commute had gone smoothly. But lately, something had gone wrong nearly every week. Three weeks ago, the skidding elk. The following week, he had run out of gas just short of Grand Junction and had to hitch his way to school. On his return trip, he had spun out on an ice patch and a van full of snowboarders helped to pull his Sidekick from the ditch. Then today, the skid on the cliff, the dead fawn in Lake City, the crushed cottontail and now this.

He bundled up his coat and set about changing the tire. Short on cash, his credit card maxed out, he'd have to make the trip back to Sanctuary on Thursday with one headlight and no spare. He could just stay in Grand Junction, of course—Len and Sydney wouldn't mind—but Casey certainly would. The previous Thursday, when he had heard of a storm brewing to the east, Flynn had called from Grand Junction to suggest he stay there overnight and start back the next morning. When she responded with a frigid silence, he hung up and drove through the blizzard, arriving home frazzled and exhausted at two in the morning. She awakened him at sunrise with a hot cup of coffee and a list of projects: clean out the horses' stalls; fix the fence on the back side of the pasture; drain, clean, and refill the water trough. "It's *so* good to have you home," she said.

Flynn was grateful the sun was up, which made tire-changing easy, but his stomach was growling. Back inside his car, he glanced at the clock: he had just enough time to grab a bacon-and-egg burrito from the Carl's Jr. in Delta and still make it to his first class. He told himself to be careful, to take it slow. In the future, if he moved to Grand Junction, he would be able to walk to campus. On Thursday evenings, instead of gearing up for yet another four-hour drive, he could go out for a beer with his friends, and on weekends he could go hiking in the Black Canyon. He could secure a second job, save his money, pay off his lawyer, and take normal flights when he visited his kids instead of the cheap, double-lay-over red-eyes.

Once he cleared Cerro Summit and saw the road ahead was bare, the sky blue and clear, he pulled over, got out of the car, and switched the wheel hubs from "Lock" to "Free." When he looked up he saw two airplanes over the mountains, one pulling the other. When the lead plane released the towline and tailed off to the left, the glider behind it curled right and arched up, catching the thermal like an eagle, on his own now and doing fine.

*

ON THURSDAY AFTERNOON, FLYNN TAUGHT HIS LAST CLASS OUTSIDE ON THE campus lawn, and as he walked out to the parking lot at 3:30 to begin his trip home, he was in his shirtsleeves, and the sky to the east looked clear. Across the road was a grove of aspen trees, their yellow leaves unevenly fringed with brown, as if a thousand butterflies had perched at the tips of their branches. Back at Casey's, the aspens had long ago gone bare.

After gassing up the car with Casey's Conoco card and stopping at the MacDonald's in Delta for the two double-cheeseburgers-for-two-dollars special, he saw storm clouds over the mountains to the southeast, so he changed the setting on his wheel hubs, then removed his Dr. Martens and put on his hiking boots. He never knew how bad it would be until he got there, and the weather reports rarely accounted for what a mountain summit could bring. On one trip back he had hit heavy snow over Cerro Mesa and had to stay overnight at the only motel in Cimarron, arriving home Friday morning to find not a trace of snow in Sanctuary and a pouting Casey on the couch. On another occasion he had called first, and Casey told him not to worry, it was all clear there; but by the time he got to Lake City there was a snowstorm so severe he had to spend the night in his car. Slumgullion Pass was never officially closed; people assumed that only locals drove over it, and locals knew enough to get home by dark and not to cross the Continental Divide during a storm. And the mountain was never plowed at night.

As Flynn turned east at Montrose, the bank sign showed 74°. A half hour later, he was in the middle of a blizzard. On Cerro, a few pick-ups and eighteen-wheelers were grinding and sliding their way up and down highway 50. Everyone else had turned back or chained up.

Everything inside Flynn told him to turn around. To be safe. To be sensible.

He forged ahead.

The snow ended abruptly on the eastern side, and after a few miles of dry road, Flynn knew the cut-off would be passable. He sailed over the straightaway through Cimmaron, blasted past Blue Mesa Reservoir (its surface a sparkling navy-blue in the twilight), and turned right onto the cutoff, the dirt road spattered here and there with patches of snow. Flynn slowed to avoid the sharp rocks jutting up through the dirt, as he no longer had a spare.

The sky was darkening. The sun had not set but disappeared. Flynn turned on the car stereo, but there was only static. He flipped on his high-beams, then remembered only one was working. He slipped in a CD—one that Casey had made for him, with songs by Patty Larkin,

Kate Bush, and Paula Cole—but ejected it after only a few notes. He tapped the steering wheel and looked in the rearview mirror. The sky behind him was streaked with pink and purple clouds. Ahead, it was gray and menacing.

He mentally added two hours and pictured his kids getting into their beds, Rachel tucking them in. Kissing Nathan first, Janey second. Rachel's former high-school boyfriend, Sam, standing in the doorway, wishing the kids goodnight, his finger on the light switch.

WHEN THE FIRST RABBIT SCAMPERED OUT, FLYNN ACCELERATED, NARROWLY avoiding it. The first time he had seen the hares, when cross-country skiing with Casey at 11,000 feet in the Wemenuche Wilderness, he had felt great affection for them. Now he saw them simply as prey, animals put on earth for the sole purpose of being devoured. They spent every second of their lives scared.

The second hare bounded out from the sagebrush and scampered safely to the other side. Flynn didn't slow down or swerve. It was now the luck of the draw. He would continue toward Lake City, driving straight and true, and if a rabbit ran under his wheel, so be it. Judging from the dark sky ahead, Slumgullion would be in snow, and the later he got there, the more snow there would be. He couldn't slow down for every damn rabbit that got in his way.

The third was unlucky. It darted out and ran ahead of the car, angled off the road, then right back into it. Flynn felt the slight bump under his back tire.

The fourth met the same fate, scurrying out from the left, racing ahead of the car, then breaking right. Flynn knew, more than felt, that it hadn't found its way to the other side. The fifth was spared by a hop off the road at the last second, but the sixth was crushed as it came out of the brush. The seventh and eighth made it out safely, but Flynn clipped the ninth with his rear tire. He knew it might not be dead, but he left it to the coyotes.

Ahead of him, the rising moon was being swallowed by the storm cloud.

The tenth hare jumped out about a mile before the cut-off ended.

It angled toward the middle of the road and Flynn slowed slightly, to keep it just ahead of him. Then, as the rabbit veered to the right, Flynn accelerated, running over it just before it reached the safety of the brush.

"Fucking rabbits," he said.

ON THE STRETCH OF 149 FROM THE CUT-OFF TO LAKE CITY, FLYNN LOST THE moonlight and knew for certain he was entering a storm. He had to be careful now, with only one headlight. He saw deer eyes in the brush. They too were prey. They too slowed his forward progress.

He accelerated.

LAKE CITY WAS AN EARLY CHRISTMAS CARD. OVER A FOOT OF FRESH SNOW had fallen, and it was sure to be worse up Slumgullion. Flynn slowed through town, following the tire tracks of others who had come before him and were now safe inside their warm homes. He passed the restaurant he had taken Casey to for her birthday, run by a chef who had studied in France. Casey had ordered the most expensive items on the menu—escargot dumplings, roast lamb, profiteroles—and picked out a sixty-dollar bottle of wine. As the chef came out after their meal to compliment her on her selections, the waiter brought back Flynn's credit card, shaking his head. They had driven home in silence through the snow.

Flynn lost the last of the tire tracks at the southern edge of town and began his ascent up Slumgullion through the unplowed snow. With his hand clenching the stick shift he drove up the switchbacks, dreading what he might find on the other side of the summit. The snow was falling like a surrealist's dream. He had no money for a motel; if he got stuck, he'd have to spend the night in his car again.

As he continued to climb toward the summit, Flynn was plunged into darkness. At first he feared that his remaining headlight had gone out. But then he realized that the snow was higher than the grill of his car. He was plowing up the mountain.

He gripped the wheel with both hands. In the deep darkness, the color of the snow had changed. What had been an enchanting white was now a ghastly gray. He nudged the gas pedal forward, his eyes adjusting to the darkness. It was insane, he knew. He could easily drive right off the cliff. But turning around would be dicey. Plus, Casey was expecting him.

In March, on their way back from Telluride in a storm like this one, five feet of snow had fallen, the main road had closed, and they had stayed two nights at an inn in Pagosa Springs. They spent the first day sitting in the hot springs and trudging to the bakery in town; they spent the second day continually checking CDOT, wondering when the highway would open, until finally Casey decided they'd head south and cut across New Mexico, at least four hours out of their way, to get home. They talked a lot in Pagosa—about Casey's book tour, her river trips, her upcoming television interview. But at no point did Flynn mention his children, or all the work he had done that summer—documenting phone records and emails, filing affidavits, writing lengthy emails—to re-establish joint custody. And at no point did they discuss Casey's abortion. The only time she seemed to refer to it was when she told Flynn she saw her life as a picture she had worked hard to create in the hopes that someone would step into it, and now that he had, she was determined to keep that picture intact, to preserve it at all costs.

FLYNN PLOWED THROUGH THE DARKNESS TO THE SUMMIT, AND ONCE THE road leveled off and he saw a bit of light on the snow in front of the car, he got out and high-stepped it to the front, his legs sinking like posts into the deep snow. It was only up to his grill now. He brushed off the headlight and got back in the car.

On his way down Slumgullion, the heat directed onto his wet legs, he took his time. The snow banks on the side of the road, from previous plowing, acted as guardrails, and the fresh snow on the road embraced his tires, keeping them straight and true.

At that moment, Casey was probably sitting on the couch with Sage, watching the Weather Channel. She was content to be by herself, as long as someone was on their way home.

If Flynn were to continue past the turn-off to her ranch, he'd be in New Mexico before midnight. It would be warmer there, too. And he would have all kinds of options. He could head east through Texas, then Tennessee, then north for two days up to Binghamton, where he could take Rachel to court, win custody of his children, and start a new life together with them, a life in the woods. He smiled to himself, then felt his throat close up.

"Natty," he said. "Janey girl. Don't forget your dad."

The car hummed through the snow.

From Slumgullion to Spring Creek, the snow stopped falling, and there was less and less on the road until he hit Spring Creek Pass, where the pavement was actually visible in stretches. But a tremendous wind now shook the car. He had expected this: a week earlier it had blown so hard that it had pushed the Sidekick sideways across the ice and spun it around, facing him back the way he had come.

Past the Oleo Ranch, it started snowing again, a different storm, coming at him low and hard from the side, harsh and icy. The pavement was slashed with drifts, like enormous yard line markers on a narrow football field. Flynn blasted through the first three drifts, finding them deeper than they looked. He rounded a curve in the road and saw more ahead, much longer and wider, twenty or thirty feet from beginning to end. He accelerated, counting on the momentum of the car to get him to the other side. One by one he plowed through, feeling the wheels slide sideways as he did.

Back in Grand Junction, it was probably about fifty degrees and calm. Here it was near zero, and howling bad. Flynn cracked open the window and the car rocked with the incoming gale.

The seventh snowdrift was at least five car-lengths long, and Flynn slowed to a halt before it. There were no good options. He could try to blast through, or sleep all night in the car and risk death by snowplow in the morning. The curve in the road behind him meant that the plow would have little time to see a stopped vehicle shrouded with snow.

Flynn went in reverse until he was back against the drift he had just gone through. Then he accelerated, hoping to power through the next one as he had the others. But after hitting the front edge of the drift the car shuddered to a halt, the rear wheels spinning. A few attempts at forward movement only spun the wheels further into the ice. The car skidded sideways, then back, sideways, then back, until Flynn finally stopped trying.

He put his gloves on and got out. The icy wind annihilated his face. Three high steps brought him to the rear of the car. He chipped off the ice on his tail lights, dug out the snow from around his rear tires, and saw that even if he had remembered to put a shovel in his car, he wouldn't have a chance. The ice under the tires was solid and thick, and his wheels had worn two wide and deep grooves. He stepped back to the car, grabbed a couple of shirts from his overnight bag, and shoved them under one tire, then jammed his dirty canvas jacket under the other. For the next hour, he tried repeatedly to get himself out of his icy trap. He ruined his shirts and jacket, but the car didn't move an inch.

He sat in the driver's seat. He had a half a tank of gas. Sitting in idle, even all night long, would probably use only a quarter tank. He would be all right . . . until a truck came around the curve in the morning and slammed into his snow-covered car. He tried to calculate how far the walk would be to the Oleo Ranch, but then he remembered that around here, that's how people lost their toes. The tips of his fingers already throbbed under his gloves. He took them off and held his hands to the vents.

After a while, he pushed back his seat, took off his wet hiking boots, socks and pants, and changed into his jeans, dry socks, and the Dr. Martens he had worn to teach earlier that day. He dropped the heat down to low, directed it onto his feet again, and settled in. The weather didn't bother him. What bothered him was that he should have moved to Grand Junction by now. The weather was just waking him up, that's all. It was teaching him a lesson, again and again, one he had yet to heed.

It was 8:03 p.m. There wouldn't be another vehicle all night, not in this storm. At the first sign of daylight he could hike back to the Oleo Ranch and see if anyone was home; but for now, he'd be safe in the car. Or could the drifting snow clog the exhaust pipe? Would that be possible, or would the exhaust continually melt it? He got out again, ducking into the screaming wind, and used his hands to dig out a trench around the pipe. Then he fought his way back into the car, took off his gloves, removed his Dr. Martens, and changed his socks again. He got his sneakers from his gym bag and put them on. He stared at the rearview mirror, half dreading, half hoping for, headlights. Within minutes the snow would build up again over the exhaust pipe, but the heat from the pipe would probably continue to melt it. He cracked open the passenger window, just in case, then opened his own about an inch as well. The wind whistled and ripped into the car, rocking the vehicle. He slouched down in his seat, wrapped a sweatshirt around his neck and mouth, tugged down his hat, and closed his eyes. In the fabric of his sweatshirt, he smelled the Gunnison River and Escalante Canyon, where he had hiked on Wednesday.

He wondered what he would do if his kids were in the car with him—Nathan in front, Janey in the back. He was glad they weren't there; he was glad they were safe with Rachel, who always took good care of them. She was a good mother—that much he could say about her. She loved them to death. And she had a stable life. Right now, considering the condition he was in, he had no business daydreaming about being their custodial parent.

At 3:17 a.m., Flynn awoke to stillness. The fuel gauge had barely moved. The snow had covered his driver's-side window, but the storm had passed, and it had been more bluster than bite: not much accumulation, but the wind had blown a great deal of it against the car.

He tried to open his door, but it wouldn't budge.

He put on his hiking boots, now dry from the heat vent, clambered over to the passenger seat, and stepped out the door on that side to check the exhaust pipe. As soon as he did, he saw a streak of cosmic dust slicing across the sky. He watched, shivering in the sharp cold, as several bluish-white meteors streaked in unpredictable curves, one slicing off to the south, another to the north, all originating from the same domed area to the east, in the hook of Leo. Then a pause, then many all at once—some darting, others taking four full seconds to streak and dissipate. For a long time Flynn watched the meteors, his bare head lifted, his mouth open. *My god, the kids would love this.* He felt for the first time the actual movement of the earth through space, and understood that it was ceaselessly surging forward, blasting its way around the sun. Any pause, any stasis, would mean instant death.

Before he got back in his car, Flynn checked the exhaust pipe, and brushed the snow off the tail lights so an encroaching plow would see them. Then he glanced up once more to watch the meteors, but they were almost too beautiful to bear.

He got in, took off his boots, and put his sneakers back on. Nobody in White Plains would ever witness such a sight, for as long as they lived. Nobody.

Flynn had been living in Colorado for almost a year. That feeling he used to get, when he would fly in on weekends to visit Casey, was with him all the time now. He had thought it was in her, but it wasn't. It was in the land.

BY THE TIME ANOTHER VEHICLE CAME BY, IT WAS 7:21 A.M., AND THE SUN WAS about to rise. The truck slowed as it approached Flynn's car, then pulled up alongside him. It was the same man Flynn had seen in Lake City three mornings earlier. He was a carpenter, headed to South Fork to pick up some lumber. He had chained tires and a tow line.

"How was that deer?" Flynn asked.

"Nice and tender," the man said, glancing at Flynn's sneakers.

They got back into their vehicles, and the man eased ahead of Flynn's car, backed up, got out, pulled out his tow chain, hooked the Sidekick to his truck, and got back in. He proceeded to pull Flynn out of the snowdrift, then through nine or ten more. Sitting in his car behind the stronger truck, Flynn sometimes accelerated and sometimes slipped the car into neutral, allowing himself to be pulled.

When the snowdrifts ended and the road cleared, close to the Rio Grande headwaters, the man stopped his truck, came back, and released him. Flynn felt that something had happened. He got out of his car, shook the man's hand, squinted into the low sunlight, and breathed in the crisp air.

The man threw the tow chain into the bed of his truck, waved, and drove off.

Flynn looked around. It was a bright day. Off to the side, a herd of elk stared at him, waiting to see what he would do.

FIELD OF BATTLE

Up to that point it had been a pretty crappy day. I am known as a pretty chill kid, but if I was honest I would tell you that sometimes I get into these dark moods and I can't tell you why. What I mean is, nothing triggers it. My dad might say it's because I'm dehydrated, or I haven't eaten my fruits and vegetables, but he's not around much anymore. And anyway it still happens no matter what I eat or drink.

My sister was in kindergarten at the time, so maybe she had a different schedule than I did—well I can't remember why she wasn't there, but I do know I came home first that afternoon. My mom always kept the key in a magnetic holder by the garage door, so I would let myself in and get jumped on by the dogs, only one of which I ever liked and that was Mollie the Collie, but my mom backed the car over her a few weeks before the day I'm talking about so Mollie was gone by then, it was just Tigger and Jeter, who were what my mom calls barkaholics, really annoying. So that day I got off the bus, which totally sucks by the way because there are some complete idiots in my town, total douchebags. They do stuff like stick gum in your hair or punch you hard in the shoulder when they walk past you on their way to the back of the bus. In town they harass the Mennonites, in school they harass the nerdy kids, but on the bus they harass everyone. Oh, and also this day I'm talking about was about a week after I had a terrible embarrassing thing happen when I was at school and I'm not going to talk about that.

So it was a crappy day, like I said, meaning normal for where we live, cloudy and drizzly, like not snow and not rain either, and when I got home I kicked Tigger and Jeter away and there was a blanket concealing a lump on the dining room table and a note that said "Game on!"

When I looked under the blanket, I found a huge brand-new Nerf gun.

Now, this wasn't just any Nerf gun. This was a fifty-round beast of a machine. I grabbed it and held it in my hands. It was the gun I would have requested for my birthday if I had thought of it. I pumped it until it wouldn't pump anymore and looked toward the living room.

Sam was in there. Sam was Mom's boyfriend, and he lived with us off and on. This was one of the "on" periods. He had reddish hair and a goatee, and he liked goofing around with me. He had two kids of his own, older than us, and he was kind of in my dad's position. What I mean is, his wife was angry with him and didn't let him see his kids very much.

I tiptoed through the dining room and kitchen, holding the Nerf gun in the shooting position. The dogs were barking but I didn't pay any attention. I was focused. I was ready for battle.

This much I knew: Sam's gun options were slim. He probably had my single-shot Nerf spring-action rifle, and maybe also the Nerf assault rifle with three different bullet types. I doubted he had bought a fifty-rounder for himself. In other words, I was pretty sure I had the bigger gun.

As I went through the kitchen to the living room, I noticed that all the cushions—from the couch, the blue chair, and the loveseat—had been removed. I looked to my right toward the stairwell, then to my left, and I saw what Sam had done. In the sun room was a gigantic cushion fort, and a gun barrel staring right at me.

I jumped back behind the wall as the shooting erupted. I counted shots; Sam fired four bullets from what looked like my Nerf assault rifle, which meant he had six left. I took a deep breath, shouldered my weapon, and rapid fired toward the cushion fort as I ran across the room and dove behind the love seat. I would position myself there for the remainder of the battle.

I checked my gun. During all the excitement I had expended half my rounds, about twenty-five Nerf bullets. Shooting such a big gun was so enticing that my finger had stayed on the trigger for too long. I crouched behind the love seat for a while, trying to come up with a strategy. He was completely protected behind the cushions; there was no way I could hit him from my position. I needed a full-fledged ground assault.

I lifted my head to draw his fire, then did it again, and each time I counted how many bullets he shot. When I was sure he had fired all ten,

I jumped out again, let out a warrior yell, and charged the cushion fort. I quickly kicked out all the cushions and found Sam struggling to reload and pump the gun. I had him! I unloaded the remainder of my arsenal and he dropped his weapon and died an agonizing death. Then he started laughing and I collapsed onto the cushions and started laughing too.

I didn't want the game to end, so I declared a timeout for us to reclaim our ammo and start again. I found a really good spot to hide, inside the Christmas box where the fake tree was stored in the attic. It was such a great spot that Sam didn't find me for at least fifteen minutes. The whole time I was in the box, grinning, my gun poised. I couldn't wait to leap out and shoot him. But I wound up waiting so long that I finally had to get out, run downstairs, and jump back into the field of battle.

We played like this until my mom came home, yelled out, "What are you knuckleheads doing? I just cleaned this house!" and the game was over.

§

I FINALLY FIGURED OUT HOW I COULD TALK TO THE KIDS. EVERY DAY, THEY would get home from school at around 3:15, and then they'd be alone for about an hour, watching TV, until Rachel came home from work. A neighbor whose daughter went to the same school was on call in case anything happened. The last time I had seen the kids, a visit that had to be arranged by my lawyer, Nathan had divulged all this, so I took him aside and told him the ringer on his house phone was shut off. I told him that every day at 3:30, he should stop whatever he was doing and watch the phone; if he saw the light blinking, that was me calling him, and he should pick it up. He asked me if he should just turn the ringer on every day when he came home, but I said no, because he might forget to turn it back off afterwards, and his mother would know what was up. So he said he would remember to watch the phone.

Some days he forgot, and on other days 3:30, 1:30 Mountain Time, would slip past me. But on this day he answered on the fourth ring, out of breath. I asked him how he was doing, and he told me he didn't mean to get in trouble at school, and please not to worry about the letter I was about to get. During recess, he and his friends were sword-fighting with orange construction cones and he had been written up for distracting the students who were watching them out their classroom window. A few days later, on a morning after the floors had been waxed, he and those same friends had taken turns running full speed down the hall, sliding on their bellies and crashing headfirst into the lockers. I laughed and told him I didn't care; both those things seemed like a lot of fun.

Janey got on the extension, also out of breath, and interrupted Nathan to tell me that a few days earlier her cat had caught a mole and had been playing with it like it was a toy, and she had saved the mole and put it in a box with grass, but it had died. When she told me about it, she starting crying as if it had just happened. I told her she was very nice to try to save the mole, but that she probably shouldn't do that again, because they had claws and germs. I told her she shouldn't be so angry with the cat; it wasn't the cat's fault—that's just what cats did.

Nathan interrupted and asked me if I was still with the lady who bought them puppets, and I said no, I was living with my friends Len and Sydney now, but not for long. In fact I would be seeing them very soon. I had found a job at a university near them and was moving back east.

PENNSYLVANIA

ALL THE WRONG MOVES

The houses on Severance Lane were stooped and weary, slouched behind gnarled trees whose roots heaved up the sidewalks. Flynn found the address he was looking for, with a mailbox that said *Siczlytsky* and a *For Rent* sign on the garage. He rang the doorbell and glanced around. It might be a nice enough neighborhood, but it was hard to tell with the sky so gray.

When nobody came to the door, he rang again, then peeked inside the bay window and saw an old woman sleeping in an armchair with the television on. He tapped on the glass, then rapped, until the woman finally jerked awake.

She opened the door, squinting at the general vicinity of Flynn's head. She was a plump, wrinkled sock, more muppet than woman, with a blonde mop for hair, watery eyes, jittery hands. She wore yellow pants, a pink blouse, and red shoes. She could have been a youthful ninety or an insane seventy. On her blouse was a blue-and-white sticker:

HELLO
my name is
Helen

"He's gone," she said. "My boy." She lurched past Flynn down the stairs, clutching her car keys, her wig tipping to the side. Flynn trailed her, ready to catch the wig if it fell off, but as she got to the powder-blue Cutlass at the curb she stopped and turned. "Are you the young man who called about the room?" She reached for his face, and Flynn jerked back at first, but then let himself be touched—his cheeks, his hair, his chin. Her hands smelled vaguely of salami.

"This way," she said, scurrying toward the garage.

Inside, the walls were plastered with yellowed newspaper clippings about Jack Siczlytsky, a high-school wrestler. Helen patted one of them before opening the door to the basement.

Downstairs, there was a washing machine with petrified sponges on top, waterlogged boxes stuffed with photo albums, and a bathroom with a moldy shower stall, a cracked toilet seat, and a rusted sink. Flynn ducked under the pipes, ready to tell Helen he wasn't interested, that when the head of the English Department search committee had told him about this room for rent, just one block from campus, he hadn't realized it was in a basement, but now that he'd seen it, he knew he'd never spend a single night in this hellhole. But when she couldn't stop shaking as she tried to open the lock to the room, she handed him the key and said, "It's a hundred dollars a week, and I really need the money now that my boy is gone."

Flynn opened the door. The room smelled vaguely of mold and cat urine. There was a twin bed on a metal frame against the wall, an old refrigerator with a microwave on top, a plaid couch, and a coffee table with placemats depicting Pennsylvania landscapes: a herd of deer, a creek bordered by azaleas, a dirt path cutting through a forest. "That's what it used to look like," Helen said, pointing out the window. Now, she said, it was where everyone did their shopping: Walmart, Kmart, Lowe's. "Still looks like this," she said, "up in Nicholson, Tunkhannock, those parts. That's where my boy— " Her eyes welled, and she looked about the room with a vacant expression.

"I've lost someone too," Flynn said, but then felt like an imposter.

"Eighty-five a week," she said, fingering Flynn's shirtsleeve. "It would be nice to have a man in the house. The washing machine. . ." Her fingers fluttered on his arm. "Eighty? Seventy-five?"

Flynn placed his hand on top of hers. He had driven two thousand miles, and he was exhausted. It was either this place or a hotel that would cost seven times as much. "All right," he said. "Seventy-five. But just for a few weeks. And I'm sorry, I'm not good at fixing things."

TWO MONTHS EARLIER, JUST AFTER FLYNN HAD ACCEPTED THE POSITION AT Sacred Heart College in Scranton, he and his friend Sydney hiked up the eastern ridge of the Colorado National Monument. Sydney hated to hike—she hated any physical activity, including sex with her boyfriend Len if she had to be on top—but she had agreed to go on the hike once she found out Flynn was leaving.

On Serpents Trail, every switchback provided a higher, broader view of the Grand Valley. The city of Grand Junction shimmered in the heat, with Grand Mesa guarding the valley on the other side. In the distance, the Gunnison and Colorado Rivers meandered separately before joining forces on their way towards the Grand Canyon. Before they reached the top of the trail, Sydney stopped suddenly, sat on a rock, and took out a pack of Virginia Slims. "And you could have all this," she said, waving the pack at the landscape. "And every day you make it more impossible."

Flynn sat down next to her. "I'll miss you too," he said. When he had first arrived at Mesa State, Sydney had given him the cold shoulder: in her view, Flynn had just waltzed into the dean's office and stolen the full-time instructorship that had been promised her. But after he had made friends with Len and started staying at their house two nights a week, watching baseball on the couch together and talking about their kids (Len was fifty, with three children from his first marriage), Sydney eventually warmed to Flynn, and in the months that followed, theirs had grown into the closer friendship.

"Leaving this place for Scrotum, Pennsylvania," she said as she lit a cigarette and looked out over the Grand Valley, "is like leaving Penelope Cruz for Judi Dench."

"Scranton," Flynn said, plucking some leaves off a sage brush and rubbing them into his hand. "And Judi Dench is gorgeous."

"All right, it's like leaving *me* for Joyce Carol Oates," she said, jutting out her chest. Sydney was a thirty-year-old writer who taught creative writing and 20th Century American literature, while Len taught Spanish part-time and had a small landscaping business on the side. When Flynn had broken things off with Casey, they had let him move in for good, in exchange for doing some of the cooking and helping Len on weekends. Flynn enjoyed the landscaping work so much he would have done it whether or not there was free rent at stake.

"My kids will be only an hour away," Flynn reminded her. He had applied to six teaching jobs within a 100-mile radius of Binghamton, New York, and landed three interviews and two job offers. He'd taken the Sacred Heart job because it was the closest, and if he found a place to live north of campus, he'd be even closer. "I could see them every weekend," he said. "I could go to Parents Night and Open House and school plays and all that stuff."

"Only if Mama Bear lets you," Sydney said. "Don't forget, you'll be closer to the cave now."

It was eighty degrees out, even though it was early April. To the west, in the vast and lonely Utah desert, it was probably closer to ninety. To the east, over the Rockies, it was snowing. Flynn started to worry about Casey and the horses, but then he remembered that six days after he had left the ranch, a new boyfriend had moved in.

Sydney pointed to the bright landscape below them, then to the anvil-shaped cloud that had been swelling and graying over the course of their hike. "You're never going to see this again," she said. "It's probably sleeting right now in Scrotum."

Flynn nodded. He had spent six years in upstate New York and knew all about the weather there, the gray that settled in around October and didn't leave until late April. It would be the same in northeastern Pennsylvania. But he felt certain he could bring the Colorado sunshine—or the *feeling* of the sunshine, anyway—with him when he moved.

A shard of it beamed onto the Alpine Building downtown, while at the same time they heard the rumble of thunder, from the same gray cloud Sydney had pointed out. They were exposed on a ridge at six thousand feet, with no tall trees nearby. Flynn heard his father's voice in his head: *What are you, nuts? Get inside where you belong.*

"Ah, it's just a bunch of rocks," Sydney said, waving at the scenery. "You won't miss it." She put her hands up to her eyes, and when she removed them, her face was red. "Who am I going to talk to now?" she said, her voice cracking. "Nobody else listens to me."

FLYNN HAD SIGNED A SPECIAL CONTRACT WITH SACRED HEART: INSTEAD OF starting in September, when the fall semester began, he was to start May first and work over the summer to clean up the mess that was the

English Department. They'd dropped from forty-one majors to twenty-three, and the six full-time faculty members despised one another. On his first day there, during finals week, Flynn was introduced to them, some of whom he had met in his teleconference interview: three men with beards, another with a toupee, and two women: one stinking of alcohol, the other wearing clothing from the Truman Administration. "Sweet Jesus," muttered the toupeed man, who'd been the department chair for the last fifteen years. "They've replaced me with John Travolta."

The alcoholic shook Flynn's hand with alarming vigor and asked if he needed anything. When he said he supposed he could use some water, she ran downstairs, bought him a bottle from a vending machine, found a cup with ice, and rushed it back to him. The toupeed man rolled his eyes.

After that, the faculty members disbursed, as they had grading to do, and Flynn was taken downstairs to get things squared away at the Dean's Office. An attractive woman with over-washed hair typed in all his information, and when she asked him for his marital status he said, "Divorced."

"Oh," she said.

He'd been free and clear of his marriage for over a year, although he still owed thousands of dollars to his lawyer and had barely seen his children. When he had flown out for his first official visit as a divorced father a year earlier, on Memorial Day, he had emailed Rachel his information and left her phone messages, but when he pulled up in his rental car, he found nobody home. After trying again on Father's Day, then calling his lawyer and arranging for a hearing at Broome County Family Court (in which he participated by phone), he managed to see Nathan and Janey for a full weekend in August, then on Labor Day weekend, then Halloween weekend (sleeping on the couch at Rachel's house while she went away with Sam, her boyfriend), then Thanksgiving week at his mother's, and a brief visit on Christmas Eve—all with conditions, all preceded by negotiations, but all visits nonetheless. When he had told Rachel about his new job in Scranton, she had immediately petitioned for an increase in child support and sent him an email: *Don't think you're going to just waltz in here and be their father again.*

On his second day at Sacred Heart, the woman from the Dean's Office came to Flynn's office with a small but weighty loaf wrapped in tin foil. She wore a tight top stretched over impressive breasts. Behind her, Flynn's toupeed colleague appeared in the doorway, raised his eyebrows, and went back to his office. He was a Victorian scholar named Joseph, and he'd been forced to abandon the chairmanship when the squabbling among the faculty had erupted into a full-fledged war.

"I'm kind of famous around here for my banana bread," the woman said, placing the loaf on the corner of his desk. She looked to be about five years older than Flynn. "I know what it's like," she said, "all alone in a strange area, no friends . . ." She reached to give his shoulder a sympathetic pat, and when she did, the fabric of her blouse strained to the brink of tearing. "Anyway," she said, placing her hands on her hips, "if you'd like a nice home-cooked meal as you're settling in, you know where to find me." She laughed, seeming a little embarrassed, but then winked.

"Thank you," Flynn said, and watched her walk away.

When she was safely downstairs, Joseph stepped back into the doorway. "Botched boob job," he whispered. "One's bigger than the other. I saw you staring."

Flynn put his head in his hands.

"Her husband left her for a younger woman," Joseph said, leaning against the doorframe, "so she went in for an upgrade." He rolled his eyes again, and Flynn realized he was gay. "But this ain't Malibu, right? There's only one plastic surgeon in the county that's any good, and she went to . . . the other guy."

Flynn felt a pang of sympathy for the woman. "I feel like— "

"Don't sweat it, sweetheart," he said. "We've all looked. How can you not? She *showcases* them in the storefront window. She should hang a *For Sale* sign on her chest: *Going Out of Business, twenty percent off.*"

Flynn held up the aluminum-wrapped loaf. "I *love* banana bread," he said.

Joseph pursed his lips. "Wait," he said. "You're single?"

Flynn nodded, and Joseph let out a low whistle. "Then let the games begin."

"When a woman makes you banana bread," Sydney said when Flynn called her that evening, "it means she wants your banana. It means, 'I would bake for you every night if you would only marry me'."

"It felt more nurturing than sexual," Flynn said.

"If by 'nurturing' you mean she wanted to breastfeed you," Sydney said, "then yes."

Flynn stared at one of the placemats, which showed a creek lined by tall trees, a heron standing in the water. "Syd, she doesn't even know me."

Sydney sighed into Flynn's ear. "How is it possible for a man to reach the ripe old age of thirty-eight," she said, "and still be such a moron about women?"

Flynn looked out the window, at the blanket of gray sky, and told her how long it had been since he'd seen the sun.

"It's a hundred fucking degrees here," Sydney said with a yawn. "We could use a little of that gray." She told him she was sick of her students talking about the sunshine, about the vast and powerful beauty of the West. "It's a *desert*," she said. "Yesterday one of them asked me where *I* go to see something beautiful, and I said, 'I don't have to go anywhere; I just look in the mirror.'"

Flynn heard the tinny sound of sirens in the background, and asked if she was watching an *ER* rerun. Sydney moaned nostalgically. "The Clooney era," she said.

"You should have volunteered as an extra," Flynn said, "back when you lived in L.A. You could have been a patient consulting Noah Wyle about breast reductions. He'd have laid you out in O.R. and taken a look." He closed his eyes and imagined Sydney's breasts, unveiled on the operating table.

As raindrops began to pelt the tiny windows, Helen's cat mewled from outside. "The OR of *ER*," Sydney said, "would be a hell of a lot better than the PA where you are."

AFTER HIS FIRST DAY AT SACRED HEART, FLYNN SENT RACHEL AN EMAIL requesting a visit the following weekend, and he cc'd his lawyer. It wasn't his scheduled visitation, but he hadn't seen them since March. He was excited about his move and couldn't wait to tell them they would soon be able to see one another almost every weekend, and he would be coming to their school events, and he had some weekend trip ideas: to Cayuga Lake, where Briggs, his former roommate, now lived; to New York City, so they could walk through Times Square, go up the Empire State Building, visit his old friend Peter, and show them where he and their mother first lived together; to Boston and Concord, where his favorite writers used to live; and to White Plains, so they could see their grandmother, Auntie Annie, Uncle Mitch, and their cousins.

When he didn't hear back by Friday, he couldn't stand it anymore. It was as if a primitive lust for the smell of their skin had taken over his being. He drove up to Binghamton, speeding the whole way, but when he arrived at Rachel's house and rang the doorbell, nobody answered. He saw her new car, a yellow Jeep Wrangler, in the garage, so he kept ringing, and for a moment he saw Nathan's face pressed to the upstairs window. He stepped back and called his son's name, again and again, then shouted it from the driveway like a repressed Marlon Brando; but when the neighbor across the street came out on her porch, looking alarmed, he finally gave up. He found a napkin in his car, scribbled a note to the kids, went up to the neighbor and asked if she would deliver it to Nathan the next time she saw him outside. She said she would. She introduced herself and told him that she was the one who watched the kids after school, and that Nathan had told her about the 3:30 calls. "It's awful," she said. "What Rachel is doing to you. I've seen you, coming here . . . " She kept glancing over his shoulder as she spoke, and when Flynn tried to shake her hand to thank her, she shook her head quickly and hustled back inside. When he got home, he looked up the neighbor's number and called her, and she told Flynn that after he left, Rachel had sprinted over to her house, insisted on seeing the note, and ripped the napkin to shreds.

"What on earth did you do," she asked, "to make that woman so angry?"

Here's what Flynn did: he left. He betrayed his wedding vows. He was the love of Rachel's life, and he had dumped her without any warning, and it only made things worse that he did so years after he realized he didn't love her. In fact, that had been the meanest part, to have kept his eroding feelings to himself for so long instead of taking action right away, back when they still may have had a chance. If one of them was to blame for the disintegration of their marriage, it would have to be the one who hadn't been honest, the one who had hidden his feelings instead of declaring them, the one who eagerly sacrificed his personal needs so that he could resent the other, the one who had never told the other that his love for her was from the very beginning a wounded butterfly, and whether by holding it tenderly, ignoring it completely, examining it at arm's length, or chafing its wings, he had soiled it, and killed it, by degrees.

WITH MOST OF THE FACULTY OFF FOR THE SUMMER, FLYNN WORKED ALONE at his office until well after the staff had gone home. He ate jalapeño potato chips and strawberry Pop-tarts from the vending machine. He drank Jolt soda. He engaged in meaningful conversations with the cleaning woman.

When he drove north on Interstate 81 to scope out towns where he might live, he passed enormous pyramids of ash, a billboard with pictures of dead fetuses, and a half-mile-long car dump the highway had been built around. He exited onto Route 6, since on the map it looked like a small road heading into a quiet town, but he found himself on some other Route 6, with a large shopping mall and a string of chain stores and chain restaurants alongside the road: Denny's, Toys "R" Us, Babies "R" Us, Long John Silver's, Burger King, Walmart, TGI Fridays, Denny's, Dunkin' Donuts, Casual Male, Suburban Casuals. He turned right and headed back towards the highway, passing Chipotle, Red Robin, Panera, Michael's, TJ Maxx, Home Depot, Taco Bell, Royal Buffet, and Ruby Tuesday. Pulling into the parking lot of the Viewmont Mall—on the hill Helen had pointed towards, the area that had once looked like the place-mats—he tried to imagine how long ago the trees had been cut down, how long since there had been a view from this mont. Down in the valley was the city of Scranton, stretched south by a string of old coal-mining towns, the Susquehanna filtering through them before widening and surging into Wilkes-Barre. There were smokestacks, landfills, and a grand junction of highways: I-81, I-84, I-80, the Scranton Expressway, I-380, the Pennsylvania Turnpike. Flynn thought of his father, who had worked for a company that made cabinet parts and had traveled north from White Plains to towns like Poughkeepsie, Monticello, and Nyack. Had northeastern Pennsylvania been part of his territory? Had he driven here to Dickson City and sold parts to these stores on the new Route 6? Had he pulled over at this same spot and gazed out at this same barren landscape?

APPARENTLY THERE WEREN'T TOO MANY EDUCATED SINGLE MEN IN THE greater Scranton area, because in his first month there, Flynn met many available women. His first date was with the Dean's Office administrator, whose offer of a home-cooked meal turned out to be limp noodles with broccoli washed down with cheap chardonnay. Most of the conversation centered on her overweight daughter, how the girl would never find herself a husband unless she lost forty pounds. She showed Flynn pictures—a bright-eyed college graduate, curvaceous and lovely. Flynn wondered if he should be dating the girl instead of her mother.

The second was with the Admissions Director, whom he'd met to discuss his ideas on improving the English major: forming a book club, starting up a visiting writers series, hosting a Halloween party where students and faculty would dress as literary characters. At the end of their meeting she'd told him that a group of employees met every Friday for Happy Hour at a bar called the Dead End. "Oh, and none of us bring our spouses," she said.

A few Fridays later, he joined them. They drank pitchers of Yuengling, sang along to loud music, and in the middle of "Paradise by the Dashboard Light," the Admissions Director grabbed Flynn by the arm and pulled him outside. After making out by the dumpster for a while, they got into their cars and Flynn followed her to her house. She kept the lights off as they made their way into her bedroom, then lit some candles, turned over a framed photograph on the end table, put on some Indian music, took off her clothes, stripped Flynn of his, swayed in a drunken fertility dance, and mounted him. Flynn, who had hastily put on a condom that instantly deadened all his nerve endings, held on as she pressed in for several orgasms in rapid succession, dramatically throwing back her head each time. In between her third and fourth, Flynn lay diagonally across the bed, his head close to the end table, and as she shifted her hips to bring it all home again, he smelled something acrid and sweet: his hair had caught fire. He interrupted Dramatic Orgasm #4 to smack at his head and peel away flakes of his hair.

His third date was with an artist. Flynn had gone to the Everhart Museum to check out an exhibit of "Homegrown Art," and one wall featured tall canvases of dark, sensual nudes conveyed in chalk. Just as he spotted his colleague Joseph in the room with a silk-shirted younger man, the artist herself approached Flynn. She was a graduate student at the University of Scranton, and her skin looked soft under her flimsy dress. As they introduced themselves and talked about her work, she thrust out her pelvis and let her hair fall over one eye.

The next morning, she called Flynn and told him she was on the front steps of his house, talking with his grandmother.

"How did you—"

"I asked around," she said.

Flynn ran out the garage door to find Helen berating her for dressing like a harlot. She was wearing a low-cut sun dress with sandals; her toenails were scarlet. She turned from Helen, her face flushed, and told Flynn she had come by to see if he wanted to go for a drive. She seemed on the brink of tears.

"Hang on," he said, and he ran down to his room to wash up and put on a clean shirt. On his way out he grabbed a condom, just in case.

The artist drove north. It was a mild day, and the sun was out at last. As they passed through woods jammed with old-growth hemlock pines, with gurgling creeks matted by leaves, the artist gasped—"Those trees!"—then pulled over, popped open her trunk, and pulled out an easel.

An hour later, Flynn had taken a long hike in the woods and a short nap on the leaves, waking up when an orange salamander crawled onto his face. Meanwhile, the artist had produced a haunting portrait of the forest. The canvas was splayed with vertical lines, tall trunks paralleling one another and branches intersecting, dimly backlit and crowding off the edges. The trees looked achingly sad, stripped of strength and violated, yet also resilient. "I can't give this to you," she said, "even though it reminds me of you." Her dress was unbuttoned almost to the waist, her arms and face striped with chalk, her hands maroon. When Flynn slipped his hand onto her rib cage she instantly pulled him down with her onto the bed of leaves, and slid aside the straps of her dress as if he were a baby yearning for her milk. As Flynn reached for the condom in his pocket, he thought, *How about that? Helen was right.*

The next day, he went to Joseph's office and told him he had found the place where he wanted to live. Joseph, the one who had originally emailed him about the room at Helen's house, apologized for how that had worked out, then took out a map of northeast Pennsylvania and helped Flynn to locate where the artist had taken him, near Tunkhannock Creek. There were patches of green: a state park, and wooded areas interrupted by small towns. "If you don't mind the complete lack of civility and loathsome turkeys in your backyard," Joseph said, "then that's where it's at, baby." He recommended a realtor friend at Endless Mountain Realty. "Your kids will love it," he said.

That evening, while walking to a convenience mart to find something for dinner, Flynn dialed Sydney's number. "They call them the Endless Mountains," he told her, "but I assure you, they are neither."

He had emailed the realtor and asked if she knew of any places in that area for rent, preferably in the woods, preferably by the creek. The woman wrote back that she couldn't think of any off hand, but she'd do some investigating. "Maybe you can expand your options?" she had asked.

"There are no other options," he had said.

"Like endless love," Sydney said. "Can you imagine that ring of hell?"

Flynn sighed. "I could be having endless *sex* right now," he said, "but the women I've been meeting are either married or psychotic." He and the artist had stopped for dinner on their way home, and when Flynn had noticed mozzarella sticks and chicken fingers on the menu, he told her about his kids, and she had flashed a look of revulsion. *Well that's the end of that*, Flynn thought. He told her he loved his children madly, and with any luck they'd soon be an intricate part of his life again, so it looked as if this would be their first and last date—and with that she put down her fork, told him she couldn't believe he had just used her like that, then stormed out of the restaurant, leaving Flynn to hitchhike all the way home. But then she called him all night, increasingly inebriated and hysterical, until Flynn finally shut off his phone at one a.m. When he turned it back on the next morning, he had six tearful voicemails and twenty-seven texts.

Now, as he walked down the bumpy sidewalk talking to Sydney, Flynn found himself looking over his shoulder for a half-naked woman with wild hair, chalky arms, and a shotgun.

"Be careful out there," Sydney said. "The mass of Catholics live lives of quiet desperation."

"The cleaning lady gave me a list of the women at school who want to marry me," Flynn said. He told Sydney about his other dates, including his tryst with the Admissions Director when his hair had caught fire.

"What on earth is wrong with the missionary position?" she said. "There's a right way and a wrong way to lie on a bed, you know. Do you aspire to be a contortionist?"

"I'm making all the wrong moves, Syd."

As Flynn paused outside the convenience mart, holding his cell phone to his ear, a large man with a cratered face exited the store balancing a six-pack of Yuengling, a box of Krispy Kreme donuts, and a carton of cigarettes. "I've just discovered the Pennsylvania Food Pyramid," Flynn said.

"At least you're getting laid," Sydney said. "My Latin lover is currently asleep on my lap, where other things should be happening." She took a drag of her cigarette and sighed. Len was twenty years older than Sydney, but Flynn knew that Sydney was the one who typically abstained. "I keep hoping that if I emit some primal odor," she said, "his loins will stir and the slumbering brute in him will awaken."

"Sex is the last thing I need now," Flynn said. "What I need now is a home."

"Well, you could have had one," Sydney said, and then cut off whatever she was going to say next. She was probably thinking of the Sociology colleague she had fixed him up with after he moved to Grand Junction, or of her and Len's insistence that they really did like having him in the house with them and he didn't always have to make himself so scarce, or maybe something like *With me, you big dummy*. When he had first gotten the job at Mesa State, Sydney had just separated from her husband and moved in with Len, so it had never occurred to Flynn to throw his own hat into that crowded ring.

"Listen," she said, changing her voice. "As soon as you have your kids with you, you'll be home. No matter where you are."

Flynn nodded. "But I have to find a better place," he said. He watched as one car after another swerved to avoid an enormous pothole. "I want a proper home for them. I need to anchor down here, Syd."

"Ah," Sydney said. "That's what Leonardo is. My anchor. I'm petting his hair as I'm talking to you. What's left of it, anyway."

The phone beeped—another text from the artist: *You will pay dearly for this betrayal.*

"Here's something," Sydney said. "*My* lover's hair will *never* catch fire."

"I need that," Flynn said, imagining living in the kind of place where he, Nathan, and Janey would be happy, and finding a woman who valued the kids' presence in his life. "I need an anchor."

Sydney sighed, then described a Hemingway story she had taught in her summer class that morning, about a father and son on a drive together. While the son sleeps in the passenger seat, the narrator thinks of his father—about his sharp eyes, his weak chin. The two of them didn't get along, but there was one thing they had in common, their love for the outdoors, and that's what the main character keeps thinking about, now that his father is dead. "And sex," she said. "He thinks about sex, too. Because you guys can't turn that button off, can you?"

Flynn cleared his throat. "I'm familiar with the story," he said. His favorite professor—a man Flynn held in the highest esteem—had considered it the best short story ever written.

"Well then if you remember," Sydney said, "when the boy wakes up, out of nowhere he starts asking about his grandfather; he asks if they could go to Grandpa's grave. And at first the narrator says uh, I don't know, son, it's a long way away. But then, by the end, he's saying yeah, okay, I guess we'll have to do that. I guess we'll have to go to Grandpa's grave."

Flynn stared at the blue gallons of windshield-wiper fluid outside the convenience mart, three rows long and four deep. He hadn't been to his father's grave in almost ten years—since the day he asked Rachel to marry him. He hadn't even talked much to his kids about their grandfather, except to tell Nathan whom he was named after.

"The moral of the story being," Sydney said, her voice dropping low into his ear, "sometimes you don't know what you need until someone tells you what you need."

IN THE MIDDLE OF THE GUNNISON RIVER IN ESCALANTE CANYON, SOUTH OF Grand Junction, two enormous boulders are wedged together in the clear, rushing water, creating a giant stone recliner. This was where Flynn used to go when he was missing his children. He would sit there and listen to the water, watching for bighorn sheep. On the day he left Colorado, he had awakened before dawn and turned off at the canyon road to say goodbye to the river. He climbed down the embankment, removed his hiking boots and socks, and waded into the icy water just as the rising sun slanted its rays through a split in the canyon wall. He heaved himself onto the rocky recliner and listened to the canyon awaken: the screech of a hawk, the whistle of a marmot, the wet spanks of a beaver's tail. He imagined what it would feel like to hold Nathan's spindly body again, to breathe in the sweet scent of Janey's skin. He inhaled deeply, trying to remember her smell, and when he did, another image came to him, the smell of his father's jacket the last time he had seen him—cigarette smoke, the slight scent of mothballs, and something else . . . the faintest whiff of his deodorant: Aramis.

It was in his bedroom. A summer morning. His father had come in to apologize for having to miss Flynn's baseball game that afternoon. Flynn had often tried to remember what he had said back: "That's okay, Pop, don't worry about it"? Or was it more like "What, *again?*"

As the river water rushed past on both sides, Flynn imagined sliding down the smooth rock, his body getting colder and colder, until he was submerged in the icy flow, his long hair floating behind him like algae. As the sun climbed up the canyon and warmed the water, he would drown in a rush of brilliance. And he would see his father again.

WHEN HE GOT BACK TO HIS ROOM AND MICROWAVED THE PIZZA ROLLS, FLYNN stared at a picture on his wall, taken when he was with Nathan at Rye Beach. Flynn stood knee-deep in the Long Island Sound, holding his son, who was two at the time, in his arms. Flynn had always kept the picture because of how Nathan looked—a depth of sadness in his eyes. But now Flynn found himself staring at his own image: alarmingly pale, with short hair, a strange moustache, and a stooped posture.

He went into the bathroom and gazed into the cracked mirror. He looked completely different now from the man in that photograph: his hair long and thick, his complexion healthy. Something had happened to him in Colorado, something good. Whatever it was, maybe he could pass it on to his children. But if he stayed here, in the basement of Helen Siczlytsky's house in Scranton, eating microwaveable food products and drinking Dr. Pepper, he would soon turn into that man again.

AFTER THE PHONE CALL WITH RACHEL'S NEIGHBOR, FLYNN HAD FILED AN online petition with Broome County Family Court and a hearing was set for the tenth of June, two weeks away. When she received the notice, Rachel called and swore to him that she would *never* let him see the kids again; and sure enough, on his next scheduled visitation, the Friday of Memorial Day weekend, he drove up to Binghamton, but found nobody home. He texted her. *This shit is getting old, isn't it?*

Never forget, she texted back, *you brought this all on yourself.*

After trying again the next day with the same result, he drove home, and on Tuesday morning he called a support investigator at Broome County to tell her what was happening. At 2:00, he left his office and drove up to Rachel's house again, hoping to see the kids during the hour they spent at home with their neighbor after school. He waited for an hour on the front stoop, then saw Rachel's new yellow Jeep Wrangler barreling down the road. He stood up, but instead of pulling into her driveway, she accelerated past the house. In the back seat, Nathan and Janey leaned forward, and Nathan, closest to the window, lifted his hand.

Minutes later, Flynn received a text: *NOT GOING TO HAPPEN, BUDDY.*

THE NEXT WEEKEND HE DROVE UP ONCE AGAIN, AND THIS TIME THEY WERE home, with a family gathering going on. He rang the doorbell and heard someone come to the door, but it never opened. He rang it again and again as he heard windows being shut. He walked around to the back, feeling like some pathetic character from a movie, and found all the shades and curtains being drawn. He peeked in and saw Rachel's family in the living room, the kids playing with their cousins on the family room floor—a board game, like *Life* or *Trouble*. But they had stopped the game and were all looking up. Nathan's chin was lifted, his eyes alert.

Flynn banged on the window. He banged on all the windows. He pounded on the back door, calling out for Nathan and Janey, his throat closing up, not caring that he was crying.

Finally Rachel's brother opened the door and held out his arms, as if to prevent Flynn from perpetrating a violent act. "You better split," he said, shaking his head. "She just called the cops."

"I love you Natty!" he screamed at the top of his lungs. "Janey, Janey where are you?"

THE NEXT SATURDAY, THE TWENTY-SECOND ANNIVERSARY OF HIS FATHER'S death, Flynn did not drive to Binghamton, and he did not call Rachel. Instead, he went to Lackawanna State Park, where the grass was tall and moist, the sky low and gloomy. He sat on a bench and watched the swans.

His father's eyes had never been sharp. They had been soft and tired, a faded green. He had been a gentle man who had suffered a heart attack in his car while on a sales trip to Peekskill, hours after leaving Flynn's bedside—a man who had traveled half his life but had never gone anywhere. After the discovery of his car on the side of the highway (even in the midst of a heart attack, he had had the consideration to pull over onto the shoulder and put the car in park), after Flynn's sister drove him home from his baseball game and there were police cars in front of his house (her mother running up to him, putting her mascara-smudged face in front of his and saying "This is it, my life is over now, do you understand?"), what had remained, following the stifled confusion that dropped in at the wake and persisted for years after, was not the softness of his father's eyes or the weakness of his chin, but the sound of his voice: mild and muted normally, but sharp and terrifying when angry.

Now, if Flynn could have anything in the world besides his children's breath on his neck, it would be to hear his father's voice again, saying his name.

THE FOLLOWING MORNING, FLYNN CALLED THE BROOME COUNTY FAMILY Court and asked the support investigator why, after six phone calls and four emails, no action had been taken on his case. The investigator informed Flynn that she had spoken to Rachel, and since Flynn had gone to Rachel's house on days that were not scheduled in the visitation agreement, it had been perfectly within her rights to deny him access to the children. It was in the agreement, she said. As for Memorial Day weekend, Flynn had neglected to provide Rachel with sufficient advance notice of his arrival, so she had presumed he wasn't coming and had taken the kids to her sister's. When Flynn asked the support investigator if she had considered the possibility that Rachel hadn't told her the truth, if perhaps during her years of experience as a child-support investigator she may have discovered that divorced couples occasionally lied, if she would like to see the emails and copies of his phone records that would prove Rachel had plenty of advanced notice, and if it would maybe be a good idea in the future to get *both* sides of a dispute before coming to a conclusion, the investigator sighed, and Flynn realized that he was not, to this woman, a father who needed to see his kids; he was just another deadbeat dad who had left his children and now wanted to see them again at his convenience.

Which, he had to admit, was true.

The investigator told Flynn he needed to be patient, wait for the hearing date, and not engage in any more "erratic behavior" like "trying to break into" his ex-wife's house. When Flynn explained that he had only knocked on the windows, and asked if his behavior might be understandable, considering how long he had gone without seeing his children, the woman said, "Well what were you doing way out there in Colorado?"

He started to respond, but then stopped. How to describe the effect of the mountains on him, that big sky, the smell of pine and sage, the sight of those quaking aspens, after so many months of being treated like an outcast to his own children, a traitor begging for forgiveness, a beggar pleading for a crumb of time with the children to whom he had for five years devoted nearly every waking hour? Or the powerful influence of the woman he moved there for, who told him his children were better off without him, that he was already being replaced by their mother's boyfriend? It would have been a much longer stay had he not realized it was the land he loved and not the woman; for once that happened, he had left her, his life unraveling again until he discovered, at the core of himself, and with the unknowing help of Sydney and Len, the embryonic stirrings of something new, a different way of being. It had been tight for a while, after his move to Scranton, right there in his chest. But now, with each new dispute, with each day of gray, drizzly weather, with each interaction with the miserable colleagues he had inherited, that feeling was tolling from him, out of his body and back west, back toward the mountains, back up to that cornflower blue sky.

THE NEXT DAY, THE WOMAN FROM ENDLESS MOUNTAIN REALTY CALLED FLYNN to tell him about a house in the woods that wouldn't be advertised until that weekend, but the owner had agreed to show it to him. Flynn met her in the parking lot outside her building and followed her up Route 11 about a half hour to Nicholson. They passed an enormous concrete railroad bridge, and after several missed turns, she found the dirt road she was looking for, called Tom's Lane. It ran deep into a pine forest. They passed acres and acres of trees, slowing as a gaggle of turkeys ran out into the road and clumsily tried to take flight. After passing an alfalfa farm with "Tom" on the mailbox, Flynn saw a creek that ran alongside the road, curved sharply away, then back. He hoped the house would be there.

It was. They pulled over at a wooden sign that said *Hemlock Ridge*, by a house sided with red slats, its front porch bursting with plants, a rickety terrace jutting out from the second floor. The woods surrounding it were stuffed with towering pines, the sun barely filtering through. A shirtless middle-aged man was in the garage, lining up a two-by-four on a band saw, and as the realtor went over to speak to him, Flynn took a look around. In the front was a garden with tomato plants, ready-to-eat lettuce, green onion shoots, flowers in full bloom, and a mound of compost off to the side. In the back was a makeshift slate stairway down to the creek where a red canoe floated, tied to a tree. Flynn inhaled the cool, clean air.

On the other side, he found a tree house in progress and a hammock stretched between pine trees over two hundred feet tall. He dropped into the hammock with a sigh. When he heard some wheezing, he looked up to find an old black Lab limping toward him; when the dog reached Flynn it went up on its hind paws and pushed down on the hammock with his front paws, trying to climb in with him. Flynn petted the dog's bony head and closed his eyes, listening to the whisper of pine needles, the wheezing of the old dog, and his heart pumping blood to his body, like creek water rushing.

"It's six hundred a month," the realtor said when she found him there. Flynn smiled at the mud on her high heels. She flinched as a humming-bird trilled by her ear. "There's such a thing as too much nature," she muttered.

The owner came over then, wiping his hands on his jeans. He had a ruddy face, and blond hair that grayed at the temples. Flynn realized how rude he was being, lying in this man's hammock, but as he tried to get up, the man gestured for him to stay put. He stuck out his hand.

"Rand," he said.

"Flynn."

"I guess the place is yours," Rand said, nodding at his dog. "Noah's never wrong."

After they signed the rental agreement, the realtor drove off, and Rand ducked inside, returning with two bottles of Rolling Rock. They walked over to the garden, where Rand pointed out what he had planted. "It's a good place to be sad," he said. He had been married down by the creek, and he and his wife had been happy for a while, but then he had boozed it up pretty bad until she finally had enough. Now, he was going out to Idaho to live with a woman he had met over the internet. "I'll be there a year," he said. "Whether it works out or not." He was a respiratory specialist with a one-year contract at a hospital in Boise. As Flynn nodded, still looking around, Rand took a cigarette and lit it. "I'm leaving every-thing here," he said, shaking out the match. "Even Noah, if it's all right with you." His eyes welled up as he took a drag. "He's too old to make the trip." When Flynn nodded, reaching down to pet Noah's head, Rand frowned, pointing to the Colorado license plate on Flynn's car. "Now why would anyone want to move from there to here?" he asked.

Flynn looked around, imagining the kids running through the woods, the old dog trying to keep up with them. He imagined all of them going for a walk and spotting some deer, maybe a black bear. He imagined Janey looking under rocks and discovering all manner of bugs and worms. He imagined Nathan dashing through the trees with a stick, pretending to slay dragons. He imagined all of them swimming together in the creek.

ON THE FIRST OF JUNE, FLYNN PACKED UP HIS SIDEKICK AND WENT UPSTAIRS to say goodbye to Helen. He found the kitchen door wide open, and Helen sound asleep in her armchair, with a *Matlock* rerun playing at high volume. He wrote her a note, put a check on the table for an extra week's rent, patted her fat, wrinkled hand, and shut the door. As he skipped down the steps, he heard her shout out, "My boy!" and hesitated. Was this how his mother was feeling, after not hearing from her son in over a year?

He got into his car, started it up, and pointed it north.

When he pulled up to Hemlock Ridge, he put away the groceries he had bought but left the rest of his car packed and went for a walk with Noah. It was about a half-mile to the end of the road, the old Lab wheezing and resting every hundred feet or so. Azalea bushes and wildflowers grew in the high grass, and mosquitoes swarmed above a fetid puddle near the creek. The road ended at an old farmhouse, with wildflowers growing in the field.

For dinner, Flynn grilled two cheeseburgers, found a six-pack of Rolling Rock the owner had left behind, and went out to the second-floor terrace in back. There was a porch swing out there, built for two. He opened a beer, set the smaller cheeseburger on the ground for Noah, and bit into his. He watched the ducks drifting on the creek, listened to the woodpeckers, breathed in the moist air. As the sun went down, the color of the water changed.

At twilight, some squirrels scrambled from the eaves behind him and leaped over Flynn's head, sailing into the trees by the shore.

When a blue heron swooped upstream, low to the water, its great wings creating strange *whumps* that ghosted past the house, Noah lifted his head.

Flynn thought about calling Sydney, but decided instead to stay in the swing, to sit quietly, with the empty space beside him.

THERE WAS NO MOON, SO WHEN DARKNESS CAME IT WAS SUDDEN AND SOLID, the air heavy with the imminence of rain. Flynn went through the house and stepped outside, intending to walk down the road and look for stars, but not ten feet from the doorway it was pitch dark, so dark he couldn't see anything in front of him. He took small steps, waiting for his eyes to adjust, and Noah hesitated alongside him, but the darkness was thick and unyielding, so finally Flynn just stood still and listened: the hoots of owls, the cracking of branches, a breeze that presaged storm. In the distance, thunder rolled in, majestic and rich. He stood quietly, thinking. He would start a new life here. He would change his way of thinking, his way of behaving. But not by fighting in court or having meaningless sex or talking to his friends or working late at a job he already hated. He would change from the inside out. He would learn how to be at peace with himself.

He closed his eyes when he heard the splatter of drops on dirt. It was going to take a while. But he would start here.

Then it was upon him: a rain that peppered his head, shoulders, and back, steadily swelling into a downpour, a barrage. Noah whimpered, wanting to go back inside, but Flynn remained in the middle of the road, his eyes closed and head lifted, until he was drenched and shivering. The sky split open and the rain teemed onto him, battering his face and body, sliding down the ancient trees all around him, spattering all the hunched and hiding beasts in the woods, nurturing the garden, turning the road to mud.

Above the din, he could hardly hear himself cry out the name of both his father and his son.

GHOST IN THE OUTFIELD

WELL, IT CERTAINLY WAS THE WEIRDEST EXPERIENCE I'VE EVER HAD AS A coach, and I've been at it for almost thirty years. This was back when I was running the varsity at White Plains High, must have been '89 because we were all, the whole team, talking about the Mets having a legit shot at winning the whole thing again. And then of course they didn't.

I didn't know much about Hawk's old man, except that he wasn't old at the time, just a year older than me, around forty-five maybe. As for Hawk, he was a good kid. Really good kid. Could *not* hit the curveball, but fortunately for us, not too many high-school pitchers had mastered that pitch (except for that kid up in Saugerties, Freer was his name, he was something else). Then again Hawk couldn't hit the fastball too good either. What he *could* do was catch a baseball. That's how he got the nickname, in case you were wondering—it's not just short for Hawkins. He'd get a big jump at the crack of the bat and then swoop in on the ball like a great big bird of prey. Before games I'd chat up the other coaches and they'd say, "I got this kid, he's batting .380," and I'd say, "Well I hope he can hit it over the fence, because if it stays in the ballpark, Hawk's gonna get it." He'd pluck line drives out of the air, he'd get to fly balls over his head—if it was hit anywhere in his range, he'd get to it. Ever see the famous catch Willie Mays made in the World Series? I've seen Hawk make that catch. Twice.

Looking back, I should have paid more attention to the kid. I never took the time to show him how to hit the curve, how to know when to expect it, how to sit on it. I'd remind him to keep his shoulder back and follow the ball into the plate and all, but his knees would buckle and he'd swing too soon. But at the time, I didn't care, I had a hell of a lineup: Montoya leading off, then Hickson, who wound up playing for the Cubs' farm system before blowing out his knee, then Labrusciano batting third, he got a free ride to Maine, hell of a program they used to have up there, then this kid Danny Kozloski at cleanup, big kid with an uppercut like Joe Frazier, could hit the ball out of any park, led the state in home runs that year, recruited by all the best schools but he joined the Marines instead and got shipped out to the first Gulf War and that was that, poor kid.

Hawkins, he wasn't going anywhere, not in D-I anyway. But he didn't need it. He had brains, that kid. Fifth or sixth in his graduating class. I heard he walked on with some SUNY team upstate, but I can't remember which. Anyway I just penciled him in at centerfield and batted him ninth, every game. Then, whenever a player connected on a line drive or a long fly ball, I'd look out towards centerfield and say "You got it, Hawk, go get it, boy," and he always did.

When he was a kid, I used to see him and his dad at Silver Lake Park when I took my sons there. His big sister, Annie, she babysat for my boys when they were little, she'd be there too—she was a hell of a shortstop for the girls' team. She played infield and Flynn would be in the outfield. He'd run up and get the balls that scooted under her glove, and she'd catch the balls he threw in from the outfield. His father would hit one, yell out, "Third! Runner's going to third!" and Annie would cover the bag and wait for the throw. Hawk never had the strongest arm, but even then, even when he was a scrawny kid, he could put the ball right on the bag. Might take a few hops, but right on the bag.

Which is why that play that day was so weird. He *never* threw to the wrong bag. Smartest player I've ever coached. I didn't have to tell him anything, it was like having an assistant coach on the field. Once in a while he'd say something to his teammates, like Montoya would be on the on-deck circle and Hawk would say, "Rico, check out third base," and Montoya would get to the batter's box, see how far back the third baseman was playing, lay down a bunt in that direction and practically jog to first for a single. Or when he was out in the field, a player would come up to bat, and Hawk would signal the left fielder to go back a few steps and over toward the line, and the right fielder to come in, and then I'd remember that the batter was a kid who always tried to pull the ball.

That day, the day we're talking about, afterwards one of the guys, I think it was the Valentino kid, he was our catcher, he told me that every time he checked the outfielders he saw Hawk looking toward the stands. It was the Brandon girl, she was from Jamaica or Haiti or one of those places. Black as night. Remember this was in the eighties, we didn't have too much interracial stuff going on, but apparently the Hawk was smitten. According to Valentino, she was sitting in the stands with a guy on the basketball team, kid named Harrison, and I guess Hawk was a little, you know, befuddled by all that. So that might explain the bad throw, Valentino said. It's amazing what you remember about some little things whereas, my god, years can fly by without remembering much of anything.

Hawk Senior, we knew him as Nate, he was an acquaintance of mine from high school. Kind of mild-mannered. A mild-mannered guy. I got into all kinds of trouble as a kid, but Nate, he was one of those quiet guys who never ruffled feathers. Run silent, run deep. A little uptight, I'd say. Member of the Knights of Columbus, if I recall correctly. Always a nice hello whenever I saw him at church. I didn't see him much besides that. He sold furniture parts, correct? On the road. On the road a great deal. I can't remember the company. But he was gone a lot, to shopping malls mostly. I'm guessing here. If he were alive today he wouldn't have to drive so much because that kind of thing is all done online now, or by phone or email. Anyway, one of those guys who seemed a little afraid of his wife, you know? One of those guys who more or less escaped the household once in a while. I mean, it was his job, he was a salesman, but still. You know what I'm saying.

Anyway, we wouldn't see him very often at the games, but when we did, young Hawk would look a little more lively in the batter's box, know what I mean? Not that this would help him much—he'd still be really cautious for the first few pitches and then whiff on the inevitable two-strike curveball or high fastball. But it did seem to bring his fielding up another notch, his dad being there. He had a funny whistle, the old man did. Whenever his station wagon pulled up, he'd give that little whistle as he took his seat in the stands, and if Hawk was out in centerfield he'd look up, then focus back on the batter, but you could tell he was more alert. The next season, the year after his dad died, I would hear Hawk whistling that same whistle, his father's whistle, to the other guys, or just to himself out there. *Chirp chirp*. Like a ghost in the outfield.

Okay so on that day, let me get to this now, on that day, his father wasn't there, he was out on the road, and here's what happened. We were playing Mount Vernon, a big game for us. Mount Vernon was always good, not just in baseball but in all sports, because they had more black athletes than we did. I'm not being racist, I'm just being honest. In any case we were playing a big game and there were plenty of people in the stands, so I thought, I thought after that game, maybe that's what rattled Hawk, or maybe like my catcher said it was the Jamaican girl, or maybe it was just, you know, a typical lapse in judgment—we're talking high-schoolers, after all—but here's what happened, I remember it like it was yesterday. The kid on Mount Vernon, he was a speedster, even faster than my guy Montoya, I can't remember his name but he broke the stolen-base record that year. Anyway he was on first. It's the fifth or sixth inning, and the game was either tied or we were down by a run, I'm not sure, and I've got Numbnuts McMillan on the mound—great arm, no brains. So the next batter drills a single up the middle, but right before that happens Hawk's sister Annie screeches into the parking lot in her mother's Dodge and comes over to the dugout like she has a load in her pants. She's bawling, her face is all red. At the same time, Hawk fields the ball cleanly, comes up ready to throw, but instead of firing to third and nailing the big-balled speedster going from first to third (because Numbnuts didn't believe in trying to pick off runners, he believed in showing off his arm strength, so the speedster—god, I wish I could remember his name—he got a big jump), my boy Hawk, he bluffs a throw to third and then tosses it to second, conceding the extra base. I was like, what the hell, kid? Would have nailed him at third with two feet to spare. Now instead of a runner on first with one out we got first and third, no outs. I might have let out a curse, I'm not sure. Big moment, big game, one of the "turning points," and it's the little things, you know? That's what I've learned as a coach, it's the little things that affect the outcome of a game, positively or negatively, and the success or failure of the whole season rides on those little turning points, more or less. Life too, come to think of it. Life too. Anyway next thing I know there's Annie Hawkins in my face saying something but crying too much for me to understand so I signaled the ump for time and ran out onto the field. Numbnuts thought I was taking him out, which I probably should have, but I was trying to tell Hawk to come in, something had happened, you know, and I had a feeling what it was, but I thought it was probably their grandmother or dog or something like that. The poor kid was crestfallen, I mean he was almost in tears on his way in, he knew he'd blown the play and he thought I was mad at him, but all I did was point to his sister and he broke into a sprint.

We lost that game—not that it mattered. Well, actually it did matter, because we dropped down in the league standings and . . . well, it doesn't much matter now. The next man up put down a perfect squeeze and the big-balled speedster—Hale, that's it, Devon Hale was his name—he scored, and we lost, but Hawk, he lost his dad that day, heart attack. Lost his dad. Too young for that to happen. I remember the obituary. Nathan Hawkins, husband of Marian, father of Anne and Flynn, et cetera et cetera. Dropped dead in his car, I don't know the details. Only forty-three, forty-four? Too young.

Oh, one more thing: at the wake. I've never mentioned this to anyone, but something a little wacky was going on with the mom. The wife. Marian. She wasn't sad or crying. She was pissed. Royally pissed. Not exactly the weeping widow. Wouldn't go up to the casket, and didn't want her children to go up there either, but Flynn, he went right up there and put his hand on his father's face, ran his fingers through his hair, put his hand on his father's hands and then he started freaking out a little and it looked like he was about to climb into the casket or something so some of us ran up there and pulled him away. My ex-wife, my wife at the time, Lynnie, she burst out crying at that. Then Flynn tried to hug his mother, it was like a group hug with the family, and she gave it a shot, cigarette in her fingers, but to me—and this is just speculation now—to me, she looked like a woman scorned. Hell hath no fury. That kind of thing. My first thought was, what do you know, was Hawk Senior getting a little road action? Did he have a heart attack in a motel bed, something like that? Because to me—and I should probably keep my mouth shut here—to me it *felt* like something of that nature. It felt like she knew something nobody else knew.

I could be wrong, of course. My wife always tells me I jump to conclusions. I'm a conclusion-jumper, that's what I am. But let's just say it was a feeling and I'll leave it at that. Again I probably shouldn't have mentioned it.

The following season, Hawk's senior year, he was in a slump for most of it. Worse than usual at the plate. But he could still catch anything in the outfield, so I kept him in the lineup. And we won the league, mainly because Kozloski averaged almost a home run per game, he probably still has the league record, but we lost in the state playoffs. I had an outfielder right behind Hawk, Tyler Tennyson, we called him TT, he was a superstar-in-waiting, that kid, and he went on to be the best high-school outfielder I've ever coached, but I've always had a seniors-first policy, at least in high school. Also, I mean, come on, I'm going to bench the kid whose dad died? I'm kind of a stickler, but I'm not heartless. I more or less took him under my wing that year. Once I asked him, because I was still thinking of his mom at the wake, "Hey, did your parents get along well? You know, before . . . ?" And he goes like this, kind of a shrug. He said they got along fine, he guessed, but he didn't have much to compare them to. "If you're asking if they loved each other," he says, "I'd probably say yes. But I really have no idea."

Then he paused for a minute. This was practice, we were at practice, on the sidelines I mean, and he was watching TT shag flies in the outfield. "Skip," he says, "TT's better than I am. He should be starting in center. That's what the guys are saying."

I shook my head and patted his shoulder. "You're going to bust out of this slump," I said. "Just you wait."

He puts his head down then, and for a while he doesn't say anything. I remember thinking I should probably put my arm around the kid, but we were at practice, you know?

"Skip," he says, "I'm really sorry about that game last year."

"Oh no, come on Hawk," I said. I nudged him out toward the field. "Water under the bridge. Mental error. Part of the growth process." I mean, we were at least halfway through the season by then, and nobody was even thinking about last year anymore. "Go on, get out there," I said. "Go shag some flies."

Then he said something I've never forgotten. "If I had to do it all over again," he says, "I'd still throw the ball to second."

"What?" I said. "Why?" I was still watching TT glide around the outfield, making everything look easy. Hawk might have been a better fielder, but only slightly, and TT was a killer at the plate. Lefty with a big looping swing. Terrific ballplayer. I brought him with me when I got the Rutgers job, and he was drafted by the Cardinals, fourth round, but nothing ever happened. Never knew what happened to him. Some kids, they just disappear.

"Because," Hawk says, "I wouldn't have hit the bag at third. I was about to throw the ball right at Dante Harrison's head."

I look at him. "The basketball player?"

He nods. "Would have hit him, too," he says. "He was talking to my girlfriend. He tried to put his arm around her."

"Your girlfriend?" I say.

He shakes his head. "It was a secret," he says. "Our parents wouldn't have approved."

I didn't say anything. I would have probably been the same way if one of my kids had brought home a black girl, especially one as dark as the Brandon girl. It's not natural, you know? That's how I thought back then, anyway. Now, I don't know what to think. The world's changing. My oldest, he married a nice Jewish girl. Who would have thought? Lynnie was furious about it, but it's all working out. She's good to him, that's all I care about. But jeez Louise, a Jew! I must be getting soft in my old age.

"So that's why I threw it to second," he said.

Now what would you say to that? "Because of the black girl?" I said. "We lost a game because of a black girl? We lost the league title because —"

He looked at me kind of sadly. "Exactly what my dad would have said." Then he put his glove on and jogged out into centerfield.

I felt bad about that for a while, let me tell you. But that's the way I thought at the time. What the hell? Live and learn.

Anyway, next thing you know—God's honest truth—next thing you know the kid goes on a tear. Ends the year with a ten-game hitting streak, something like that. Even belted a curve ball once—he just sat on it and ripped it into the gap in left center. Big grin on his face standing on second. Such is life, right? Who can predict these things. Who can predict.

IN LOVE WITH LOUISE

FLYNN WAS LATE TO THE HALFWAY CAFÉ. HE AND JUDY LEE HAD COME directly from their new work site in Clarks Summit, and she had screwed the directions. He was about to give her hell about it, figuring it would make for an ice-breaker of sorts, but then he set eyes on Louise, fiddling with her long spoon at an otherwise empty booth, her shoulder just touching the pink wall.

Whoa.

She was clearly too young—late twenties, if that—and far too pretty for the likes of him. And too classy. He considered fleeing the premises, but then she half-stood and reached out her hand. He took it, then held on a bit longer than he needed to, on account of her slender fingers.

Judy Lee rolled her eyes.

Flynn apologized for being late, Judy Lee excused herself to take a phone call from her needy girlfriend, and after Flynn ordered a beer and some food, Louise said something like *Well, here we are!* and laughed.

The *lilt* of it. Like summer rain on a field of wildflowers. Flynn had heard some interesting laughs in his thirty-eight years—his friend Sydney's was like a pleasant, low-lying fog, while that of a young artist he had recently known (in the Biblical sense) was like a staggered-emission garden hose. Louise's laugh? Think poppies.

Next thing he knew, he was reaching across the table, to get those fingers back in his hand. An audacious act—he was jumping the gun, and you would think he'd know better, given his age—but he held on anyway, afraid to speak lest he'd blow it right then and there.

But then he did. "Nice fingers," he said.

And she quickly withdrew.

But as she forked some whipped cream off her shoo-fly pie, she flashed the barest hint of a smile.

When Judy Lee returned, Flynn took the opportunity to wash up. In the restroom mirror his eyes looked a little droopy, his teeth slightly yellowed (from all the coffee, no doubt); but still and all, he was looking Okay en route to Better. His hair was graying at the temples, he had his mother's crow's feet by his eyes, and there were early warning signs of turkey neck, but otherwise, the moves he'd made recently—renting a sweet house in the woods, quitting his faculty position at Sacred Heart, taking his ex-wife to court to improve his visitation agreement (and being introduced to a guardian *ad litem* who would intervene on the children's behalf in future disputes), finding work at Sunshine Orchards, and then starting up his own business on the side—had done him a world of good.

He scrubbed his hands, trying to get at the stubborn dirt under his nails. He had told Judy Lee he hated blind dates, but in truth he had never been on one. Ever. Never mind the typical scenario where both people hated each other on sight and then had to be pleasant for two hours; that's not what he was worried about. What if it actually *worked*? What if he managed to earn his way into this longfingered young woman's heart over the course of a milkshake and she invited him to her family's Labor Day cookout? Then what? He imagined Louise's mother (a proper lady, the kind who summered at the Vineyard) and father (silver-haired, with a polo shirt and chinos) taking in the sight of him, Flynn Hawkins, a divorcee on the brink of forty, with two kids living with their malcontent mother in Binghamton, to say nothing of the Abandonment of His Children in Late December of Oh Nine and the Sacred Heart Scandal of Two Thousand Twelve. In graduate school he had read a number of sonnets on this topic, lyrical bums who had fallen in love with women far beyond their reach: instead of admitting defeat and propositioning the local peasant's daughter as a viable alternative, they persisted in their outlandish yearnings, certain that one day their fair damsels, once aware of how sensitive and heartsick they were, would leave their aristocratic husbands or tyrannical fathers and offer their soft hands and delicate fingers to the callused, dirt-encrusted mitts of the gardeners who loved them more than any fancy-pantsed princes ever could.

That's what Flynn aspired to be: someone's prince. And that's what he was now: a gardener. Landscaper, if you will. Not just mowing and trimming, although he had started off that way, after shifting to part-time at the Orchards back in late July. No, to be perfectly forthcoming, he considered himself an artist of sorts, although he would never say so out loud. Once he got around to designing business cards, they would read, "Flynn Hawkins, Landscape Artist: *Put your lawn in order.*" Then a simple floral design, a swoosh of green topped by a red dot. He'd stencil the same design on the side of his truck—not the ancient Dodge Ram he had picked up in exchange for his old Sidekick, but the gleaming silver Tacoma he had seen one morning in the Toyota of Scranton lot.

Business was slow, but after some Valpak coupons yielded nothing and an ill-advised Groupon deal nearly ruined him, the flyers he'd stuck in people's doors, along with chatting up the regulars at the Orchards, had generated enough work to pay his rent and stay current with his child support, and pretty soon he had enough left over to hire Judy Lee to help him with the big jobs. Once he arrived on site, he almost invariably got the job, for he generally underbid the competition and adopted a professorial manner (i.e. kind and knowledgeable, mildly flirtatious) when dealing with customers. He'd take a look around, listening to what the owner wanted, but at the same time sensing what the yard, if you will, was asking for. Then he'd lock his brown eyes onto the woman's (and it was always the woman) and relate, in sonorous tones, his vision: a shock of limerock rubies bookending the front stoop, some hillside black beauties circling a fountain out back, some arborvitae near the kids' play area to block off the neighbors' view. He'd hope for *All right, Mr. Hawkins, have at it; here's a check to start you off*, but more typically he'd get *How much?* and have to downgrade to something like lilacs along the back fence, forsythia on the borders, and fieldstone near the garden. However, while most people in the area had yet to recover from the economic downturn, there were still pockets, in places like Clarks Summit and Waverly, where folks could afford the full realization of his vision. The Lieberthals had a lavish spread on Country Club Road; if Flynn did good work there, word of his talents would spread throughout the Land of the One Percent, and the cash would follow.

It was a big job: the Lieberthals had just purchased the place and were looking for a complete re-haul of both yards, low walls and pathways included. This work, plus his regular weeklies and monthlies, would carry Flynn all the way until first frost. He'd be able to get the kids some high-class Christmas gifts for once: maybe a new computer for Nathan so he could improve his grades at school, and one of those kiddy keyboards for Janey, the kind where you program the drumbeat and chord sequence and then learn the melody on your own.

He opened the bathroom door and peeked out at Louise, her lips pursed around the straw. Now here was a woman he'd like to garden for. She'd come out onto the front porch in white pants and a sky-blue blouse, tuck her blonde hair behind her ears, and remark on how breezy it had gotten since daybreak. Flynn would nod, suggest that rain was in the offing, and say, *Well then, let's see about this yard of yours*. Once out back, he would envision not only the yard, but a life. He'd imagine rigging up a hammock between the aging maples, reviving the overgrown peach tree by pruning the non-scaffolding branches, and setting up the grill near the back steps in order to facilitate the transport of beef. Louise would lean out the back door, hand him a glass of iced tea and say, *The corn's ready, dear, how are those steaks coming?* and Flynn would say, *Your medium-well needs another minute or two, but mine's raring to go*. After she extracted the corn from the pot she'd call out, *My prince, would you like a beer with dinner or will you join me in a glass of shiraz?* And he'd say, *Angel, nothing complements a rib-eye better than an ice-cold pale ale*.

Well now, he thought as he headed back toward the booth, what on earth would such a woman be doing meeting a run-down ex-professor like him at a half-empty diner in Old Forge, PA? By now she ought to have settled down with a good-looking young businessman with considerably more cash in his checking account than the $124.52 Flynn currently had, post-child-support-payment and pre-Lieberthal-deposit-check.

It was all Judy Lee's doing, by the way. Flynn had met her at the Orchards when he answered their ad for a slightly-above-minimum-wage job that began at five a.m. After his disastrous year at Sacred Heart, he had decided he would finally walk the talk, abandon the professoriate, and lead a simpler life. So he did it: he walked into the dean's office and told Sister Mary Michael (ignoring the potato-chip crumbs on her vestment) that he would tolerate no longer her general lack of support (referring both to the alleged scandal and to his personnel decisions, as she had refused to place his alcoholic colleague into a rehab program, nudge his most graybearded piece of deadwood into early retirement, and fire the thrift-store-aficionado whose teaching evaluations were the worse he'd ever seen) and was quitting his position, indeed the entire profession, at the end of the school year. He had started off at the Orchards doing grunt work (planting, watering, weeding, and covering beds when frost was predicted), but quickly worked his way into snipping the leafy greens, pruning trees, seeding and watering (in the greenhouse), and manning (side-by-side with Judy Lee) the Farmer's Market booth on Saturdays. After the market closed, and every Thursday after work, they headed over to Gin's Tavern for happy hour, keeping up the practice even after Flynn abandoned the farmer's market gig and dropped down to part-time in order to start his own weekend business. He typically passed the time at Gin's telling stories of his pathetic love life—like the time his hair had caught fire in a married woman's bed, or the time he attempted cunnilingus in a woman's bathtub and nearly drowned, or the night he showed up at the wrong house for a date and sat on a stranger's porch for a half hour before the police showed up. As soon as he was done, Judy Lee would bring up the name of an old high-school friend of hers named Louise, who was now working at the Orchards in place of Flynn. When he suggested he was probably too old for any friend of hers, Judy Lee said in case he hadn't noticed, there weren't a lot of decent men of any age in northeast PA, at least not many who weren't still living with their mothers and drinking a case of PBR per day.

And apparently she'd been telling Louise, I've got this friend; he's a gardener, but don't go by that—he used to be a professor, PhD and everything. Louise told him as much after he finally returned to the booth at the Halfway Café, wolfed down most of his food, watched the girls finish off a second slice of shoo-fly pie, and widened his eyes at Judy Lee as she went off to use the restroom after first giving Flynn a look: *Here's your chance, stud.*

"She's been going on and on about this handsome friend of hers," is what Louise said.

"Well, now you know the truth," Flynn said, pointing to his droopy eyes and keeping his lips together when he smiled. "This is as good as it gets, right here."

Louise fingered a drop of milkshake from the bottom of her straw. "I've seen worse," she said. And then she laughed again, and again Flynn saw poppies—an entire field of them.

FLYNN'S RENTED HOUSE WAS ON A DIRT ROAD IN THE MIDDLE OF A HEMLOCK pine forest in Nicholson, Pennsylvania, and there was no lawn to speak of. He had signed a year-long lease when Rand, the owner, moved to Idaho, but after ten months Rand had emailed Flynn to say he loved it out there and might never come back—and Flynn wrote back to say that was just fine with him. The enclosed front porch, which Flynn had dubbed the Contemplation of Life Room, featured a spider plant with fourteen offspring, a picture of his kids on the trail at Lackawanna State Park, a white wicker couch and table, a tweed armchair, and an end table with two photographs: one of his mother when she was a young woman, arm-in-arm with his father, the other of Nathan and Janey in Batman and Robin costumes. After coming home from his meet-and-greet at the café, Flynn had let Noah outside, dumped the contents of his to-go container into the dog bowl, cracked open a cold Rolling Rock, and checked his messages. The first was from Rachel, pre-emptively cancelling his visitation with the kids that weekend due to an unexpected visit from her sister. The second was from Judy Lee, promising information of immeasurable value.

He decided to sit on the Rachel callback; no good would come of that exchange. He called Judy Lee instead, after drawing a hot bath. It had been a long day.

"*Nice to meetcha?*" she said as soon as she picked up. "You big dork."

That's what Flynn had said to Louise upon leaving the café. Considering his rattled condition, it could have been a lot worse.

"So whatdja think?" she said.

"I don't know, JL," Flynn said as he set Janey's Sponge Bob Bath Time Soap Paints on the floor, settled into the hot water, and put his feet up on the rim, one by the Bob the Builder bath mitt and the other by the

Ariel doll that changed colors when it got wet. "She's way out of my league." As he said this, Noah came upstairs and nosed his way into the bathroom, lapped up some tub water by Flynn's knee, and then lay down, a lump of mac-and-cheese still clinging to his upper lip.

After Judy Lee divulged the substance of the conversation she had with Louise in the diner while he was doing god-knows-what-for-forever in the bathroom, Flynn said that while he had never had a successful relationship with a woman, and while he surely needed to take steps in the right direction, a girl like Louise was probably more leap than step.

"She's from Wilkes-Barre!" Judy Lee said. "You have a PhD! Do you have any idea what a catch that makes you?"

"One's point of origin is irrelevant," Flynn said, as barking erupted from outside (that would be Buddy, the Golden Retriever from Tom's farm, down the road) and Noah heaved himself up to see what all the commotion was about. (The last time Buddy had come by he was dragging a bloodied deer leg, and the two dogs had gone down to the creek to share in the feast.) "Same for one's terminal degree," Flynn added, for he had known many an insouciant and insipid professor, and had long understood the achievement of his doctorate to be more a matter of persistence than of genius. Outside, Noah's bark joined in with Buddy's, which probably meant *bear in the woods*. "She does, however, have a great laugh."

"I'll text you her number," Judy Lee said.

Don't bother, Flynn almost said, but he heard his friend's anticipated disappointment clear through all the barking. "Exquisite fingers, too," he said. God, the woman was gorgeous. But it was an old habit of Flynn's to immediately see himself as unworthy of such beauty, to predict the flaws such a woman would find in him and take himself out of the equation right from the get-go.

"Her last boyfriend was a businessman," Judy Lee said, which only made things worse, as Flynn pictured a clean-cut young man in a navy-blue suit. "A real dickhead," Judy Lee said. "She's looking for someone more down-to-earth."

Flynn blew out a breath, then remembered his resolution to rethink who he was and how he behaved. After all, hadn't he just drastically changed on the outside, from an academic who wore tweed jackets to a man who loved nothing better than to mix sheep manure and peat with his bare hands? He was surely changing on the inside as well. And if that was the case, perhaps he *would* be attractive to a woman like Louise.

"Well," he said, "you can't get much downer-to-earth than I am right now."

After they hung up, Flynn took a swig of beer and slid deeper into the tub. His arms looked strong and tan against the enamel—swarthy, even. He had never been so fit and healthy in all his life. Every day he had taken home fresh fruit and veggies from the Orchard, so for four months that's all he had eaten; and working outside every day had re-animated muscles from their atrophied state. He hoped he had looked good to Louise. Nobody that lovely had ever given him a second look, not with such blue-gray eyes anyway, and on the drive home he had convinced himself he hadn't a prayer, but according to Judy Lee, Louise had been "quite excited" afterwards. "She said you have a nice smile," she told Flynn. "She said you have 'soft eyes', whatever that means." At the time, he couldn't formulate a response, but now, as he sat up to look at his reflection in the bathtub faucet, he supposed that yes, you could say they were soft.

THE NEXT DAY, AFTER PICKING UP JUDY LEE FROM THE ORCHARDS, HE ASKED her if she knew of a good sushi place. They were at the Dunkin' Donuts drive-through in Clarks Summit on their way to the Lieberthals', where the plan was to plant tulip bulbs and bleeding hearts along the front porch, aerate the back lawn, install two garden beds he would fill now and plant in the spring, lay the groundwork for a Zen garden in the northeast corner (by way of weeding, laying down landscape fabric, and wheelbarrowing a ton of pea gravel), pull up the multitude of weeds in the northwest corner (Flynn refused to employ chemicals like Roundup, given their heinous effect on bees and the nation's food supply), spread some organic 50/50 mix, layer onto that some untreated mulch, and plant a variety of bulbs.

Earlier that morning, while thinking of Louise and loading his truck full of tools, bulbs, cedar two-by-fours, and the huge roll of landscape fabric, Flynn had felt loose-limbed and carefree. It felt good to work with his hands, and to have his evenings free (no papers to grade, no books to re-read, no desperate student emails); he was seeing his children fairly regularly (thanks to court orders, the assistance of the guardian *ad litem*, and the mollifying effects of Rachel's boyfriend); and best of all, he was starting to enjoy his own company. His only concern on this day was the Lieberthals' two big mastiffs, who loved to run around, dig up the backyard, and generally get in the way of whatever Flynn was trying to do. It being a weekday, Mr. Lieberthal would be at work, and Mrs. Lieberthal (whom Judy Lee had dubbed Her Royal Thighness due to her affinity for short skirts) had thus far showed no predilection for governing her precious puppies' precocious, at times riotous, behavior.

Judy Lee raised her eyebrows while accepting her ham-egg-and-cheese bagel.

"She said it had to be a 'friendly date,'" Flynn said, "but I vetoed that."

"I'm afraid it can't be a *date* date" is what Louise had said when Flynn called, for she was, technically, still in a relationship (an important detail Judy Lee had neglected to mention during her lengthy promotional campaign), although it was "in its death throes." When Flynn said he couldn't imagine containing himself enough to keep things friendly, Louise had laughed her poppy laugh, thought about it for a moment, and then said okay, she supposed it could be a *"friendly* date date." Flynn was so happy he didn't know what to say next, and when he did speak, he said something like *Should we ask Judy Lee?* but he had drunk three beers for courage prior to making the call and his tongue got in the way so it must have come out *Should we have sushi?* because Louise said, "Oh I love sushi!"

After biting into her sandwich, Judy Lee said there were a couple of good options nearby; she preferred Atami—"right over there," she said, pointing across the street. "But wait," she said, "you've never had sushi?"

Flynn proceeded to convey to his friend his miserable food history: the overcooked-meat-and-potatoes of his upbringing, his avoidance of any meal worth more than eight dollars in grad school, the baked-chicken-and-Ore-Ida-french-fries dinner his ex-wife had expected every week, the lack of fresh seafood in the mountain towns of Colorado, all the fast-food he ate during his time in Grand Junction.

"Do you even know how to use chopsticks?" she asked.

Later, in the Lieberthals' backyard, she demonstrated for him, snapping off two twigs and using them to pick up a leaf. But when Flynn tried it, he was all thumbs. "Never mind," Judy Lee said, taking the twigs from him and tossing them on the ground. "They'll probably let you use a fork. But how pathetic, using a fork to eat sushi. You should be deeply ashamed."

 As it turned out, he was. At the restaurant that evening, Louise used her chopsticks with great dexterity, but Flynn, he just couldn't get the hang. He fumbled for a while, his face burning—the entire date, the slim remnants of his pride, his last best shot at true love, all of it falling apart before his eyes. But what did Louise do? She smiled, set down her chopsticks and said, "I prefer to eat sushi with my nice fingers."

She looked even prettier than she had at the Halfway Café, so pretty Flynn could barely look her in the eye, and several times he tried to tell her so, but the first time the waiter came by, the second time she dropped her napkin, and the third time a sushi chef yelled out something. She wore a white blouse and a bright blue cardigan that turned her eyes a color Flynn had seen only once before, when poking holes with his ski pole into the deep snow of the Continental Divide. Finally he blurted out that she was as pretty as an angel, and she told him that nobody deserved to be called such a thing, least of all someone who had screwed up as much of her life as she had, but that it was certainly nice of him to say so.

"Okay, a flawed but interesting angel," he said. For she was kind, kind to the core, that much was clear, and she had told him some things about herself—she was a published poet, she had worked for the Department of Justice in D.C., she liked punk music, she was addicted to home-im-provement shows—that he had found enticing.

"I'll take it," she said. "Thank you. You're really nice too," she said. "And terribly handsome. For a gardener, anyway." She took a demure sip of *sake*.

Well, how about that. Flynn had worn olive pants for the occasion, with a charcoal shirt and his freshly polished tried-and-true Dr. Martens, which he thought he might have to remove upon entering, but they'd been escorted to a table near the sushi chefs. Flynn had let Louise fill out the order form, since he didn't know *unagi* from *anago*, to say nothing of what on earth constituted a Dragon Roll. When the sushi showed up, he mimicked her actions, so when she dribbled soy sauce into the little bowl and mixed in a dollop of green paste, he followed suit—and then yelped when a chunk of wasabi burned its way down his throat.

Now, smiling deviously as Flynn turned halfway around to blow his nose, she squeezed a lump of salmon-and-rice between her fingers, dipped it into the tiny bowl, and put the whole enterprise in her mouth. As the wasabi struck home, tears filled her big blue eyes.

Judy Lee had warned him that the Japanese were dessertly challenged, so when the waiter made a lame attempt to pitch the virtues of green tea ice cream, Flynn asked for the check. Louise took the opportunity to go to the ladies' room, and as she headed toward the rear of the restaurant, her golden hair shimmering, Flynn wondered if this was what people meant by *love at first sight*. He had asked Rachel to marry him out of some inherited sense of obligation, back when they were living a mean, meager life in the East Village; there had never been anything like this, his knees knocking under the table and his deodorant long since rendered useless. This was big. Nothing in his life had prepared him for this. He wasn't sure he was up for the task.

He handed the waiter his credit card, calculated how much he had available, and hoped to God it was enough. The date was ending. He would drive this lovely human being home. He would not try to kiss her. He would simply open the door for her, maybe gently peck her on the cheek, toss and turn in bed all night, then call her the next day to ask for a second date.

But as she returned from the bathroom with lipstick reapplied and hair freshly pouffed, she asked if he wanted to get dessert elsewhere, her treat. Judy Lee had been telling her that Manning's Dairy Farm had the best ice cream in the world, she said, and she'd always wanted to verify that for herself.

During their drive out to Dalton, Flynn nodded or provided hopefully appropriate guttural responses as Louise spoke. What about? Flynn couldn't say. It was all he could do to focus on the road and cease his shivering. *It's not cold out,* he told himself. *It's only September.* When he finally looked at her (she was talking about how things had deteriorated with Jeremy, the guy she'd been dating) he saw the streetlights reflected in her eyes.

When they arrived at Manning's, Flynn took Louise's hand as they walked past the cows, and they entered the shop that way, like a couple of teenagers, just before the place closed. But as they bent to inspect the flavors and she mentioned her fondness for cookies-and-cream, he let out a weird laugh and said that had been Rachel's favorite flavor as well.

"Oh," Louise said. And straightened.

He had told her he'd been married, and that he had kids. She'd asked a lot of questions about Nathan and Janey at dinner. But this wasn't about that. This was about a moron talking about his ex-wife's favorite ice cream on his first date with the woman of his dreams. He could hear Judy Lee already: *Smooth one, Ace.*

Louise ordered blueberry and sweet-cream instead, took a few licks, and threw the rest away.

Two days later it was sunny and bird-crazy, a perfect day for tree-planting according to Judy Lee, so they stopped at Avallone's Nursery for a red dogwood, a birch, and two cherry trees, balled and burlapped. Flynn had tried to talk Mrs. Lieberthal out of the cherries, but she'd been adamant. Her husband was a New Yorker who had once worked for the Attorney General's Office in D.C., whereas she, judging from her posture, her accent, her daily misjudgments regarding skirt length and her injudicious use of eye shadow, was a New Jersey WASP, and like most transplanted New Jersey WASPs, while easy on the eyes, she was nothing if not persnickety. "Offensively sexy," Judy Lee declared in the truck, after Flynn had outlined their plan of attack and they had moved on to their daily appraisal of Mrs. Lieberthal's figure. "One of those women who turns you on, and then you hate yourself for being turned on. You might as well masturbate." Judy Lee bit into the glazed donut they'd picked up from Krumpe's. "And in the spirit of the public trust," she said while holding the donut in the air, "no skirt should ever be above the vagina." Flynn tried to remember if he had ever seen Judy Lee wear any skirt of any length. "In sum," she said, "the woman is abrasive, obstinate, and spoiled. And yet, her golden thighs redeem her."

When she finally got around to asking about his date, Flynn shook his head and told her not to bother; as she well knew, Louise already had a boyfriend, it would probably take forever for them to break up, don't even ask about the chopsticks. He described the Mishap at Manning's and told her he had called Louise afterwards to re-apologize, but her response had been nothing short of forlorn. "I should never have agreed to the date in the first place," Louise had said with a sigh. (Flynn pictured her reclining on her chaise longue in silk pajamas and a cashmere robe, reading an old copy of *he's just* not *that into you*.) "It's not your fault," she said. "I *am*, technically, still in a relationship." Her dog started yapping then, and she put her hand over the phone to say *Leave it!* which caused Noah's ears to perk up. "And so, apparently, are you," she said.

No, Flynn said, no no no, it had just been a slip of the tongue, that's all, certainly not an indication that he was still defined by his unhealthy co-dependency with his ex-wife. "Look," he said, "I don't know this Jeremy guy from Adam, but why don't you just put him out of his misery so you and I can work this thing out?"

She made a sound, a cross between a moan and a growl. "Is that what you would do to me?" Louise asked. "Just toss me aside when someone new came along?"

Now, turning the Ram onto Country Club Road and dropping down a gear, Flynn speculated to Judy Lee that the boyfriend didn't even exist. Lord knows he had pulled the same trick himself, telling a woman he was taken when he wasn't, as soon as he detected the need in her eyes, the plaintive tone in her voice, the feeling that she was seeing him as *The Answer to All Her Prayers*. And look at him: he had acted that same way to Louise, and she had intuited the danger therein. Smart woman.

"She hardly talks about him," Judy Lee said as they parked in the Lieberthals's vast driveway and got out of the truck. "That's why I never mentioned him to you. But he certainly *exists*; she's not the type to lie." She hoisted the saplings out of the truck bed and yoked them onto her shoulders. She was thin and strapping, pound-for-pound stronger than any man Flynn knew, and with her cap tugged down she looked like a teenaged boy.

"What she is," she said, "is a serial monogamist who never actually commits." She paused, repositioning the saplings. "Whereas *you*, my friend, sabotage relationships before they even happen. Or *as* they're happening." She shook her head and started walking toward the back yard. "I don't know what I was thinking," she said. She nodded toward the flagstone path Flynn had made the day before. "Hey, nice and level!"

Flynn had just grabbed two shovels and a bag of compost from the truck bed when the Lieberthals' slobbering mastiffs appeared, tumbling down the steps of the back deck and galloping towards Flynn like defensive ends with unobstructed paths to the quarterback. As the lead dog lunged at him, Flynn dropped the bag and flung out a shovel. The dog yelped as it caught him in the tender parts, just as Mrs. Lieberthal came out the sliding door.

"Mister Hawkins!" she yelled, putting her hands on her hips. She wore a half-open mini-bathrobe, her dyed-blonde hair loosed and curled, and at the sight of her, Judy Lee's jaw went agape. The mastiff, instantly cured, bounded back across the yard and scampered up the steps for some Mommylove. "That will *not* be tolerated," she said, tick-tocking her finger at Flynn. Then she pointed at Judy Lee. "Young man," she said, "drop those trees and leave my property immediately."

FLYNN WAS NEVER GOOD WITH DAYS OFF, ESPECIALLY WHEN THE GAME PLAN had been to dig in the dirt all day. He wandered aimlessly around the house, confusing Noah to no end, before settling onto the couch, reading a chapter of *Blood Meridian* (he was on a quest to read one book a week for the rest of his life, but he kept choosing bleak books with no concluding hints of redemption), then honoring his late father by indulging in an AMC Clint Eastwood marathon: *Pale Rider, The Outlaw Josie Wales*, and *Hang 'Em High*. Dinner was Triscuits with salami and Swiss cheese, followed by Tastykake cream-filled buttercream cupcakes from Lochen's Market. He spent two full days like this.

On the third day, his son called him after school, with Janey on the extension, to ask why he hadn't phoned of late. Were they going to see him soon? Did he not love them anymore? (That from Janey, of course.) Flynn told them he was just a little down, that's all, and he'd be sure to see them not the coming weekend but the one after that. He told them to have fun with their aunt and cousins and know he was thinking about them all the time and would love them dearly until they were dead. After they hung up (when Rachel came into the room and shouted, "Who're you guys talking to?"), Flynn stayed slumped in the armchair, staring at the dirty baseball glove hanging from a nail, at the old banana-seat bicycle in the corner with plastic *Star Wars* light sabers wedged under the seat. Once again he'd be unable to give them classy presents for Christmas. And once again he was allowing Righteous Rachel to prevent him from seeing his children. Eight more days seemed far too long to wait before giving Nathan a back-cracking bear hug and blowing a raspberry on Janey's little neck.

Flynn Hawkins sat in the Contemplation of Life Room and, for the first time, contemplated his life. Where, oh where, had his little balls gone? And what exactly was he doing, planting trees for rich people by day and watching spaghetti Westerns by night? He had quit academia in order to live life closer to the bone, like Thoreau, to find some honest work that left him a good kind of tired at the end of the day, and he'd started his own business so he would feel less like an indentured servant and more like an adult, not to mention bringing his taxable income down to stealth level. But where had these bold career moves taken him? When he kicked the bucket in his late fifties like most of his male progenitors, what would his offspring say about him in their semi-tearful eulogies? And what good were even his minor accomplishments (1991 All-County Baseball Defensive Team, 1994 Daytona Beach Spring Break Dance Championship, 2008 Fairfield University Professor of the Year) if he wasn't loved by another grown-up? To date, leaving aside his mother's sporadic and ill-timed expressions of affection after his father's death and Rachel's all-too-occasional and suspiciously trite declarations of such back in the increasingly distant past, no woman had ever truly loved him; and not one had *he* truly loved, not in the My-One-and-Only way. Surely the problem was with him, not with everyone else. Surely a sea-change was in order, for everything he'd done to this point had proved an abysmal failure. He needed to get out of his own head, as he had in Colorado, and live in his body, in the land, to connect with what was bigger than himself—to be *selfless* instead of *self-absorbed*, to *do* instead of *think*, to *act* instead of *react*, to *be* instead of *seem*.

He slapped the tweeded arms of the armchair and heaved himself to his feet.

Start with the body, he told himself. Eat some real food. In the kitchen, he turned the heat on under the griddle, made a thick patty of organic ground beef, and opened a can of baked beans. Then, he couldn't help it, he imagined cooking dinner for Louise: some lasagna maybe, with sausage and parsley in the sauce, or better yet grilled salmon with mixed greens—that would be more her speed. He hunted around the fridge and found some pepper-jack cheese. Since when had he given up on someone or something so easily? Was this his *modus operandi*? Here, perhaps, was the problem: to this point, he had either chosen the wrong woman and gamely stuck it out, or flirted with the right one and bailed at the first sign of trouble. But he hadn't been like that as a professor (when his students botched their rough drafts, he always worked with them to bring their writing up to speed), or as a father (he routinely told his kids that failure was the only sure-fire way to success, so they should persist in all their worthwhile endeavors), or as a gardener (if his plants and flowers were drooping, he didn't give up on them; instead he weeded, toyed with water distribution, considered sun exposure, even relocated them if necessary). Why couldn't he adopt a similar strategy regarding women? Louise had originally expressed a desire to be friends first, before dating. What had been so wrong with that? Wouldn't that have been a substantial improvement over the jump-into-bed-first, hate-each-other-later method he had heretofore perfected? And as for his kids, they certainly wanted to see him this weekend, *and* they probably wanted to see their cousins too. Why couldn't they spend one day with him, the other with their cousins?

But as he ate his undercooked hamburger smothered with cheese and beans, he remembered Louise's voice on the phone and intuited its underlying message: *Game over.*

And he knew what Rachel would say to his compromise proposal: *Game on.*

IT WAS HARD TO TELL WHICH CAME FIRST, THE HEADLIGHTS TURNING INTO the dirt driveway or the cheerful tail-wagging of Noah, the World's Worst Watchdog. Flynn tugged on a shirt, stepped over the dog, and opened the door. It was Judy Lee.

And that's when he realized what day it was.

"I waited an hour," she said as she handed him a six-pack of Yuengling and threw herself onto the wicker couch. "But the good news is, I drank for free. Two guys at the bar, trying to convert me." She ripped a can from the plastic loops and popped it open. "They backed off," she said, "after I beat one of them in an arm-wrestle."

Flynn dropped into the armchair apologizing. It was the first time he had missed their weekly tête-a-tête at Gin's.

They sat for a while, taking long drafts of beer, petting Noah, and complaining about New Jersey women. When they opened their third cans, Judy Lee told him that Louise had seemed depressed at work; she was confusing the Golden Delicious with the Jonagolds. "She was fine during peach season," she said. "But now.... What happened with you two?"

Flynn started to rehash their disastrous date and the subsequent phone conversation, but Judy Lee stopped him. "No," she said, "I mean what *happened*? The poor girl looks completely lovesick."

Flynn paused in mid-swig.

"You better do something," she said, "or they're going to fire her." She set down her empty can and got up. "By the way," she said, "I went back to full-time there. I can't wait for you to get your shit together." She looked out the window when she said this, as if searching for the friend she used to be proud of. "I knew it," she said to the crickets. "I knew you would screw this up."

THE NEXT MORNING, FLYNN PUT ON A POT OF COFFEE AND MADE A PLAN. First he called Mrs. Lieberthal, to apologize for his abuse of her precious hound and ask for his job back. When she assured him that nobody who had done that to one of her babies could ever work for her again, he said he understood, but would nonetheless insist on being compensated for the work he had completed—which, he added, was of the highest quality; she might want to go out there and see for herself. He refrained from telling her that the bleeding hearts by her front entrance would bloom and die, bloom and die, year after year, and when they did, and when her heart opened and closed with them, she would think of him and regret her decision. He refrained as well from telling her that what he had done for her, what he did for all his clients—and this was as much a revelation to him as it may have been to her—was not so much putting her lawn in order as it was implanting Beauty, all around her, along with helping, in his own small way, to keep a dying planet alive. And that was a far better way to make a living than forcing young people to read books they didn't want to read, and to write essays they didn't want to write.

He called Rachel next, stabbing at the numbers as if it were a telegraphed message: *FLYNN HAWKINS BACK ON HIS FEET STOP*. He told her he was coming to get the kids the next morning for his scheduled visitation, and as a favor to her he'd have them back by Saturday evening so they could enjoy the company of their cousins. He said he'd love to negotiate such things with her in an amicable manner and in the spirit of compromise, but it was also important, indeed imperative in the eyes of the Law, that she honor their legal visitation agreement. Therefore if two children named Nathan and Jane were not on her porch by 0900 hours, overnight bags packed and ready to go, he'd see her in Broome County Family Court *tout de suite,* which was French for Monday morning. Then he hung up on her before she could hang up on him.

He called Louise next. It was a cowardly act, knowing she was at work and wouldn't answer the phone, but he had some things to say, and if he caught her live he probably wouldn't be able to say it all.

He waited for the beep, then dove in. He told Louise's voicemail that when he couldn't see the kids after his divorce he had gone into a hole so deep he hadn't fought hard enough for his rights. He told her the primary reason why he had left Sacred Heart was not that he hated the place, as he had told her (although that was certainly true) or that he found the relationships among his colleagues to be so deeply acrimonious there was nothing he could do to remedy it (also true), but that an affianced woman from Alumni Relations had come to his apartment drunk, and after Flynn denied her access and sent her on her way, the woman wrote rapturously about Flynn in her diary, and when her fiancée (a ponytailed Fine Arts professor) read, photocopied, and then pinned pages of said diary to the office doors of Flynn's colleagues and handed the diary itself to the dean, telling her that the new atheist in the English department was having an affair with his bride-to-be, said dean, the aforementioned Sister Mary Michael, had called Flynn into her office and said she always knew he'd be trouble, and by the way she would *not* be instituting his recommendations regarding his poorly-performing colleagues and yes, as a matter of fact she *did* inform them that their new department chair wanted to fire them, so best of luck fostering departmental camaraderie from that point on. (To which Flynn replied via email, "Holy Mother of God, I quit.") He told Louise he had never, not once, committed himself in both mind and heart to a woman—that every time he had been with Option A, he had daydreamed about Option B, until they eventually switched letters—but now, as Noah was his witness, he was going to grow the hell up and mend his wayward ways. He talked through the sound-pauses of Rachel's callbacks, and thrice Louise's voicemail cut him off, but each time he redialed and started up fresh at the beep.

Then, Flynn Hawkins went back to work. In one dawn-to-dusk day he took care of the weekly mow-and-trims he had missed during his three-day sabbatical, then drove over to Kinko's, printed up a stack of flyers, ventured back out to the Land of SUVs, and tucked the flyers into about a hundred screen doors. When he got home, there were six messages waiting for him on his landline: three from Rachel, reminding him that, among other things, he could go to hell; one from a woman who found his flyer on her door and was "definitely interested" in implanting Beauty all around her; one from Judy Lee, ordering him to cease and desist the marathon Louise voicemails as they were only making matters worse; and the last from Louise herself, thanking him for his "extremely informative" messages and asking for some time to think.

Tempted to sit on all the above while imbibing a cold one (he actually went as far as opening a bottle and digging through the couch cushions to find the remote), Flynn instead remembered his resolutions, clapped his hands together (startling Noah), and drove to Lochen's, where he found a *Thinking About You* card, then wrote a note in which he told Louise he was thinking about her thinking about him, and mailed it off to her at the Orchards address. Back home, he found the guardian *ad litem*'s business card, called her, and solicited her aid enforcing his scheduled visitation that weekend. Finally, he called Judy Lee and lit into her: if she didn't want him to continue boring her to tears every Thursday pining for Ms. Just-About-Right, he said, then she'd better back the hell off and let him make an ass of himself with her blonde BFF. Upon which Judy Lee lit right back, predicting that if Louise were stupid enough to give him a second chance, one of them would sure as shit end up breaking the heart of the other, as both their track records thus far had been nothing short of cataclysmic. Then she hung up on him, but with a pathetic slap of her flip-phone versus the dramatic slam of Flynn's landline.

THREE WEEKS LATER, FOLLOWING NOT ONE BUT TWO COURT-SUPPORTED VISI-tations with the kids (eating blueberry pancakes for dinner, watching old Lauren Bacall movies, enjoying canoe rides in the creek, playing catch with Nathan on Tom's Lane, and teaching Janey how to ride a bike without training wheels, all of which wiped out Noah for days afterwards)—and following not one but two new job contracts on Gravel Pond Road (on the opposite side of the golf course from the Lieberthals), Louise called. Out of the blue. Exactly three days after Flynn had a Thursday beer by his lonesome at Gin's Tavern, abandoned all hope regarding Our Lady of the Long Fingers, and found a new therapist—who, at their first meeting, handed Flynn a well-stocked pillow, told him to imagine it as someone he was angry with, and, when he asked Flynn who it was that he was suddenly punching, tears coursing down his face, seemed unsurprised when it was neither his ex-wife nor Judy Lee nor his mother, but his dearly departed dad.

It was Sunday, and it was raining, the kind of rain that turned afternoon into evening, and he had just returned from dropping off the kids. After taking some time to think things over, Louise said, she had finally broken things off with Jeremy—not for Flynn's sake, mind you, but because the relationship was clearly not working. "But know this," she said when Flynn expressed his guarded pleasure at this turn of events, "I'm mostly responsible for the failure of that relationship. What I'm saying is, I'm no angel. I drank too much in my twenties. I've been engaged twice and twice I broke it off. I worry about absolutely everything. My father calls me 'The Obstinate One,' and my mother thinks I'm far too wide in the hips for one who hasn't borne children. My roots are already gray, my dog shits on my carpet because I failed our animal-training class, I'm living with my parents again, and I'm making a giant bowl of nachos for dinner tonight. Do you hear what I'm saying?"

Flynn snapped his fingers at Noah, who was scratching at the door, desperate to pee. If he asked Louise to hold on while he opened it, the dog would sniff the rain and stay inside anyway.

"If there's one thing I've figured out," he said, "it's that our supposed failings are what make us lovable."

"I need a while," Louise said, her voice softening, "but if you still want to spend some time together, I insist, it must be as friends."

AND SO IT CAME TO PASS THAT FLYNN AND LOUISE WENT BOWLING.

Before: Flynn decided it would be a "clean date." But then he got the jitters, so he slugged down a beer, and afterwards he opened another, just to wash down a bag of sea-salt-and-vinegar chips. Baby steps.

During: He did his utmost to stick to their agreement. He took her to Idle Hours near Dickson City, the cleanest bowling alley in the area. He high-fived her when she notched a spare, and stared at her exquisitely-shaped derriere only when she couldn't see him doing so— and such is the beauty of bowling that he could get away with this almost twenty times per game. He talked a lot about Nathan and Janey, but refrained from mentioning their mother—except once, and that was only to say that she was doing a top-notch job as primary caregiver, which was the God's-honest truth.

After: He kept two hands on the wheel, and upon pulling over at the curb at her parents' house, he fully intended to scoot out, run around the back and open her door, but as he started to exit she laid a hand on his arm, closed her eyes, and put back her head—which made Flynn wish he had cleaned the headrests that afternoon and not just the dash, seats, and floor pads.

"This was nice," she said with a sigh, and Flynn sat back as well. "Bowling is good," she said.

She said Judy Lee had been quite the grump of late, even going so far as ordering Louise not to go out with Flynn ever again. "And at first I agreed," she said. "But then I thought, there's none of us that's perfect, right?"

Flynn sighed, and checked his impulse to reach for her long fingers. His life thus far had been about a hundred weed-infested acres from perfect, but the point, it seemed to him now, was not to bemoan or curse his fate but to weed diligently, fertilize organically, water regularly, and trust the sunshine to do the rest. While he was thinking this, Louise said, "Well then," and slid a little closer to him. And as she turned toward him, her lips parted, that's when Flynn, who would have considered an airy kiss on the cheek an unexpected step in the right direction, understood that all bets were suddenly off, that they were about to do a tad more than that right there in the cab of his old Ram, at the end of their allegedly friendly date. He closed his eyes (his heart suddenly spilling out), took a deep breath (the scent of bowling-shoe deodorizer clashing with the lavender of her perfume), and felt his callused hand enveloped by the nice long fingers of the fair-haired young woman who was, tis true, no angel, but who could still, in a manner of speaking, be the answer to all his prayers.

THE PENNSYLVANIA BRIDGE

LOCATE ME IN THE GARDEN, PULLING WEEDS. IT'S JUNE 16, 2013. I AM FORTY. The sun is blazing.

Janey's kneeling at the edge of the woods, looking for bugs. Nathan's down by the creek, in his swimming trunks and flip-flops.

This is my life now.

Nathan grabs hold of the long rope I tied to the tree branch, backs up a few steps, lifts his feet, and sails out over the creek, yodeling like a cross between Tarzan and Peewee Herman. When he drops into the cold water, he screams and thrashes his arms, then looks up to see if I was watching. "Dad! Get in here!"

I smile and wave. It looks like fun. When did I decide that life was no longer fun?

I wave at him. "Too cold!"

I take a break to call Louise. We've been seeing each other on the occasional weeknight, when I make the hour-long drive to Wilkes-Barre, and on weekends when I don't have the kids. Sometimes I don't know until Friday whether or not I have them, on account of my perpetually temperamental ex-wife. But Louise has been patient about this, so far.

When Janey hears me talking on the phone she comes over, holding an old sour-cream container she found in the recycling bin. She yanks on my shorts *DaddyDaddyDaddy* until finally I excuse myself to Louise and tell her I'll call her right back.

I put my hand on my hip and look down at my daughter. "What."

She cracks open the lid and I see orange salamanders inside. She looks up at me.

I wipe my forehead with the end of my tee shirt. "No," I say, and she frowns. "Honey, their home is the woods. How do you think they feel right now, trapped in there like that?"

She shakes her head; she's already considered this. "Look," she says and points to the holes she's punched in the plastic, the grass she has placed inside.

"I used to have posters of nature in my office," I say, "but I was still in an office."

I turn my attention back to the garden. The potato patch has been infested by some kind of bindweed, which I have privately named "Rachelweed." I don't know how to get rid of it without using something like Roundup, which is against my principles. I decide to be attentive and persistent: I'll never fully eradicate it, but I can make damn sure it doesn't dominate.

From down below, Nathan screams "Cowabunga!" and launches out again. He screams again when he hits the water, but it sounds a little deeper, more adolescent. He'll turn eleven in a few months. Janey looks down the hill, like she might want to give it a try, but there's no way—she hates the cold water.

I hit "redial" and put the phone to my ear. I shouldn't have cut off the call; I should have simply told Janey to wait until I was off the phone. *Priorities. One loved one at a time.*

"You're a big girl now," I tell her. (This isn't true, of course; she's only six.) "I know you'll make the right decision."

The next morning, a Sunday, I wake them up the way my mother used to when I was a kid, by frying up some bacon and letting the smell drift upstairs. I hear Janey's footsteps first. She loves big breakfasts, especially when they involve pancakes, especially in shapes: a crescent moon, an owl, a starfish. But when she comes downstairs, she's holding the sour-cream container and her whole face is red. She's beyond crying. She's bawling. Her eyes are so big that it takes a while for the tears to well up, exit the lids, and fall to the ground.

She holds up the container. All the salamanders are dead.

THE NEXT WEEKEND, RACHEL HAS PLANNED A GETAWAY WITH SAM, HER boyfriend, so I have the kids again. I apologize to Louise (she's said she doesn't want to interfere "in any way whatsoever" with my visitation weekends) and pick up Nathan and Janey in Binghamton, an hour north. When we get back, Nathan runs inside, digs into his overnight bag, and pulls out a red cape, from a magician's costume I've never seen. He cloaks himself in it and runs up the stairs. When I come up a little later, I see him standing in the corner, perfectly still, encased by the cape. He unveils himself—"Ha-ha!"—and brandishes a plastic knife.

He is Unknown Man.

He does this all weekend. He can make himself invisible at will, and he has accumulated a variety of weapons with which to slay villains—an old film canister filled with thumbtacks (to flatten the tires of their getaway cars), a cracked travel mug filled with dust (to dash in their faces, blinding them), a long string with a grappling hook (in case he needs to scale a wall or tree)—but his favorite is the "death disk," a soup-can lid wrapped in duct tape that, when flung properly, could decapitate a 300-pound man, to say nothing of the countless evildoers inhabiting the Pennsylvania woods. He hides behind trees and leaps out like a man with his head on fire, flinging the disk. His enemies, cleverly disguised as pine trees, are instantly vanquished. He laughs triumphantly, retrieves his weapon, wraps himself in the cape, and dashes off (invisibly) to his next mission.

It starts off as a game, but it soon becomes his identity. He keeps the cape on all the time. He sleeps with it on. At breakfast (French toast with powdered sugar, blackberries, and real maple syrup), he uses it as a napkin.

I'm lying in the hammock. Janey is by her favorite tree, which she calls "Tall Tree," singing a song to herself while studying a ladybug on a leaf. Suddenly, Unknown Man jumps out from behind the wood shed and flings his weapon. The disk rises and dips at an odd angle and Janey shrieks, grabbing her foot. From twenty feet away I can see a bubble of blood. I scramble out of the hammock, imagining my daughter without a big toe—she'll spend her whole life off-balance. I look down the road, but I don't know where the nearest hospital is. What's wrong with me? I should know where everything is—hospital, doctor, all that stuff. *Ice.* I'll pack the sliced-off part of her toe in ice.

But it's only a cut, and it's not too deep. Janey's eyes are wide, though: *Mon frere, mon assassin.* I try to remember if she's had a booster for tetanus. Shouldn't I have copies of their medical records?

I scoop her up in my arms while looking around for Unknown Man. A bit of duct tape must have torn off from the aluminum lid. What would have happened if it had sliced her mouth? Her eye? Her jugular?

I clean Janey's wound in the kitchen, but I don't have any gauze. I don't even have band-aids. When I was a real father, I had a fully stocked first-aid kit at the ready at all times. I wrap her toe in a clean dish-towel and keep pressure on it until the bleeding abates. Then I carry her upstairs, set her down on her bed, surround her with her books and stuffed animals, elevate her injured foot, tie a clean napkin around her toe with a shoestring, and tell her she gets to be Princess for a Day. She asks if she can have pancakes for lunch—in the shape of a fish, maybe? With a blueberry for its eye?

"No," I say, and in an instant she's crying again..

I go outside, looking for Nathan. I need him to understand how stupid that was, flinging a sharp object in the general direction of his sister. How would he feel if somebody did that to him? But I find him by the creek, curled up in the canoe, crying. *I didn't mean it. I was aiming for the tree. Is she okay?*

THE FOLLOWING WEEKEND, LOUISE COMES UP. ON SATURDAY MORNING, WE go on a long walk in the woods, and I take pictures of her in the airy streams of sunlight. On our way back, I spot the name on a rusted mail-box belonging to a house set far back into the woods: *Siczlytsky.* I stop and stare at it as Louise keeps walking. What are the odds?

We make an early dinner together (ratatouille, made with organic vegetables she picked up at the Wegman's in Wilkes-Barre), but we stay up late, messing around, laughing at each other's lame jokes, singing and dancing to Motown CDs, and watching the tube, until it's eleven o'clock and we're both hungry again. So we hop in the car, wearing our pajamas and glasses, and drive to the only place that's still open, the Loaf and Jug. We roam the aisles in our slippers, ending up with a cache of Tastykakes—double-cream for me, peanut butter and chocolate for her—which we eat back home while watching *An Affair to Remember* and holding hands under the blanket. The next morning we stay in bed, drinking coffee and reading the Sunday *Times*, and in the afternoon we take a hot bath together in the enormous tub, with the windows wide open so we can hear the hummingbirds.

Two weekends later I pick her up in Wilkes-Barre, meet her parents (her mother is a nurse, her father a math teacher), and drive her two hours to my sister's house, where we have lunch with my family ("Much better, Flynnie," my sister yells out as we leave; "Muuuuch better"), then take Metro-North into the city, where we meet up with my old friend Peter and his husband and walk around the Village so they can see where we used to hang out, and even though most of the places are gone, it's a great day. Afterwards, I take Louise to Little Italy for dinner, then go to Café Palermo for cannoli afterwards. "I've never been with anyone so *decisive*," she says when I suggest we top off the evening with a drink at the Jane Hotel, and I have to think that one over. It's a remarkable thing, to be known as decisive. I must have gotten that from Casey.

Maybe, I think, this is what life is like: we learn from everyone we are with, even if it doesn't work out. It's unconscious. We choose people because they have something we secretly want, even if it's the very quality we don't like about them, the quality that ends up killing the relationship.

I can already tell what I'm learning from Louise. Patience. Empathy. Love. A soft voice. She processes her thoughts. She deliberates. She takes care. She protects herself.

So what did I learn from Rachel?

WHEN WE GET BACK TO LOUISE'S HOUSE AFTER OUR BIG DAY IN THE CITY AND sleep in her childhood bed, she drops off immediately, her mouth demurely closed, her face serene, and I tiptoe around the room, looking at the pictures of her when she was a girl. Then I kneel beside the bed and watch her sleep.

Look at you. Just look at you.

WE'RE DOING WELL SO FAR, BUT OUR RELATIONSHIP IS ALMOST ENTIRELY weekend-based. Almost entirely Rachel-dependent. I know this is something we should discuss, but I don't bring it up, because I don't know what I can do about it. What I say, officially, is that I'm so desperate to see the children that I don't ever want to say no to Rachel when she says they're available on my off-weekends. But the truth is, I'm afraid of saying no to Rachel, period. Always have been.

Judy Lee and I aren't friends anymore, so Louise and I make Thursday night our weekly Date Night; no matter what, we have that time to ourselves every week. And whenever the subject of the weekend comes up, Louise says that if we can spend it together, great, if not, she totally understands; but I can see it's not great and she doesn't totally understand. It's as if I'm dating the female version of my younger self: she never gives me a straight answer; she suffers from intense migraines; she sacrifices her own needs four times an hour; she cries easily. For all I know, she wishes she was still with her ex-boyfriend. He may not have been very interesting, but at least he didn't have this much baggage.

So I make a proposal. I'm in this big house with plenty of room, I say; she's living with her parents; I'm closer to the Orchards, where she works; the kids are here most weekends but otherwise it's just me and Noah. Why doesn't she just move in?

So she does. And the whole house is transformed. When her little dog, Tess, tries to get Noah to play with her, Noah looks five years younger. When we go grocery shopping together, I realize why there are so many cabinets in the kitchen. When she puts up curtains in the living room, the living room suddenly looks like a living room. When she bakes me black-cherry oat bars, I understand what love tastes like. When she takes a bath, the whole house smells like lavender. When she wraps herself in my old towels, the towels seem to regain their color. When she comes out to the back terrace in her robe, I understand why Rand, the owner, saw fit to install the porch swing.

But one evening when we're sitting there, watching the creek turn from blue to silver and waiting for the heron to swoop over the water, a squirrel scurries out from the eaves behind us, leaps out over Louise's head, and sails down to one of the trees by the creek. Another squirrel does the same thing, and then another, and then a whole platoon of them. I've witnessed this before, of course. I call them the Furry Paratroopers. It's like some low-budget adaptation of the monkey scene from *The Wizard of Oz*. But this is a first for Louise. She shrieks, ducks, whacks at her hair, scrambles off the swing, and runs inside.

I do see her point. The squirrels probably shouldn't be living in the house. Plus they keep Janey up at night, scratching over the ceiling above her.

I notice other problems, too, now that Louise is here. An attic door that leads to nothing but thin air. No screens on any of the windows. Bats in the slats. Bears in the woods. And a front door that doesn't lock. Can't lock. They're old French doors that open inward; even when they're locked, all you have to do is push hard from the outside and they swing right open.

One day, when I'm at a work site and she has the day off from the Orchards, Louise calls to tell me there's a squirrel in the living room. Tess is going crazy, she says; the dog has torn apart couch pillows trying to get at it. A lamp is broken, the screen to the balcony is bent, and the squirrel now seems to be hiding in my desk drawer.

"Where's Noah?" I ask.

"Sound asleep."

When I come home, I find Louise locked in the bedroom with Tess, with sheets stuffed into the crack under the door. Out in the living room, I see a trembling tuft of fur sticking out of my desk drawer. I open the sliding door to the back terrace, tip over the couch so that it's a boundary between the terrace and the living room, find the broom, and jerk open the drawer. The squirrel scampers out, I swipe at it, it dashes outside and leaps onto a tree branch.

I shut the sliding glass door, put the couch back where it belongs, and go into the bedroom, where I find Louise under the covers. "This house is clean," I say, in the voice of the little woman from *Poltergeist*.

Louise peeks out from the bed sheet. "This might not be the best situation for me," she says.

WHENEVER I HAVE THE KIDS FOR THE WEEKEND, SHE DRIVES BACK TO HER parents'. She doesn't want to cause any discord; she knows how desperate they are to be with me, and she knows how Rachel would react to her being there. Sometimes she stays until they arrive, so she can say hi and give them hugs, but then she leaves, waving to us as she drives away. But this, too, is getting old. So the next time I know I'm going to have the kids for the weekend, I ask Louise to stay put. You live here, I say. This is your home. They like you, and you like them. Let's be a family.

She raises an eyebrow.

When I pick up the kids in Binghamton, they do what they usually do, talking over each other, trying to give me all the news of the week even though I talk to them on the phone almost every day now, and after they settle down we play the Animal Guessing Game; but during a lull in the proceedings, with the Susquehanna and then farmland and then the low mountains and then the woods out the window, I tell them what's going on. I tell them Louise and I love each other and we're living together now. She'll be with us all weekend, I say, and every weekend from now on. Okay? We're a couple. You know what a couple is?

Nathan shrugs. "Yeah! Mom and Sam are a couple." Then he starts telling me how he was the hero of his last soccer game. But Janey curls up in the back seat and starts sucking her thumb, an old habit I thought she had given up.

I didn't tell Rachel, of course. She wouldn't have let me pick them up. Anything out of the ordinary evokes a reaction. When Nathan told her he had met Louise and her cute dog, Rachel accused me of neglecting the children for my new girlfriend, and for the next month there was a strange sequence of "family events" that meant the kids needed to stay in Binghamton. Then there was the time I drove the kids to "downtown" Nicholson, which is two blocks long, and as Janey and I went into the thrift store, I gave Nathan a ten-dollar bill and sent him to the grocery store, Lochen's, for some pasta and bread, just as my mother did when I was ten. He did great—he came out of the store beaming, and handed me the change—but when he called his mother later and bragged to her about it, Rachel told him to hand the phone to me and started screaming before it was even at my ear. How dare I let him out of my sight, even for a minute? Do I realize how many children have been abducted, this year alone? What kind of father am I? Then she threatened to call Social Services and I didn't see them for three weeks.

I see the "Welcome to Pennsylvania" sign in the distance. On our past drives, the first one to shout out that they see this sign wins one of the Jolly Ranchers I keep in the cup holder. Later, when we exit the highway and make the turn towards Nicholson, they start looking for the massive concrete railroad bridge, and the first to see it shouts out "I see the bridge! I see the bridge!" and wins another candy. But this time, the border sign passes without remark; and after we exit I-81 and turn towards Nicholson, Nathan looks up from his cartoon book, says "I see the bridge," and takes a Jolly Rancher without checking to see if it's watermelon. Janey is still sucking her thumb, still looking out the window.

Once we bump our way over the ruts of Tom's Lane and arrive at our little house in the woods, Louise steps outside to greet us. Nathan is all sweetness and smiles, but Janey goes immediately to Tall Tree, plops down, and starts ripping up grass, ignoring Noah, who brings her a stick, and Tess, who laps at her arm. When Nathan runs to the garage, grabs the big stick he calls Excalibur, and tries to get Janey to play Dragon Slayer, she just stares at the ground until he calls her a big baby and stomps off.

I approach Janey, but she looks at me as if I've violated a sacred trust. After squatting down and trying to coax her into telling me how she's feeling, only to be met with silence, I get annoyed, so I go to the car to bring in their bags.

Louise decides to give it a shot. She sits on the pine needles next to Janey. I bring the bags upstairs and watch them from the kids' bedroom window.

Louise smooths back Janey's hair, which is the same color as her own, like a wheat field in the sun. They have always gotten along, but this is different. Louise talks softly to Janey. "I know how much you love your father," she says. She puts her hand over her heart, trying to get Janey to look her in the eye. "And I promise I would *never* do anything to jeopardize your relationship with him."

Use smaller words, I want to say.

She rests her hand on Janey's arm, and that—my girlfriend's long fingers on my daughter's tender, sunbrowned skin—does something to me. "I also know how much you love your mom," she says. "And I promise I will never try to take her place."

Uh oh.

Janey looks up, as if she can feel me watching her. I back away from the window.

Louise talks a little more, and Janey nods, drops her head, and goes back to ripping grass. Louise pats her on the shoulder and comes back inside.

I meet her on the steps.

"Maybe I should leave," she says.

We go into the bedroom. I tell her it's going to take time, that's all. It's a big adjustment. For everyone.

"But what if she's this bratty all weekend?" Louise asks. "I don't know if I can take it."

I lean back. Does she know who she's calling a brat? The daughter I thought I would never see again, the one who could have wound up with a different man as her father? Does she realize how hard this must be for a kid who has been without her dad for a year, whose daily fantasy is that her parents get back together and live happily ever after?

"I didn't mean that," she says, and I exhale.

"No, you're right," I say. "She's being a brat. Nathan would agree."

"But she's only six," she says. "This is hard for her. For both of us."

Janey continues to sulk by Tall Tree, then eventually comes inside. She climbs in my lap, clings to my leg, tugs my arm, peppers me with point-less questions. She sits on the back terrace with me at twilight, watching the squirrels leap out from the eaves, then cries as I seal off the eaves with screening to prevent them from getting back into the house. That night she comes into our bedroom and tells me she wet the bed, even though her sheets are completely dry. The next night she calls out for me and says she's had a nightmare, even though she hasn't fallen asleep yet.

"Sing me the song," she says, and I sing it: *Good night, it's all right, Jane.* "Sing it again." And I do.

"Again."

At no point all weekend does she look Louise in the eye; it's as if this woman, the one who is sleeping with her father in the place of her mother, is invisible.

On Sunday, about six minutes after I drop off the kids in Binghamton, Rachel calls me on my cell phone. How dare this young girlfriend of mine tell Janey she would never take her mother's place? Janey knows damn well who her mother is! And what kind of father am I, shacking up with someone during this important time in my children's lives?

Don't I realize how much they need my undivided attention right now?

I try to interrupt: "It's the same age difference between you and Sam"; "That's *not* what she said"; "Jesus, Rache, she was just—"; "Well Sam's living there with *you*, isn't he?" But she keeps going and then hangs up on me.

For the next month, Rachel acts like I'm getting the kids every weekend, but every Friday something "very important" comes up—a birthday party, a family get-together, a soccer game, a sudden illness. It's in the visitation agreement that one party may reschedule so long as there is "advanced notice" and "agreement from both parties," but she takes a liberal view of the word "advanced," and I have a hard time legally disagreeing. Louise and I make plans; I cancel them; we reschedule. I drive up to watch Nathan's soccer game, but it turns out there is no game. The next Friday I get on the highway, but then I get a call—sorry, Janey says she's sick, and Nathan better stay home too, his head feels warm—I exit I-81, turn around, and head back home. I complain to Louise about how manipulative Rachel is being, and she looks at me as if I may have lost my balls somewhere on the highway.

One Friday, out of the blue, our friend Judy Lee calls to invite us over to have dinner with her and her partner Jade. I haven't seen ol' JL since our falling out last year, so it's an important date. But as Louise and I are getting ready to go, Rachel calls to tell me I can have the kids, no conditions this time, they miss me and it's high time they saw their father, which is code for *I'm going away for the weekend with Sam and my niece just told me she can't babysit.* I cover the phone and ask Louise what I should do.

Louise stares at me for a moment, blows out her cheeks, and marches off to her car. As she peels out of the dirt driveway, I take a deep breath and tell Rachel that one hour doesn't constitute "advanced notice"; but when I hang up on her ("So let me get this straight," she shouts so Nathan and Janey can hear, "you don't *want* to see your children?") and call Louise to find out where the restaurant is, she ignores my calls. An hour later, she texts me to say that she'll be spending the night at Judy Lee's.

The next day, I schedule a hearing at Broome County Family Court to report Rachel's many and various violations of the visitation agreement.

When she gets wind of this, Rachel files a counter-petition for an increase in child support commensurate with my recent increase in revenue, which of course has gone unreported to the IRS. But I know that she knows the judge won't look kindly on what she's been up to, so I tell her if she promises to give me the kids the following weekend, no funny business, I'll withdraw my petition. She says fine, but she's still going to make sure she gets the increase, and I say that's fine, I don't mind paying my fair share.

On Friday I make the drive to Binghamton, constantly checking my phone, and pull up to their street like a PTSD victim, certain the house will be empty. But there they are, waiting on the porch.

During our drive to Nicholson, they both talk at once, and if one·of them gets my attention for too long, the other jumps in, and before you know it they're screaming at each other, Nathan punches Janey in the shoulder, I turn to yell at him, and the car shudders dangerously onto the shoulder.

I pull over, both hands on the steering wheel. The move from Colorado to Pennsylvania was supposed to have made everything better, but nothing has gone as planned. I left an academic position with a decent salary and job security for a risky self-employment scheme with uneven pay and zero security; the kids are always fighting; Rachel is more stubborn than ever; and now Louise is MIA. I came home from work on Monday to find her side of the bathroom sink cleared out, along with a note saying she was staying at Judy Lee's indefinitely, please respect her wishes and don't contact her for a few days. It's been almost a week. The house is so empty without her.

I look in the rearview mirror. Nathan has his arms folded tight, his face scrunched. He looks like a spindlier, handsomer version of me. Janey is crying and rubbing her shoulder. I want to scream at Nathan to never, *never* hit his sister, but I've said that before. I count slowly to ten.

"It's been a long month," I say to the rearview mirror. "I think we really miss each other."

After we're back on the road for a few minutes, Nathan mumbles that he's sorry and Janey says, "That's okay."

When we get home, Louise is there. In the kitchen. I've never been happier to see anyone in my life. I look at the kids—I'm sure I'm beaming—but to them this isn't news; they expected her to be there. She has a new dress on and she's cooking Janey's favorite dish, tortellini with butter and parmesan. She hugs the kids and shows them the cake she's baked for my birthday. I had completely forgotten what day it was, and clearly so had the kids. They look at the cake. They look at me. Louise sets down the wooden spoon and whisks them upstairs.

When they come back down, I've got one bowl of tortellini set up for the kids, another (with pesto instead of butter, along with a mixed-green salad) for us. They have handmade cards, along with presents: a pair of wool socks from Nathan (which Louise had bought for me), and an illustrated three-line poem from Janey: *Happy birthday to my dad / Who makes us all so very glad / Even when he is sad.*

I kiss them and they run back upstairs to wash their hands.

"It's not their fault," Louise says, pulling out the placemats and napkins. "Rachel should tell them when it's your birthday. You do that kind of thing all the time for her. Have they ever once sent you a Father's Day card? A birthday card? Christmas?"

I lean against the doorframe, staring at her. Her blue dress has lit up her slate eyes. "You're back," I say.

She shrugs, and the smile she had for the kids has disappeared. "It's your birthday," she says.

SUNDAY AFTERNOON, AFTER I RETURN FROM TAKING THE KIDS BACK TO BINGhamton, Louise and I have a quiet dinner together. She tells me she's done a lot of thinking. She's tired of all the Rachel drama—no not *Rachel's* Rachel drama, *my* Rachel drama. Tired of feeling like a second-class citizen. Tired of being treated like an afterthought. "You're not being straight with me," she says. "You're trying to make everyone happy, but as a result, you're making nobody happy. Least of all yourself." I can tell she has rehearsed some of this, but her voice trembles as she speaks, and I realize she is the type of person who is so frightened of her own anger that she turns it inward instead of projecting it outward, and that means she has probably been storing it all up and is about to break up with me.

Then she announces that she is going out to walk the dogs.

I step outside and watch her stride down the road, her hair shimmering. She holds back Tess with one leash and pulls Noah forward with the other. There's something about the way she walks, her back upright, her hips swaying. Something about the kindness in her voice, even when she's upset. I never knew you could love every part of a person, even the parts you don't like.

I put my hands on my hips and breathe in the piney air.

I once saw a sign in a Colorado café: *Don't climb into the saddle if you ain't ready to ride.*

Before long I hear barking in the distance, then a shout, and I see Tess racing back, full speed, by herself. She scampers up to me in the garden, then loops around my feet, panting. I peer down the road and there's Louise, with Noah by her side, his gait stiffer than usual. Down that way are three trailers set close together with an American flag on a tall pole, and one of the residents keeps Rottweilers in cages. When I run down to Louise, she tells me that one of the Rottweilers got loose, tore across the lawn and leaped onto poor Noah before the owner came out and whistled him back.

"Fucking Rottweilers," I say. I hate those bloodthirsty dogs and their fucked-up owners. Every time we walk that way, they go crazy, growling and barking, rattling their cages.

"They're just scared," Louise says. "Poor things, locked in cages all day."

"What kind of animal attacks when they're scared?" I say, picking up Noah and carrying him through the garden.

"Almost all of them," she says.

I lay Noah down in his bed by the front door. Tess licks his ear and stands over him, still panting. I give him some water and put my hands through his fur, feeling for blood. There isn't any, but his heart is hammering into his rib cage. He's breathing as if his lungs can't get enough oxygen. He paws his way onto me so he's half on his bed, half on my lap, and I cradle his boney head. I tell him to hang in there. I tell him he's been a wonderful dog. I tell him that he's the one who welcomed me to this weird and magical home. I tell him Louise loves him as much as I do now, and it's been very nice of him to tolerate her scruffy little dog even though it's his house, and it's been nice of him as well to have been such a pal to Nathan and Janey, letting Janey ride him like a horse and swimming in the creek with Nathan just to keep an eye on him. I tell him (while looking at Louise) that he's been helping me to learn how to love. I tell him the Rottweiler owners are mean stupid sons of bitches, and as soon as he starts breathing normally again I'm going to go down there and kick their asses.

Louise brings him some leftover salmon from the refrigerator, but he can't eat it. She squats down next to me and cups her hand on Noah's heart. She rests her forehead on my shoulder. "This isn't good," she whispers.

Noah rests his chin on my lap, exhales, and dies.

TEN DAYS LATER, WE DRIVE DOWN TO HERSHEY PARK, THE FOUR OF US: ROLLER coaster rides, a tour of the chocolate factory, funnel cakes—the whole nine yards, as my father used to say. Janey keeps a tight grip on my hand, I keep a tight grip on Louise's, and Nathan runs circles around us, darting over to a booth, dashing through arcades, showing off how fast he is. When he asks if he can go on a ride that looks vomit-inducing, I consult with Louise and we decide he's not old enough; we suggest the super-swings as an alternative. When Janey asks for cotton candy, I shake my head no, and when she persists, Louise bends down, puts her hand on Janey's cheek, and says "Sweetie, if you have any more sugar today, you might explode!" and Janey widens her eyes, probably thinking of the kid in *Willy Wonka's Chocolate Factory*, which we had all watched together a week earlier.

At one point, we stuff ourselves into a photo booth: one picture with just the kids, one with me and the kids, one with me and Louise, and the last one of all four of us, Janey on my lap, Nathan on Louise's, all of us laughing nervously.

Toward the end of the night, Louise asks Janey to go on a ride with her, just the two of them. It's the one where you sit in a log and it plows through a wave of water at the end. Janey lets go of my hand, takes Louise's, and they head over. Nathan and I get some soft-serve ice cream and find a bench. When the ride comes to a halt, Louise and Janey are both drenched and bent over laughing. They're laughing so hard it takes them a while to get out, and the teenager running the ride has to come over and help move things along.

On the drive home, the kids fall asleep in the back, and Louise leans over and kisses me on the cheek.

We get stuck on the highway—a big accident involving an eighteen-wheeler—and don't get home until after midnight. I didn't take my cell phone, since all the people I love were with me, and when I check it I see eleven missed calls. I carry the kids up to their beds, then come back down and listen to the voicemails:

Where the hell have you taken my children?

Whatever it is you're doing, I never gave you my approval.

I need to know exactly where they are at all times!

If you ever want to see them again, buddy, you'll have to play by MY rules!

Stop ignoring my calls! Call me back NOW or I'm calling the police!

Louise's smile collapses. She can hear Rachel's voice from ten feet away. She starts cleaning the kitchen, even though we haven't cooked anything that day. She takes a plastic six-pack holder from the garbage and snips at it, so that fish won't get their mouths caught in the holes. She snips it to shreds.

I get it, of course: Rachel's scared. Scared I've stolen the kids. Scared I've turned out like one of those guys on the shows she watches. Scared about the kids' safety. Scared they're having more fun with me than they have with her. But when she's scared, she doesn't act scared. She doesn't *say* she's scared.

She attacks.

FOR THE NEXT TWO WEEKENDS, I DON'T GET THE KIDS, RACHEL DISCONNECTS the land line, and I think, dear God, not this again. I call Broome County Family Court and file another petition. The clerk says, "You again?"

On the date of the hearing, Rachel shows up carrying her trusty attaché case, and when it's our turn, we take our seats in front of the bench, and she clicks it open. It is stuffed with documents. All morning we've been sitting there at opposite sides of the courtroom as the judge has calmly resolved disputes, looking rather bored, but after Rachel and I make our statements, he tells us to give him a minute. He looks over a document, which I imagine is our custody agreement, then half-rises from his seat, points a long finger at Rachel, and tells her he's absolutely sick of hearing about her uncooperative behavior. He tells her she'd better darn well start complying with the law and let the children enjoy their court-appointed visitations with their father and stop jerking everyone around, wasting the court's valuable time. Does she understand how important their father is to them? Does she have any idea how he spends most of his days, trying to get deadbeat dads to pay child support and see their kids once in a while, wishing that they could be even a little like her ex-husband sitting right there next to her, who has never missed a child-support payment in four years and who obviously just wants to be with his children as much as he can? Does she wish to lose custody? Because that's what's going to happen.

He sits back down. "Have I been clear?" he says.

"Yes," Rachel says. "Yes, your honor." And he has to lean forward to hear her.

AFTERWARDS, RACHEL DOESN'T LOOK ANGRY; SHE LOOKS SCARED. SO I ASK her if she wants to get a cup of coffee.

We walk over to a place called Java Joe's, and I order us coffee and bagels—cinnamon raisin, her favorite. Rachel's hair has grown out a bit, and she is coloring it now to hide the gray.

"Listen," I say after we sit down. "You've been a great mom. The kids are healthy and well-adjusted, and that's all because of you. In spite of me. So I just want to say thanks for all you've done." I cut my bagel in half and take a sip of my coffee. "But Jesus, enough already, you know?"

I bite into my bagel as she stiffens and tells me I have no idea what I'm talking about, living all carefree in the woods doing whatever the hell I want. She tells me about all the work she's had to do, all the stuff I know nothing about: Nathan's misbehavior at school, Janey's screaming fits, keeping the house together when her adjustable mortgage rate shot up, all the while taking care of her sick mother and dealing with all kinds of expenses: over a hundred a week in groceries, the clothes they keep growing out of, unreimbursed medical bills . . .

I nod. I listen.

When she's finished, I tell her I hear her, loud and clear. Got it. So many things I didn't know about.

I spread some jam onto the other half of my bagel. I clear my throat. I tell Rachel I appreciate all she's done. I remind her that once upon a time, I was the one who took care of the kids, day and night, and she totally trusted me with everything. So. When they're with me now, she might consider that I do know what I'm doing. Therefore those crazy phone calls? They need to stop. "I understand you're worried about them," I say. "And I also get that you're still angry with me. But you can trust me with them. I know how to take care of them."

I want to say more. I want to say that the whole thing—our living together in New York, our marriage, the decisions I made after I left her, the terrible way she used the kids to get back at me, the weak and impotent ways I reacted—it was all such a mistake. So many mistakes. I want to tell her I loved her once, or thought I did, but I didn't have any idea what I was doing. Neither of us did.

She looks away, towards the barista. She's lost a lot of weight since the divorce; her cheekbones are coming out again. "Did you hear about what happened? The retired cop?"

I nod. It was in White Plains. A man whose wife filed for divorce came home from work and shot his two children and three dogs before shooting himself.

Rachel shakes her head, then almost sips her coffee, but doesn't. "That poor woman, she came home to a horror show. And before he did all this, he cut her out of his retirement and life insurance." She stares at her coffee. She seems short of breath.

"Rache," I say. "I would never—"

She looks right at me. "Give me one reason," she says. "Give me one fucking reason why I should ever trust you."

I sit back. I try to see myself the way she sees me. As the man she loved more than anyone, the husband who didn't tell her a damn thing before he just up and left. The man who said *I love you* when he didn't, who said everything was fine when it wasn't. The man who moved to Colorado to shack up with some famous writer instead of fighting her for custody of the kids.

I shake my head. I can't come up with one fucking reason.

She takes a bite of her bagel. I've finished mine and my coffee mug is drained.

"I've been both mother and father to them," she says, and as she talks, her face and neck redden. "I deserve some respect. You can't just come back into their lives and expect to pick up where you left off." She thumps the table with her fist. "I've kept them *alive*," she says, her eyes welling up. "I've done *all* the *work*. You have *no* idea." Now she's crying, but fighting it every step of the way, and I realize what I've learned from her.

Ferocity.

Passion.

Personality.

A certain say-what-you-mean-ness. Don't-ever-fuck-with-me-ness.

Bear Love.

"It's going to take me a while," she says, "but yes. I will learn to trust you again." She puffs out her cheeks. "And I'll tell you what, Hawk. What I've found out. I am *so much better off without you*."

She puts the rest of her bagel in her mouth and chews.

I wait. I need to treat this woman with kindness, not hostility. Not mockery. I owe her that.

"You scared me," she says. "You know that? You still do." She swallows the bagel and swigs down the rest of her coffee. "You're all friendly and smiling, but then . . ." She shakes her head.

I feel, in this moment, that in some way I have, all these years, actually needed her to be angry with me. That way, it's been easy for me to play the victim. Poor me, I have a crazy ex. She's insane! A lunatic! What's a nice guy like me to do?

Now? I don't know what to do with this person in front of me.

"I'm working on it," I say. I've been seeing a therapist. Last time I was in therapy, years ago, when I was still married, all I did was cry every week. This time, I've been getting down to business. Why I am the way I am.

It hasn't been pretty.

"I know I used to brag about how protective my parents were," she says, her voice now husky. "But really, I hated it. And here I am being the same way with my own kids."

She folds her arms. "I was protected," she said, "and they gave me a safe place to grow up, but, you know . . . it wasn't really safe safe. It was just protected. So I was always afraid of being alone, on my own. Now, being on my own, you forced it on me, but . . . I realized I'm okay, I can do it. In fact, it's made me stronger. Better. So"—she cracks a smile as she wipes away a tear—"thanks, I guess. Asshole."

She lets go of the mug and holds out both hands, palms open. "In the meantime, Hawk, I am the way I am, I can't change that. I worry about them. All the time. Every minute they're with you. So all I'm asking for, *all I am asking for,* is to know *where they are* and *what they're doing* when they're with you. Is that too much for a mother to ask?"

I think about it, then shake my head. "No," I say. "No, that's not too much to ask."

THE FOLLOWING FRIDAY, I GET THE KIDS, AND WE TAKE THEM TO JUDY LEE'S house. I text Rachel where we're going and I bring my cell phone with me. Jade, Judy Lee's partner, makes a great dinner (rainbow trout with Brussels sprouts and rice) that Nathan and Janey don't like, then microwaves some popcorn and puts on an old movie called *Darby O'Gill and the Little People.* It's a terrible film, but it's an old favorite of Jade's, and she apparently put a lot of thought into its selection, so I pretend to enjoy it. The kids sit on the floor with a blanket and pillows, stuffing their faces with popcorn, getting it all over the floor. They love watching movies, any movies, and they have no taste whatsoever.

I don't follow the plot. Instead, I chat with Jade and watch the backs of the kids' heads while half-listening to Louise's conversation with Judy Lee in the kitchen. I'm trying to relax—here we are, doing a normal thing families do, visiting friends and watching a movie together—but Louise's voice has dropped to a whisper.

The film stars a young Sean Connery, singing a jaunty song, and it's okay the first time, but then it gets sung again and again throughout the film:

She's my dear my darlin' one, my smilin' and beguilin' one
I love the ground she walks upon, my pretty Irish girl

By the time it's sung by a bunch of leprechauns, Nathan and Janey are giggling and singing along quietly to each other. I can see what's coming.

ON THE CAR RIDE HOME, THEY SING THE SONG OVER AND OVER IN THE BACK seat, louder and louder, collapsing in laughter, but they don't remember the words, so they just sing it like, "She's my dear my darlin' one, na na, na na, na na, na na," sometimes in their human voices, sometimes in their leprechaun voices. Janey laughs so hard she falls onto Nathan, and Nathan tickles her until she can't stand it anymore and starts screaming.

Louise smiles back at them, but then spends the rest of the drive looking out the window.

THE NEXT MORNING, IT'S RAINING, SO THE KIDS SET UP SHOP IN THE CONTEMplation of Life room. They sell various items to their "customers," meaning Louise and me.

Poems:10 cents

Neck masagg:20 cents

Fortun: 10 cents

Oreo cookie: 5 cents

Mind reeding:10 cents

News papr: 25 cents

Majic trick: 25 cents

Pichures:10 cents

Creecher cards: 5 cents

Chores:25 cents

Janey is a good retailer. She sits at her table for hours, clearing her throat when she hasn't had any business for a while. She sells her products below market rate and is always courteous. Nathan is more of an entrepreneur. He has built a robot named "Newman" using cardboard boxes and duct tape, and he gives Newman its own booth in order to double his sales potential. When he finds out that Janey has raked in sixty cents more than he has, he decides to run a lottery: he rips up paper, charges ten cents per ticket, and writes our names on them; the more tickets you buy, the better your chances of winning. Then he crumples them up, tosses them on the floor, and calls Tess into the room, and whichever ticket Tess sniffs first is the winner—free dishwashing for the whole weekend, a free room cleaning, one hour of garden work, instant

260

garbage takeout—and he pockets the cash. Afterwards, when he shows off how much money he's made, shaking the coffee mug full of change in front of Janey's nose, she knocks it out of his hand and it spills all over the rug. When Nathan screams at her and shoves her to the floor, I snatch him up and carry him upstairs, my jaw clenched.

AFTER DINNER, IT'S STILL RAINING, SO ONCE THEY REACH THE ONE-HOUR limit for TV watching, they come back into the Contemplation of Life room and beg us to play *Sorry*, the only board game in the house. I say okay, but Louise makes a face.

Nobody hates a board game the way Louise hates *Sorry*. She'd rather put on some music, read books, and do just about anything but play a game that pits everyone against one another. When most people draw a Sorry card, they celebrate; but when Louise draws one, she sits back and makes a noise with her lips. She doesn't want to "sorry" anyone, ever. She can't bear to "sorry" one of the kids, even if Nathan or Janey is about to win, so she always "sorries" me. If I have no pieces out on the board, then the kids both tell her to "sorry" the other, and it turns into a game of Which Child Do You Love More.

This time, Janey pulls ahead, but then she gets "sorried" twice in a row—first by Nathan, then by me. After my "sorry," she flings her game piece across the room, kicks the game board to the floor, folds her arms tight, and starts squeezing out tears. Nathan, who was next in line for victory, throws his cards into the box, calls her the most Annoying Sister Who Ever Lived, and stomps up the stairs.

Louise gathers all the pieces and puts them in the box. It's the third or fourth time this kind of thing has happened. "I hate this game," she says.

I shove the board into the box, close it, get up, and stuff the whole thing into the garbage.

SUNDAY NIGHT, AFTER I'VE TAKEN THE KIDS BACK TO RACHEL'S, LOUISE IS waiting for me in the wicker chair, her hands folded. The windows are open, and a nice breeze is coming in through the screens I installed.

"Let me guess," I say. "You're leaving."

She shakes her head, like she can't believe my attitude. "I just wanted to talk!" she says, and hugs the little pillow to her chest. Her face tightens.

I've learned this about Louise: when she's mad, the last thing in the world she'll tell you is that she's mad.

And this: she can cry without moving a single facial muscle.

I imagine her as a little girl on her childhood bed, gazing out the window at the rain, tears streaming down both cheeks. And when I picture her like that, I realize I am as much in love with that girl I didn't know as I am with this woman I am just getting to know.

She looks up. "Is this what you do?" she says. "Give up on things when they start to get difficult?"

I stand near the door, by Noah's dog bed, which Rand asked us to save for him, in memoriam. Yes, I thought. Yes, this is what I do. Because I *expect* everything to fail. Because when things fail, then I can do my thing. I can go into a hole and feel alone and hurt, just like I did after I left my marriage, just like I did during 9/11, just like I did when my dad chose to go to work instead of coming to my baseball game and then died. Yes, that's right: If I was a better son, he would have wanted to come back in time for my game, and he'd still be alive today. And yes, I know how stupid that sounds.

Louise goes upstairs—to pack, I presume. I follow her, because I can never just let someone do what they want to do; they should do what *I* want them to do.

"Hey." *Be tender,* I think. *Be kind.* But she doesn't turn around. I stare at the back of her: her blonde hair, the shape of her shoulders. I take a breath.

How many chances does a man get to set his life straight?

"I don't know what I'm doing," I say, and I've never said a truer thing in my life. (*I'm a pathetic piece of shit,* I'd like to say next, but my therapist has been encouraging me to "practice self-love and self-forgiveness.") "I need your help," I say.

For Casey, my ex-girlfriend, the way to run a relationship was to first create a picture, and then find someone to step into that picture. And I did, I stepped into her picture. But here I am doing the same thing, only it's me creating the picture, here in the woods of northeastern Pennsylvania, and I've been asking Louise to step into it. For me, it's been my version of Sanctuary; but for her . . .

It's like asking poppies to grow in mud.

She turns around. She's at the top of the stairs; I'm at the bottom. "If you want out," I say, "I understand. I do." And as I say it, I imagine it: having my kids with me more often, continuing to improve my relationship with my ex-wife, Janey having me all to herself, lots of free time to read and watch baseball. An easier life.

Too easy.

Because, you know—I'm starting to figure this out, and yes, it may be too late—what is love, after all, what is life, but a striving *against*, and not settling for, our inevitable doom? What is it if it's not a constant assertion of our longing for home, for intimacy, in the face of our unfathomable annihilation?

I think of my father, sitting in the armchair all weekend, watching TV, and I understand: he had accepted his doom, around the same age that I am now. He had given in and given up.

He had been destroyed and then defeated.

I think of him in his coffin and I have to catch my breath, my hand on my chest.

"As for me," I say after a while, "I'm in. I'm all in." And it's kind of like raising a flag.

I lift my hand from the bannister. "But I really do need your help."

Louise sighs, and sits down on the top step. "How can I possibly help you," she says, "when I don't know what I'm doing myself?"

THE NEXT TIME WE HAVE THE KIDS, IT'S THE WEEKEND BEFORE HALLOWEEN, Janey's favorite holiday. She's going to be a ninja, and she and Nathan will go trick-or-treating in their mother's neighborhood on Wednesday, but for now, Louise is upstairs making monster drawings with her. I'm on the couch with Nathan, half-watching a football game, half-grading essays. I'm teaching part-time now at Penn State Worthington-Scranton, a way to earn some money during the off-season—and yes, I freely reported my increase in income to the Broome County Family Court, along with my 2012 tax returns, and my support payments have increased accordingly.

Once their scary drawings are taped all over the house, along with fake spider webs that Louise bought at a place in town called Endless

Collections, she and Janey wash their hands. They have a follow-up activity: baking a Halloween cake.

They do it together. Louise shows Janey how to pack and level off a cup of flour, lets her crack the eggs (then shows her how to pick out the bits of eggshell from the batter, as if that kind of thing happens all the time), and boosts her up onto the counter so she can reach the vanilla extract. When it comes time to put the cake in the oven, she shows Janey how to put on oven mitts and lets her slide it in. It's chocolate, Janey's favorite. When Janey says she wants to tell her mom she's made a cake, Louise helps her to call, then holds the phone to Janey's ear because her little hands are caked with batter and icing. When she hangs up, Janey looks at Louise and says, "My mom said to say thank you, and she wants me to bring home a big piece for her!"

Well, well, well, as my father used to say. *What do you know.*

Meanwhile Nathan and I sit with the mixing bowl between us, each with a spoon. Tess sits at attention, hoping we'll share, but Louise has warned us not to because chocolate is bad for dogs. When it's ready, the girls present the cake. It has white frosting with "Happy Halloween" in orange letters, but the best part is the enormous black spider with wire legs that Louise placed on top. It looks as if the spider is guarding the cake, daring us all to take a bite.

WE HAVE THE KIDS AGAIN THE FOLLOWING WEEKEND, SO ON FRIDAY AFTERnoon I give Louise a kiss and head out to the car, but when I call out that I'll see her in a couple of hours, she doesn't say anything back.

I turn around.

When I come inside, her face is flushed. "You never ask me to come," she says. It's as if the words have been stuck in her throat for the four months we've been living together.

I coax her into the car.

For the first half of the drive, she talks. She wants to be included more. But she also respects the kids' need to be with me for the short and precious times we have together. But then she winds up feeling like an outsider.

When she stops talking, I drive for a while in silence. I feel tired.

Exhausted. Every time we have the kids, Janey clings to me, Nathan wants me to approve of everything he does, and whenever the kids and I do something—go to the park, watch a minor-league baseball or hockey game, play miniature golf—and I ask Louise to join us, she says something like, "Don't worry about me, you guys go enjoy yourselves."

"If you want to be included," I say to her now, "then say yes when we ask you to come.'

"But—"

"And if *you* want to do something," I say, "just you and them, then go ahead and ask them."

It's gone from mist to a light rain outside, so I adjust my wipers. "*They're* not going to initiate it," I say. "They're children. You're the adult. So just ask! They do stuff with Sam," I say. "He doesn't wait for an invitation."

I know what this sounds like, but it's as if I can't stop myself. It just comes out of my mouth. Plus, I know I'm right. I'm always right.

Louise looks out the window. We've crossed the border from northeast Pennsylvania to upstate New York, and believe me, there's nothing to look at. Finally she sighs, as if she can't believe she has to spell this out to her idiot boyfriend. "Sam *lives with* Rachel," she says. "And the kids *live there with him.* He's a regular part of their lives; they see him all the time. I see them, what, two or three weekends a month? And that's when they want you all to themselves, every second. And I don't blame them. You're their father. They need you. They miss you. If *I* initiate something, then that's time they wouldn't get to spend with *you.*" She sits back and fingers the window button. "So how do I do this?" she says. "Where do I fit in?"

I don't have a good comeback, so I drive for a while, imagining what it might be like if I had no kids, and Louise had two children with another guy who now had custody of them, and I moved in with her, and her kids saw her only two or three weekends a month, and they clung to her all that time, competing for her attention, asking her questions as if I weren't in the room. I imagine how I would feel in that situation.

The trees outside look barren. "I'm sorry," I say. "This must be hard for you."

We talk some more, and I listen to her without telling her what to do, without trying to come up with a solution. It's more difficult than it should be.

I try to think of a couple I know, or have known, who's done this kind of thing. Then I try to think of any couple I know, any normal couple, who do everything right—who love each other and get along well. When I think of my parents, I almost laugh out loud. My mother talks about her married years as if it were the Golden Age, but I remember my father slapping my mother on the leg so hard that she cried out in pain; I remember dinner ending early one day because he said something vile and bitter under his breath; I remember when he yelled at her so loud I heard him from my friend's back yard, six houses away; I remember my mother putting out her cigarette on my father's forearm and him howling like an animal.

"He was a loser," she said after the funeral, when a bunch of people I had never seen before gathered at our house. "But he was *my* loser."

I realize that instead of keeping stuff like this in my head all the time, I should tell Louise what I'm thinking. So I do. I tell her about my parents. I tell her about how sarcastic they were, how they never showed affection. I tell her about the muffled arguments I heard through the wall of my bedroom, next to theirs. I tell her how angry my mother was after my father's death.

And she listens.

She tells me how her own parents weren't exactly role models, living separate lives: her mother working overnight shifts at the hospital, her father constantly tinkering in the wood shed. Not the kind of relationship she wants, she says. What she wants is union. What she wants is to be a couple. As for the kids, she says, they're sweet, they're beautiful, and Janey is starting to warm to her. She feels great affection for them, and can see how it will turn into love someday. "But first we have to be a real couple," she says. "Then we can create the picture together, all four of us."

She's staring at me now, and I'm looking at the road. I try to see myself the way she must see me, as a man who has never fully committed, a man who is acting like his ex-girlfriend, thinking that being a couple means two strong independent selves co-inhabiting the world one of them has created.

Then I try to see myself the way my kids see me now: as a Treat Dad.

The way my favorite professor, my second father, probably sees me, as a young man who abandoned him when he needed me most.

The way a big-eyed woman I dated briefly sees me, as a guy who was afraid of *realismo mágico*.

The way my old friend Peter sees me, as a great guy who made terrible decisions.

The way my ex-girlfriend Casey sees me, as someone who couldn't match her strength with his own, and therefore blamed her for his own decisions.

The way Sydney and Amita see me, as someone who didn't have the balls to pursue them out of respect for their boyfriends.

The way my mother and sister see me, as a misguided romantic.

None of them has seen me the way I see myself, as a nice man who tries his best to make everyone happy and is constantly put upon and taken for granted.

When I do this, when I pull back my vision as if I'm in center field, watching the entire game take place before my eyes, I see a man who still can't hit the curveball. A man who still hasn't truly loved. A man who constantly feels sorry for himself and blames others for his misfortunes. A man who has screwed up every relationship he's had because he's been afraid to engage, to invest, to expose himself, to admit to his flaws, doubts, and mistakes and embrace the other person's shortcomings and idiosyncrasies. A man who does mean petty things to the people he loves, in mean petty ways—subtly, not openly.

The worst kind of warfare.

It's not very attractive, let me tell you.

But seeing myself like this—it's a start.

I reach out for Louise's hand, and I'm terrified she won't take it. But she does, and then she puts her other hand on top of mine. She's right: you don't create a picture and wait for someone to step into it. You create a new picture together. And then—look—as soon as you decide to do that, you're already creating it; you're already in it.

When we get to Binghamton, we exit the highway, make the two left turns, turn right onto the road parallel to the Susquehanna (there's a more direct route, but seeing the river relaxes me, and I want to show it to Louise), then make another right, drive about a mile (past two houses, a cornfield, and a vineyard), and pull into Rachel's driveway.

I put the car in park and stare out the windshield. Typically, when I pick up the kids, I don't see Rachel. Typically, I leave her a voicemail to tell her when I'll be arriving, and she has the kids waiting on the porch, bags packed. They may be a little embarrassed, or cold, but they don't care, as long as they get to come to Daddy's House in the Woods.

But this time, there's a crowd out there: Rachel, her parents, her boyfriend Sam, her brother, and the kids. All sitting out on the porch.

Louise stiffens. I practically guaranteed her she wouldn't have to see Rachel.

"I'll just wait in the car," she says.

But Rachel comes out to the driveway to greet us, so Louise exits the car, stands straight, and puts out her hand. Only Rachel keeps coming. She marches right up to Louise and plants a kiss on her cheek, pats her shoulders. "Good to finally meet you," she says. "The kids say such nice things. That cake was delicious!"

Then she turns to me. "Hey there, Hawk." She gives me a quick hug.

On the porch, Janey grins. Nathan widens his eyes.

I put my arm around Louise as we follow Rachel to the porch. "What'd you put in that cake?" I say.

I kiss the kids, introduce Louise to everyone, peck Rachel's mom on the cheek, hug her dad (and realize how much I miss him), and half-hug her brother, which triggers some awkward laughter. I shake hands with Sam, and we smile like we're in some kind of secret club. I mean, we practically wink. He's divorced too, with two grown kids, and according to Nathan, he's been telling Rachel to stop harassing me when I have them for the weekend, to let the children enjoy their time with their father. I like Sam. Sam's been a good addition to the family.

I grab the kids' bags and gesture for them to get in the car, but Rachel says, "Oh wait," and rushes inside. She comes out with a Tupperware container of chocolate-chip cookies and hands them to Louise. "Here," she says. "Jane and I made them together. You better take them with you or else I'll eat 'em all and get fat." She laughs, and everyone else laughs too.

I don't trust it, of course. It's all a show, some kind of weird competition. But I'm going with it. I thank Rachel for the cookies and tell the kids to kiss their mother goodbye.

On our way back, everyone is quiet for a while, but then Nathan suggests we play the Animal Guessing Game. We go a few rounds, all of us winning at least once except for Louise. Then in the last round, with Nathan in charge, after nineteen questions, Louise has the last guess—"Is it a fox?"—and Nathan shouts out that she's right, she's the winner, even though she can't be: foxes aren't bigger than hound dogs, which was one of the first clues. I look back at Nathan and he grins wickedly. Then he leans forward, taps Louise's arm, and hands her a watermelon-flavored Jolly Rancher.

Janey is looking out the window, the warm breeze blowing back her hair.

"You guys want to go for a swim when we get home?" I ask.

"Yes!" Nathan says, but Janey shakes her head.

"We shouldn't," she says. "We'll disturb the ducks."

"No we won't, they like it!" Nathan says. He taps me on the shoulder. "Are you coming?"

"Absolutely," I say. "In fact, let's all get naked and jump in the creek."

"Ew," Janey says.

"Are you coming too, Louise?" Nathan asks. He's half-talking, half-screaming.

Louise smirks, then tucks her head between the window and the seat and looks back at Janey. "Janey, dear," she says, "while these two heathens are flapping around like goons in the cold water, why don't we go to the art center and make a picture poem for your father?"

The art center is the garage, and a "picture poem" is one of Janey's favorite things to make. They get out the paint set Louise bought for her, find a piece of scrap wood, paint it, and then, when the paint is dry, paste a piece of colored paper with one of Janey's original poems on it. The ones she's made so far are hanging in the Contemplation of Life Room.

"I'll make you *both* a picture poem," Janey says.

"You mean each," I say, "or both?"

"*Both*," she says. "One for you and one for her."

"Then each," I say.

"No, *both*. But none for Nathan," she says.

"Oh, like I care," Nathan says. "Like I'm devastated. Like I'm dying to have one of your stupid picture poems."

"Nathan," Louise says, before I can open my mouth. "Your sister's picture poems are gorgeous."

"Yeah," Janey says. "Gorgeous."

"Maybe we can think of a goofy one to make for your brother," Louise tells her.

Nathan sticks his tongue out to Janey, and Janey sticks hers out to him. Then she leans up and whispers to Louise. "With monkeys," she says.

We drive in silence after that. I keep checking to make sure Nathan isn't hitting Janey. He has this move where he swipes his fist sideways on the seat, thinking I can't see it—but I always hear Janey cry, "Ow!"

"Hey Dad," Janey says out of nowhere, "why don't we ever go to Grandma's?"

I look out at the trees, thinking of my mother's house in White Plains. "I don't know," I say. But I do know. Thus far, I have not been able to add my mother into the very full bucket I've been carrying around. The bucket would be too heavy and I'd have to set it down. But to Janey and Nathan, my mother is not a weight. Not a chain-smoking grouch. Not an embittered woman who can't believe I ditched my career as a professor to become "a common gardener." My children's grandma, as they know her, is light as a feather. She's the person who gives them candy and takes them to the Olive Garden for mozzarella sticks. She's the person who calls them beautiful and precious, her little angels. She's the person who gives them a ridiculous amount of presents at Christmas, as if trying to make up for holidays lost.

"I'll give her a call," I say.

"And Auntie Anna Banana too," Nathan says.

"And Marianna and Robbie," says Janey.

"Okay," I say, shooting Louise a glance. "Okay. How about next weekend?" And they smile and nod. Louise looks at me as if she's seeing a different person in the driver's seat, one that she might come to respect.

I look out at the road, at a lake we are passing, at the swans floating in the middle, and I picture my mother as she was before my father died: pretty, with blonde hair and cheekbones. She is at my bedside, I am sick with something, and she is rubbing my chest with Vic's Vaporub. She smells vaguely of cigarette smoke and the perfume she wore the night before, when she went out to dinner with my father. This is the only time I ever feel her hands on me, when I'm sick. I close my eyes, feeling her palm on my chest, listening to her humming an old song.

"Dad, do Grandpa's whistle," Nathan says. I look at him in the rearview mirror and I try to whistle, the two chirps, but my throat closes up and it doesn't come out. And then I'm lost.

I will always wonder why he didn't come to my game that day. I will always assume he was disappointed in the way I swung a bat. I will always wish I had fought through his defenses and hugged him as fiercely as I wanted to. I will always wish he could have seen my beautiful children, that he could sit on the couch between them and watch an old Western with them, or take a ride with all of us, right now, to get some fresh ice cream at Manning's dairy farm. I will always want to see his soft green eyes one last time. But all that, it just binds me up into knots. I can't keep doing it.

"Dad, do the whistle!" Nathan says, but Louise shoots him a look and he slumps back. She puts her hand on my cheek and swipes a tear with her thumb.

I blow out a big breath and smile when Janey, who constantly stares out the window, sees the "Welcome to Pennsylvania" sign and shouts it out; she gets a grape Jolly Rancher, which she holds up like an Olympic medal. And when we make the turn at Nicholson and the kids catch sight of the concrete bridge, they both cry out, "I see the bridge! I see the bridge!" But this time they turn it into a manic song, to the same tune as the song from the annoying movie we watched at Judy Lee's:

I see the bridge, I see the bridge, I see the Pennsylvania Bridge,
I see it here, I see it there, I see the bridge, it's everywhere!

I turn onto Tom's Lane, keeping an eye out for turkey and deer, as they sing it over and over in their leprechaun voices, knowing I hate it, cracking each other up. Louise even joins in for a chorus, just to mess with me. And I imagine my father watching us somehow.

I scowl at their singing and aim at the ruts in the dirt road hard, to bounce them up off their seats, and they all shriek with each bump and tell me to stop.

But I'm only pretending to be annoyed. I've never heard a more beautiful song in my life.

ACKNOWLEDGMENTS

"DIAMOND DASH," THE FIRST CHAPTER OF THIS BOOK, WAS ACCEPTED (IN essay form) by Stephanie G'Schwind at *Colorado Review* way back in 2003—my first-ever publication. Since then I've published many more stories, some of which appear as chapters of this book, and I've received a great deal of help from my friends along the way.

My dear wife, best friend, and finest editor, Cynthia Kolanowski, has read each chapter more than once, and more than once has provided astute commentary that has improved the book. Without her help, it would still be a book, but not an especially good book; and without her love I would still be a man, but not an especially good man.

Other readers are so numerous that I'm afraid to name them here for fear of leaving out one or two, especially since fifteen years have passed since I started this book. But since the members of my Boulder writing group edited most of these stories, I'd like to single out Arsen Kashkashian, Colin Tracy, Norah Charles, and Jody Reale for their advice and friendship. Jim Seitz, Sydney Argenta, Dan Vaccaro, Kate Jordan, Steve Edwards, Marcelle Heath, Charles D'Ambrosio, Alyssa Finer, Shara Johnson, Yu Yang, Dawn Dennison, Laura MacAlister Brown, Michael Karson, Beth Davis, and Katy Craig provided suggestions for individual stories; the Jentel Arts Foundation and Brush Creek Arts Foundation, both in Wyoming, provided peaceful and beautiful environments in which to compose, revise, and organize them; and Paul Matthew Carr of Webworkz Digital Strategies provided a beautiful website (david-hicks. com) on which I could feature them.

And where would I be without my writing buddies? My love and gratitude go out to Jacqueline Kharouf, Rachel Byrne, Olivia Tracy, Amanda Avallone, Rich Cadwallader, Jill Talbot, Janna Goodwin, and Stephanie

Vessely—and a special thanks to Sophfronia Scott, whose dedication and spirit have been motivating me to keep at it, through thick and thin, for years now.

Hugs to Lauree Ostrofsky (of simplyleap.com), who helped me to own my identity as a writer; my agent, Victoria Skurnick of the Levine Greenberg Rostan Literary Agency, for her advocacy and affection; my editor and publisher, Caleb Seeling, for believing in my book, for making it better through his edits, and for designing such a beautiful cover.

And finally, hugs and kisses to my children, Stephen and Caitlin, for co-authoring two of the stories in this book, and for unwittingly helping to co-author the story of my life—which, thanks mainly to them and Cynthia, seems to be building towards a happy ending. May it, like the final chapter of this book, be just a tad too long.

DAVID HICKS grew up in Harrison, NY and is a professor of English at Regis University in Denver, where he co-directs the Mile-High MFA program. He and his wife Cynthia enjoy hiking with their dog Rosie and meeting his children Stephen and Caitlin for big breakfasts at Cozy Cottage, Jelly, and Sassafras. David has published many stories in such fine journals as *Glimmer Train, Colorado Review, Saranac Review*, and *South Dakota Review*. **WHITE PLAINS** is his first novel.

Thin Blue Smoke

A Novel about Music, Food and Lo[...]
by Doug Worgul

978-1-942280-11-8

LaVerne Williams is a ruined ex-big le[a]
ballplayer and ex-felon with an attitude p[...]
lem and a barbecue joint to run. Ferguson
is an Episcopal priest and fading literary [...]
with a drinking problem and past he's [...]
ning from. A.B. Clayton and Sammy Me[...]
are two lost souls in need of love, underst[...]
ing and another cigarette. *Thin Blue Smo[...]*
an epic American redemption tale. It is a [...]
ry of love and loss, hope and despair, God
whiskey, barbecue and the blues. Hilarious
heart-rending, sacred and profane, this [...]
marks the emergence of a vital new voi[c]
American fiction.

MORE GREAT BOOKS FROM CONUNDRUM PRESS

Glassmusic

A novel by Rebecca Snow

978-1-942280-01-9

In the serene fjordlands of Norway in the early
twentieth century, Ingrid has led a blissful childhood until she becomes holder of her family's
secrets. Her father, a blind preacher who minis-
ters through sacred music played on glassware,
increasingly relies on Ingrid to see for him even
as it threatens to tear apart his marriage. And
after she witnesses an assault against her sister,
Ingrid must decide when to speak and when to
remain silent. *Glassmusic* explores the sometimes
devastating realities of loyalty and jealousy, with
philosophy, music, and love serving as guides.